THE PAIN
AND
THE SORROW

A Novel of Old New Mexico

Loretta Miles Tollefson

PALO FLECHADO PRESS

ISBN: 978-1-952026-01-0

This novel is a work of fiction, not biography or history. The thoughts, words, and motivations of the 'real' people in this book are as much a product of the author's imagination as are those of the fictional ones.

Library of Congress Control Number: 2019920880

Palo Flechado Press
Santa Fe, NM

Cover Art by Fresh Stock

Other Books by Loretta Miles Tollefson

Old New Mexico Fiction
Old One Eye Pete (short stories)
Valley of the Eagles (micro fiction)
Not Just Any Man
Not My Father's House

Other Fiction
The Ticket
The Streets of Seattle

Poetry
But Still My Child
Mary at the Cross, Voices from the New Testament
And Then Moses Was There, Voices from the Old Testament

A Note on Spanish Terms

If you speak or read modern Spanish, much of the Spanish in this novel may look wrong to you. That's because the dialect used in this book reflects the Spanish spoken in northern New Mexico in the middle 1800s: a unique combination of the Spanish used by the settlers who arrived in the late 1500s, indigenous words from Mexico (primarily Náhuatl) and the peoples already in the region, and imports from French and English that came in with the French and American trappers and traders. I've tried to represent the resulting dialect as faithfully as possible. My primary information source was A Dictionary of New Mexico and Southern Colorado Spanish by Rubén Cobos (University of New Mexico Press, 2003). Any errors in spelling, usage, or definition are solely my responsibility and do not reflect in any way on Mr. Cobos' excellent work.

For María Gregoria Cortez Kennedy Chavez

After the evening meal, Gregoria and the rest of the ranch crew gathered around the massive stone fireplace in the ranch's main room. Gregoria settled into her rocking chair with her sewing while most of the men clustered around the fire. Suddenly, the room's heavy wooden door swung open and a ranch hand appeared, pulling off his buckskin gloves. "Clay Allison's dead!" he announced.

The men were too busy gaping at him to notice the look of shock on Gregoria's weathered face. Her sewing dropped to her lap and she closed her eyes as her hands gripped the arms of her chair.

"What happened?" someone asked.

"Fell off a wagon in East Texas. Broke his neck," the newcomer said as the men around the fireplace moved aside to make room for him. He held his hands to the flames and shook his head. "What a way for a gunslinger to die."

"Well, that's one more piece of scum off'n the face o' the earth," a scrawny man with a squint commented as he poked a stick at the fire.

An old man in the corner took his hand-carved cottonwood pipe from his mouth. "I ever tell you about the time I was in Herberger's saloon in Elizabethtown and Allison rode his horse into the bar?"

A lanky man near the fire tossed another log onto the blaze. "You've mentioned it a time or two."

"He was right crazy when he was drunk."

"He was right crazy when he wasn't," the scrawny man said. "I was part o' that group lookin' for the goods on Reverend Tolby's killer durin' the Colfax County War. That got nasty in a hurry."

Gregoria took a deep breath and opened her eyes. The men were shaking their heads, gazing into the flames.

"Gunslinger and a half, that one," the lanky man said.

"Cool and collected," someone agreed.

"He was somethin' of a lady's man, though," the old man observed. "Liked the look of a well-turned ankle."

"But he was always a gentleman," Gregoria said. They all looked at her in surprise. "Even to women who others wouldn't have called ladies." She gazed into the flames for a long moment, then lifted her sewing from her lap. "I liked him."

"I think all th' ladies liked 'im," the lanky man said. "He did have a way about 'im."

"And that cold kinda handsome," said the old man with the pipe.

A smile flickered across Gregoria's face. "His face didn't seem cold to me, the night I met him," she said. "It was kindness itself. He was quite courteous and respectful. Gentle, even."

"Clay Allison kind and gentle. Now that's something I woulda liked to of seen," the scrawny man said.

The men all shook their heads and one of them spit a slurry of chewing tobacco into the fire.

Gregoria glanced at the spitter with a bemused expression. "He was quite the gentleman," she said. A shadow crossed her face. "At least to me." She looked down at her sewing, gazing blindly at the cloth and thread, thinking of all that had led to her meeting with Clay Allison so long ago. And what had come after.

Missouri, 1852

"Here boy, gimme another drink." The teamster slammed his glass on the battered wooden table in the center of the half-empty saloon. "You!" he bellowed. "Boy!"

Charles Kennedy shuffled toward him. At thirteen, he was a big boy who gave promise of being a massive and bitter man. Always ragged, life had already lowered his shoulders into apparent submission and the brow below his dark mass of hair into resentful creases. His blue eyes were habitually squinted and rarely looked directly into another man's face.

"And get one fer yerself," the old man sitting with the teamster told the boy. He grinned at the teamster. "See what he does."

Charles nodded sullenly and returned in a few moments with two glasses.

"Go on," the old man said. "Drink it."

Charles tossed the whisky back with one gulp and grinned.

"Now ask him where he comes from," the man said to the teamster.

"Where you from, boy?"

"Tennessee."

"You a mountain boy?"

"No sir. My pa owns a hundred slaves, raises horses." He thrust his chin forward belligerently. This was untrue. He'd run away from his parents' hardscrabble Tennessee mountain farm two years before and begun drifting slowly west.

The teamster laughed. "And my pa is President Fillmore!"

The boy's fists doubled.

3

"Have another drink," someone said from behind him. A hand thrust a glass of whisky into the boy's hand and he gulped it down.

"Try again, kid. Where ya from?"

"I'm from Tennessee!" he bellowed, glaring blindly at the men around him. "Ya goddam sons of bitches. Ya sons of hell!"

The bartender looked up from his work. "You, Charlie," he said. "I told you about swearing at the customers, now didn't I?"

The boy swung around to face him and went silent, his broad face red with anger, fists clenched. The men at the tables laughed uproariously. The boy swung back to face them, then turned to stalk out of the room. But he was too drunk. He lurched against an empty chair and it clattered sideways onto the wooden floor. There was another burst of laughter.

"You hadn't ought to rile him like that," the bartender said mildly. "He's got a temper, that one."

"Seems harmless enough," the teamster said.

"He's just a driftin' kid," the old man said dismissively. "He'll outgrow his foolishness."

~ ~ ~

The boy waited in the shadows of the alley beside the saloon. The whisky had worn off now and he flipped the knife in his hand, over and over. A cold fury filled him. Those bastards. Filling him with drink. Taunting him. Laughing in his face. They had money so they could do what they wanted. Make everybody bow and scrape. Say what they pleased.

He threw the knife, hard, across the alleyway. The blade bit deep into the wooden planks of the building opposite. He'd be bigger than them, one of these days. Bigger in size. Bigger in money. Bigger'n all of them. Bastards.

RANCHOS DE DON FERNANDO DE TAOS, 1854

Even a two year old knows when her world has changed irrevocably. María Gregoria Cortez watched numbly as her father knelt beside the bed where her mother and infant brother lay so silently. Never before had she seen an adult weep.

"Papá?" she asked, but he gave no sign that he heard. She turned toward the door that led into the adobe casita's other room. There, three women in black went somberly about the business of preparing food, as befitted a house in mourning. None of them acknowledged the child as she entered. She passed to the outer door and stood staring at the bright blue New Mexico sky, the great bulk of the Sangre de Cristo mountains looming down at her. A shiver passed through her small body, in spite of the heat of the day.

~ ~ ~

Small in stature, José de Jesus Cortez had always been a quiet man, given to obedience rather than command. His wife María Antonia had made the decisions in the household. Now she was gone, she and the boy child the priest had christened José Ramon before he and his mother had been swept away in a single week's time. She had died of the fever that sometimes comes to women after childbirth, the baby of some unknown infant cause.

José de Jesus sat listlessly on a small wooden stool outside his rented two room casita, his habitually hunched shoulders more curved than ever. The food the neighbor women had left after the deaths was almost gone now, but he was so tired, so weary. Even the warmth of the sun on his face could not rouse him. The burden of life was too much for him. He might walk to the church in Don Fernando de Taos later and pray. He felt the need of a church, not Rancho's village chapel. But he wasn't sure he could travel the few miles it would take. The weariness, the hopelessness, was overwhelming.

La niña came to stand beside him. He patted her hand gently. María Gregoria. What would her life be, the child of a sinner such as he, whose wife and son had died so suddenly? At any moment she also might be taken. Perhaps it would be for the best.

"Papá, tengo hambre," she said. I am hungry.

He nodded and patted her hand again, but did not move from his seat.

Ranchos de Don Fernando de Taos, 1860

Always a religious man, after the death of his wife and son, José de Jesus Cortez began to spend even more time at the morada, the chapel, with his fellow Penitentes, and Gregoria had to make shift for herself. Because of their poverty, there was no schooling for her, of course, not even in household matters. But she was an observant child and by the time she was eight years old, she had learned from watching the village women the essentials of life: how to sweep the house and prepare simple meals of tortías y habas, corn tortillas and beans. She'd developed her own method of seasoning the beans with the few herbs she was able to grow in the tiny garden plot next to the wood pile behind the casita. She thought the beans tasted well but her father only grunted when she asked him, so she had stopped asking. She watched him anxiously, doing her best to silently lighten his load of pain, her spirits rising inexplicably when his face cleared even a little.

She was happy when he brought his friend Diego home, a man who talked much and appeared to alleviate José's darkness. But then the man stayed behind one day from the morada.

He spoke to Gregoria sweetly, then more sharply, then grabbed her by both arms and carried her swiftly into the casita's back chamber. He placed her on her father's cot, the bed where her mother and brother had died, and began to unfasten his calzones, his pants. As young as she was, she knew what it meant. She shook her head and eyed the blanket that covered the doorway behind him. "Por favor señor," she begged.

He chuckled and leaned over her. "Por favor," he mimicked. "Por favor." He grabbed her long black braids and pulled her back, forcing her flat on the bed, yanking her legs apart. Then he was on top of her. She closed her eyes and whimpered as he hurt her, then hurt her again. She bit her lip against the pain. Then suddenly, it was over and he was standing again, fastening his calzones, when the casita door opened and her father crossed the outer room and pushed back the blanket that covered the door.

~ ~ ~

"Lo siento," José groaned. I am sorry. He crouched on the floor, refusing even the comfort of the low wooden stool. "Que Dios me perdone." May God forgive me.

Gregoria went to him and put her arms around his thin shoulders, but he pushed her away impatiently. "Dios lo siento," he groaned again.

She stood in the middle of the floor, fighting tears. The dark space between her legs still burned from the contact with her father's friend. She was ruined. She knew that. Even at eight and without a mother she knew the basic facts. A girl who had been raped was soiled forever. No decent man would want her.

"Lo siento," her father groaned again. Gregoria frowned, not sure if he was apologizing to her or to God. "I must pray," he said. He stood, stretching his legs, and sighed deeply. "And ask Diego's forgiveness." He moved toward the door without looking at her.

It was God and his friend he was apologizing too, the child realized dully. For having such a puta for a daughter. A girl who could make a man do such a thing.

8

WESTERN FRONT, 1862

"Kennedy," a voice said as he passed the last fire.

Charles stopped and peered into the circle of flame-lit soldiers and gear. "Yeah?"

Faces turned toward him, carefully blank. "Oh. Wrong Kennedy it is," an Irish voice said. "We were speakin' of Patrick, that young scamp."

"You're up next for patrol," a voice said from the opposite side of the fire. The Lieutenant rose and officiously placed his hands behind his back. "You can relieve Scanlon on the southern end."

Charles felt a surge of anger. His fists clenched. He'd stood guard last night and the night before that. But he only nodded and turned abruptly back toward his tent to retrieve his rifle. The Lieutenant had it in for him, the bastard. Thought that because Charles was big, he didn't need sleep.

His route to the southern end of the line required Charles to re-pass the fire site. He heard a chuckle as he went by and his jaw clenched. The hand gripping his rifle tightened reflexively. War was hell, but not just because of the fighting. There were too many people, too many orders, and not enough women or money for them. The enemy wasn't all on the other side. "Bastards!" he growled under his breath.

9

Colorado Territory, Summer 1865

"You said you'd see us to Oregon!" The man sounded angry, but he'd taken off his hat as if in supplication. There was a sudden murmur of female voices from inside the big Conestoga wagon, then silence, a silence that echoed the empty prairie around them.

"Said I'd go 'long with ya," Charles said. "Not how far."

"But why go south, man? It's hot as hell down there, from what I hear."

Charles shrugged his massive shoulders.

"It's the mines, I suppose. Hell man, that Santa Rita in New Mexico Territory is no place for a Christian. And it's another 400 miles, at least." The homesteader replaced his hat and turned to look at his wagon and ox team. "What're we gonna do without you?" he asked plaintively as his wife came around the back of the wagon and stood beside him.

"I wish you luck, Mr. Kennedy," she said.

Kennedy looked at the wagon's team and his own mule. "I'll take payment in grub," he said to the man.

The homesteader's lips tightened. "The deal was we'd feed you, not stake you to leave us. You won't be here to bring in more game."

"Don' want game. Just coffee an' salt."

The woman turned and went to the back of the wagon. She said something to her daughters inside. The men were silent, examining the oxen and the ground while they waited, Kennedy raking his fingers through his unkempt black beard. When she came back, she carried a small packet wrapped in cloth.

"Here's what you asked for and some biscuits besides," she said. "Good luck, Mr. Kennedy."

Charles grunted, took the bundle, and turned toward his waiting mule.

The homesteader and his wife stood watching until Kennedy was well out of earshot.

"You sure seemed anxious to let him go," the man said then. "We'll be short on meat now."

"Better to be short on meat than have him lurking around the edge of the camp at night, leering at our girls," his wife answered grimly.

New Mexico Territory, Fall 1865

Charles had been forced to sell the mule the month before for food and drink, but it was just as well. A man on foot was more difficult to spot, could creep up on his prey more easily, although the dry New Mexico heat and the rocks made the trail tougher going.

He'd shadowed the Mexican out of El Real de San Francisco for two long hot days before grabbing him from behind, knifing him in the back, taking his gold, and leaving his body in the dry hills southeast of Santa Fe. Then he'd skirted the city and headed north. Taos was far enough away that no one was likely to connect Charles' few nuggets with the disappearance of a peón from a dirty gold-mining settlement too small to even be called a village. A place where everything was in transition from somewhere else, including the ever-elusive flakes of gold.

Finally found a way to get some of it for myself, Charles reflected. Probably how the Mexican had got it, for that matter.

"Dirty greaser," Charles muttered. He moved angrily northward through the endless dry arroyos and rocks, the sun beating down relentlessly. "Need a drink. Need a woman."

Northern New Mexico Territory, Spring 1866

Charles trudged steadily down the rocky road skirting the Rio Grande river gorge south of Taos. As much as he hated it, he was returning once again to the back-breaking labor of the gold placer mines of El Real de San Francisco.

He grunted bitterly. If they could be called "gold fields." He expected to be only one of a few americanos digging at the dirt in the hillsides, hauling the mixture of sand and ore into the valley to be washed with the little water available, staring for hours into the watery sludge for a glint from the miniscule golden flakes hidden there.

It was dirty work, long back-breaking hours, and little likely to show for it. But he was out of money and there wasn't much else he could do to raise any. New Mexico Territory was like everywhere else. What the mexicanos called the ricos—the rich men with connections—controlled everything, and Charles didn't have the capital or the connections to compete with them.

"Damn ricos!" he swore as he trudged out of the barren, rockstrewn hills above the rushing river.

He paused for a moment, studying the green fields below. The valley widened here and the river current slowed. Over time, the Rio Grande had deposited rich silt from the mountain slopes to the north onto the valley floor. The resulting nuevomexicano village of Velarde looked prosperous, with its gardens of chile, pumpkin, and other vegetables and its orchards of plums, apples, and pears. Horses and cattle dotted the green pastures.

Charles felt a surge of resentment. "Someday," he muttered. Land of his own, acres that promised this kind of wealth. No more manual labor for him. He'd walk with his son beside him and boss his peóns. Or maybe the boss of his peóns. He laughed harshly and raked his fingers through his beard. Or his son would boss the peóns, and Charles would sit by the fireside and eat and drink like a rico.

But sitting required money. And getting money was painful. Scrabbling in the dirt for gold took the blood from your veins and the strength from your bones. Then you had to spend it for food so you could scratch out more gold. And drink to give you the courage to go on. The injustice of it filled him with rage. Other men didn't work half so hard for so little.

"Ricos!" he spat. He started down the narrow road to the valley, a scowl squinting his eyes into narrow slits. These rico mexicanos clung obstinately to this land while Americans like him had nothing.

He strode angrily past the orchards, glaring at the ripening fruit. The local children moved out of his way and old women tending their gardens crossed themselves behind his back, murmuring spells against the evil eye. The men in the orchards kept their heads turned away, but still they watched him. There was no telling what a crazy americano might do.

EL REAL DE SAN FRANCISCO, JUNE 1866

The hillside placer mine outside El Real that Charles thought of as his own had been taken over by a half-dozen ragged ex-Confederates from Georgia. He circled the site warily for three days, looking for a way to take it back, but the Georgians were too many for him and they always had someone on guard.

"Damn Rebs," he growled as he stalked down the hot and rocky hillside toward the hamlet of El Real. "Lose at home, come here an' steal!"

~ ~ ~

Charles paused in the doorway of El Real's single adobe saloon, letting his eyes adjust. The only light came from two narrow rectangles cut into the wall at shoulder height. Originally designed as rifle slits, they acted as unshuttered windows for the rough wooden counter that served as the bar and the four battered tables for patrons.

As Charles' eyes adjusted, he saw that there were a dozen men sitting in the semi-darkness, where a year before there'd been only one or two. The grime on their faces and holes in their clothes said some had been mining for a while. But not all of them. The new-comers were the ones with shirts without patches and boots that were more dusty than scuffed. Charles edged to the far end of the bar and nodded to the barkeeper.

"Mr. Kennedy," the man said formally. "It's been a while since we've seen you. The usual?"

Charles nodded. He glanced around, threw back his drink, and gestured for another as he studied the room out of the corner of his eye.

The two men at the table nearest him were arguing quietly but intensely. He could just make out their words.

"I just do not think it wise to take on someone we don't know or who hasn't been recommended to us," the younger one said. He looked to be in his late twenties and had a small reddish-blond mustache and a narrow, high-bridged nose.

"We can't do this alone, Brian," the older man said. He pushed back his hat. The light from the window slits glinted on the strands of gray in his hair. He glanced at Charles and leaned toward his companion, lowering his voice. "Every location has a dozen men vying for it. We'll be lucky if our gear is still there when we get back to camp."

"But we can't find just anyone, Curt," the younger man said. "They could be working for somebody else and just wanting to frighten us off."

Curt nodded and resettled his hat. "It's a problem, I'll grant you that."

"I think we need to get some advice."

"Yes, but where?"

"From somebody who's been in the Territory more than two weeks."

"As far as I can tell, that would be the barkeeper."

Brian grinned. "He'll know who can hold their liquor, anyway."

Without looking at the table, Charles eased toward the other end of the bar. He gestured to the barkeeper.

"Another drink?" the man asked, moving toward him.

"Nah." Charles jerked his head sideways, toward the two men at the table, and leaned across the battered wood. He lowered his voice. "They ask you for a name, I'm on the north end of town."

"You and a dozen other good men."

Charles laid a gold coin on the counter.

"But sure, I can tell 'em."

Charles nodded and went out the heavy wood door. He stood for a moment, blinking against the sharp sunlight. Another coin out of his pocket, he thought grimly. It'd better be worth it.

~ ~ ~

"You been in the Territory long?" Curt asked over his shoulder as Charles followed him up one of the many gullies northwest of El Real. The smell of piñon sap mixed with the dust scuffed up by their feet and tightened their throats.

"'Bout a year," Charles answered. Greenhorn, he thought. Shoulda asked that before he agreed to take me on.

They'd discussed the important issue though: a quarter split for Charles, three quarters between the other two. Charles would provide protection. His bulk alone was likely to scare off all but the most determined of claim jumpers. He'd also advise about locations and digging methods. He permitted himself a small smile. It'd be mostly talking and being ready to shoot anyone who got too inquisitive. No shoveling dirt or washing gravel.

The younger man was tending a small fire when they walked into camp at the edge of yet another gully, this one with a trickle of water at its center. He came forward. "How do you do?" he asked, holding out his hand. "I'm Brian Carrigee."

Charles nodded and put down his pack. "Charles Kennedy," he said. He looked around. "Where's the placer?"

17

Brian frowned, dropped his hand, and went back to the fire.

"It's just up the hill," Curt said. "We'd be glad of any suggestions."

"Would you like some coffee?" Brian asked.

"Too hot," Charles said. He looked at Curt. "Placer?"

The two of them worked their way up a narrow quarter-mile path edged with juniper, scrub oak, and piñon. Curt pointed to a large hole in the hillside roughly three by five feet and three feet deep. "We started there," he said. "I'm told that the lower hillsides are the most likely locations. But we haven't had much luck and there's not enough water for washing it out."

Charles looked up. A thirty-foot high granite boulder loomed over them. He jerked his head toward it. "Look behind there." He turned and headed back to the fire, where he checked his ammunition, grabbed a tin cup from a rock beside the fire, poured himself coffee, then sat down on a large rock next to his pack.

"How d'ya haul out?" he asked Brian, who was stowing flour and sugar in a pack.

Brian lifted his head, stared at Charles, then turned away. "We have a mule hobbled nearby," he said over his shoulder.

"Closer, ya wanna keep it." Charles lifted the tin cup to his lips.

"He's already cropped all the nearby grass," Brian said. He ran a short end of rope through the pack's straps, then began lashing the bundle to the upper branch of an old scrub oak, out of bear reach.

Charles shrugged. "Better t' cut grass than catamount find him."

Brian turned, stared at him for a long minute, then went to collect the mule.

Charles contemplated the coffee pot. Really didn't need coffee this time of day. But he wasn't paying for it. He grinned. He could feel his bag of coins getting fatter already.

~ ~ ~

By the end of two weeks with the greenhorns, Charles was feeling less sure about how fat his moneybag was likely to grow. Curt and Brian had little endurance for the endless digging that placer mining required in the dry Southwest. After a couple morning hours with pick and shovel, they'd stumble back to the campsite to rest, remain there most of the afternoon, waiting for the cooler evening hours, then climb reluctantly back up to the digging site.

As soon as darkness began to fall, they'd be back in camp, where Charles had been all day, guarding the supplies and mule. The next morning, they'd coax the mule up the path, load him with bags filled with the gravel results of the previous day's efforts, and ease him back down the hillside. They'd add the bags to the stack at the campsite, then return to the boulder. They'd pound at the rocky ground behind it until the dryness and heat became too much for them once again, then return to camp to rest.

They seemed relieved when Charles told them they had enough bags of gravel to find some water and wash out the gold. He told them where to look for water in El Real and tersely described the process they'd need to use, and they headed out, the mule between them, into the dry heat of the day.

Charles chuckled and stretched out next to his pack for a nap. They'd be gone at least two days. He tucked his rifle under his arm and eased his pistol into position in case he got visitors. There'd been none so far. Probably needed to have some while the

19

greenhorns were gone, so they'd know his protection was valuable. He chuckled again and closed his eyes.

~ ~ ~

"Is he asleep?" Brian muttered irritably as the two men paused in the junipers and scrub oak at the edge of camp. "It's broad daylight." Charles lay propped against a large rock, black hair tousled over his closed eyes, rifle tucked under his arm. Empty tin cans littered the ground.

Curt murmured something and moved into the clearing and across. Just as he reached Charles's feet, Charles lunged suddenly upward, the end of his rifle barrel inches from Curt's face. "Tryin' t' get killed?" he snarled.

Curt's hands were in the air, palms forward. "No! No, of course not!" he protested. "I thought you were sick or something."

"You and some others." Charles jerked his head northward. "Georgia fellas come visitin'. Good thing I was here."

Brian was pulling packs of supplies off the mule. "Someone in town told us those Georgia fellows were run off by a group from Missouri," he said.

"Come by on their way out," Charles growled.

"The man we talked to said they'd been gone for a week." Brian set the packs down near a juniper at the edge of the clearing.

Charles glared at him and shifted his gun, but Curt said, "Never mind that now, Brian." He turned to Charles. "That cleaning process is hellish. And here I thought digging was bad." He shook his head and grinned. "But we made out pretty well. Do you want to divide now or shall we wait until we have a larger pot put together?"

"How much ya get?" Charles asked.

Brian moved forward. "Don't you trust us?"

Charles scowled. "Should I?"

Brian's face darkened, but Curt was already pulling out the bag of coins. "Three hundred dollars, all told," he said. "And some gold dust we didn't have converted to coin."

"Hundred for me," Charles said. "An' half the dust."

"We said a quarter," Brian said. "That makes your share seventy-five."

"Not much, for what I did," Charles said. He jerked his head toward the digging site. "You'd still be diggin' below."

"Let's make it ninety and a third of the dust," Curt said. He crossed to his pack and pulled out a small scale and a bag of weights. "Do you want it now or later?"

"Now."

Once the gold was divided, Charles picked up his pack and carried it a quarter mile from camp. Then he doubled back to just beyond earshot. He worked his way into the middle of a thicket of scrub oak, then pulled his trousers down just enough to uncover his money belt. He distributed the coins and bag of dust into the belt, then refastened his pants. Just within sight of camp, in case anyone was watching, he made a show of putting down his pack to fidget with a leather pouch tucked deep inside. If they wanted something of his, they could have the pebbles in the pouch. They were nothing but fools' gold, but he wasn't fool enough to let anyone see where his stash was really hidden.

~ ~ ~

Curt and Brian were standing toe to toe, deep in conversation, when Charles stepped back into the clearing. Abruptly, they stopped talking, and Brian turned away and began collecting the scattered tin cans. Curt crouched down and began building a fire.

21

"I'm going to boil some coffee," he told Charles. "Would you like some?"

Charles nodded and put down his pack.

"So how long have you been away from Taos, Charles?" Curt asked. "About six weeks?" He added some small sticks to the flames. "We heard in town that Uncle Dick Wootton has finally finished his toll road over Raton Pass. That'll sure make it easier for wagons on the Santa Fe Trail Mountain Route. It should increase traffic on that route considerably, which I would think will mean travelers to Taos, as well, since it'll be closer. Travelers will cut off from Rayado, won't they? Thought you'd be interested to hear it."

Charles shrugged noncommittally.

Curt lifted an eyebrow. He poured water from a tin bucket into the coffee pot and added crushed coffee beans. There was a long silence as the mixture began to steam and then simmer. When it was ready, he poured out a cup for Charles and handed it to him. Charles grunted in acknowledgement.

Brian had finished collecting and burying the tin cans and gone to collect firewood. He walked in with an armload of old scrub oak branches as Curt put the pot back on a flat rock next to the fire.

"Coffee?" Curt asked.

Brian nodded and bent to arrange his branches in a neat pile. He looked up at Charles. "That scrub oak patch back there looks like someone climbed right into the middle of it and stood there a while," he said. "You afraid of someone seeing you put your money away?"

"Other business," Charles said.

Brian straightened and gave him a hard look. "No evidence of that kind of activity."

Charles grunted. "Nothin' private?"

Curt chuckled and handed Brian a mug of coffee. "You have to hand it to him, Brian's pretty observant. He served as an Army Scout, you know. It's a habit with him, now."

"I didn't see any bullet casings around here, either," Brian said. "Or foot prints. There's no evidence of an altercation with that Georgia crowd, or anyone else, for that matter."

"Didn't need t'shoot," Charles said. "Ground's soft and dug up. Can't tell prints apart." He leaned forward to reach for the coffee pot. "Diggin' tomorrow?" he asked as he refilled his cup.

~ ~ ~

"We could use some real meat," Curt said, two weeks later. "We're going through the canned goods more quickly than I thought we would."

"Go into town, clean more gravel," Charles said. He was sitting on a granite outcropping at the edge of the campsite, rifle in hand.

"We don't have quite as much collected now as we did when we went in last time," Curt said.

"We do have three shovels," Brian observed.

"I guard," Charles said.

"Perhaps we could increase your share," Curt suggested.

"You and I will need to discuss that first," Brian said sharply. "And at some length." He looked at Charles, then back at Curt. "A discussion between the two of us."

"Half fer me. You split the rest," Charles said.

"One man gets half?"

"Know what I'm doin'." He shifted his rifle.

Brian scowled and looked at Curt, who shrugged at Charles. "Brian and I are partners," he said. "I can't go against his thoughts on this."

"Then I guard and advise." Charles tilted his rifle and examined the stock. He rubbed a notch on the top with his thumb.

"We haven't received much advice lately," Brian said. "Except to keep digging."

Charles eased off the rock, rifle in the crook of his right arm. He moved closer to Brian, reminding the younger man of his size. "What we agreed."

"That was the agreement," Curt acknowledged. He came alongside Charles, facing Brian, and put his hand on Charles' left arm. "Although we certainly could use some—"

He never finished the sentence. Charles flung his arm up and back at the same time. Curt lurched backward, his feet digging into the soft dry soil and catching on each other. He fell with a thud, his head making a hollow sound as it hit the boulder where Charles had been sitting.

Brian sprang up, took two steps toward Curt, saw blood, and turned back to Charles. His eyes narrowed and his hand reached toward the holster on his belt, but Charles' rifle was already in position. The barrel roared and a bullet slammed into the base of the younger man's throat. Brian put a hand to his neck. And then he crumpled beside his partner.

Charles lowered his rifle and looked down at the two men. Then he moved to Curt. His skull was bashed in on one side, his eyes already glazing over. Too bad. He'd liked Curt well enough. His only fault was the bastard he'd partnered with.

~ ~ ~

Charles dug a rough hole in the middle of the scrub oak thicket, then dragged Brian's body there and Curt's to the original hillside digging pit. After a moment's hesitation, he decided to bury their weapons with them. Both men had carved their initials into the stocks. Too easy to spot, too many questions. He covered Brian's body with dirt and oak leaves, stomped them down thoroughly, then led the reluctant mule through the branches and tethered him there to add his own markings.

While the mule moved restlessly inside the thicket, Charles went to the hillside above the original digging pit. He used a shovel to leverage the smaller boulders on the slope until they gave way and crashed down over Curt's body, filling the hole and scattering debris above and beyond it. A casual observer would think miners had undercut the rocks above and started a slide.

Finally, he led the mule back out of the thicket and took him back to the campsite. Charles glanced around. Take everything, he decided. Make it look like they'd cleared out. Someone else'd move in soon enough, when nobody came into El Real with more gravel to wash.

He considered the mule. She was just a gray mule. No brand or clipped ear or white patch. It'd be rough to tell who she'd belonged to, once she was away from here.

He gathered the three bedrolls and combined them into one fat one, with an extra blanket stowed under the mule's packsaddle, camouflaged as part of its usual cushioning. He untied the food packs from the scrub oak and loaded them onto the mule. Then he cut open Brian's personal pack. He tossed the clothes aside. None of them would fit his large frame. Hafta dig another pit, he thought irritably.

At the bottom of the pack was a small leather bag and a slick new black leather wallet. Charles emptied the bag of coins and counted them. Two hundred twenty-five dollars. Curt had been a trusting cuss, leaving the mining proceeds in Brian's hands.

The wallet held more money, in greenbacks. Four hundred and twenty-three dollars. Charles ran his fingers through his beard thoughtfully, then reinserted the bills and tucked the wallet inside his shirt.

He reached for Curt's pack and dumped it upside down, shaking it sharply. More clothes, the scale and weights, then a battered brown leather wallet. He grabbed it greedily.

This wad of bills was much thinner. Thirty-two dollars. Charles shook his head in disgust, then grinned. With the ninety he already had, there was seven hundred seventy dollars.

He began to tuck the bills back into the wallet, then stopped and turned the battered brown leather in his hands. It was less likely to draw attention than the black one. He combined the greenbacks into the older wallet and placed the black one on the fire. As the leather began to curl, he heard movement behind him. He whirled where he crouched, reaching for his revolver, but it was just the mule pulling at juniper branches.

~ ~ ~

Charles and the mule worked their way down the trail toward El Real, but turned east when the path connected to the dusty road, cutting across country. There was just enough moonlight to pick a way through the juniper and piñon. He headed slightly south, skirting the occasional campsite, moving steadily toward the plains.

By the next morning they were well away from the mining settlement, still moving south and east. They made the grasslands on the eastern slopes by afternoon. There Charles shot a small antelope, then moved into a ravine where he and the mule would be less visible against the skyline. The gully had seen more seepage than flooding in the last few years, so there was grass for the mule, old flood debris for a fire, and a small stand of coyote willow.

He cut and peeled a willow stick, threaded a strip of antelope flesh onto it, then sat back on his heels while he held it over the fire.

He patted the wallet tucked inside his shirt, then grunted at himself disparagingly. It was still not enough for the kind of spread he wanted. When the Territory was still part of Mexico, American and other ricos with connections had corralled huge swaths of open country into their own hands, then passed it on to their children and their spouses. After the American occupation, the government had allowed most of the land grants to remain in place. Which meant people like Lucien Maxwell and his friends controlled a vast number of acres, along with the people who lived on and worked them. The ravine Charles was crouched in probably belonged to Maxwell or one of the other ricos. He was going to have to cross part of Maxwell's grant to get back to Taos, for that matter. Charles grunted in disgust.

He blew on the strip of antelope meat to cool it slightly, then slid it off the stick with his teeth. Too bad he didn't have some bacon to fatten it up a bit. Maybe he'd take a swing through Las Vegas and see if he could buy himself a haunch of pork. Or liberate one from an outlying farmyard. He grinned, then sobered, considering the risks. Should probably wait until he was nearer Rayado or Maxwell's store on the Cimarron. On the other hand, there were women for hire in Las Vegas, and it'd been a long time.

SANGRE DE CRISTO MOUNTAINS, FALL 1866

There'd been nothing to fear in Las Vegas, after all. Charles was just one more dusty traveler in a New Mexico Territory town. The mostly one-story adobes that clustered around the plaza were hot and dry under the cloudless sky. The pigs penned up behind the houses on the outskirts had been well guarded and he was forced to use one of Curt and Brian's coins for a small saddle of pork. He spent an hour with a prostitute, then headed out.

He camped in the hills west of town and ate some of the pork with the remainder of the antelope. Then he headed north, skirting the Mora Valley wheat fields and easing up into the rocks and piñon of Guadalupita Canyon. He swung wide of the few cabins that crouched haphazardly in the canyon bottom and forced the mule upward, along the rocky slopes, using the boulders that perched there as cover.

When they reached Coyote Creek, he edged closer to the canyon bottom. This made travel easier, though wetter due to the frequent beaver ponds that slowed the stream. Charles eyed the beaver mounds speculatively, raking his fingers through his beard, then remembered there was no market. Though if a man needed skins for his own use, this'd be a good place to collect 'em. In the icy water in mid-January. A man'd have to be desperate to endure those conditions for a few measly pelts. And stupid. He grunted irritably and clucked at the mule, moving onward.

The usual route from here to Taos followed Coyote Creek towards Osha Pass, then along the rough track the Sibley Expedition had used in '25. He was still following the creek when he heard a voice on the slope above him.

"Jare!" it called in a strong Texas drawl. "Howdy! You there! Do I know ya'll?"

Charles squinted up the hillside and recognized the man's face from the El Real saloon. One of those newcomer miners with more clothes and voice than sense. Charles scowled and turned the mule slightly eastward, as if he'd wandered off his course and was now correcting it.

"Jare!" the man called again. "Hey ya'll! What news? Can ya'll hear me?"

Charles lifted his hand in acknowledgement that he'd heard, but didn't turn his head. He yanked at the mule's lead rope, hurrying him around a clump of juniper and out of the man's line of sight. Greenhorn. With that voice, lurking Utes or Apaches were bound to hear him and investigate. Charles grunted approvingly. Then the loud mouth wouldn't go back to El Real and start making connections between the disappearance of Curt and Brian and the sight of Charles leading a mule into the Sangre de Cristos.

He clucked at the mule and angled north and east, onto the ridge above the creek. With fools like that on the track, he'd do better to stay off Osha Pass, cut across to Taos by another route.

~ ~ ~

Man and mule stood on a rocky outcropping near the head of Coyote Creek and looked northwest, into a broad valley dotted with small ponds. Cattle and sheep clustered around the water holes or grazed beside the narrow streams that meandered through the valley's thick grasses toward the creek. A few men clustered around a campfire to Charles' left while herd dogs trotted casually among the livestock, monitoring conditions.

"Black Lake," Charles muttered. He'd heard about this place. A number of Taos' Spanish families still herded their livestock into the mountains early each summer, each clan using a different route and grazing area. The use of this particular valley was reserved to the Martínez family, the relatives of the infamous, defrocked, and unrepentant Taos padre.

Most travelers would have headed into the valley to rest their animal and chat with the herders, but Charles continued along the east bank of the creek and the valley. At the northern end, the forest thickened again and Coyote Creek turned west. Following it would take him to Osha Pass. Instead, Charles bore north, working his way around rocky outcroppings and through long stretches of quaking aspen and ponderosa pine.

There was little underbrush—the ponderosas and aspens had seen to that, blocking the sunlight below them to prohibit the growth of anything much beyond grass and wildflowers. The elk herds had done their part, too. There was plenty of sign, both in round black droppings and in aspens streaked with bloody-looking sap where the big animals had rubbed away the white bark.

Eventually, Charles crested the top of a ridge that had a view of something besides more trees. He paused and studied the layout.

The land sloped steadily downward. It was still thick with ponderosa, aspen, and fir, but he could glimpse what appeared to be another grassy valley ahead, much longer than the one behind him. Thin ribbons of water wound through it, glinting in the sun.

Charles looked up. The sky was blue and crowded with large white cumulus clouds, the kind that could turn black and stormy at a moment's notice, producing a sudden squall of rain. Rain was something he hadn't seen lately. He grunted approvingly, clucked at the mule, and began angling down the rocky slope, picking his way between the trees.

This'd be the south end of Moreno Valley. Why the hell moreno or "black" he didn't know. He'd seen a Sibley map once that labeled it Eagle Park. He squinted upward and grunted. No eagles today.

He studied the line of mountains to the west, between him and Taos. Apache Pass was somewhere near, on the mule track that headed west, then dropped into the Rio Fernando Valley. It created a fairly direct connection between Taos to the west and Rayado to the east and points south, including El Real. As a direct connection to the Santa Fe trail at Rayado, it got its share of travelers. Something inside him stirred uneasily. Then he remembered that there was another pass farther up the valley. Palo Flechado, they called it. Arrowed tree, whatever the hell that meant.

~ ~ ~

Charles and the mule were in the valley by noon, following a small creek that meandered north in endless switchbacks. Evergreens were scattered along its banks or in small clusters near occasional ponds. The grass was thick and studded with wildflowers. The mule snatched mouthfuls as they moved forward.

The openness and lack of cover made Charles uneasy. A man could see a good ways off, but he could also be seen. He squinted north and west for signs of the pass. There'd be a stream. The other side would have water flowing toward Taos. He came to a small creek that meandered down from the western slopes, but a herd of sheep and goats grazed on either side of its banks and was monitored by two men and several mangy dogs. Charles moved north.

A breeze came up and the clouds overhead darkened. A pale gray screen of rain obscured the northern end of the valley.

31

Charles angled west, heading toward the ponderosa pine that marked the meeting of valley and foothills.

He crossed another stream flowing from the trees. Its edges were soft and undercut, and the mule balked at the lack of support under her hooves. Charles gave the rope a stiff yank and the mule lurched forward in spite of herself, hooves tearing at the muddy bank.

At the next stream, Charles turned directly west, following the stream toward the trees. If this wasn't the pass he wanted, it would at least get him closer to Taos than where he was now. And out of the open valley.

At the forest edge, he glanced back at the valley, then turned more fully and took another look. He raked his fingers through his beard, considering. He knew there was a cut on the valley's northern end, in the smaller mountains to the east, where the Cimarron River began. A low grassy ridge cut across the valley, hiding the opening from view, but he'd heard that the Cimarron flowed east from there, through a rocky canyon to Maxwell's place on the Santa Fe Trail.

Charles glanced southward. He couldn't see the herds and men that he'd passed. The ground dipped here in a kind of grassy hollow. It would be a good place to live if a man didn't want much company. Small chance anyone here'd know about events in El Real. A man could do pretty much what he wanted in a place like this.

He stirred restlessly. Except for women. A man needed an outlet. The pressure in his groin had been relieved only slightly by the Las Vegas prostitute. His physical needs were too strong to go womanless so long.

He grimaced. As cheap as prostitutes were, the cost added up. "Cheaper to keep one o' my own," he muttered. "Somewheres safe, out o' other men's way."

But this was Maxwell's land. Had been Charles Beaubien's, the old French trader turned Territorial Judge. Lucien Maxwell had married a Beaubien daughter, then started buying out her siblings when the old man died. It cost money to go to law.

"Rico!" Charles spat contemptuously, then turned to trudge up the rocky path.

~ ~ ~

The path followed the creek, which was becoming more like a mountain brook, less like the meandering streams in the valley below. Its bed had suddenly straightened and its water ran clear over gray stones. A bathing robin paused to wait for the man and mule to pass, but Charles didn't notice it.

The question was how to keep his money and a woman, too. A female wouldn't be much use in El Real or on the trail. Needed a roof and bed, damn 'em.

His senses tightened. There was someone ahead, coming towards him. A stranger, tall and dark with quick eyes, riding a horse with a silver-mounted bridle, right hand holding a rifle with a highly polished stock. He reined in as Charles approached.

"Señor," the stranger said, nodding politely.

Charles nodded and grunted, then paused. "From Taos?" he asked. "This Palo Flechado?"

"Sí." The nuevomexicano laid his rifle across the pommel of his saddle. "To both inquiries." He smiled. "You go to Don Fernando de Taos? It is a lovely day on which to travel."

33

Charles glanced around. Sun glinted on the long green needles of the ponderosa pines that stretched overhead. The air moved slightly, cooling the sheen of sweat on his face. "Ways to Taos, though," he said.

The stranger nodded. "I must admit that I could wish for a resting place." He gestured at the trees around them. "Someplace indoors with a meal and a fire."

"Hafta ask Maxwell," Charles said irritably. "His grant."

The other man shook his head. "You are mistaken, señor." He pointed toward the valley. "The grant ends at the crest of the mountains on the eastern side." He waved a hand at the trees and the grassland beyond. "This is all for the taking. The americano Congress has said so."

Charles looked at him sharply, but there was no bitterness in the man's voice. The smile seemed genuine, though brief.

"But if I make haste, my horse will sleep in Señor Maxwell's stables tonight." The man nodded again and lifted his rifle away from the saddle. "I bid you good day."

Charles nodded and watched the rico's horse work its way down the rocky trail. This was the only logical route for anyone travelling from Taos to Lucien Maxwell's Cimarron spread and the Indian agency there. In fact, it was the shortest way to connect to the mountain route of the Santa Fe Trail, if you were horseback or afoot. Charles looked around. So it didn't belong to the lands old man Beaubien had acquired from the Mexican government, after all.

He proceeded more slowly now, thinking about the rich traveler's wish for a place to rest, the length of his journey from Taos. He still had a good thirty-five miles before he reached Maxwell's. Someone living along this route, with a roof and food and drink to offer, could relieve the occasional pilgrim of his money and goods and never get caught. They'd have to truly be pilgrims—men unknown in Taos, or to Maxwell and his cronies. Greenhorns like Brian and Curt, hunting adventure or gold. It was something to consider. As long as you had a woman available.

DON FERNANDO DE TAOS, EARLY 1867

"You tellin' me Thomas Means got hisself lynched 'cuz he beat on his wife?" The old man drained his drink and gestured to the barkeeper for another.

"Almost killed her," Charles Kennedy replied, running his fingers through his unkempt black beard.

"What was she doin'?"

"Spendin' money. Runnin' up credit."

"Merchants lettin' her do it?"

"Guess so." Kennedy turned his back to the bar, leaned against it, and surveyed the room.

"Way I heard it, he was shootin' up the street," a voice said. Charles and the old man turned their heads. A scrawny man with three missing teeth was leaning against the bar to their right, grinning at them. "Got arrested for firin' off his pistol in the plaza," the man said. "Lynch mob liberated 'im from jail, hauled 'im inta the neighboring room, an' hanged 'im from the vigas."

"A man's got no rights nowadays," the old man grumbled.

"Not in Taos," Charles said.

~ ~ ~

Charles fingered the coins in his pocket and thought morosely about women and money. It was warm in the saloon, a relief from the January chill outside. But he needed more than drink and a roof against the winter. He needed a woman. The pressure was building in him and he needed an outlet. But he needed land, too, and there'd be no money for land if he kept buying prostitutes.

36

His eye fell on the girl collecting empty drinking vessels from the tables nearby. She was young, perhaps fourteen, but already blossomed. Her breasts had formed nicely and poked pleasantly against her blouse. He could see her hips moving under her skirts, which clung to her thighs. Either she intended to attract male attention or poverty kept her from wearing petticoats.

Charles watched her with interest. Her skirt, in typical nuevomexicano fashion, was cut just below the knee and her calves curved nicely above small bare feet. She kept her eyes down, as if afraid to look around the room and meet the gaze of the drinking men. She had long dark hair, more straight than curly, and broad cheekbones, making her look almost Indian despite her creamy Spanish skin. When she clutched the roughly carved wooden noggins the bar used as drinking glasses to her chest, her loose blouse pulled down slightly, revealing smooth curves.

Charles licked his lips. "You. Girl," he called.

She looked up at him, large dark eyes wary.

"Come 'ere," he said.

She stood still, staring at him.

"Here," he insisted. He held out an empty noggin. "Take it."

She came closer. She already held three containers against her chest with her right hand. She reached her left for Charles' noggin. He made as if to give it to her, then dropped it to the floor and grabbed her wrist instead, pulling her toward him. "Pretty," he said. "'Fraid o' me, pretty?"

"No señor," she said, but she nodded "Yes" as she said it.

He chuckled. "Su gracia?" What's your name?

"Gregoria," she said reluctantly. "María Gregoria Cortez."

"Like a Rose," he said. "Call ya Rosa. Pretty like a rose."

She smiled at him then. "Gracias," she said.

37

He patted her bottom. "Come home with me."

She looked at him in confusion. "Qué?"

His grip tightened. "Slut. You know what."

"Me duele," she whimpered, trying to pull away. It hurts.

He loosened his grip. "No americano, huh? E'en better." He turned toward the bar and lifted his voice. "Barkeep, this girl got a papa or mama t' speak for her?"

"Papa," the barkeeper said. "Not much o' one, though."

~ ~ ~

José de Jesus Cortez was a broken man and he knew it. The last of his meager strength had gone with his wife and son, and he had not been able to exert himself to recover from the blow.

José's fellow Penitentes were a comfort to him, but his daughter was a problem he didn't know how to solve, so he didn't try. It was easier to go to the morada or accept scraps of work from other members of the brotherhood. Anything was less painful than to look at her face, so much like her mother's, and know he was failing her, too. No daughter of a Christian man should be working in a saloon. It was only slightly better than prostituting herself, becoming one of the traídas y llevadas, the women of the streets. But he felt deeply that this, too, was inevitable and somehow his doom. After all, she was already ruined.

The day Charles Kennedy followed Gregoria home from the saloon, José felt a slight stirring of hope that straightened his spine just a little.

"Take her with me," Kennedy told him.

José looked at his daughter staring at the floor in the casita's dim light. She had a wistfulness about her that her mother had never possessed. "She is a good girl," he told Kennedy. "She will not go with you without la diligencias matrimoniales." To say she was good was not so very wrong, he told himself. There had never been an incident since the one six years earlier. The americano would not understand the difference. This was likely to be her only chance. And the formal ceremony of marriage was necessary. The americano must be tied to her as firmly as possible or he would discard her when he wearied of her. Or learned the truth. José put the thought firmly from his mind and did his best to look the black-bearded man in the face.

Kennedy grunted. "Wedding costs money."

José frowned, pretending not to understand. He looked at Gregoria, who was staring at the casita's dirt floor. Her breasts curved pleasantly beneath the red cotton chal, the shawl she'd inherited from her mother.

"I got money," Kennedy said impatiently. "Don't wanna waste it."

They both looked at Gregoria, who glanced up into Charles' face, and returned her gaze to the floor.

"She is a good girl," her father repeated. He gestured around the room. "She cleans and cooks. She has discreción."

"A real rose," Kennedy growled. "How much?"

Father and daughter glanced at him in surprise.

~ ~ ~

The ceremony was a simple one, late on a cold Thursday afternoon on the last day of February. Father Gabriel Ussel was tired, had a head cold, and was burdened with preparations for the Lenten Season which began the following week. He wanted only to go to bed. He viewed the small group before him with distaste.

The father had rounded up a distant cousin and a Penitente friend to act as witnesses. Did the girl have no female family members or friends? he wondered.

But Padre Ussel had done his duty, had collected the requisite family information from the prospective groom and bride and assured himself for the record that they weren't related in any way. It was highly unlikely, he thought dryly, given the slight Southern drawl in the americano's voice and the girl's lack of English. But then, after ten years in the Americas, the French-born Ussel still struggled himself with both English and New Mexican Spanish. This was a foreign place to him. Always would be, he supposed.

The Padre squared his shoulders and got on with the task at hand. There wasn't much required of him. Just the words and the blessings. The groom wasn't wasting money on masses and celebrations, and the bride's father certainly had no coins to spare.

Ussel gestured the little group into position and nodded to the big black-bearded man and the slender girl to kneel. She shivered as she did so and he looked down at her questioningly.

She shook her head. "Lo siento," Gregoria said. "No es nada. Hace frío hoy." I am sorry. It is nothing. It is cold today.

DON FERNANDO DE TAOS, SPRING 1867

At first Gregoria thought her luck had finally turned: Charles bought her cotton cloth for new dresses and there was enough food to eat. He even bought her a small pair of coquetas, dangling silver earrings inset with tiny turquoise chips. Having him call her "Rosa" was a small price to pay for food, clothing, and an occasional piece of jewelry. She'd never liked her name anyway. It was a man's name dressed up to appear a woman's. It made her feel ugly. And so when Charles Kennedy said "Call ya Rosa," in his gruff voice, she had smiled with pleasure. At last, someone who recognized her, someone who saw her for who she was.

But he seemed primarily interested in her body. The Taos casita he rented for them consisted of two tiny dark adobe rooms in a back alley lined with similar houses, half of them empty. Gregoria saw it for the first time immediately after the ceremony, but she caught only a glimpse of the front room as her esposo led her into the back chamber. The floor was of hard-packed clay, the bed a ledge of adobe jutting from the wall and covered with three wool trade blankets. Charles lifted her onto it and began unfastening his trousers.

"Get 'em off," he said, thrusting his chin at her.

Gregoria stared up at him and began pulling off her blouse.

"Wastin' time," he growled. "The skirt." He pulled his shirt off over his head and she gazed at him as she stood to wriggle her skirt down over her hips. He had a massive chest, covered with black hair and well muscled. She let her eyes drift lower, then lifted them back to his face.

41

He grinned at her. "Never seen one before, huh?"

He didn't wait for an answer, but reached for her arms, maneuvered her to the bed, and began assaulting her with rough kisses. He stopped only to pull her blouse over her head. His bearded lips went to her breasts. "Pergates," he said. "Ah, pergates."

She smiled. As he entered her a few moments later, she focused on the fact that he liked her breasts. Still, she felt herself stiffening in mute protest. He pulled back and grinned at her, narrowed blue eyes glittering in the dark room. "First time, huh?"

She nodded, knowing the lie was important, and bit her lip. Certainly the pain made it feel like the first time.

~ ~ ~

A week later, Gregoria slipped out from under the blankets while Charles was still sleeping. She dressed quickly in the dark and went into the outer room to light the fire and prepare the morning meal. Within a day of their marriage she had organized the kitchen area and asked Charles for the supplies she needed. He had grumbled, but he'd bought them. By now she could move comfortably in the morning dimness to light the fire and gather her utensils. The tortías were almost ready when he came from the inner room. She had wrapped them carefully in a cloth to keep them warm.

"Buenos días mi esposo," Gregoria said shyly, looking up from the cast iron griddle.

Charles grunted in reply and went out. When he returned a few minutes later, Gregoria was standing at the rough-built table, slicing queso into a dish. She turned her head to smile shyly at him and he reached for her, one large hand fondling her breasts from behind as the other unfastened his breeches.

42

"Almuerzo," she said. Breakfast. But it was too late. She could feel his member pressing against her buttocks. She bit her lip. She had already learned what to expect. She placed her knife beside the cheese and gripped the table edge. Charles lifted her skirt and she bent forward obediently. At least he is only one man, she told herself, not half a dozen leering and reaching for me at all hours of the day.

When he was done he slapped her bare rump, dropped her skirt, and turned away, fastening his clothes. "What's t' eat?" he asked. She looked at him blankly. He scowled and lifted his hand to his mouth in a eating gesture.

"What food?" he demanded.

Gregoria gestured toward the table. "Tortías y queso," she said. Corn tortillas and cheese. She unwrapped the stack of tortillas, showing him the food. I must learn to relax, she told herself. Then it won't hurt so much.

"Need meat," Charles said as he sat down on the table's single wooden bench. "I'll hunt tomorrow." He squeezed her thigh with one hand as he reached for the food with the other and Gregoria smiled at him obediently.

~ ~ ~

Gregoria was bent over the adobe fireplace, carefully stirring the meat in the stew pot, when a shadow crossed the casita's open wooden door.

She looked up. "Papá!"

"Buenos días mi hija," he said humbly, his hat between his hands.

Gregoria felt a twinge of guilt. Though they lived only a few miles apart, she had not seen her father since the day of her marriage. She had food and a roof and new clothes. He was still ragged and tired and hungry-looking. She rose and went to him, her hands out. He clasped them in his thin fingers and looked questioningly into her face.

She led him to the table, filled a wooden bowl with stew, and brought tortías. She sat across from him and watched as he tried to eat slowly. It was clear that it was his first true meal in days.

They were still at the table when Charles came in. He grunted at them and went into the back room. Gregoria could hear him moving around the room, then he called "Rosa!"

She turned her head. He was standing in the doorway, gesturing toward his groin. She saw the bulge beneath the cloth and raised her eyes toward his beseechingly, but he motioned at her impatiently. She glanced at her father, who was still focused on his stew, then rose and went into the other room.

Charles grabbed her arm and pulled her to him before she could get the door properly shut. He pushed her toward the adobe bed. "Please," she whispered. "Mi papá."

"Mi papá," Charles mimicked sarcastically as he pushed her down and yanked at his pants. "Mi papá. Think he doesn't know?"

When he had finished with her, Charles went into the outer room and returned with her father's empty bowl. "Gone," he told her. He tossed the bowl at her head. It bounced against the wall and fell onto the bed beside her. "No more," he said. "Didn't marry you t' feed him."

"Lo siento," she said as she reached for the bowl. I'm sorry.

~ ~ ~

Gregoria carried her few purchases back from the market slowly, nausea roiling her stomach. Agua, she told herself. That's all I

44

need. And perhaps a little mint tea. She bit her lip. Surely I cannot be with child this soon.

As she entered the alley, she saw that the door of one of the empty casitas was open. Two men were unloading household goods from a clumsy wooden-wheeled carreta while a black-clad old woman with a black chal over her head leaned on a cane and gave directions. She nodded curtly to Gregoria, then went back to directing the men. An old man came out of the house and stood watching.

They are clearly respectable people, Gregoria thought. Not beggars like my father. Not like the woman in the casita next to the one we live in, who is clearly one of the traídas y llevadas, the women of the streets.

Surely Charles wouldn't object to her knowing this old woman in black. She was so often alone, while he hunted or disappeared on what he told her was "business." She waited until the carreta had rumbled out of the alley, then went to knock timidly on the rough wooden door.

~ ~ ~

Somehow it all came out. María seemed to divine Gregoria's situation almost instantly and brusquely asked her when the child was to be born. She didn't ask how el americano treated her, but the assumption that he didn't treat her well was implied in the contemptuous way the old woman said "el americano."

Why good nuevomexicana girls married los americanos, María could not understand. As if diligencias matrimoniales, marriage documents, meant anything to these men. Gringos knew nothing of loyalty and duty. Look how they had fought each other in the recent war. She sniffed.

45

They were sitting on roughly carved wooden stools in the alleyway, just outside the door of María's casita. The old woman patted Gregoria's hand sharply, then stood up. She went to the door and looked in, contemplating the adobe fireplace in the corner. Then she turned back to Gregoria. "Adelante," she said abruptly. "Tengo algo para ti." Come in. I have something for you.

Puzzled, Gregoria followed her into the house. María was pulling a mixing bowl, flour, and lard out of her kitchen supplies. "Bísquete," she said abruptly.

Gregoria frowned, puzzled.

It was something los americanos loved, María explained impatiently. Gregoria's esposo would like them. If he should ever leave Gregoria without money, she could sell them to los gringos and support herself and the child. María baked and sold them in the plaza when she and her esposo were short on cash. She had learned how to bake them from an americana she had once worked for in Santa Fe—the Baptist minister's wife.

It was a great secret, the process for making el bísquete. María would not share it with just anyone. She showed Gregoria the sourdough starter she kept always underway and demonstrated how to mix the batter and let it rise. When it was ready, she gently placed the carefully shaped biscuits in a cast iron dutch oven and set the covered pot next to the fire. She heaped burning coals over the pan and led Gregoria back outside to wait. "Hace mucho calor," she complained. It's very hot.

When the biscuits were ready, she gave Gregoria a small piece to sample, then sent her home with a bit of starter. Gregoria took them unwillingly. She wasn't at all sure she could master this art. On the other hand, Charles might be pleased to know she could make a gringo food.

~ ~ ~

46

A man of few words, in the two months they'd been together, Charles had often been impatient with the language difference between Gregoria and himself. She did her best to understand what he wanted so he wouldn't have to repeat what he said. But she thought he would like it better if she could learn to understand and speak americano.

Carmelita, the woman who lived in the casita next to theirs, spoke the americano words. Gregoria often heard her in the evenings, talking with the trappers and soldiers who visited her. Gregoria knew what she was—she had grown up among too much poverty to not know what women did when they could not marry or find employment as servants. But Gregoria was lonely. María was often occupied with her ailing husband and the other two casitas in the alley remained untenanted. When Charles was gone—which was often—she had only the few herbs she had planted for company.

While the laughter coming from the house next door made Charles scowl, Carmelita seemed friendly enough. Certainly enough to cause Gregoria to look up and nod when the other woman came back from the market one morning as Gregoria sat outside her door with her sewing. Charles had been gone on a business trip for two days and Gregoria had not glimpsed María in the past week.

"Jare!" Carmelita said gaily. Hello!

Gregoria smiled back at her shyly.

"What are you making?" Carmelita asked in americano.

Gregoria frowned in confusion. Carmelita pointed to the work in Gregoria's hands and raised her eyebrows questioningly.

"Una camisa," Gregoria told her. "Para mi esposo."

"A shirt for your husband?" Carmelita asked.

Gregoria nodded uncertainly.

"Ah, mi cuata," Carmelita laughed. My friend. "You must learn americano or that man will leave you before long. And I sure don't want him." She shivered dramatically and laughed.

Gregoria laughed back at her and nodded.

"Shall I teach you?"

Even in English, Gregoria understood the offer. She nodded and then frowned. "No tengo dinero." I have no money. Charles paid for everything. When he was gone, she shopped only where he had credit, and then carefully. She worked diligently to stay well within the limits he'd set for her.

Carmelita laughed. "Ya somos dos." That makes two of us. She winked at Gregoria. "You can help me in some other way, one of these days."

Gregoria understood this kind of bargaining—putting someone under obligation to you, with payment at a future time in some unspecified way. Favors and counter favors were the coin she had grown up with, poverty's unquestioned currency. She nodded at Carmelita shyly. "Trato hecho," she agreed. It's a deal.

~ ~ ~

Charles was leaning against the saloon bar nursing a drink when the barrel-chested Irishman bounced in the door. He was only a few years younger than Charles and shorter by half a foot, but he carried himself with an authority that seemed to energize the very tables themselves.

The man nodded to Charles and gestured to the barkeeper. "Whisky," he commanded. "It's celebratin' I am."

The barkeeper poured the drink and set it in front of him. "Celebrating generally calls for more than one drink," he observed with a grin.

The man winked at him. "That's as may be, but I've got a wee bit of a ride before me and want t' get back with my news."

"Back to where?"

"Baldy Mountain, man! Willow Creek! Have ye not heard? That valley yonder is bustin' wide open and it ain't hardly spring yet!"

"Oh, the gold flakes they've been finding?"

"More'n flakes, man! An' a good quality they are, too!" The man's chest seemed to enlarge as he thumped it. "I'm just from the assayer's office and they're tellin' me what I brought in is worth a good mite. An' there's more where that came from! That mountain's heavin' up nuggets the size o' pigeon eggs, just layin' there waitin' t' be collected!"

Charles swung his head to look sharply at the smaller man, then studied his own drink as the Irishman rattled on. Baldy Mountain was part of the Cimarron headwaters, at the northern end of the Moreno Valley. There were miners swarming the hills already and more coming in every day. They were all gonna be rich, the man told the barkeeper, and Taos would see the benefit of it, too, if its merchants made something of an effort. There were so many people flooding in that Maxwell's store in Cimarron couldn't keep what they needed in stock. Miners needed supplies and Taos was closer than Las Vegas. The road between Taos and Baldy would be crawling with customers, if the merchants played their cards right.

When the Irishman began talking about an eventual stage line between the Valley and Taos, Charles slipped away. He reckoned that it'd be a long while before the rocky track he'd travelled last fall was fit for a stagecoach. But there'd still be travelers on it. Travelers with gold.

Loretta Miles Tollefson

Don Fernando de Taos, Summer 1867

Gregoria hoarded her growing knowledge of biscuit-making carefully, along with the americano words she was learning, concealing both activities from Charles. She couldn't have said why she did this, except that she wanted to surprise him. The americano words came slowly because the lessons with Carmelita were sporadic, dependent on whether Carmelita had visitors to entertain or other prospects to pursue and if Charles was home. Still, Gregoria gathered her crumbs of knowledge steadily, waiting for the moment when she could present her esposo with an entire sentence or two. She wanted to surprise him, to again see the glint of interest in his eyes when he'd called her "Rosa" for the first time.

And los bísquetes—they didn't seem quite right to her, somehow. She continued to experiment, but she had to be careful, because the wheat flour necessary for them was expensive compared to the corn from which she ground the meal for tortías. And the biscuits took time to rise and bake, so she could experiment only when she knew Charles wouldn't be returning any time soon.

María was seldom available to answer Gregoria's questions—since the day she'd shown Gregoria how to prepare el bísquete, she'd been rarely visible, occupied with her husband and her many family obligations, nodding curtly when she passed Gregoria in the alleyway almost as if she was embarrassed to know her or regretted the information she'd given her.

But Gregoria had that information and continued to experiment with it. As she sat sewing in the sun that early summer afternoon, she considered whether to attempt another batch. Charles had said he was going to Santa Fe and would be back in quince días, two

50

weeks. She had been keeping careful track of the days, both when she could expect him to return and the time since her last menstruo.

She turned the work in her hands and smiled. She was certain now. Soon she would be using the scraps of cloth left from making this shirt for Charles to create much smaller garments. So she would have two surprises for him. With Carmelita's help she would learn how to say "Soy preñada" in americano. She hummed a long forgotten tune as she went back to her work.

~ ~ ~

But when Charles returned and Gregoria faced him, carefully speaking the americano words "I am pregnant," his response was not what she had hoped. He scowled at her blackly.

"I have good news," she said again, slowly, afraid she had said the words incorrectly. "I am with child."

"Where'd ya learn that?" he barked.

She stared at him in confusion.

He grabbed her elbow. "Who taught ya American?"

"Carmelita," she stammered.

"Who?"

She gestured toward the door. "La vecina." The neighbor woman.

"That whore!" he roared. "What'd ya trade?"

She didn't need to know the specific meaning of the words to understand what he was asking. "Nada," she whimpered. "Nada."

He let go of her arm and slapped her cheek so hard that she lurched away from him, toward the table. She steadied herself, her hand on her cheek, as he roared, "Ya know what ya say?"

51

She put her hand on her belly. "I am with child." Her voice shook, then steadied. "Soy preñada." She pushed herself away from the table.

"Ya bitch." The fury on Charles face said it wasn't only her choice of language that angered him. He shoved at her, knocking her against the table. Gregoria grabbed at it again, but it moved away from her this time and she fell awkwardly onto the hard clay floor.

He kicked at her then, aiming for her belly. Instinctively, she rolled away.

"Don't run, bitch!" he roared, kicking out again. This time his boot connected, slamming into her belly, and she gasped from the pain. "Lyin' whore!" he yelled. "Ya don' cuckold me!" He reached down, grabbing her shoulder, hauling her upward. "Get rid of it!" He shoved her, slamming her onto the floor again, then straightened. His boot moved again toward her belly, then stopped. He turned and reached for his hat. "Bitch," he muttered as he jerked the outer door open.

Carmelita was standing on the doorsill, her hand raised as if to knock.

"Whore!" Charles roared at her. "Turned her int' a whore!"

Carmelita backed away from him, hands up as if in surrender. She watched him stomp out of the alley, then slipped into the house. Gregoria crouched on the floor, arms across her belly. She looked up at Carmelita tearfully. "I thought he would be happy," she said.

"With one like that, you never know." Carmelita shook her head.

"He told me to rid myself of it."

Carmelita nodded. "I heard him."

"What should I do?"

"He may change his mind."

Gregoria shook her head. "I do not think so."

"I have a special tea. How long has it been since your last bleeding?"

"Diez semanas." Ten weeks.

Carmelita nodded. "It should work. I think it will be safe for you to try."

The concoction of inmortal and poleo chino, spider milkweed and pennyroyal, that Carmelita brought Gregoria the next day was barely palatable, even with the precious sugar she'd added to it. Gregoria drank it four days running, but nothing happened.

Charles had not returned since the day he'd stormed out of the casita. Gregoria wondered bleakly whether he would ever come back and how long it would be until the rent was due again. What would she do then? Go back to the saloon with a baby in tow? Then there would be no escaping the men's hands or other body parts. When they had thought her a virgin, they had leered but not been insistent. Now they would not hesitate.

~ ~ ~

Gregoria sat on a low wooden stool just outside the casita's heavy wooden door, her head bent over the bowl of peas she was shelling. I must keep moving, she told herself. I must not be despondent. I must act as if my world has not collapsed around me, must not go running to my father. After all, what could he do for me? And aren't Charles' suspicions reasonable, given where he originally found me? I lied to him, told him he was my first man. Did he somehow divine the truth? She bit her lip and listlessly ran the alverjones in the bowl through her fingers.

53

"What's that?" a male voice growled above her head. "Jus' peas? No meat?"

"Charles!" Gregoria put the bowl on the ground beside her and jumped up, her face radiant. Behind him, a mule laden with packs twitched its ears. Gregoria looked into Charles' face timidly. He handed her the lead rope as if he had left only yesterday.

"Back there," he ordered, gesturing toward the area behind the casita. He swatted Gregoria's rump. "Then inside. With th' packs."

She smiled and nodded and led the animal down the narrow passageway beside the house. She brought it a bucket of water, then removed the heavy packs. Charles had returned to her. She stroked the mule's neck happily and it nickered at her. "Mula bonita," she told it. Pretty mule.

When she entered the house with the second pack, Charles came forward to take it from her and her heart swelled with happiness. He had forgiven her. She glanced sideways at him as she brought out tortías and ladled stew into a bowl. "I was not expecting you," she said apologetically. "Lo siento. It contains little meat. It was only for me."

He folded a tortía and dipped it into the stew. "Meat enough soon," he said. He satisfied his first hunger, then reached for her, pawing at her skirt as he pulled her toward him. "Meat enough here."

Gregoria was so relieved that he'd returned that she giggled in spite of the roughness of his touch. The fingers of his left hand dug into her thigh as the other fumbled with his clothes. "Hun'ry," he groaned. "So hun'ry." He bent his bearded face toward her neck and bared his teeth. "Hun'ry for breast!" he growled. "Pergate!" She giggled again as she braced herself for the feel of his teeth.

~ ~ ~

Gregoria's forehead wrinkled in puzzlement as she watched Charles leave the casita. There was an inner excitement to him that she hadn't seen before, a kind of tension.

She began straightening the bedding. He had returned to her. That was all she needed to know. He loves me, she told herself. It is only that he has never learned how to say so.

And when she told him the child had not gone from her body, he would love it, as well. She was sure of it. He had only been angry because he was surprised and because she had learned the americano speech from Carmelita, who was, after all, not a good woman. She must be more careful not to anger him in that way, not to use his language unless she was sure it would please him.

Gregoria bit her lip. She had liked learning americano. It made her feel intelligent and strong. Perhaps, with time, he would forget where she had learned it. She must be more careful.

He came back late that afternoon carrying two jugs of Taos Lightning and leading another mule, this one with an empty aparejo, pack saddle, on its back. Gregoria was perched on the stool outside the door, peeling potatoes this time, when he led the animal up the street. Out of the corner of her eye, Gregoria saw María's door open slightly, then quickly shut.

Charles handed Gregoria the rope and gestured toward the back of the casita. "Tie 'er up," he ordered.

Gregoria put the wooden bowl of potatoes on the ground and stood, knife still in her hand. She looked into Charles' face. He still seemed tense, but there was an irritability about him now that hadn't been there earlier.

"Now!" he growled. "Hurry up!"

Loretta Miles Tollefson

She dropped the knife into the bowl and led the mule around the casita. When she returned to the house, she found that Charles had closed and fastened the shutters and lit a candle. He motioned impatiently for her to shut the door.

"Qué pasó?" she asked. Is something wrong?

"Qué pasó?" he mocked her. "Whole street don' need t' hear!"

Gregoria looked at the shuttered windows and then back at Charles. Her hand went to her blouse. Perhaps he was in need of her.

He grabbed her wrist. "Stupido," he growled. "Not now." He jerked her around to face the dishes and food supplies she'd arranged on the crude wooden shelves near the table. "Pack up," he ordered. "We're leavin'."

She opened her mouth to ask why, then thought better of it. He was taking her with him. That was all that mattered. "La carreta, it will arrive soon?" she asked. She wondered how much time she had, if she would be able to slip out and tell María or Carmelita adiós.

"No cart." Charles moved to the door and peered outside, then paced back to the center of the room. "Two mules." He grabbed her wrist again, squeezing it hard. "No talkin' to nobody. No one followin' or trackin' us."

She looked into his face, trying not to notice the pain. "Is there a problem?"

He gave a short laugh and dropped her wrist. "Don' wanna be followed." He slapped her rump. "Got a new start. Be all mine." He put his big hands on her shoulders and ran them possessively down her breasts to her hips as he leered at her. "All mine."

~ ~ ~

56

By midnight Gregoria knew why Charles had piled everything onto the mules instead of hiring a cart.

They were heading east out of Taos, deep into the cañon of the small but steady stream of the Rio Fernando. Although the rocky track was ostensibly wide enough for a wagon, it would have been difficult going for a wooden-wheeled carreta. Only iron-bound wheels could withstand the impact of the stones the mules side-stepped so easily. Trees crowded the roadway: the tall narrow-leaved cottonwoods that filled the cañon bottom—so many more than the ones that lined the waterways at home—and the ominously dark evergreens that clung to the rocky cañon sides wherever the massive sandstone boulders gave them space.

The mules were roped together, one behind the other. Charles held the lead rope in one hand and kept a grip on Gregoria's arm with the other. "Don' fall," he'd said roughly.

"Gracias," she'd responded. He takes care of me, she thought. Then his hand tightened and she realized: He thinks I will run away.

But where would she go in this tree-filled, steep-sided cañon? She would fall and then the wild animals would come. Better to go with him quietly, pretend his hand wasn't hurting her arm. He would relax after a while, when he realized she went with him willingly.

She had never been in the forest before. She was a town girl, after all, and the mountains were dangerous for women. The moon-shadowed trees frightened her. She clutched her chal around her shoulders with one hand and tried not to gasp with pain when the unforgiving stones on the rough track twisted her bare ankles beneath her. A coyote yipped on the cliff overhead and she shrank toward Charles. He chuckled harshly but didn't push her away. She concentrated on the path before her, keeping her eyes down, away from the frightening sounds and the black trees looming in the night.

They trudged through the darkness for hours, the rocky path cold underfoot. Finally, the sky ahead began to lighten. Gregoria's heart lifted a little at this, and she began to look around her again. The small Rio Fernando was to their right, its water moving steadily away from them, back toward Taos.

There were even more trees now, especially of the blackshadow evergreens. Clumps of aspen were scattered among them, brightening the cañon's slopes as their white trunks and translucent green leaves glowed in the early morning light. They and the evergreens towered above her, overwhelming in size. Gregoria tilted her head back, looking upward. The canyon walls constricted the amount of sky she could see, a stark contrast to the wideopen plains around Taos.

Gregoria shivered. "The trees, they are so tall."

"Get used to it," Charles answered. His face had that air of suppressed excitement again, the irritability gone. A new start, he had said. She shivered again and pulled her arm gently from his grip. He frowned down at her.

"I can see the path now." She readjusted her chal and smiled up at him. "It will be easier for you."

He nodded and forged ahead. Gregoria followed slowly, picking her way carefully up the rocky path. She blinked, trying to focus. She hadn't slept since the night before and she wasn't used to this much walking. Her legs ached.

When the second mule nickered as it passed her, she realized she was falling behind. She twisted around to look back down the trail. It was rocky, but clearly a path. Following it would take her back to Taos. She shuddered. There were wild animals on the rocky ledges above them and probably wild men as well. Apaches, Comanches, and the mexicanos and americanos who traded with them illegally.

She craned her neck, looking around the loaded mules for Charles' broad back. If she fell too far behind, he might not wait for her. She quickened her step.

~ ~ ~

Hours later, as it grew dark, Charles led the mules off the rocky track, into a small clearing on the left. A fringe of trees blocked it from easy view of the trail. Through a haze of exhaustion, Gregoria saw a small fire ring, a few rocks positioned nearby like chairs. Someone had been here before them. There was even a small pile of branches for firewood. Charles jerked his head towards the wood as he began unloading the mules. "Food," he ordered.

Gregoria nodded numbly and went to the packs. There were tortías and jerked meat. She started a small fire and began warming the tortías.

Charles hobbled the mules and came toward her, and she smiled up at him.

He grunted and turned away. He was a good man, she told herself. He simply didn't know how to apologize. Her hand moved to her belly. How would she tell him that the child was still inside her? But he was moving restlessly at the edge of the fire and she turned her attention to the food.

~ ~ ~

They pushed on the next morning, though Gregoria's legs were stiff from the previous day's exertions. Charles' mood had

59

changed again. There was a grimness to his face that warned her not to ask where they were going or how long this trek would continue. They stopped briefly for a noon meal, then Charles rose abruptly and Gregoria struggled to her feet to follow him. She had begun to feel as if she had always been trudging behind him up this rocky path, that they had always been climbing steadily upward, that they would always do so.

Then suddenly they reached a flat place in a small, sparsely grassed meadow and began to descend. The mules quickened their pace and Gregoria stumbled on rocks that rolled with a clatter over the edge of the mountain. She stopped, gasping, swaying from weariness, afraid to go on. Ahead of her, Charles turned and growled, "Hurry up!"

Gregoria took a deep breath, steadying herself. "It is so steep," she said meekly, but he'd already turned back to the path, continuing downhill.

Gregoria hurried after him until she was abreast of the second mule. She edged between it and the mountainside and it shook its head at her, then grudgingly moved closer to the far edge of the path. She put a hand on its halter. "Mula bonita," she said coaxingly. The animal snorted mildly but didn't pull away as they continued downhill.

There was comfort in the animal's presence and Gregoria felt herself relaxing, her feet moving in rhythm with the mule. Her eyelids closed in spite of herself and she stumbled, rocks rolling across the path and down the mountainside. Startled, she jerked awake. Ahead of her, Charles paid no attention and she breathed a sigh of relief. Finally, the path grew less steep and a little less rocky, although Gregoria had no sense of how long the slope before her would continue or what lay beyond it. She was too weary to care. She was only partly conscious of the gurgle of a stream to her right.

Then suddenly the mule stopped and the girl was startled into wakefulness. Charles and the other mule stood beside her, gazing at a grassy valley that lay just beyond the trees. Charles raked his fingers through his beard.

Gregoria could see more mountains on the other side, but the valley itself seemed to continue to her right and left, past the grassy ridges that blocked her view. The stream they'd been following gurgled to her right, flowing into the valley. Overhead, three bald eagles circled as they soared ever skyward, sunlight gleaming from their white heads. Just below, to the left of the rocky roadway, lay a grassy hollow. Half a dozen brown-speckled cattle grazed at its northern edge. A few upright posts marked the beginnings of a corral.

Charles clucked at the mules and led them down the slope to the posts. Gregoria, following, saw the remains of a fire and a small pile of fire-length wood. She stopped beside it. Charles dropped a pack full of food beside the fire ring. He gestured toward a small ponderosa nearby. "Tie 't up when yer done," he said. "Out o' bear reach."

Gregoria shivered. Bears? But she did as she was told.

PALO FLECHADO PASS, SUMMER 1867

When Gregoria woke, she was alone. The sound of an axe echoed from the mountainside. She sat up, her body stiff and aching from the hard ground and the long trek from Taos. She pulled grass from her hair and straightened her blouse, then stood and shook out her skirt. She found the water bucket at the base of the tree where she'd tied the food pack and took it to the brook on the other side of the cart road. She splashed water on her face, drank a little, then dipped the bucket into the stream to fill.

When she returned to the campsite, she saw that Charles had left two tortías and a scrap of jerky lying on a large rock near the cold fire ring. She perched on the rock and began to eat. She looked around. If Charles was cutting wood, that would imply that they were staying here for at least a short time. Were the cattle his? Had he built the corral? Had he been here during the weeks he'd said he was going to Santa Fe? She shook her head. There was no point in asking, even if she could formulate the questions in americano. He would only be angry. I must be patient, she told herself.

She finished eating and her hands fell to her lap as she absorbed her surroundings. Sunlight slanted across the foothills to the east and touched the bunched needles of the ponderosa pines that grew along the mountainside edge of the hollow. The grass around her was long and lush, and interspersed with narrow-leaved plants that drooped with slender tube-shaped red flowers that hung facing the ground. A hummingbird investigated a blossom as she watched.

Wild roses blossomed near the stream. Butterflies hovered over the flowers. On the slope that rose beyond the stream, ponderosa and aspen reared above a scattering of scrub oak. There would be acorns. Gregoria wondered how difficult it would be to find them. She knew they were edible if you were careful to soak them in water first. And, of course, everyone knew that rosehips were good to eat. She stood, rummaged in the packs for a small basket, and headed toward the stream.

If she and Charles were to stay here, she would need to hollow out a deeper place to fill her water bucket. She examined the stream bed, looking for a likely spot as she followed it toward the rose bushes. She found a few shriveled hips from the previous winter and collected them, then looked more closely at the water's edge. There were strawberry plants sprinkled across the turf. The birds had been here before her, so there was only a handful of fruit, but she smiled at the berries anyway, and gathered them carefully. She lifted them gently into her basket, carried them back to the campsite, and sat down on the rock by the fire ring to admire them.

Suddenly, Charles' form blocked the sunlight.

Gregoria looked up at him, eyes shining. "Fresas!" she exclaimed, holding the fruit toward him.

He leered at her. "Other berries I want. Man builds appetite, chopping trees."

~ ~ ~

When they began constructing a cabin the next day, Gregoria knew they were staying. Charles set her to work digging rocks from under the trees on the hillside and piling them into a low foundation wall with a doorway that faced eastward. He went deep into the woods to fell the wall timbers, avoiding the trees nearest the house. He didn't explain why he'd chosen this location, although he did point to the mountains across the valley with a scowl. "Maxwell land," he'd told Gregoria, glowering. "You stay away."

She'd nodded, knowing she'd never have a reason to stray that far across the valley, anyway. She knew of Lucien Bonaparte Maxwell, the son-in-law of Taos' old Judge Beaubien. They said Maxwell was a quixotic man with an unreliable temper. She was glad Charles had chosen to stay well away from his lands.

Even though the hollow was beautiful and she loved the look of the valley as it swept before and to either side of her, the mountains behind her and on the other side of the valley seemed foreign to her and she shivered when she looked at them. The landscape here was very different from Taos. In the east, the sky brightened long before the sun actually appeared in the mornings, blocked as it was by the mountain peaks. And twilight didn't linger. Behind the cabin, the afternoon shadows from the mountainside had an ominous quality as they lengthened across the grass. Then the tree-covered slopes would cut off the early evening sun before its time and, abruptly, night would fall.

Gregoria learned quickly to fill the water bucket long before shadows began to linger in the hollow. Lurking things hid among the trees on the other side of the creek, especially now that she'd scooped out the rocks and silt to create a deeper hole for her bucket. She'd seen raccoon tracks and deer, and the imprint of what looked to be a large cat. When she'd described the markings to Charles, he'd merely grunted.

"Catamount," he'd said dismissively. "Wear that red shawl, he'll know you ain't food."

Gregoria had stared at him. The red chal that had been her mother's had faded over the years to a soft rose. I will go only in daylight, she told herself now, as she put another foundation stone into place. And there are two buckets. I will fill both of them and leave one outside the door with a dipper, so we may drink without coming inside. With two buckets of drinking water, I will not have to go so often to the stream. She nodded to herself, stood, hands on her hips and arched backward, stretching her back muscles.

"More rocks, that end," Charles said sharply, coming up behind her. He'd been out to check on the cattle, which liked to roam out of sight over the valley ridge northeast of the hollow. Charles looked irritable. The cattle annoyed him, somehow. He went to the pile of tools at the base of the largest ponderosa and lifted his axe. He looked toward the cattle and swung the axe slowly, feeling its weight, then turned and headed across the wagon track, onto the tree-covered slopes south of the hollow. A few minutes later the sound of an axe biting into wood began to echo from the hillside.

Gregoria pushed loose strands of hair from her face and returned to her work. She picked her way through the trees on the hillside behind the cabin to a spot where stones as large as her head lay half-exposed under the dirt and pine needles. She used a dead aspen branch to pry the rocks free, then carried them one by one to the hollow and stacked them carefully onto the wall Charles had marked out.

The dirt came with the rocks and rubbed off onto her hands and clothes. Gregoria looked at them anxiously and bit her lip. How would Charles finish the cabin's inner walls so she could keep it clean? The smooth adobe walls of the Taos casita had been easily wiped down or repaired with more mud when they became pitted or cracked. These rocks were full of indentations. Some of them

65

flaked badly when she dropped them into place on the foundation wall. She tried to avoid that type, but there were only so many that she could lift.

And Charles would be angry if she used only small ones. She'd already had one scolding from him and that was enough. Her left cheek still burned where he'd pinched it. I must learn to be more careful of how I do things, she told herself now. To think about what he would like and to do it before he becomes angry.

~ ~ ~

As the walls of the cabin went up, a small but steady trickle of men and mules began to appear on the rocky road between Taos and the valley and the gold fields at its northern end. Occasionally, a traveler stopped to ask if he could camp nearby. As long as they were willing to stay beside the road, Charles would nod his agreement and keep working. He growled at Gregoria more when this happened, did not introduce her or invite the traveler to share a meal, and seemed in more of a hurry to get the cabin constructed.

He'd built a rough shed for them to sleep in and to store their goods. It had two doors, one leading into the stone foundation and one opening to the north and the cooking fire. It is so kind of him to find a way to give me shelter at night, Gregoria thought gratefully.

She was especially thankful that she no longer needed to tie the heavy food packs in the trees out of bear reach. She shivered at the thought. Although she hadn't actually seen a bear, she was in no hurry to do so.

The stone foundation was in place and the first few rows of logs arranged on top of it, but the selection of straight trees of the right length and width, and their felling and debranching, took time. While Charles sawed and chopped on the mountainside, Gregoria used a knife to peel bark from the logs he'd dragged in with the mules. Charles thought her work unnecessary, but she persisted, fearing the bugs that would invade their food supplies and the general dirtiness she would have to contend with, if she did not. The shed's green unpeeled walls were already dropping bits of bark and dirt onto their blankets. Gregoria shuddered when she thought what they would be like when winter came. And so she peeled, despite Charles' disapproving grunts.

She was alone, Charles on the mountainside chopping trees while she peeled bark from a fifteen-inch thick aspen, when she felt the stab in her abdomen. Puzzled, she stopped working and looked down at herself. The pain came again, sharper this time, and she gasped, her knife slipping to the dirt.

Again the pain. Gregoria dropped into a crouching position beside the log, clutching it for support. She tried to think. How many weeks had it been since Carmelita had given her the tea? She couldn't remember. The pain stabbed again.

Gregoria gulped back unbidden tears and looked toward the cart track from Taos. There was no one in sight, gracias a Dios. Charles would be so angry if he found a stranger bending over her, trying to help.

She had assumed Carmelita's remedio had been ineffective, but still she had delayed telling Charles the child still lived within her. She'd known she would have to speak eventually, when her growing belly made it impossible not to do so. She had hoped he would be confused about the timing, think it was a second pregnancy she spoke of, one that had begun after they left the casita.

Another pain ripped through her belly. Gregoria jerked forward, clinging to the dead aspen, her fingers digging into the ridges in its gray-white bark. She felt a pressure now, an asking to be voided. It is coming, she thought wildly. She struggled to her feet and made her way into the shed. There, she leaned against the wall and gasped for air, fighting the pain, gripping the knobby logs for support.

I must get rags, she told herself. I must go outside, into the trees behind the shed. A thicket of oak, a space where I can bury what is coming. A deep shudder passed through her.

The tears came then, but she fought them back. I will not think of this as a child, she told herself sternly. I tried to remove it and now it is being removed. I should be glad. Charles told me to do this. It will save much explanation and anxiety.

A wave of pain swept through. "May God forgive me, I have killed it as he wished," she murmured. Then she closed her eyes, steeling herself to her task. She gasped her way through another contraction, then stumbled to the packs in the back of the shed to collect the rags she would need.

~ ~ ~

The walls of the house continued to go up, although Charles often swore in disgust at Gregoria's limitations as a woman, and a small one at that. She hadn't told him about the miscarriage. Better that he think the child had been cleansed from her body the day after he'd told her to do so. Better that he not have something else to be angry about.

She'd been so weak after the child expelled itself that she'd decided to limit her bark-peeling project to removing the bark only on the logs in the areas where her kitchen supplies would be stored and where she and Charles would sleep. This meant that she now waited until the logs were in place in that section of the half-built cabin and then peeled them from the inside surfaces only.

She had her head bent to this work late one afternoon when Charles came into the hollow, passed the empty cabin doorway without a word, and headed to the hollow's east slope, where the mules and cattle were grazing. He returned with the larger of the two mules, collected rope from the shed, then headed back across the road to the slope south of the cabin. An hour later, he was back, the mule dragging four aspen logs lashed together with rope.

"Rosa!" he bellowed.

Gregoria looked up from the wall of what would be the kitchen area, her peeling knife in her hand. "Yes?" He was maneuvering the mule to get the logs into place and didn't answer. She watched as he settled the logs onto the ground, parallel to the southern wall.

"Blanket," Charles barked over his shoulder. He began un-wrapping the ropes from the logs. "Need firewood."

Gregoria stared at him in confusion.

"Blanket!" he bellowed at her. He began forming the rope into a rough loop over his massive shoulder. "An' shorter rope."

She went into the shed and gathered a blanket and rope, then slipped outside to build up the fire, using a stick to rake the coals together. If they were to be gone for any length of time, it would be difficult to prepare an evening meal.

Charles appeared. "Fire out," he ordered.

She turned her head. "Lo siento," she said. I'm sorry. "I thought we would eat before we go."

He came closer, and began scattering the coals with the edge of his boot. "Don' got all night."

Gregoria bit her lip but rose obediently. She followed him around the cabin and across the road, lugging the blanket and rope. She scrambled after him as he led the mule up a steep incline, then paralleled the road westward about half a mile. They stopped in a small flat stony space, where four more aspen logs lay ready for hauling.

The tree branches had been chopped off, then into three and four foot lengths. They were scattered haphazardly across the clearing. Charles gestured at them. "Firewood," he said. "Use the blanket."

Gregoria was still winded from the climb. It had been ten days since the miscarriage and she still had stretches of weakness. She gasped for air as she stared at Charles, her mind processing what he was saying. In Taos, firewood arrived on a carreta behind a mule. The man who delivered it stacked it for her and even split it into smaller pieces, if she gave him a meal. Since she and Charles had been at this place, she had collected dry wood under the trees edging the hollow to supplement the small pile beside the fire ring. She hadn't thought about where the fire supply would come from when all that wood had been burned.

"Comprende?" Charles asked sharply.

Gregoria nodded and looked around. So this was how it would be. Her breathing slowed and she nodded again. Summer would end and they'd need a winter supply ready to hand. She began moving some of the thinner branches to one side, then spread out the blanket. The question was how to position the wood so the blanket could be pulled. A kind of travois, she thought.

While Charles lashed the four aspen logs together and attached them to the mule's harness, she experimented. If she angled the branches across the square blanket, then folded it over like a tortía, she could grasp the two corners and pull it behind her. This seemed to work fairly well. She looked up to see Charles watching her. She smiled at him, proud of her ingenuity. He grunted disparagingly and turned away.

Gregoria looked at the blanket again, studying it. She would secure the edges with the short length of rope, she decided. That would make it easier to pull.

~ ~ ~

Charles had led the mule out of the rocky space on the mountainside and was well down the first slope leading back to the hollow before Gregoria had managed to tie her rope securely to the edges of the blanket full of aspen branches. It was growing dark.

She grasped the makeshift rope handle and pulled her bundle behind her as she scrambled downhill. The blanket's heavy wool seemed to catch on every bush, thick clump of grass, and half-buried rock that she passed. It would need to be thoroughly cleaned, she realized, her heart dropping. There would be pebbles in it, and stickers from the bushes. She was suddenly overcome with exhaustion and she paused, her chest heaving. But Charles would be angry if she lingered, and it was growing dark. She pushed her weariness aside and stumbled after him through the lengthening shadows.

Despite her exhaustion, Gregoria felt her heart lift when she glimpsed the cabin walls through the trees. She stopped again to catch her breath, just inside the line of trees on the other side of the roadway, and looked at the house gratefully.

The cabin itself was already in shadows, but a last bit of sunlight shone brightly on the tips of the eastern mountains. The doorway faced the glowing light, the hollow stretching before it.

The hollow's south-facing slopes will be warm when the spring sunlight arrives, Gregoria thought, her heart suddenly lifting. I might be able to plant a garden there. And perhaps wild strawberries where the water seeps from the snow at the edge of the slope.

Loretta Miles Tollefson

She smiled and her shoulders straightened in spite of her weariness and pain. Charles was building it for her. He wanted her with him. It would be a good house. She was sure of it.

~ ~ ~

No venda la piel del oso antes de haberle cazado. It was an old saying: Don't count your chickens before they are hatched. You would think I'd have known better, Gregoria told herself. When had anything ever been perfect, except for those few days right after she and Charles had married? And even then, there were shadowings.

Now she stood alone in the center of an empty shell. The two windows at the front of the cabin were covered with thin cloth, so air filtered through them but little light entered. A perpetual draft blew between the unchinked logs. A pile of blankets and furs on the floor in the far left hand corner served as a bed. To its right was the door to the shed, then a drafty fireplace of rough stones that projected into the room. There was no furniture. Yesterday Charles had muttered something about a table and stools, then taken his rifle and a mule and gone hunting.

It is my pain at the loss of the child that makes me so despondent, Gregoria told herself. Even though I know it was for the best, still it pains me.

They needed meat and the game would not present itself at the door to be shot. But she was alone in the mountains and even in mid-summer the mornings were cool enough to make her glad of a fire. The weather would only become cooler. Gregoria bit her lip. There would be snow soon and it would not melt in these mountains as easily as the snow did in Taos.

She shook her head ruefully. Throughout her childhood, Gregoria had gazed at the white-peaked mountains to the east and

72

wondered what it was like up there, envying the freedom of the men who herded cattle and sheep each summer into the cool highland meadows to graze. Now she lived in one of those highland valleys and she shivered with the cold and the loneliness.

But at least Charles brought me with him, she told herself. And the cabin is larger than anything I have lived in before. I will think of the good things, not the bad. Her shoulders straightened and she brushed away her tears. She could at least try to produce a properly tamped-down floor, if only in the kitchen area. Both of the buckets were almost empty. She would need more water from the stream.

~ ~ ~

As she knelt beside the pool waiting for the second bucket to fill, Gregoria heard the creak of leather harness on the rocky trail from the pass. She looked up. A bare-headed young man with curly brown hair rode toward her on a small sturdy black horse. Behind him stretched a long line of burros, each with a pack towering on its back. There seemed no end to the small animals with their big loads as they streamed down the mountainside.

Gregoria was so startled at the sight that she stood motionless until it was too late to cross the road to the cabin without being seen. The young man saw her and smiled. "Is this the Kennedy rancho?" he called.

Gregoria nodded wordlessly.

He jerked his head backward. "My boss back there, he has business with Mr. Kennedy." The burro immediately behind him stopped to nibble on the grass by the roadside and the line of animals behind it began to fold in on itself. The young man looked back anxiously. "Myself, I cannot stop," he said apologetically.

"These burros need the most constant attention." He smiled at her, turned his mount, and gave the lead rope in his hand a shake. "You there!" he said to the front burro with a laugh. "There's plenty more further on! You must leave some for the others!" The gray beast lifted its head and moved reluctantly on, and Gregoria watched them, bemused.

She was still waiting for the line of burros to end, so she could cross the road, when an older man appeared in the midst of the mule train, riding a tall brown gelding. He lifted his hat from his head as he rode toward her.

His face was thinner than the younger man's, but kind. He nodded to her courteously. "Señora Kennedy?" he asked.

She nodded.

"My name is Adolph Letcher." He spoke thickly, a German burr to his tongue. When she didn't respond to his name, he gestured toward the brown-speckled cattle grazing on the far side of the hollow. "I wish to speak to your husband about the bill for the beef and the loan of money that I gave him this Spring."

She frowned. "He is not home."

"Ah." He sat silently, looking down at her for a long moment, the burros behind him watching patiently. "You will tell him I have been here? The three months, they have expired."

She nodded, not sure what he meant. "I will tell him."

"The amount, it is one hundred fifty five dollars, not including the interest," he said. "I am moving my stock to Las Vegas, so he must come there to pay me." The gelding stirred restlessly and the man tightened its reins. A burro brayed. "You will tell him?"

"Sí, señor."

He put his hat on his head, nodded politely, and prodded his horse into action. The line of loaded burros followed obediently.

As Gregoria watched, the beginning of the line turned southward, following the young man on the black horse.

Gregoria carried her buckets into the cabin and began sprinkling the floor with water, to settle the dirt. One hundred and fifty five dollars. She wasn't sure what interest was, but clearly it meant that Charles owed this man more than the amount he had named. It was a great deal. More than she could even imagine.

He had bought the cattle and also borrowed money from this man, this Señor Letcher. She stood for a long time, staring blankly at the floor. Charles had said nothing of this debt. Perhaps he thought it was not her concern. She must be as careful as she could with the food supplies, to make them last as long as possible, to keep from spending more. Perhaps they could sell the coquetas he had bought her.

It was an enormous debt. What a burden her esposo must find it. And he had said nothing about it. She had no doubt that he had done this for her, so she could have a home away from the town and what he thought were corrupting influences. She shook her head and tackled the floor with redoubled vigor, eager to present him with a clean cabin when he returned.

~ ~ ~

Every cleaning cloth Gregoria owned was filthy with dirt. She'd dragged the firewood chopping block into the cabin and stood on it to reach as high as she could to wipe down the cabin walls. They weren't perfectly clean, but they were certainly less grimy than they had been.

The crude fireplace Charles had constructed of stone from the hillside was black with soot. The rocks were simply stacked, with no mortar between them, and contrary winds tended to blow

75

smoke back into the house. Gregoria was standing in front of the fireplace, looking up at the grime, when Charles darkened the open door.

"Charles!" She turned and smiled at him. "Hola!"

"I'm gone, door's shut," he growled at her.

"Lo siento," she said. "I was cleaning. I needed the light."

"Clean enough." He pushed the door shut with his foot and came toward her. "What I want don't need cleanin'."

Before Gregoria could open her mouth, he had grabbed her, carried her to the pile of blankets and furs in the corner, and dropped her with a thud.

Gregoria felt the edge of a rock under the bedding. I must re-move that, she thought. Before he notices it. I should have been doing that instead of trying to clean what cannot be truly cleaned. He doesn't care about that anyway. This is all he cares about, she told herself as he pulled at her skirts and undid his trousers. They were thick with elk blood, and clumsy.

"Let me help you," she said, reaching up.

"Slow me down," Charles said impatiently. "What ya want?" Then his body was free of the encumbering leather and he was on her. "This's what I want," he snorted into her hair. "What I want." She smiled as he moved clumsily inside of her. He wanted her. She would think of the good things.

~ ~ ~

With Gregoria's help, Charles rigged a frame of aspen poles in the shed and strung up the elk carcass. She watched as he began peeling back the hide, cutting with the smooth, rapid motions of long practice. Then he folded the bloody mass into a bundle and carried it to the stream, Gregoria following.

Below the pool she'd dug, a downed pine had recently created a miniature waterfall. Charles knelt beside the icy water and submerged the hide, pushing it down with his hands. He sloshed the skin up and down, working the blood and gore into the water, letting it wash downstream. "Rocks," he said over his shoulder. "Heavy."

Gregoria began searching the ground nearby for stones that she could easily pry out of the soil and carry to him.

"Hurry up!" he growled. "Water's cold!"

"Lo siento," she said. "How many do you wish me to bring?"

"Five, six."

She brought him two, then ranged across the stream, out of his sight. Most of the stones were hidden under leaf and pine needle litter or half buried in earth. She needed a stick to pry them loose and she couldn't find one thick or long enough for her purpose. Finally, she found a small rockfall at the base of a steep incline. She collected an armful of stones and lugged them to the stream.

"Where ya been?" Charles growled at her. "Tellin' yer lover goodbye?"

Gregoria bit her lip, remembering Señor Letcher and the young man with him, but said nothing. She bent to place the rocks within Charles' reach, but one of them fell from her arms. It struck the back of his hand, then rolled into the stream, throwing water into his face. "Bitch!" he howled, leaping up. In a single step, he was across the stream and reaching for her.

She shrank away. "Lo siento!"

"Siento? Sorry? Always sorry!" He gripped her by the shoulders. "I'll make ya sorry!" He glared into her face, then his expression changed. He glanced at the empty road and the trees on the hill. "Right here," he said slowly, reaching one hand to his pants as he walked her backward toward the trees. "Rocks an' sticks an' dirt." He grinned. "Lo siento," he said mockingly as his trousers fell open.

He pushed her against the rough bark of a ponderosa, then paused and looked around. His hand clamped down on her arm and he yanked her toward a granite boulder half-buried in the earth, its craggy sides roughened further by patches of pale green and yellow lichen. He wrenched her around, forcing her back against the boulder, and reached under her skirts.

"Won't even feel it, all yer padding." He yanked her skirt higher, exposing her skin to the granite. "Won't even feel it." He laughed deep in his throat as he took her. Between his grunts she could hear the stream water sloshing over the elk hide, buckling it under the waterfall, bits of blood washing downstream. She forced herself to relax.

~ ~ ~

When he was done, Gregoria leaned back against the boulder submissively. Her buttocks and legs stung from the rough surface, but she took a deep breath and moved forward, letting her skirt fall back down over her hips. "Por favor, tu mano." Please, your hand.

He held it out to her. It was slightly bruised and there was a red scrape on the fleshy spot below his little finger. She grimaced and touched it gently. "The pain. It is great?"

He shrugged. "Es nada," he said. It's nothing. He began fastening his clothes. "Need food."

She bit her lip, nodded, and shook out her skirt. "There are tortías," she said. "I cooked them this morning. And some meat from the elk?" She raised her eyes to his face, carefully submissive.

When he had eaten the first edge off his hunger, she told him of Señor Letcher and his visit, careful to explain that she'd been collecting water for washing when the burro train had appeared. To her surprise, Charles only grunted and went back to his food. She opened her mouth to suggest ways they might cut back on food expenses, then thought better of it. After all, that's why he hunted, wasn't it? It was her duty to find ways to help silently, without making it appear a sacrifice. And to be more careful in everything I do, she thought ruefully, remembering the rocks splashing into the water, hitting his hand. And what had come afterward.

~ ~ ~

For three days Charles had done little besides lie on the bed of blankets and furs in the far corner, guzzle Taos Lightning, and sleep. Gregoria crept around the cabin as quietly as possible, bringing him food and lying on the bed when he fumbled at her. She stayed outside as much as she could, allowing him to sleep while she perched on the firewood chopping block in front of the cabin.

As she watched the sunlight slant across the hollow, she decided that it was probably too late this year to plant a garden. She studied the northern slope, where the sun warmed it from the south, where she would plant next spring. The grass was thicker there, indicating good soil and moisture. She would need seed, of course. But she had some, she realized with a small jolt of pleasure: the dried peas and the beans and corn that she cooked with. Surely some of it would grow, even though they were from plants grown in warmer conditions. She gazed for a long while at the spot she'd selected, mentally placing each type of plant where she

79

thought it would do best, then rose to check on the elk hide that still swayed in the stream below the fallen pine.

When she reached the brook, she stopped short, sucking in her breath. Large cat tracks indented the mud at the stream's edge. Gregoria shuddered. Catamount. Again. What the americanos sometimes called mountain lion. In fact, something had pulled the elk hide to one side, trying to drag it out of the water. There were punctures along the hide's edge. Teeth marks?

Gregoria's heart thumped in her chest and she glanced at the trees lining the hillside on the other side of the stream. Nothing moved. She took a deep breath, forcing herself calm. It wouldn't do any good to point out any of this to Charles. He would just grunt dismissively and tell her to wear her red chal. She bit her lip, used her foot to push the hide back into the stream, and turned toward the house.

As she turned, Charles appeared in the doorway, buttoning his shirt. Gregoria arranged her face into calmness and moved toward him. "Hola!" she said as she drew closer. "You are well?"

He grunted without looking at her, eyeing the sun overhead. Then he stepped out of the door and reached for the axe. "Vamos," he ordered. Come on. He strode across the hollow toward the road. Gregoria hurried to shut the cabin door and follow.

Charles didn't look toward the stream and the hide, just headed up the road for perhaps a half mile. Then he stopped abruptly beside a cluster of young aspens. He swung the axe, once, twice, three times, and the first tree fell. He halted and looked at the small grove, combing his beard with his fingers, then turned to Gregoria. "Mules," he ordered abruptly. "An' rope." He jerked his head at the aspens. "'Nuff for these."

She nodded and turned back toward the cabin.

"Hurry up!" he growled behind her. Then the axe began chopping again.

They were beautiful young trees, she thought sadly. Why had he chosen them in particular for firewood? Or were they for furniture? They would support a bed frame, she thought.

But two hours later she realized that Charles wasn't harvesting the saplings for either furniture or firewood. Instead, he shoved them into a rough square on the ground, using the two corral posts already in place as the first corners. Once he'd laid out the logs, he set Gregoria to work digging two more holes while he chopped another log into fence post lengths.

It took two days, but at the end of it there was a rough corral just north of the cabin. The mules and cattle would be more comfortable there, Gregoria thought. Especially when winter came. It would be easier to monitor them and they'd be safer from the mountain lion. She shivered, thinking of the predator at the stream, but she was careful to keep Charles from seeing her fear.

Perhaps I am being over-anxious, she told herself. After all, Charles has far more experience in the wilderness than I ever will. And he must have seen the cat tracks himself or he wouldn't have created the corral. But the thought of the big cat still sent a chill into her stomach that she couldn't argue away.

After the corral was constructed Charles went to work on a rough shanty beside it, a kind of lean-to that could act as a stable. As she trimmed the branches he was using to cover the shelter's roof, Gregoria considered asking for something similar to protect the firewood stacked in front of the cabin. Then she thought better of it. He would only be cross with her.

I should be glad of the wood that is there, she told herself, and not ask for more than he has already done. Surely, when the snow comes it will not cover the wood completely.

81

Besides, she didn't have the stamina to face his anger. She woke each morning to nausea that could only be assuaged by cold water from the stream. And she was very tired. More than seemed reasonable, even with all the labor of the corral and shanty construction. She paused in her work, counting the days, then smiled. The tiredness lifted a little and she half-turned toward Charles, who was standing on a block of wood beside the shanty walls, shoving roof branches into place. He scowled at her. "Hurry up!" he growled.

Gregoria turned back to her work, moving more quickly now. There would be time enough to tell him her news. How had Carmelita taught her to say it? She thought he wouldn't be so angry this time. After all, they had been alone here on the edge of the valley all this while.

PALO FLECHADO PASS, AUGUST 1867

The construction of the corral and shelter seemed to have sparked a new level of energy in Charles, because he turned almost immediately to creating wide planks from a white fir, then using the planks to fashion a rough rectangular table and a bench for each side. He also chopped four-foot sections of ponderosa and carved high-backed stools from them. These were so heavy that Gregoria could barely move them around the room. She had to grasp them from the back and walk them awkwardly across the dirt floor. Even then, she struggled to keep them upright, but this only made Charles chuckle sardonically.

Once he'd finished the stools, Charles began creating food platters from the remaining pieces of log. Gregoria smiled at this, acknowledging his care for her, and went back to stuffing moss in the cracks between the cabin logs, working to block the drafts that would only get stronger as the cold came on.

I am like an ant, she thought ruefully. Worrying about winter, not even noticing the sunshine of today. She went to stand in the doorway for a moment. It was very beautiful: the trees at the edge of the hollow so tall and mysterious, the purple and yellow wildflowers dotting the grass that flowed eastward toward the mountains on the other side of the valley.

Gregoria touched her belly. If she'd counted correctly, there would be a child when the valley flowers began blooming again. She hadn't told Charles yet, preferring to wait a little longer, until the signs were more unmistakable. She wasn't sure why, but it seemed safer somehow.

Behind her, Charles slapped a completed platter on the table. She turned.

"Fill it," he ordered.

She smiled at him, pushed the door shut, and moved to her cooking supplies. She wrinkled her nose at the smoke from the fireplace as a gust of wind blew it into the house. Tomorrow she must create some clay and begin chinking the worst of the cracks between its stones.

~ ~ ~

Gregoria was behind the cabin, using a small stick to push mud between the rocks in the chimney, the day the man Stinson arrived.

He had come from the valley, not down the mountain, and the cabin blocked her view, so she didn't know he was there until she heard voices. The stranger's voice was placating and Charles sounded irritable. Gregoria paused in her work, wondering if she should show herself, then thought better of it. If they wanted food, Charles would call for her.

Sure enough, he bellowed "Rosa!" a few minutes later. She hurried around the cabin without washing her hands.

Charles looked at her with contempt. "Food," he said. He jerked his head toward her hands. "Wash first."

A short dark-haired man with a narrow face was looking out over the hollow, past the rattletrap buckboard that he'd arrived on. Gregoria saw a grin cross his face and she flushed, but she only murmured "Lo siento" and turned away.

"Tortillas!" Charles said sharply. "An' meat."

She nodded and went toward the stream to wash. When she came back, the men were on the other end of the hollow with the cattle, the stranger running his hands over their haunches and

84

scratching their heads. She went into the cabin, heated the cast iron skillet, placed two elk steaks in it, and began mixing fresh masa. As she began forming the first of the tortías, the door opened.

"I'll give you one fifty," the stranger said, a nasal twang in his voice.

Charles barked a short laugh. "Worth three."

"One seventy five."

"Wastin' time, Stinson." Charles lumbered across the room, ignoring Gregoria, and picked up his whisky jug. "Drink?"

"Don't mind if I do." Stinson took the jug, wiped its mouth with his sleeve, and lifted it to his lips. He took a drink and handed the jug back to Charles. "That's true Taos Lightning," he said with a grin. "Come to my saloon in Etown and I'll give you stuff a deal smoother than that."

Charles grunted and took a swig. "Two hun'red." He jerked his head toward the yard. "An' the wagon."

Stinson shrugged. "That's a little steep, but I'll take it," he said. "I'll send my man Albert to collect 'em tomorrow morning. He'll bring the buckboard and payment then."

"Hun'red now," Charles said.

The smaller man studied him. "Fifty."

"Seventy-five."

Stinson nodded and pulled out his wallet.

"No paper," Charles said. "Gold."

Stinson pulled a small leather bag from another pocket. "You have a scale?"

Charles turned, went into the shed, and came back a few moments later with a small scale and set of weights that Gregoria had never seen before. The men went to the table, the gold was weighed out, and the men shook hands.

Gregoria lifted the skillet and tested the meat. "The meal, it is ready, mi esposo," she said, but the two men ignored her.

"Albert'll be here first thing tomorrow," Stinson told Charles. "He's a red haired fellow, mid-twenties, answers to Bert."

Charles nodded and hefted the gold in his hand. "With one twenty-five worth o' gold."

"That's right." Stinson put his hand to his forehead in a mock salute. "Nice doing business with you." He turned toward the door and Charles followed him out.

Behind them, Gregoria lifted the elk steaks onto a wooden platter and placed the warm tortías beside them. Well, there will be plenty of food for tonight and it will only require that it be heated, she comforted herself.

~ ~ ~

Several weeks later, Gregoria woke to an unaccustomed chill and sat up. She would need to light the fire quickly. Charles would be angry if the room was cold. She huddled into her clothes and moved to the cabin door. The tamped-dirt floor was cold under her bare feet. She lifted the latch and inched the door open. Snow. Several inches. She felt a sudden panic. It was still fall. The aspen leaves had turned golden but had not begun falling in earnest, yet already there was snow. A wave of weariness swept over her.

She took a deep breath and straightened her shoulders. She'd been barefoot all summer, as was customary for Taos women of her class. Her feet had been chilly at times, but not unbearable. In Taos, this much snow would have kept her housebound, but only until mid-day. By noon, it would be melted enough to walk in the middle of the hard-packed clay streets. That seemed unlikely here.

The white flakes fell implacably from a heavy gray sky that held no promise of clearing.

She turned back into the room. Her sandals were in one of the bags by the bed. She would need light to find them and that would waken Charles to a cold room. She saw with relief that there were still coals glowing from last night's fire and that a few wood chips lay near the hearth. She gathered them together and laid them gently on the coals. Her breath steamed as she blew on the coals, coaxing them fully to life.

Finally, the chips began to smolder, then glow. Charles was still asleep. Gregoria cracked open the door and peered out, careful to block the cold from coming into the cabin. The firewood lay where she had stacked it against the side of the house, covered with a layer of white. She took a deep breath and plunged out into the snow.

~ ~ ~

Even after the fire was blazing, she was still cold. Gregoria prepared the morning meal with numb fingers and waited for Charles to rouse. The dullness of the light slowed his senses and it was mid-morning before he rolled over and muttered, "Damn! No fire?"

"Lo siento, mi esposo," Gregoria said. I'm sorry, my husband. "There is much snow and it doesn't want to warm up." She bent closer to the flames. "Perhaps we can move the blankets closer."

"Snow?" He roused, went to the door, and peered out. "Hell!" He turned back to the room and sat down on the bedding.

"Should've stayed here. Kept me warm," he grumbled. He scowled at her. "Where's th' food?"

She gestured to the table. "It is ready, except for the tortías. I will cook them now, so they will be hot for you."

He grunted morosely, pulled on his clothes, ate his meal without speaking, then pulled a blanket from the bed to wrap around his shoulders and huddled next to the fire. Gregoria found her sandals, went outside to bring in more wood, then began organizing the room so they could bring the bedding closer to the heat. Charles watched her gloomily.

She wondered anxiously when he would speak. His silences worried her. They often ended in a sudden blow to her shoulders or back, even her face. Only then would she learn that she had done something that angered him, that he had been following her movements for hours with only fury in his heart.

But this time she was saved by the muffled sound of a wagon leaving the rocky roadbed and bumping over the snow toward the cabin. Charles' head lifted and he dropped the blanket from his shoulders, dangerously close to the flames, and went to the door. His rifle was tilted against the wall nearby and he reached for it as he lifted the latch.

From the other side of the room, Gregoria could see little but swirling white and the bulk of a man in a heavy overcoat.

"May we shelter?" the stranger asked. He gestured toward the wagon behind him. "My wife and child are with me, or I'd try to continue, but this snow—"

Charles moved back. "Of course, of course," he said heartily.

Gregoria glanced at him in surprise. She'd never heard this tone in his voice before.

"And I'll need to stable the mules." It was almost an afterthought, the man already turning back toward the wagon.

"My coat," Charles barked at Gregoria. He'd put the rifle down and was pulling on his boots.

She brought him his heavy blue army coat and he shrugged into it. "Food," he barked at her as he went out the door.

Before she could move in response, a woman entered, carrying a well-wrapped young child and clutching a shawl and blanket over her heavy wool coat. They were both shuddering with cold. The tow-headed boy was a toddler, big enough to walk only after he'd been unbundled. His mother checked his hands and feet carefully, then sat him on a wooden stool in front of the fire before she began unwrapping herself. In the meantime, Gregoria folded the blanket Charles had dropped and placed it on the bed in the corner.

"I am so grateful to you," the woman said to Gregoria. "There was no snow in Taos when we started for home this morning and very little on the other side of the pass. This storm was unexpected, to say the least." She shook her shawl out in front of the fire, then wrapped it around her shoulders again. She pushed curly black hair away from her round, tanned, and freckled middle-aged face and smiled at Gregoria. "I'm Alma Kinkaid. We live in the valley." She gestured northward. "We saw your cabin when we went by on the way in and I wanted to stop, but William was in a hurry." She shook her head. "I wish we had. It would have been nice to get acquainted before we lighted on your doorstep." She smiled again, into Gregoria's eyes. "I'm sorry we had to meet in this way."

Gregoria shook her head, trying to place this woman. Her child was obviously americano, with that pale hair. And the woman's name was americano. But her skin was brown enough to be Mexican, although her hair was curly enough that she could be negrita. And the freckles were a puzzle. But none of that mattered in light of her friendly smile and eyes. Gregoria smiled back at her. "Mi casa es su casa," she said, giving the formal welcome. My house is your house. "I am glad you are here," she added shyly in americano.

The door opened and the women turned. The man entered first, his square face anxious. He nodded to Gregoria as he took off his hat, revealing hair only slightly darker than the child's.

"Ma'am," he said. "I apologize for the inconvenience." Smiling, Gregoria shook her head and he turned to his wife. "Are you all right? I should have turned those mules around at the top of the pass and gone back to Taos."

"But we're so close now," she told him. She smiled at Gregoria. "Besides, it will give us a chance to get to know each other."

"Load all right?" Charles asked from the door.

"Yes, it should be fine," the blond man said. He put out his hand. "I'm William Kinkaid. This is my wife Alma and our son Alfred. We live up the valley."

Alfred looked up from the fire. "Warm fire," he told his father. He smiled happily, then frowned. "Alfy hungry."

"I can make tortías," Gregoria said. She looked at his mother. "Will that be all right?"

"That would be wonderful," Alma said gratefully. "He loves tortillas. Don't you, Alfy?"

The child nodded and watched eagerly as Gregoria placed the cast iron griddle on the fire. He slid off the stool and edged toward her. "Alfy help!" he said. "Alfy pat. Mama show me."

"Which means he doesn't know how to do it well," Alma said ruefully. "I'm not a very good cook." She smiled and sat down on the stool the child had vacated. "But we all love tortillas, don't we Alfy?" She pulled him toward her, away from the flames, which were reaching for the front of his shirt.

Gregoria saw what she was doing and smiled. "But you are a good mamá," she said shyly.

"I try to be," Alma said confidingly. She glanced at the men, who had moved toward the cloth-covered window and were talking weather and mules. She lowered her voice confidentially. "At my age, I'm not likely to have another child, so I want to ensure that Alfred is as safe and well cared for as possible." She smiled at Gregoria. "It is natural. You will know what I mean when yours arrives."

Gregoria glanced involuntarily at Charles. To hear her news in this way would make him very angry indeed. But he was standing at the other end of the room, in conversation with Mr. Kinkaid. As if he felt her glance, his head turned. "Rosa!" he said sharply. "Food ready?"

"Lo siento," she said. "Un momento." She turned back to Alma Kinkaid, who smiled at her.

"He doesn't yet know?" the other woman asked quietly. Gregoria shook her head and Alma smiled again and nodded conspiratorially.

~ ~ ~

They ate slowly, Gregoria relaxed in a way that she hadn't felt in a long time, absorbing the kindness of this woman and her soft-spoken husband. The men talked about mules, weather, and the number of travelers between Taos, the Moreno Valley, and Lucien Maxwell's place on the Cimarron.

"I hear you're raising cattle, as well," William Kinkaid said. "Joseph Stinson told me he got those beeves he drove in this summer from you."

Charles nodded noncommittally. "Lotta work, cows."

91

"Worth your while though, if you got half of what Stinson made on them."

Charles grunted and reached for more tortillas.

"Beef's a prime item with miners," William continued. "Stinson told me the butcher gave him a hundred a head."

Charles stopped chewing. His head swung toward the other man, then jerked toward the fire. Gregoria saw his jaws tighten and her stomach clenched, but he only said, "Too much chasin' after 'em." He thrust his chin toward the fire, then the table. "Offerin' lodgin' and food'll be easier."

"So that's your plan? It's a good location for a way station."

Gregoria glanced at Charles in surprise, then dropped her eyes to her food. So that was why they had moved to this particular spot, why the cabin was so much larger than what they truly needed, why he'd constructed the corral and its shelter. It wasn't just for her and the animals. A small spot of disappointment poked at her chest, but she pushed it away. It would be nice to have company from time to time. Especially if they were like these folks.

"I am glad we are neighbors," she told Alma shyly, speaking the americano words slowly. "Su casa? It is in the valley?"

"We're toward the northern end," Alma explained. "Near the beginning of the road to Maxwell's ranch. It's only ten miles or so from here, but the snow was so bad we weren't sure we could make it. And Alfred was so cold."

"I shouldn't have taken you to Taos this late in the year," William said contritely. He shook his head and turned to Charles. "You never know when snow will strike here, once summer is past."

"Or even in the summer," Alma said with a smile. She turned to Gregoria. "We've been so busy getting in the crops, we couldn't get away until now. My younger brother usually helps us, but he was away this year, trading." She shifted Alfred on her knee. "But now I'm glad the snow came when it did, because it gave us the opportunity to meet you."

Gregoria smiled at her. "I am glad also."

"You wanna stay, we have room," Charles said.

William looked at his wife. She glanced down at Alfred, who was tearing his tortía into small pieces and eating them slowly, his eyes closed in blissful concentration. "I think we can go on," she said, smiling. She looked up at her husband. "If the snow has let up, that is."

William Kinkaid said, "Excuse me, ma'am," to Gregoria, rose, and went to the door. He fumbled with the latch and Charles got up to assist him. The men stood silently in the opening. The women followed them, Alma carrying Alfred on her hip. The snow had stopped and the sun was shining, glittering on the whiteness that covered the hollow and the grasslands beyond and weighted down the branches of the ponderosas overhead.

"Ay!" Gregoria exclaimed.

Alma gave her a bemused look.

"There is so much," Gregoria said shyly.

William chuckled. "You'll see more snow than this before winter's out," he told her. "There's only about six inches out there now."

"Road'll be slick," Charles said.

"If we get home before nightfall, we'll be fine," William answered.

The men went outside and Alma began gathering the wraps she and the child had worn into the house. Gregoria started clearing the table.

"I wish I could help you," Alma apologized. She crouched down to button Alfred's coat. "But William wants to be home before the sun sets." She glanced toward the door. "That snow is quite wet and will melt quickly, which means the road will become muddy very soon and then icy after sundown."

Gregoria nodded. "I understand." She smiled shyly at Alma. "I am glad that you stopped."

Alma tied a shawl around Alfred's head and stood up. "So am I." She came to the table and reached for Gregoria's hand. "I'm very glad to have met you." She held Gregoria's hand between hers and looked into her eyes. "I hope you'll come to visit us some time." She nodded toward Gregoria's belly. "And that you'll let me know when your time comes, so I can help you."

Gregoria nodded wordlessly. Tears sprang unexpectedly into her eyes. No one had ever spoken to her like this before. So kindly. So sincerely and directly. Her heart filled with a confused joy.

The door opened and the men came in. The women turned toward them. William's mouth was tight and Charles looked sullen. Anxiety gripped Gregoria's throat.

"Tol' ya I was a way station," Charles said.

William shrugged. He laid two coins on the table. "Are you ready?" he asked Alma. He nodded to Gregoria. "Thank you for your hospitality, ma'am." He looked at Charles. "Next time, you might want to be a little clearer up front."

Alma turned to Gregoria and smiled. "Goodbye. And please remember what I said."

Gregoria smiled and nodded, but her eyes were on Charles. The muscles in his neck were tense with anger, his mouth grim under his beard. He pocketed the coins on the table and followed the Kinkaids out the door.

They said their goodbyes, the men barely civil, and the mules worked their way carefully to the rocky roadbed. Gregoria followed Charles back into the cabin.

"Didn' think neighbors should pay," Charles grumbled.

Gregoria silently continued clearing the table.

"Said I was settin' up a way station!"

Gregoria wrapped the remaining tortías in a clean cloth. There was enough for another meal, if she was careful.

"Four bits! Damn arrogant bastard! An' that Stinson! Six hun'red dollars!"

The indoor water bucket was almost empty and there was a thick layer of ice on the one outside the door. Gregoria poured what she could into the kettle and put it on the fire, then went to collect her chal. She wondered what it would be like to walk in six inches of snow. And how did Mr. Kinkaid know that, just by looking at it?

She slipped out the door. Behind her Charles growled, "Clearer up front. Bastard!" Her heart sank. If he felt like that about Mr. Kinkaid, there was little chance she would ever see Alma Kinkaid again.

The woman had looked at her so kindly. As an equal. That had never happened to Gregoria before. Not from a woman like Mrs. Kinkaid. After all, Carmelita was a prostitute. And old María had been kind enough, but abrupt and impatient. As if Gregoria was a charity case, not an equal.

She crouched next to the pool of water, careful to keep her skirts tucked away from the snow. Fortunately, the water hadn't iced over. As she waited for the bucket to fill, Gregoria's shoulders slumped. She might have known that friendship with a woman like Alma Kinkaid was impossible. She wasn't good enough to associate with someone like her.

Tears welled into her eyes, but she shook them away impatiently. She must prepare herself for future visitors. She must begin a bread starter and bake bísquetes americanos as María had taught her. There was flour and sugar in the packs they'd brought from Taos. She thought she could remember enough of what she'd learned. She would offer the raised biscuits to visitors when they arrived. Then surely they would be happy to pay and Charles would be willing for them to return. She hoped Charles would not be angry with her, would not leap to wrong conclusions when he discovered she knew how to bake such a thing.

PALO FLECHADO PASS, WINTER 1867

It was snowing again, but now two feet of it lay on the ground and the roadbed was slick with ice. The man rode in on a mule. It was the only reason he'd gotten as far as he had, he told Charles cheerfully. He was a thin young man with a ready smile and a shock of uncombed black hair above gray eyes. His pale face had a sprinkling of small pink freckles, making him seem younger than he was.

Charles had risen grumpily from the bed in the corner when the knock thudded on the door, but once the man had agreed to pay for a night's lodging and brought in two bulging packs, his face lost its scowl. He went out into the snow to bed the mule in the shelter at the end of the corral.

"Come a ways?" he asked as he came back inside.

The young man nodded, his hands to the fire. "Well, just Taos on this leg, though it seemed a deal farther."

"This leg?"

"Oh, I've been hither and yon. Bought some goods in Taos for Etown, but it took longer'n I thought it would to collect 'em. I didn't reckon on it bein' this cold." He laughed. "They says there's seven thousand men up there, waitin' for Spring so they can look for more gold. I aim to mine the miners, I guess you could say." He nodded at his pack. "They say Cap'n Moore's makin' a killing. I aim to cut a slice off his pie. Speakin' of food, I hope I ain't puttin' you out none."

"Food and lodging, all one price," Charles told him. He turned. "Rosa, food."

97

Gregoria nodded and went to her food supplies. But the young man wasn't completely focused on his goods and his plans. She could feel his eyes on her even as he went on talking to Charles. She fumbled with the tin of flour, hoping she'd remember all that she'd learned, thankful she'd begun the biscuit starter three days before. She bit her lip. Maybe she should just make tortías. But she'd already prepared the starter and it would go bad if it wasn't used soon. She stirred it anxiously. She hoped it would rise as it should.

As she worked, she listened to the young man describe his itinerant life, first coming west from Missouri with one of the Santa Fe wagon trains, then trading with the Navajos, and now heading to Etown to take advantage of the gold miners. Gregoria wondered how Alma and William Kinkaid felt about the miners in the valley. But perhaps it was large enough that they weren't in each other's way. She had no real sense of where their farm and the place called Etown were actually located, although she knew the mining camp was north of the Kinkaid's.

~ ~ ~

"How much they get?" Charles asked. The two men were sitting on the crudely carved stools in front of the fire. Charles got up and went to a shelf on the opposite wall, near the table. "Whisky?"

"Sure thing," the young man replied. He leaned to the fire. "I tell ya, this warmth sure feels good. I was almighty glad when I saw the lights at your windows."

"How much gold?" Charles asked.

"Well, they say the Aztec Mine's already made a hundred thousand. 'Course, that's Maxwell's deal on the east side of Baldy, up off Ute Creek. Him and Matthew Lynch and Tim Foley.

They brought in a 15-stamp mill t'clean the gold out o' the rock."
He turned to look at Gregoria, as if to bring her into the conversation. She kept her head down, arranging biscuits in the cast iron dutch oven. "They say it's real pretty quartz crystal. Got gold threads runnin' all through it."

Charles grunted and the young man turned back to the fire. "But you know how it is," he said. "It don't really matter how much there is. There'll be plenty o' people huntin' it even when it plays out. I figure it's safer t' bring in supplies t' sell than t' actually mine. And minin's hard work."

"Is that," Charles agreed, running his fingers through his beard.

Gregoria put the lid on the dutch oven and carried it carefully toward the fireplace.

The young man started up. "Lemme help you with that."

She shook her head. "No es nada." It's nothing.

"But I insist." He took the pot from her hands and placed it next to the fire. He scraped coals aside, set the dutch oven into the empty space, then raked coals up against the pot and over its flat lid. "See, I've got practice," he said. "I've been batchin' it for a while now."

He smiled up at her and she found herself smiling back, then caught herself. He moved more coals onto the heap, then sat back on his heels. He grinned up at Charles. "I'm one o' those rare men that actually likes t' cook," he said. "May just set myself up with a restaurant in Etown if prospects look good."

Charles grunted and stared into the fire. Gregoria retreated into the kitchen area and hoped the young man wouldn't follow her there. She breathed more easily when he stood, sat on a stool, and reached for the whisky jug. She shivered a little in the draft from the cloth-covered window and began slicing portions from the venison haunch she'd roasted the day before. They were going to need more meat soon. There was very little left on the doe hanging in the shed behind the house.

When the men had eaten their fill, Gregoria began cleaning up and Charles tossed blankets for their visitor onto the floor in front of the fire. As she and Charles moved to their own bedding, he gestured impatiently at her to sleep next to the wall, his usual spot. It would be awkward in the morning, rising before him, but she submitted silently. It is his protective instinct to keep me safe, she told herself.

And his protectiveness was evident again the next morning, when the young man hovered nearby while Gregoria cooked, sitting on the stool by the fire and asking her questions about how she worked the masa for the tortías, telling her how something he called crepes were prepared. Gregoria was interested in spite of herself. Surely Charles would understand she only wanted more knowledge about this strange kind of cooking, to better feed the guests that would come to their door.

"And they are with huevos? Eggs?" she asked as Charles came back inside from dealing with the mules. She looked up and saw him pause as the young man leaned forward to answer her. She pulled back, but it was too late.

Charles' hands flexed and his eyes tightened. "My woman," he growled, coming forward. "Stay 'way."

The young man half-turned on the stool, a smile on his lips. "I was just—"

Charles' fist clenched. Then he punched, slamming into the younger man's head. The gray eyes widened in shock, then the man toppled toward the fire. Gregoria screamed, snatching her skillet out of the way and pulling back at the same instant. She started up, but Charles had already grabbed the man's shoulders.

As he pushed the tousled black head into the fire, she screamed again.

"Charles! You're hurting him!" she cried.

But Charles didn't seem to hear. He was grunting with exertion. "My woman," he growled. "My woman." He pushed harder against the younger man's struggling.

The black hair caught fire, the room filling with the sharp smell of it. Then the back of the man's shirt was alight. Gregoria felt as if she couldn't breathe.

Charles released the man's head and began slamming his fist into his chest. "My woman," he growled again as the stranger struggled, gray eyes wide with panic.

Then the man stopped moving and his eyes went blank. His hair still smoldered in the flames. Fire licked at his shoulders.

Charles stood, yanked the man out of the fireplace and onto the dirt floor, and stomped out of the house.

The stink of burnt hair was strong in the room and the man's shirt still smoldered. Gregoria knew before she felt for his breath that he was dead.

Tears streamed down her face and she sank onto a fireside stool. She had done this. Her interest in his words had done it. She knew Charles was unreasoning in his jealousy. How could she have let this happen? This was her fault. "Lo siento mucho," she murmured to the young man's blank eyes. I am so sorry.

An hour later, she was still hunched on the stool, staring at the body between her and the fireplace. A shudder of fear went through her. Charles would be so angry with her for flirting, for causing the jealousy that made him do such a thing. She shuddered again at the thought of what he would do to her, then felt a stab of guilt. At least she was still alive. The cheerful black-haired young man with the gray eyes had died because of her.

But Charles didn't seem angry, or even upset about the young man's death, when he finally came back into the cabin. He went directly to the body and began going through the stranger's pockets. He pulled out a wallet, opened it, and ran his thumb over a wad of greenbacks. He grunted in satisfaction, set the wallet aside, and continued rummaging. Finally, he pulled up the man's shirttail.

"Yup," Charles said. He fumbled at the man's trousers, then pulled a money belt from his waist. He hefted it, then extracted a coin. "Gold." He hefted the belt. "Not much. Spent on goods."

"His family will be glad of it." Gregoria lifted herself from the stool and moved to the end of the fireplace. "His possessions belong to them now."

"Ain't here." He picked up the wallet, pulled out the greenbacks, and tossed the wallet into the fire.

Instinctively, Gregoria leaned forward to retrieve it, but Charles slapped her hand away. "Leave it," he growled. "Safety in fire."

He stood, went to the door, and looked out. The snow had stopped. Sunlight glinted cheerfully in the cabin yard. Except for where Charles had walked toward the corral, the snow's surface was smooth. There was no sign that a man and mule had crossed from the roadway the night before.

Charles turned back into the room, picked up the young man's body, heaved it over his shoulder, and headed for the door leading into the shed. "Come on!" he barked over his shoulder. Gregoria grabbed a chal and followed.

Charles dumped his burden against the shed's back wall. The traveler's packs of trade goods had been set near the door to the cabin. Containers of sugar and flour and a collection of canned goods lay beside the one on the left. Bright red cotton fabric peeked from the top of the other.

"Hurry up," Charles said sharply.

Gregoria turned and Charles motioned toward the corral.

"Mule," he said. "Into the trees."

She frowned, puzzled. Charles gestured toward the forest behind the shed. "The pass," he said impatiently. "Turn 'im loose."

It was protection, Gregoria realized. Against the questions that might come. She nodded numbly and turned toward the shed's outer door.

"Wait," Charles said. He bent down and yanked the young man's boots off his dead feet. "Take these."

Gregoria frowned as she took them. "What shall I do with them?"

"Wear 'em," Charles growled. He turned away. "Stupid," he muttered, looking down at the body. "Vamos," he growled. Go.

Gregoria pulled off her sandals and slipped the boots onto her feet. They were too large, and stiff where they rubbed against her ankles, but they would provide protection from the snow. "Lo siento," she murmured to the corpse on the stony floor.

"What?" Charles demanded, turning his head.

Gregoria shook her head. "Nada."

As she headed downhill toward the cabin an hour later, she kept to the trees. The stiff leather boots, too large for her feet, rubbed harshly against her ankles, but they were certainly better protection against the snow than bare feet or sandals. The pain reminded her of her guilt. When would someone come looking for the dead man and what would Charles tell them? She bit her lip and again wiped the tears from her face.

As she opened the cabin door, the grate of shovel against rock came from the shed. A grave, she supposed. It was the only place, with all the snow outside. Gregoria shuddered and looked at the fire. The wallet had fallen out of the blaze and lay smoldering, half burnt, to one side. She picked it up gingerly and carefully opened the charred leather. There were papers inside. She drew them out and studied them.

Because she couldn't read, she had no idea what the papers were for or what they said. Yet she felt that it was wrong to burn them. But she knew that if Charles discovered she'd kept them, he would be angry. She stared at the black marks on the white paper, wondering what to do.

"What's that?"

Gregoria looked up. Charles was standing over her, the shovel still in his hand.

"The wallet was too thick. It did not burn."

He pulled the papers from her hand and glanced at them. "Allan Lamb," he muttered. "Sheep to the slaughter." His big hands came together, crumpling the papers into a ball and tossing them into the fire, well into the flames. "Safety in fire." He glanced at her. "Good thing you can't read."

"What do you mean?"

He nudged at the nearest fire log with his boot. "Woman. Injun, too. No one'd believe you."

She frowned. "I am not Indian."

"Cheekbones say Injun." He leered at her. "Little Injun Rose." Then he sobered. He jerked his head toward the shed. "That food. Use it first."

She nodded, the tears springing again into her eyes. "Lo siento mucho," she whispered.

"What fer?" He looked at her sharply, then away, fingers combing his beard. "Keep yer eyes to yerself, I won't hafta protect ya," he growled. Then he slapped her rump sharply and went to sit at the table and count the money from the wallet and money belt.

Gregoria frowned, confused but also relieved that he wasn't angry with her, then slipped into the shed to retrieve the food. When she returned, the greenbacks and coins had disappeared. Into Charles' hiding place, she supposed. There was a long narrow gap in the wall behind the bed, where two of the logs were slightly larger than the one between them. He'd tucked his bag of coins there, next to an old brown leather wallet of greenbacks. And there were more coins and gold dust in the shed, though she wasn't sure just where. He didn't think she knew about them. She shivered. Not that she wanted to know. At least, not what he had just hidden. It was blood money. Tainted. The thought of it turned her stomach and gagged her throat.

Just as the goods in her arms chilled her heart as well as her arms. But she would use them and soon, because Charles had told her to do so. If only she could forget as easily as she could use up the food.

~ ~ ~

There was a trickle of paying guests in the next few weeks, Gregoria careful to avoid their eyes, and then winter closed in and travelers on the rocky track ceased altogether. Charles and Gregoria lived quietly, he sleeping most of the day, she creeping from fire to food supply to the woodpile just outside the door and, when the buckets were completely empty, to the stream. Charles had turned the mules out of the corral to fend for themselves and, when the weather lightened enough to permit it, Gregoria went to them in the hollow or the shelter of the trees, to speak a few words of comfort.

She still had not told Charles she was pregnant and he didn't seem to notice the changes her body was undergoing when he called her to the bed for pergates, as he called it. She went to him obediently, but her mind tended to wander while he was busy with her body. The name of the young gray-eyed man kept repeating itself in her head. Allan Lamb. Allan Lamb. Perhaps it was because he had been kind to her, had told her about tortías with huevos in them, had tried to include her in his conversation with Charles.

Gregoria was thinking of him again as she crossed the hollow that mid-December morning, her chal tied tightly over her chest, shoulders hunched against the cold. She had been to see to the mules, but even they could not take her mind from the terrified look on Allen Lamb's face as Charles shoved his head into the fire. A shudder went through her that had nothing to do with the weather. She looked down at her feet. She still wore the man's boots. She was glad their visitors had ceased for the time being. She must be more careful, for Charles' protection as well as that of their guests.

Another shudder ran through her, this time followed by a stab of pain through her groin. She gasped and her hands went to her belly. It was too soon, far too soon. She bit back her tears and groaned despairingly. This too would end in sorrow. She began walking, quickly before the pain returned, biting her lip as she strained toward the cabin. As she reached the corral, the pain came again and she leaned against the rail and retched into the snow. Another spasm jerked her up and she clutched at the railing, then pushed herself onward. She would need rags and a bucket. If she were careful, if Charles was asleep—

But he wasn't. He sat up in bed as she came in and gestured impatiently. "Pergates!" he barked.

She shook her head, hands clutching her belly. "I cannot," she gasped.

He scowled at her. "What?"

"My time," she gasped, hoping he would think she spoke of her menstruo.

"Don' matter." He leered at her. "Make it better." He lifted himself from the bed and came toward her.

She backed away, against the closed cabin door. "I cannot," she repeated. Tears sprang into her eyes. "Por favor."

Charles' hand came up threateningly and she closed her eyes, bracing herself. "Por favor," she begged. Then the pain cut through her abdomen and she bent into it, gasping.

Charles' hand gripped her arm, forcing her to stand. "What?" he demanded.

She shook her head. "My time," she gasped.

He scowled. "Never sick." His grip slackened. "Baby?"

She nodded, gasping into another spasm, and moved away from him, toward the bed. "The bucket," she gasped. "And rags for the bleeding."

He brought them silently, standing over her as the pains came again and again until her body had expelled the clot of matter and blood that might have become a child. He turned away then and left the cabin. Gregoria sank back onto the blankets, too exhausted even for tears. In a moment she would clean herself and get the shovel from the shed. Un momento.

~ ~ ~

Winter set in with a vengeance after that, the cold sharper than anything Gregoria had ever experienced, icicles hanging from the mules' coats as they crowded together under the corral shelter, the

107

snow in the hollow as high as Gregoria's knees. She learned quickly to wrap her hands in old rags before she ventured outside to break the ice on the stream or to carry in wood. The weather cleared a little in late January. With the thinning snow came William Kinkaid, on his way to Taos and asking if there was anything he could bring them.

"Flour," Charles said, without looking at him. "Hun'red pound."

"You sure do want to get that in Taos," William said as he warmed his hands at the fire. "The stores in the valley are charging mining town prices."

"More'n one?"

"There's Captain Moore's and then the Middaugh boys. The butchers are busy, too. The rise in beef prices is good for me, though. It makes all that feed I've forked out this winter worth the effort." Charles' face darkened and William Kinkaid looked at him apologetically, then turned abruptly to Gregoria. "The mercantiles have that printed cotton," he said. "That angaripola. But Alma won't buy it, no matter how pretty it is. She says Etown prices are even higher than Maxwell's." He grinned and touched his shirt pocket. "She gave me a list of what she wants from Taos. Is there anything I can get for you, ma'am?"

Gregoria looked at Charles. "Jus' flour," Charles said. He moved to open the door, as if he were impatient for Kinkaid to leave.

Instead, William fumbled in his shirt pocket. "I almost forgot. Alma sent a packet of garden seeds. She wanted to bring it herself, but Alfred's been feeling poorly." He glanced at Charles and the door, then handed a carefully folded piece of white paper to Gregoria. "She said she thought they'd grow in the hollow. There's summer squash, peas, beans, and salad stuff, too, I think.

She's been fussing with seeds since she was a girl, trying to find ones that'll mature in our short growing season and also stand up to July hailstorms. Oh, and she also said to warn you that corn doesn't do well up here." He turned to Charles with a small smile. "You know women and their gardens."

Charles grunted and looked away. Gregoria took the envelope. "I had been thinking about a garden," she said shyly. "Tell her gracias. Muchas gracias."

He patted her arm and Gregoria saw Charles stiffen. Then William moved past him into the yard without making eye contact and swung up onto the buckboard.

Charles closed the door and turned to glare at Gregoria. "Stay 'way from him," he growled.

"Sí, mi esposo," she said as she tucked the envelope into her skirt pocket.

"Gimme that."

"It is only seeds for a garden," she pleaded.

"Give it me!" he roared.

Outside, William Kinkaid heard Charles' voice rise. He glanced at the cabin door, then clucked at his team, urging them forward.

Alma had said she wanted to befriend the wife. "I think she's going to need us," she'd said quietly, looking at her hands. She'd looked up, eyes tense. "Please try to be polite to him, Will. I know it may be difficult."

So he'd stopped and he'd brought the seeds and he'd offered to bring flour back. But he didn't like the man. The house felt dark. And dangerous, somehow. He was glad Alma had felt Alfred couldn't make the journey. That house was no place for a woman and child, even for a short visit.

Inside the cabin, Charles wrenched the paper from Gregoria's fingers and ripped it open, scattering the precious seeds across the dirt floor. He turned the paper, examining it thoroughly. There was a short list of the different seeds Alma had sent, nothing more.

Gregoria knelt on the floor, carefully gathering up her gift, biting her lip to keep back the tears. I cannot read, anyway, she thought hopelessly. Even if the man had given me a note, it wouldn't have done any good. And why would he even look at a girl such as me, when he is married to a woman like Alma?

Charles threw the paper on the floor and went out. Gregoria gathered up what seeds she could find and carefully refolded them into the torn paper. She thought again of the spot she had marked out in her mind on the side of the hollow. It would be safe there from wagons or other activity, although she would have to keep the mules away. If she added manure from them and any visiting animals, as well as what she could find of old elk and deer droppings, she thought what she planted would do well there.

Now, thanks to Alma Kinkaid's kindness, she had vegetable seeds to plant. Squash and peas and greens. Gregoria smiled as she slipped the refolded paper carefully into her pocket. She would begin spreading manure there tomorrow, if the weather permitted. What she spread could begin mixing into the soil while she waited for the real warmth to arrive, when she could actually plant. Charles wouldn't mind once she brought him the first salad to eat with his elk meat, she told herself. When she could flavor it with something besides juniper berries. And perhaps— Her hand went to her belly. Perhaps there would be another mouth to feed by then. Just perhaps. She had reason to hope again. She grimaced, remembering the young man with the gray eyes. He had no hope. I must be more careful in future, she reminded herself.

The Pain and The Sorrow

Loretta Miles Tollefson

Palo Flechado Pass, Early 1868

Abijah Edwards had been a merchant in Taos for half a dozen years and those years had been good to him. With a natural gift for languages, a hearty manner, and a shrewd business sense, he had the skill to stop a man's line of credit and still make him feel welcome in his shop. But Edwards' ambition had never been to stand behind a mercantile counter all his life. At the age of forty, with no wife or children, he was becoming restless. His attention had been caught by the mining activity on the other side of the Sangre de Cristos and he was eager to explore the potential for investments there. When the Sangre de Cristos' usual brief February thaw hit, he extracted what he could from the mercantile safe while still leaving himself a good working capital, then set off up the rocky track that led eastward.

He made good time, but he was unused to fending for himself in the wild. The jerky he carried with him had begun to pall when he came upon the cabin at the foot of Palo Flechado Pass as darkness began to descend.

Edwards reined in his horse and contemplated the cabin. It didn't look like much, but the door was slightly ajar, and even from the roadway he could make out the scent of venison and raised bread. A bridled and saddled horse stood in the snow outside the corral, indicating that they already had guests. He clucked at his mare and she stepped willingly down into the hollow.

A burly man with a rough black beard appeared in the doorway as Edwards looped his bridle reins around the corral's top rail.

"Food and lodgin'?" the man asked. "It'll cost ya."

112

"Gladly," Edwards answered. He followed the man inside. A pretty young Mexican woman bent over a large pot of stew at one end of a rough stone fireplace. A scrawny young man sat on a crudely carved stool at the other end, smoking a pipe and pretending not to watch the girl.

"Rosa!" the burly man said. "'Nother plate."

The girl looked up, nodded, and returned to her cooking.

The man gestured for Edwards to put his hat and coat on a nail driven halfway into the wall by the door. "Drink?" he asked.

"A spot of whisky would go far to chasing away the cold," Edwards said, smiling at the man companionably. "My name's Edwards. Abijah Edwards."

"Kennedy," the man said. He looked toward the fire. "Rosa! Whisky!"

The girl straightened, went to a shelf near the table, and produced a jug and two wooden noggins. Kennedy poured the drinks out silently and the men drank. The young man by the fire stared into the flames.

There was a long silence, then the girl raked the coals from a cast iron dutch oven, lifted the lid and turned to Kennedy. "The dinner, it is ready, mi esposo," she said.

The men sat and she served. Edwards found himself watching her, silent in the firelight, her dark hair gleaming, her skirts short in Taos fashion. Even in the February cold, she wore only sandals on her feet.

After the meal the silent young man with the pipe took his leave.

"Cold out there," Kennedy warned, but the man shook his head, paid for his meal, and slipped out without a word.

Edwards, sitting on a stool by the fire, watched him go with amusement. "Loquacious young cuss, isn't he?" he asked as Kennedy closed the cabin door.

Kennedy grunted and went to the table. "Drink?" he asked, lifting the jug.

"Don't mind if I do," Edwards said. As Kennedy refilled the noggins, Edwards looked around the room. "Nice setup you have here. I'm betting you get a good deal of traffic to and from Taos."

Kennedy grunted again. Edwards twisted around to look at the girl. "Though it must be lonely at times. Do you get into Etown at all?"

"Naw," Kennedy said. "Busy here." He handed Edwards the noggin of whisky and sat down before the fire.

"Given the season, you don't seem to be doing too badly for customers," Edwards observed. "The loquacious one and now me. Is that pretty much your traffic load?"

Kennedy scowled and squinted at his face. "Why?"

Edwards shrugged. "Just curious is all. Guess it's the merchant in me."

Kennedy frowned at the fire. "Taos?"

"Edwards and Co., that's me," the merchant said. "On the north end of town, toward Taos Pueblo."

Kennedy grunted again.

"This isn't a mercantile trip, though," Edwards said. "I'm thinking of divesting a little, getting into mining." He glanced toward the girl at the table. She was certainly a pretty young thing. Then he turned back to the husband. "Who would you suggest that I talk to in Etown?"

Kennedy scowled. "Joe Stinson," he said irritably. "Long's you got funds."

"Oh yes." Edwards grinned. "I'm figuring mining's like everything else in this Territory. Without money in hand, a man doesn't have much reason for talking."

Kennedy's eyes tightened and one hand raked through his black beard, but he only grunted in acknowledgement. Edwards threw him a look, glanced at the pretty wife again, then turned to gaze into the fire. The two men were silent after that, the only sound the woman in the background, arranging her dishes. Kennedy offered more whisky at one point, but the merchant politely refused. When they retired—Kennedy and his wife in the corner, Edwards in a blanket before the fire—Edwards kept his pistol belt near at hand.

In the middle of the night there was movement between the bed and the doorway. Edwards wakened and stirred, and Kennedy paused, then continued to the door. When they all rose the next morning, the traveler indicated that he needed no breakfast. He'd head out early to Etown. He went outside, saddled up, and came back in to say goodbye, but found Kennedy gone.

"I understand Henry Lambert's got quite a restaurant going," he told the girl heartily. "Thought I'd try there for an early lunch." He smiled at her downcast eyes as she followed him across the room and opened the door for him. He stepped out the door. "Thank you for the food ma'am. You're a mighty fine cook."

"Leave 'er alone," Kennedy growled from behind him and Edwards turned to find himself facing a rifle barrel. Kennedy and the gun blocked his way to the corral and his horse. "Rosa! Door!" Kennedy bellowed and the cabin door shut with a thud.

The merchant lifted his hands. "I was about to ask how much I owed you," he said. "No harm done."

Kennedy scowled. "All of it."

Edwards frowned in confusion.

"Yer wallet." Kennedy's rifle jerked slightly closer.

The merchant nodded. "I'll just toss the wallet to you and you can take what you want," he suggested.

"Do that," Kennedy growled. "No tricks."

Edwards shook his head. "No tricks," he agreed. He kept his right hand in the air as he slipped his hand into his vest pocket. The hand came out swiftly, holding a pistol, but Kennedy was prepared. The rifle roared and pain seared Edwards' side, wrenching him toward the closed door.

He caught himself and burst away, running instinctively across the hollow to the road. The rocky roadbed felt secure under his feet and he turned blindly, heading toward Etown, but the black-bearded man's gun roared again and then there was only blackness.

~ ~ ~

"I sure could do with some raised biscuits," Peter Kinsinger said over his shoulder to his brother Joseph as they trudged east out of the San Fernando River valley and over Palo Flechado Pass. He hitched his end of the pole that supported the elk carcass between them into a more comfortable spot on his shoulder. "I hear tell Rosa Kennedy knows how to make 'em real well. It's only a coupla miles away now."

"You could wait for Elmira's biscuits," Joseph said. He hadn't liked the looks of the Kennedy cabin when they'd gone by on their way into the pass. They now had the meat they'd been hunting and he was tired of the snow and the cold. "She and Desi'll be waitin' on us, fer sure."

Peter turned his head and grinned. "I'm a little chilly, ain't you? An' thirsty. A little liquid refreshment seems in order."

116

Joseph chuckled. Peter's Elmira was a stickler about drinking. Peter found it easier to stay away from the Etown saloons than to experience Elmira's tongue when he stumbled home from them. But a man did deserve a drink every once in a while. And, given the weather, there'd likely be no one at the Kennedy cabin to carry tales. "It is mighty cold out here," he acknowledged.

The road leveled out at the top of the pass and they headed downhill, careful of the icy patches. They were about halfway down the mountainside when they heard the echo of a rifle shot, then another.

"Sounds like Kennedy's huntin'," Peter said.

"May not get that drink after all," Joseph replied. "I hear his woman don't open that door if he ain't there."

"Too bad," Peter said. "I sure am thirsty."

Joseph chuckled. "It's still a ways. Maybe he'll be back before we get there."

But when they came within sight of the Kennedy rancho forty-five minutes later, both brothers forgot all about liquid refreshments.

A man's body lay sprawled in the middle of the road at the edge of the Kennedy hollow, the rocky track dark with blood. Charles Kennedy was crouched beside him. The Kinsingers eased their elk to the snow beside the road and hurried forward.

Kennedy looked up at them. "Injuns," he said.

Peter and Joseph looked at each other, then Kennedy. "Is he dead?" Peter asked.

Kennedy nodded. "Fought 'em off." He straightened and gestured toward the cabin. "Bullet holes in th' door." He nudged the dead man with his toe. "Greenhorn ran."

Joseph crouched to turn the man over. "I don't recognize him," he said.

117

"Taos," Kennedy said.

Joseph stood up.

"When'd it happen?" Peter asked.

"Coupla hours," Kennedy said.

The Kinsingers nodded, eyes raking the hollow and trampled snow, careful not to look at each other or Kennedy.

"Well, we have meat t' get home," Peter said. "We'll tell 'em in Etown t' come get the body. I 'spect his Taos friends'll want to give 'im a proper burial."

Kennedy nodded. He stood next to the body, running his fingers through his black beard as he watched the Kinsingers return to their elk, hoist its pole onto their shoulders, and trudge past him. Then he turned and went into the cabin.

~ ~ ~

The brothers were out of sight over the rise to the north before either spoke.

"Injuns my hat," Peter said over his shoulder.

Joseph spat into the snow at the side of the road. "Sure is a convenient excuse though, ain't it?"

"We didn't see anything different," Peter pointed out.

"Wouldn't wanna get crosswise o' that one," Joseph agreed.

They trudged morosely up the valley toward Etown.

~ ~ ~

Gregoria moved forward anxiously when Charles opened the cabin door. "It is well?"

"Injuns," he said. He jerked his head toward the road. "Shot Edwards."

Her eyes widened and she put her hand to her mouth.

"Greenhorn," Charles growled. He crossed to the bed and tossed Edward's wallet onto the blankets.

Gregoria watched silently. It is because of me, she thought wildly. His eyes kept following me and now he is dead. And here is yet another wallet. She bit her lip, wanting to make the same protest she'd made about the wallet Allen Lamb had carried, but not daring to speak.

Charles pulled out a fistful of greenbacks, then reached into his pocket for a small bag of coins. When he had finished counting them up, he grinned, then glanced sharply at Gregoria and carried his loot into the shed.

Palo Flechado Pass, Spring 1868

Miners were pouring into the Moreno Valley from every direction, including Palo Flechado Pass. Besides the Etown mercantiles and butcher, there were plenty of places of entertainment and even a hotel. It was no place for a lady, though, the travelers who stopped at the cabin assured Charles, even as their eyes lit with excitement at the stories they'd heard. Better wait for things to settle a bit before Rosa visited.

"Though they'd be mighty glad t'see her," an old Scottish prospector said one evening as he tamped tobacco into his pipe.

"Too far," Charles growled from the other end of the fireplace.

The old man paused in the process of lighting his pipe and nodded. "'Tis a ways from here still," he acknowledged. "Twelve mile. But a woman's got a need for ribbons and such like." He turned to smile at Gregoria, who was standing at the table, mixing up another batch of biscuits. "'Specially a fresh young one like herself."

Gregoria saw Charles scowl and averted her eyes, but it was too late. He stood up, towering over the other man. "Leave 'er be," he growled.

"No harm intended," the miner said mildly. "I'm just an old man with an appreciation for the finer things o' life." He gestured around the room with his pipe. "You have yourself a nice arrangement here, next to the main road an' all. You're a right clever man, settin' up here like you did. You should do well for yourself. How many people you calc'late ETown'll get to?"

Charles sat back down reluctantly. Gregoria's head stayed carefully averted, looking down at her work. "Sayin' ten thousand," he said. "Seems high."

The Scot nodded. "You just never know, though," he said. "And whatever the numbers are, I'm thinking it'll go good for you here."

The men chatted on and Gregoria allowed herself to breathe again as her hands kneaded the bread dough.

~ ~ ~

And then she was sure. Early on an April morning Gregoria told Charles shyly that she was with child. He responded with only a grunt, so she wasn't sure how he felt about her news. He showed more animation early that afternoon when she came in from checking on the mules and collecting water and told him she'd seen elk sign in the melting snow near the stream. Their meat supply was low and there'd been no sign of elk or deer in the past week.

Charles collected his rifle, pulled on his coat, and headed out. Behind him, Gregoria left the cabin door slightly ajar, enjoying the small fingers of warmth that crept in with the fresh air. Shadowed as it was from the afternoon sun, the road from the pass was ice-packed once again, following a recent spring snow. There seemed little danger of anyone visiting today. She hoped Charles would not be angry that she had not kept the cabin as tightly shut up as usual while he was gone.

The warming air created a steady drip of water from the edge of the cabin roof. Gregoria positioned her largest pot to capture it and save herself a slippery walk to the stream. She heated the water she already had in a smaller pot and began giving the table and chairs a good scrubbing, while trying to avoid getting water on the floor. Even with the thaw, it was prone to developing icy patches.

She was bending over the damp table, using a piece of wood to carefully scrape it clean along the grain, when there was a series of thuds on the door jamb. She looked up.

A burly man with an unkempt white beard blocked the sunlight. At least one other man stood behind him. Gregoria bit her lip, then dried her hands on her skirt as she moved toward the door.

There were three men and one burro, well loaded. The man in the doorway was the oldest.

"Buenos días," she said. "You are looking for shelter? We have food. There is a cost."

The men took off their hats as they entered the room. The youngest one shut the door behind him. He was just a boy, really. In his late teens. "Yes, ma'am," the old man said. "We'd take some supper, if'n you have it. Not to put you out, ma'am."

She shook her head. "There is plenty," she said. "Mi esposo—" The sound of a rifle reverberated from the hillside on the other side of the stream. "He returns soon," she said. "With elk meat, I think."

"That's fine, ma'am," the man said. "Is there someplace to store the burro?"

She looked at him blankly, then realized what he meant and said, "I will show you," and moved toward the door.

"You can just tell me," the boy said, intercepting her. "We don't want to put you out, ma'am." He put his hand on the door latch just as she reached it.

As he swung the door open, there was a shout from the other side of the stream.

"Rosa!" Charles yelled. "Damn it! Rosa!"

Gregoria and the young man looked out from the cabin's entrance at the same time. Charles stopped in his tracks and frowned angrily. Gregoria stepped quickly across the threshold, disassociating herself from the boy.

"We have guests," Gregoria called to him.

He stepped across the stream and moved toward her, rifle in hand.

"Tres hombres," she told him.

Charles looked at the burro, then the young man. "Panning?" he asked.

The old man was in the doorway now, behind the boy. "That's right," he said heartily. "Lookin' for gold. 'Spect you've already checked the streams hereabouts, ain't ya?"

"Had my fill," Charles said. "Need shelter?"

"Yessir. The three o' us. My son-in-law, my youngest, an' myself." He moved aside as the other man came out the door. "Name's Chester Landry. This here's my daughter's man Henry Cutter an' my son Jim Bob."

"Kennedy," Charles said. He gestured toward Gregoria. "Rosa. My woman." He jerked his head at her, then the stream behind him. "Elk's on th' hill. Hurry up or critters'll get it."

Mr. Cutter moved forward. He was a thin man with a pale face, frizzy red hair, and a red beard as wide as his shoulders. His brown eyes were mild but there was a tightness in the skin around them that said they could turn instantly hard. He lifted his hat to his head. "I'll just go along and assist with that, if you don't mind," he said to Charles. "That'll give you and Jim Bob time to take care of the burro."

"Yessir, that burro is one tuckered out beast," the old man said heartily. "I'll go 'long with you, Henry." He turned to Charles.

123

"Matter of fact, if you'll point us in the right direction, we can prob'ly find the meat ourselves and save you all a trip."

Charles scowled, then nodded. He gestured toward the stream. "Path's there."

"I— We use a hide to pull it over the ground," Gregoria told the old man without looking at him.

"It's a yearling," Charles said. "It'll carry."

Which they did, returning forty-five minutes later with a gutted animal positioned between them on a stripped aspen pole. Charles grunted in acknowledgement and directed them into the shed, where he hung the carcass, stripped the hide, and cut off a portion of the haunch for their dinner.

~ ~ ~

"There's just nothin' like fresh elk meat," Chester Landry said as the men sat around the wood-plank table. He nodded to Gregoria as she placed a wooden platter of raised biscuits in the space between their plates. "Elk meat, beans, an' fresh-baked biscuits. What more coulda man want?"

"Caviar," Jim Bob said. "Champagne."

"A house with carpets," Henry said.

"Now that's not you wantin'," his father-in-law said. He grinned. "That's what that daughter o' mine's wantin'."

"And I'm wanting a happy wife," Henry said, pushing his hair away from his forehead.

Chester Landry laughed. "Like I tol' you before ya'll got hitched, I ain't sure she's ever gonna be happy."

Henry shrugged and reached for a raised biscuit. "I can but try."

Charles grunted disapprovingly.

"You don't agree?" Henry asked.

"Woman's like goat." Charles stabbed his knife into the meat on his platter. "Food, shelter, baby. All she needs."

The three other men looked at each other, then the old man said, "Me, I need gold t' be truly happy. And that's what we're headin' t' get." He turned to Charles. "You hear about what they're taking out o' the east side o' Baldy Mountain? They say it's a big one. Just like Sutter's Creek. Maybe bigger."

Charles snorted. "More travelers, anyway. Good fer me."

"I'd say you're in a prime location for that," Chester agreed.

"And a pretty wife is always an attraction." The boy smiled at Gregoria, who turned abruptly away to add more wood to the fire.

"Not yer business!" Charles growled.

Gregoria sucked in her breath and stood stone-still, staring into the fire. But there were three of them and only one of Charles, and Chester Landry said merrily, "This one has always had an eye for the gals. Just likes t' look, though!"

"Not at mine," Charles said.

"No, sir. Sorry, sir," Jim Bob said. He looked at his father. "I think I'll bed down with the burro tonight. Keep him company."

Chester nodded and the boy stood, nodded to the room in general, put on his hat, and went out. The rest of the men finished their meal silently and then the visitors arranged their blankets in front of the fire.

Gregoria crept into bed. Charles followed soon after, reaching for her breasts before he was fully undressed. She looked anxiously toward the fireplace, but he growled "What?" and began groping her breasts and pulling at her night clothes. She bit her lip and lay as quietly as possible as he moved over her, grunting. There was no sound or movement from the two men in front of the hearth.

The next morning the three men and burro left just after sunrise, eyes carefully avoiding Gregoria as they paid Charles for the lodging and food.

"Come back now," he called after them as they trudged across the hollow in the clear morning light. The old man paused. Without turning around, he raised his hand in response. The others kept walking, the youngest in front, breaking the way through the icy slush that had formed overnight from the half-melted snow.

"Gonna be more." Charles looked down at the coins in his hand. "Now Spring's come." He rubbed his thumb thoughtfully across the coins. "Need more whisky."

~ ~ ~

Two days later they had another visitor, but this one wasn't looking for either whisky or food. When the young man followed Charles through the cabin door, Gregoria recognized him and turned instantly away. It was the man with the laughing brown eyes who'd headed Señor Letcher's train of burros the previous summer.

He didn't appear to recognize Gregoria, but kept his eyes focused on Charles' massive back. "Adolph Letcher asked me to stop on my way and collect from you," he said.

Charles swung around, his face darkening. "Collect?"

The young man pulled a set of papers from a coat pocket and consulted it. "The loan he gave you last spring was for seventy-five dollars and the balance on the cattle was eighty-one. Then there's the interest, of course. It comes to one sixty-two twenty-one if you pay me today."

Charles grunted and went to the shelf that contained his whisky jug. "Drink?" he asked.

"No, thank you," the young man said. Gregoria could feel his eyes on her now, but she kept her face carefully averted.

"I'm prepared to give you a receipt for the payment," he said to Charles.

Charles snorted derisively. "Won't."

"I hope I misunderstand you, sir," the young man said stiffly.

"Not payin' today." Charles lifted the jug, took a swig, and replaced it on the shelf with a thud.

"May I tell Mr. Letcher when he may expect payment?"

Charles shrugged without turning. "When I'm ready."

"And this is what I am to report to him?"

Charles turned then, moving menacingly toward the younger man, but Lecher's messenger stepped smoothly back and toward the door. A moment later, he was bowing stiffly and lifting his hat to his head. "I will inform Mr. Letcher of your statement," he said formally.

Charles followed him outside. Gregoria forced herself to turn back to her work. She heard a muffled sound, then the click of horseshoes on stone and the man's voice, louder now. "You are aware, of course, that every delay in payment increases the amount of interest accrued. The total amount owed will increase accordingly." Then the horse moved off, its saddle leather creaking.

Charles muttered something unintelligible, stood for a long moment in the yard, then reentered the cabin. Gregoria bit her lip and returned to her work.

~ ~ ~

As the aspen buds began to green and unfurl and the rains to soften the soil, Gregoria began turning dirt for her garden, remov-

127

ing as much of the clinging grass roots as she could and working in the manure she'd collected. Two passing miners cut down the encroaching bushes on the north edge of the hollow in exchange for a meal, although Charles growled threateningly when they suggested that the payment include whisky, as well.

The pile of brush they left was rather formidable. Gregoria took some of the evergreen branches inside, to use as a sort of bed form under the pile of blankets in the corner. The rest she chopped at a little each day, creating kindling, praying that the wood's damp greenness would dry quickly, so it would be usable soon. She didn't have much time for this work, as the road had now completely lost its slick surface of ice and there was at least one paying guest at almost every meal. She found herself at the table preparing biscuits more than she would have really liked. That's where she was late on the afternoon that the Navajo man showed up.

He was carrying a small wooden box as he came into the cabin. He held it out to Charles with a questioning look.

"What ya got?" Charles growled.

The man placed the box on the table and opened it reverently. Inside, resting in a cloth-covered indentation shaped to its barrel and grip, lay an engraved ivory-handled pistol. "Colt," he said.

Charles nodded. His hand moved toward the gun, then stopped.

"Bullets also." The man lifted a cloth to reveal ammunition carefully tucked into a separate compartment beside a small powder flask and what looked to Gregoria like cleaning tools. A key for the box lay in a separate indentation.

"You take," the man said to Charles.

"What fer?" Charles' eyes narrowed. "Where's it from?"

The man gestured toward the west and Taos. "I trade many blankets."

Charles grunted.

"You take," the man said again.

"What fer?"

"Whisky." It was more of a breath than a word.

Charles shook his head. "No whisky to Injuns. It's th' law."

The man touched the pistol's grip with a gentle finger. "Iv'ry," he said. "Many blankets." He looked at Charles. "Little whisky."

Charles shook his head. "No whisky t' Injuns."

The man put his hands together in a supplicating gesture. "You good. Trade whisky."

Charles shook his head impatiently. "I tol' ya. No whisky."

The Indian reached for the box, turning it so that the Colt's silver engraving glinted in the firelight. "Pretty. Many blankets. Iv'ry," he said. He moved the box slightly toward Charles. "Little whisky," he said coaxingly. "Just little."

Charles backed away. "I told ya! No whisky!"

Gregoria went to the fire and lifted the lid of her stew pot. "Food?" she asked without looking at the men.

"Whisky!" the Navajo man said. He stepped toward Charles, his face urgent now. "Whisky!"

"No whisky!" Charles wrenched the pistol case out of the man's hands, then shoved it hard into his chest, sending him reeling across the room and against the log wall beside the door.

The man pushed himself upright, then moved suddenly forward, his submissive demeanor gone. He half-crouched, hands out, looking for a hold.

Charles tossed the pistol case onto the table and swung his arms, parrying the blow. With one sweep, he lifted the Indian from the floor and sent him crashing against the wall's stone foundation.

The man lay silent, head bleeding. Instinctively, Gregoria moved toward him, but Charles waved her back. He stepped to the wall, bent to touch the man's neck just below his chin, then grabbed his head in both hands and yanked sharply left. Gregoria heard a sharp crack and her own breath caught in her throat. Charles straightened, went to the table, lifted the pistol from its case, and held it up to the light. "Iv'ry," he said approvingly.

He tucked the pistol into his waistband, then went to the door and looked out. Darkness was settling across the hollow and the valley beyond it, a pink light still gently touching the eastern peaks. Charles turned. "That brush," he said, jerking his head at Gregoria. "Light it."

She stared at him uncomprehendingly. "Light it!" he bellowed at her. "Stupido!" He jabbed a finger at the fireplace. "Fire!"

She turned automatically, picked up a piece of kindling, and held it to the flames, waiting for it to catch. When she looked around, Charles was halfway out the door, the body of the Indian over his shoulders. Gregoria followed him with her flaming stick. He climbed the edge of the hollow, dumped the man's body beside the pile of brush, and began pulling branches over it.

"Light!" Charles bellowed and she went closer, raising her torch higher so he could see. But then he wrenched the stick from her hand and thrust the flame into the brush. "More wood," he ordered. He moved around the pile, thrusting the burning stick into it at strategic locations. "Need heat."

The bile rose in her throat as Gregoria turned away, but she numbly brought him pieces from the wood pile until he gestured at her to stop. She crept into the cabin then, while he watched the fire burn. She lay on the bed, arms holding herself, tears gagging her throat. It was only an Indian, she told herself. He started the quarrel. It is against the law to sell whisky to Indians. But it wasn't enough to stop the tears from coming, tears for the two men before him as well as the Navajo man. The tears did not cease until she choked them down hours later, when Charles came in from his task.

~ ~ ~

The bottle was shaped like a little glass log cabin and was the color of cottonwood leaves in the fall. The salesman held it up to the light streaming from the open cabin door. "Pretty, huh?" he winked at Charles. "The stuff in it is pretty good, too. Ninety proof and pure as the day is long." He unscrewed the cap, then tightened it. "It's refillable."

He handed the bottle to Charles, who turned it over. "Booz?" he asked, looking at the raised letters on the glass.

"It's made by the Booz Company in Philadelphia, Pennsylvania," the man said. "I can let you have four boxes at a dozen a box. They're just the thing to attract customers. Adds a little class to the place."

Charles scowled at the bottle in his hand.

"Adds even more class," the man amended hurriedly. He waved his hand at the room. "You've got yourself a great little rancho here, spit shined and cozy and capital food. All you need is some bottles like these to add that extra touch."

Charles grunted and put the bottle on the table. "You stayin' the night?" he asked.

"If you need to sleep on it, I'm stayin'!" the salesman said heartily.

Gregoria turned away, stomach clenching against the bile, and went to check the biscuits rising in the pan near the fire.

But Gregoria was careful to avoid any interaction with him and the salesman slept with his guns at his side, so there was no violence that night. The next morning Charles sullenly dug out some of his greenbacks and paid for a single box of the golden glass.

"'Course, I'm assuming you have a license to sell from these," the man said as he slid the money into his billfold. He moved out of the cabin into the sunlight, toward his waiting buckboard.

"License?" Charles growled as he followed. "What fer?"

"For doin' business, man! Especially for sellin' liquor!" The salesman ran a hand over the back of the nearest mule, then turned to look at Charles. "Haven't you heard? Santa Fe is sendin' out inspectors. They're tryin' to increase Territorial revenues by requiring business owners to buy licenses." He grinned. "Whisky from a jug is one thing. After all, most everyone has a jug or two for their own use." He gestured toward the back of his wagon and shrugged. "But these Booz bottles, they make it pretty clear you've got liquor to sell."

"Don't need no license."

"Well, they think differently in Santa Fe." The salesman moved to the back of the buckboard and settled his remaining boxes into place. "But that's between you and them. I just sell the bottles." He winked at Charles and climbed onto the wagon. "I don't ask what you do with them."

Charles grunted in reply and the man tipped his hat to Gregoria. "Ma'am," he said. He snapped the reins over the back of his team. "Giddup now!" he said and the wagon began moving carefully toward the road.

"License!" Charles said bitterly. "Bet Stinson don't have one!" He spat into the mud beside the door and shoved past Gregoria into the house.

~ ~ ~

As the weather began to truly warm, the road between Taos and the Moreno Valley became busy with travelers. There was even talk of improving it to make it easier for wagons to make the trip.

"Next thing you know, they'll be puttin' in a stagecoach," the old man crouched by the fireplace said. He lifted a noggin toward Charles. "I'll take a little more of that booz, if'n you don't mind."

Charles, who was sitting on a stool in front of the fire, grunted, half-turned, and gestured to Gregoria. She worked her way around the legs of the young carrot-haired man who sat on the other stool and carefully poured the liquid into the man's container. It was half-water, she knew. There was only one whisky jug in the cabin now. The others had been moved to the shed, out of sight. The Booz bottles were carefully arranged on the shelf by the table, each with a different percentage of alcohol mixed into the water that filled them. Charles had explained gruffly which bottle to serve from, depending on the customer's state of inebriation. It kept his costs down and steadily increased the coins in the bags behind the bed and in the shed. Perhaps the bags will grow fat enough to pay the debt that he owes to Señor Letcher, Gregoria thought now, as she carefully avoided the eager gaze of the old man she was serving.

"Stage takes money," the carrot-haired young man observed.

There was a knock on the cabin door and Gregoria went to open it. A young man with a doctor's bag in his hand nodded to her. "Ma'am," he said. "I understand you serve meals and drink?"

With eyes carefully on the floor, Gregoria nodded and gestured him in. Charles stood and came forward. "Meal's two bits, drink's a nickel," he said.

"I'll take a drink now and a meal before I leave," the man said. He removed his hat, revealing a head of thick blond hair. He turned to Gregoria. "I bear you greetings, as well, ma'am," he said. "Alma Kinkaid asked that I mention her name to you."

Gregoria glanced at Charles. "Gracias," she said warily.

"Yer that Etown Doc, ain't you?" the old man by the fireplace asked.

"I am Doctor Applegate." The newcomer smiled. "Yes, I suppose you could say that I'm the Etown doctor."

"You know the Kinkaids, then?" the carrot-headed man asked. He jerked his head toward the door. "Heard what you said."

"Yes, I provide care for their son."

"Nice woman, Miz Kinkaid," the old man said. "Knows a thing or two herself 'bout potions. I'm surprised she don't doctor 'im herself."

The doctor smiled gently. "She wants the best for her son." Gregoria brought him a noggin of drink—stronger than the one she'd poured the old man—and he looked into her face. "She asked me to inquire as to your health."

"She's healthy," Charles said abruptly. "Preñada, too."

"Ah," the doctor said, looking at Gregoria. "Is this your first?"

She glanced toward the fireplace, where the other men were suddenly watching her, and shook her head. She moved toward her food preparation area in the corner next to the table. The doctor followed. Gregoria glanced over her shoulder at Charles, but he had turned back to the fire, listening to the old man, who had suddenly begun a detailed story about Old Bill Williams and trapping in the Cimarron Canyon.

"I apologize for being so abrupt," Doctor Applegate said to Gregoria in a low voice. "You have been with child before now?"

She nodded and reached for her mixing bowl. She began measuring flour into it. It was the only thing she could think to do. Her americano words had suddenly deserted her.

The doctor glanced around the cabin. "And was a child born?"

She shook her head, her eyes on the flour. "Tres," she said. She reached for the package of sugar.

He moved slightly, the better to look into her face. "You have been pregnant three times and have not yet born a child?"

She paused, considering the question, then put a floury hand on her belly. "Tres," she said.

"This is the third time."

She nodded, dragged her small barrel of lard from the corner under the shelves, and began spooning the fat into her bowl.

"I can give you something to assist the child to grow."

She glanced up at him, then frowned at her mixing bowl. "No dinero." Her eyes slid involuntarily toward Charles and the doctor nodded.

"I will ask him," he said. "If he wants a child, he will buy what I offer. It isn't much."

Later, after the meal, when the old man and the carrot-haired one had gone their way and Doctor Applegate was settling his account with Charles, he said, "I understand your wife's previous pregnancies ended in miscarriage."

Charles grunted, turning the coins over in his hands.

"As a physician, I can provide you with a tonic that will enable her to come to full term."

"Huh?" Charles gave him a sharp look.

"I can give you something for her to drink that will help the child grow and be born healthy."

"A boy?"

Doctor Applegate smiled. "I'm afraid that is in the hands of the Almighty. But it will increase the chance that the child is born at all."

"How much?"

"One dollar."

It was the amount Charles had gathered from the three men that day. He half-turned toward the door, then stood staring at the wall, hand raking through his beard. In her work corner, Gregoria paused, watching. Did he not want this child? But finally, Charles counted out the coins and the doctor retrieved a bottle of dark brown glass from his bag.

"Rosa!" Charles said sharply and jerked his head toward the man. She came forward and listened carefully as he explained how much liquid she was to take and how often. Charles moved toward the fire, but she could tell from his silence that he also was noting the doctor's instructions.

"Gracias," she said when the physician had finished. But she spoke to her husband as much as to the doctor that Alma Kinkaid had sent to her.

Palo Flechado Pass, Summer 1868

Gregoria crouched in her garden, weeding the lettuce. It had rained hard the night before and the weeds came out easily, making the task more pleasure than chore. As she worked, she marveled at the way the plants grew even in this rocky soil. There seemed no end to the rocks, yet still the plants grew. She smiled at the tender greens. "Tan bonita," she murmured. "So pretty."

She stood, stretched, took a moment to watch two eagles playing overhead, then moved to the pea plants. She'd propped dead aspen branches on end and leaned them against each other to create rough supports for the vines. The green leaves glowed in the sun. Gregoria squatted down and carefully pulled weeds away from the base of the sticks. She felt badly for the weeds. After all, they had found a welcoming place to grow and now she was destroying them. "Lo siento," she said softly.

She bit her lip, thinking of the man buried in the shed, the ashes of the dead Navajo at the edge of the hollow above her head. She took a deep breath. It is the way of things, she told herself firmly. Some die, others live. And Charles loves me. That is why he is so jealous. She winced, thinking of Alan Lamb and the boy named Jim Bob. Only the quick thinking of the boy's father had saved him.

Charles also worries about money and is glad for it, no matter its source, she told herself. Even if it comes from a man who has been killed by Indians. She frowned. She was confused about what had happened to the merchant Edwards, though she could think of no reason for Charles to lie to her. Certainly, he hadn't attempted to shield her from her guilt in causing the other deaths. She shuddered and closed her eyes. But she had been inside the cabin when it happened and Indians could be remarkably silent. After all, the man with the ivory pistol had spoken few words.

She gulped back the bile that suddenly filled her mouth. The Indian's fight with Charles had been completely soundless. That was part of what had made it so horrible. Gregoria shook her head. His death was an accident, she reminded herself.

She bit her lip and went back to her weeding. There was nothing she could do about any of it, anyway. Except resolve to be as invisible as possible. And to remember that Charles loved her.

Gregoria smiled. She had much to be thankful for. Her fingers grazed her belly, feeling the slight mound where the child grew. She placed her palm on the earth, to steady herself, and gazed upward into the newly green aspens, the light bright on the ponderosas' long needles, letting herself be pulled into the greenness and movement as the breeze fingered the branches. The trees were so beautiful, so all-encompassing. It was if they were trying to tell her something. She felt herself pulled in, unaware of anything but the trees and the wind moving through them.

Then Charles bellowed "Rosa!" from the cabin doorway and Gregoria woke from her trance. She turned her head. Two men stood in front of the house, looking at her with curiosity while Charles scowled from the open door.

She shook her head sharply, bringing herself back to the present, stood up, and moved toward the cabin.

~ ~ ~

Gregoria grasped the shovel handle firmly and punched downward, cutting into the soil and roots. Once again the grasses were encroaching from the tree line onto her knee-high bean plants.

There had been a short but intense shower earlier in the day, so she'd come out in the afternoon to take advantage of the moisture softening the ground in her continuing battle with the grass line.

She worked her way along the edge of the garden bed, cutting as straight a line as she could with the curved shovel blade. She was concentrating so hard that she didn't see the small man on the big bay until he was beside the corral.

"Whoa, now!" the man said to his mount. Gregoria's head jerked up as the cabin door opened and the man's head turned toward it.

Charles came out. The two men spoke briefly and then the man dismounted. Charles looked toward the garden. "Rosa!" he bellowed. "Biscuits!"

Gregoria dropped the shovel and obediently headed inside.

While the biscuits baked in the cast iron dutch oven, she fried the last of the venison steak. By the time the food was ready, Charles and the stranger, who said his name was Evans, had shared a good portion of a whisky jug. It had no apparent affect on Charles, but Evans' tongue was loose and he seemed very relaxed. When they sat down on opposite sides of the table, he ate greedily. Both men had their knives out, cutting into the meat.

"I tell you, it's been a long while since I ate a raised biscuit like this one," Evans said to Charles. "This little wife of yours knows how to cook." He winked at Gregoria. "She's a looker, too."

Gregoria looked at Charles, who had his eyes on his plate. "Más carne, mi esposo?" she asked. More meat, my husband?

He shook his head and kept eating, eyes on his food.

"Yes sir, you got yourself a nice set-up here." Evans looked around and nodded his small head. "Cozy. And good food to entice folks in with." He grinned at Charles' bent head and winked at Gregoria. "A pretty face helps too. We don't see many of those

139

once we're out of Taos. Not in Elizabeth City." He raised an eyebrow at Gregoria. "Do you ever get into Etown yourself, ma'am?"

Gregoria shook her head wordlessly and glanced at Charles, whose head had come up, his eyes narrowed.

"Don' need town," Charles growled.

In the fireplace, a log fell onto the hearth in a shower of sparks and Gregoria moved hurriedly to adjust it. As she maneuvered the wood back into position, she heard Evans say something else. A bench thudded to the floor.

Charles growled "'Nough!" as Gregoria turned, the poker still in her hand. She saw Charles strike out with his eating knife, slicing into the man's arm, then his throat. She stared in disbelief as blood spurted onto Charles' chest, the table, and the floor. Charles half-rose, moving around the end of the table, stabbing again and again, until the other man stopped jerking. Then he straightened, tossed the knife onto the floor, and glared at Gregoria. "What you done," he growled at her. He pushed at the blood on the floor with the toe of his boot. "Shovel!" he barked.

Gregoria gasped for breath as she went blindly into the gathering dusk. She found the shovel in the garden and leaned against it, taking in long ragged breaths. She had done nothing but what Charles had told her. She had kept her eyes to herself. How was this death her fault? What could she do to keep the men from seeing her, from making remarks? She tried so hard to be invisible, but still it wasn't enough. Tears ran down her cheeks and she wanted only to indulge them, but Charles would be waiting, and angry if she delayed. Afternoon shadows stretched down the mountainside. Somewhere a catamount screamed. A long shudder went through her and Gregoria turned back to the house.

When she entered, the cabin was empty except for the firelight and a wash of blood streaking the floor across the room toward the shed. Gregoria followed it.

Charles had laid out Evans' body and was pulling off his clothes. The man seemed even smaller now, laying naked in the dirt. His pale skin glowed in the semi-dark. Charles took the shovel from Gregoria but, instead of cutting into the dirt floor to dig a grave, he began stabbing at the man's shoulders and hips, chopping into his flesh, splintering the bone beneath. Then he grunted in disgust, turned, and headed out the shed's outer door. Gregoria stared at the body in wordless shock, her stomach roiling.

Charles returned a few minutes later with the ax and went back to work, forcing the blade down with all his weight. The limbs broke free quickly and he went after the head, hacking at the man's neck bones and smashing the skull with the side of the axe head. When he was done, the man Evans lay in scattered pieces, blood darkening the ground. Charles tossed the shovel in Gregoria's direction. "Bury 'em," he said. He moved toward the outer door.

She went to the back of the shed and began digging into the floor.

Charles turned his head. "Not here!" he said sharply. Then he chuckled sardonically. "Garden," he ordered. "Ground's soft." He chuckled again and then he was gone, to untie the bay and lead it into the corral. A few minutes later, Gregoria heard a gunshot, then a thud as the horse hit the ground.

Numbly, Gregoria turned to her task, averting her eyes as she passed the corral to the garden. She heard Charles chuckle again in the soft darkness and the sound of knife on flesh, the hiss of entrails spilling onto the hard-packed earth of the corral.

141

She hacked fiercely at the grass between the garden and the edge of the hollow, digging sharply into the ground with the bloody shovel, cutting half a dozen holes, taking the cleared space closer to the trees. She let her tears fall freely, though soundlessly, into the darkness. The tears helped to ease the pressure in her stomach, just as the dirt helped to wipe the shovel clean. But my memory and heart will never be clean, she thought bitterly. They will be as stained as the floor of the shed, although less able to absorb the dark marks.

I am as guilty as Charles in this, she reproached herself. I want to believe I am not, but deep down, I know it is so. I did not turn away from the stranger quickly enough. And I stood in silence as Charles cut into him, severing his body into pieces. Now here I am, burying those pieces, while Charles butchers the man's horse. But what choice do I have? I am his legal wife. I cannot simply leave. And he would surely come after me.

Her mind flickered to her father. He had stood up to another man, for once, when he had insisted that she be legally bound to Charles so she couldn't be easily discarded by him. Gregoria's stomached tightened in despair. Her father had made sure she couldn't simply return home. Clearly, he didn't want her. Even if he did, he could barely feed himself, let alone another person. And a child. A deep shudder ran through her. She had no place to go.

Gregoria shook her head and wiped the tears away with the back of her hand. This was her life. There was no use thinking of escaping it. After all, she was tainted. She always had been. Why else would her father's friend have done what he did to her? What was happening to her was all she could expect of life. All she deserved.

She tamped the dirt on the last of the holes gently with the tip of her foot, careful not to press too hard, and her mind turned to

Charles' activity in the corral. She would be required to cook the horse flesh tomorrow. And to eat it. And after he'd eaten this easy prey, Charles would be filled with lust yet again. Even if they had guests, he would take her to himself.

Gregoria stifled the wave of horror and helplessness that swept over her and wearily headed back to the cabin.

~ ~ ~

The bottles shaped like amber log cabins had been a big hit, even when Charles refilled them with his own version of Taos Lightning, well diluted with water from the stream, and charged twice as much as for drinks from the whisky jug. When guests arrived, he always offered the contents of the Booz bottles first.

"Special order," he'd say, raising the glass cabins by their chimney sections. "Cost more."

Except for the day in early July when an old woman stopped in. Of uncertain origin, dressed in a Mexican-style skirt, heavily-scarred men's boots, and an old Confederate overcoat, she wore a battered Union cavalry hat well down on her graying and greasy head.

Charles and Gregoria were both in the cabin, Gregoria setting another batch of biscuits after the noon meal. She'd served six men besides Charles and there were likely to be more this evening. The long summer days made for more traffic on the road to Etown and Maxwell's place. Travelers to Mora also seemed to be taking the longer route through Palo Flechado Pass these days. "Liquor an' raised biscuits," one of the noon crowd had explained to Charles with a wink.

But now those guests were gone and the old woman in the worn-out hat clutched at the frame of the open door. "Well?" she barked. "I hear ya got somethin' t' sell!"

"Food, drink, an' lodging," Charles answered.

"I wanna drink!" Her eyes wavered, then focused intently on Charles, whose face darkened.

"Got money?" he demanded.

"I wouldn't be askin' if I didden! I wan' whisky!"

"Don' serve women."

Gregoria looked up from her baking, surprised that he'd turn a paying customer away. But then, it was true that he'd never served alcohol to one of their rare women guests, she reflected. Though they'd never asked for it, either.

"I said I got money!"

He moved to shut the door, but she pushed her way past him into the room.

"I wanna drink!"

"Don' serve women," he growled.

"You'll serve me, or be sorry!" The old woman shoved the battered hat back from her grimy face.

Charles chuckled menacingly and grabbed her arm. "Drunk." He yanked her toward the door, but she pulled her arm back with surprising strength.

"You got a license?" Her voice was clearer now, less slurred.

"What fer?"

"Sellin', ya fool! Ya got a license t' sell?"

He scowled. "Not to you."

"Not t' anyone, I'll warrant!" She stalked out the door, then turned to face him, hands on her hips. "I'll sen' ya a warrant!" she cackled. She paused, dropped her hands, and edged back toward the door. "'Less you wanna gimme me a drink."

144

"Go t' hell," he growled, slamming the door in her face.

Inside the cabin, Gregoria looked up apprehensively.

"Don' serve women," he said sullenly, sitting down on a stool in front of the fire. "Ma drank. We starved." He scowled at the flames and Gregoria went slowly back to her work, processing what he had said. Poverty, alcohol, a mamá who thought only of herself. It was no wonder that he was so anxious about money, so quick to drink, so abrupt with herself, so angry. An unexpected wave of pity swept over her.

MORA, FALL, 1868

New Mexico Territory's Attorney General Merrill Ashurst looked at the ragged old woman with distaste. If you could call the person before him a "she." Indeterminate sex, indeterminate age, indeterminate race. Disgusting.

He glanced up at Vincent St. Vrain, a tall, fair-haired young man who, as the Mora Fall Court Session's grand jury foreman, was keeping his face carefully neutral. In the corner, County Sheriff Romero was examining his hat, which he'd taken off when the woman came in the room. Ashurst sighed. He hated this part of his job, this taking of affidavits from people who thought the court system was established only to alleviate their petty concerns.

"So where does this man live?" he asked.

"Palo Flechado Pass, on th' way t' 'lizabeth City." The old woman jabbed a grimy finger at the brim of her battered Union cavalry hat, pushing it back so she could stare challengingly into his eyes.

"And he offered you liquor for sale?"

"Yessir," she said firmly. She leaned toward him and he forced himself not to pull back from the whisky-and-old-urine reek of her.

"And what is this man's name?"

"Canady," she said firmly.

"I think she means Kennedy," St. Vrain said. "Charles Kennedy has a hostel at the bottom of the pass. He offers food and a place to sleep for travelers heading to Etown or Maxwell's Ranch. People have been taking that route to get here instead of Apache

146

Pass, so they can stop for Mrs. Kennedy's raised biscuits. I hear they're quite tasty."

"I tol' 'im he needs a license t' sell!" the old woman said. She leaned toward Ashurst again. "He offered me a drink. Me a woman an' all." She sniffed and straightened. "Nasty brute of a man."

"We aren't here to evaluate the man's moral character," the Attorney General said mildly. He glanced at the Sheriff. "Have you investigated? Do you know if the man has a business license?"

Sheriff Romero shrugged. He was a solidly built man with a perpetually patient look on his brown face. "Ours is a large county, señor. And the land, it is Señor Maxwell's. It is for him to decide."

"There's some doubt about that," St. Vrain said mildly. "My father says Maxwell's boundaries don't cross the valley."

"He's breakin' the law!" the old woman screeched. "Don't matter whose land he's squattin' on! He's breakin' the law!"

Ashurst handed the affidavit to St. Vrain. "If you'll be so kind as to take this to the grand jury, you all can decide whether there's probable cause. Then we can get on to the other cases before us this session." He turned to the Sheriff. "If you could escort this lady to the courtroom for that consultation, I would appreciate it."

A smile flashed across the Sheriff's face and he moved politely toward the old woman and reached for her elbow. "Señora," he murmured.

"What's that ya say?" she screeched. But she went with him willingly enough.

~ ~ ~

Old Judge John S. Watts looked at the form before him and shook his head. "You're going to arrest a man for selling a gill of whisky?" He looked up at Vincent St. Vrain, who stood on the other side of the table holding the remainder of the grand jury paperwork. The Judge wiped his face with his handkerchief. A faint breeze blew through the second story adobe courthouse's windows, but the late August heat was still stifling.

"Kennedy's selling without a license and Santa Fe needs revenue." St. Vrain shrugged. "The grand jury found cause to indict."

"It's ridiculous," the Judge grumbled, but he scratched his signature on the paperwork and handed it to the jury foreman.

St. Vrain chuckled. Sheriff Romero came into the room and the younger man handed him the warrant.

"I hope you don't plan on wasting your time with that yourself," the Judge said.

"No sir," the Sheriff said. "I have a deputy for this kind of thing." He folded the paper, put it into his pocket, and smiled at the other two men. "Me, I have more important things to do and more important matters to discuss."

"Such as the boundary lines between Mora and the soon-to-be Colfax County?" Judge Watts chuckled. "Isn't that what they're naming it? Colfax? Or is that contingent on Schuyler Colfax actually becoming the next Vice-President?"

The Sheriff smiled noncommittally and the Judge grinned. "I'll meet you downstairs in about twenty minutes." He turned to St. Vrain, who handed him another set of forms. "How is your father these days?" he asked as he picked up his pen.

"He's doing as well as can be expected." St. Vrain took what the Judge had signed and handed him another set of forms. "He keeps himself busy with the flour mill and his Masonic work."

Judge Watts nodded and signed the last form with a flourish. "Please give him my respects," he said.

The two men shook hands and the old Judge headed downstairs to confer with the Sheriff about the proposed legislation that would split Mora into two counties. The details needed to be worked out before the upcoming Territorial Legislative session. The boundaries, the elections that followed, the choice of a county seat, the support of men like St. Vrain's father, with power to wield. Now those were things worthy of a man's time. But an arrest warrant for selling four ounces of liquor without a license? That was a waste.

~ ~ ~

It was a crisp early fall morning in the Mora Valley and Deputy Frederico Benitez's only duty that day was to ride north through the Sangre de Cristo mountains to deliver Charles Kennedy's arrest warrant, but he was an unhappy man as his horse ambled along the dirt track that ran between the fields of golden wheat. The weather would become uncertain the farther north he travelled. More importantly, he'd heard stories of Kennedy and his temper.

But Deputy Benitez rode on, because Sheriff Romero had told him to, and because the Sheriff paid his salary on time each month with a kind word to Benitez' wife and mother. They were, after all, related somehow, although the tangles of marriage and cousinship that his mother loved so much remained a mystery to Frederico.

He rode steadily north, the aspen leaves changing from the bright greens along the Mora River to iridescent yellow and then darker gold as his mount moved upward. He stopped only twice, once to relieve his bladder, then again to stretch his cramped legs. It was late afternoon when he reached the Moreno Valley.

Frederico looked longingly toward its northern end, where Eliza-bethtown lay hidden some twelve miles away, then dutifully swung west to the base of Palo Flechado Pass.

When he came to the edge of the Kennedy hollow, Frederico reined in and stared down at the roughly-built cabin and its ram-shackle corral. There were no animals in the enclosure. No light glimmered from the cloth-covered windows against the gathering shadows and no smoke rose from the chimney.

The Deputy frowned. Had Kennedy heard about the indictment and taken off? Benitez walked his horse across the hollow and swung off next to the wood pile. He listened for a moment, think-ing he heard movement inside. He rapped on the rough wooden door and put his head closer, listening. A squirrel chattered over-head and he looked up at it and scowled. "Kennedy?" he called. He rapped on the battered boards again, harder this time. "Señor?"

This time he definitely heard movement. But then silence fell again. Frederico stood for a long moment, uncertain what to do, then turned away. It was a small thing, this selling without a li-cense. Certainly insufficient to justify rushing into a man's home uninvited. He frowned, then turned back to face the door and raised his voice. "Señor! You have sold liquor without a license! This is illegal! The court in Mora has issued a warrant against you!"

The only response was the squirrel overhead again. Benitez frowned, then shrugged and went to his horse. He took a pencil from one shirt pocket and the arrest warrant from the other. On the outside of the warrant paper he wrote, Sertifico que el deman dado Charles Kennedy no asido encontrado en el Condado hoy dia 29 de Agosto de 1868. I certify that the defendant, Charles Kennedy, was not found in the County this day August 29, 1868. Then he signed it.

He shoved the paper back into his pocket and swung onto his horse. When he reached the road, he reined in and looked back. The house was dark and shut up. Yet he was sure there was someone inside.

The Deputy shrugged. He'd done his duty and Kennedy—or his wife—was informed. He looked up at the sky, considering his options. He was in time to reach Etown tonight. I will eat and sleep at Lambert's Hotel, he decided. The County will defray my costs and I'll be able to describe the hotel's interior to my mother and wife. He lifted his shoulders slightly and grinned. Well, at least he'd get something out of this trip.

~ ~ ~

Charles stalked into the hollow from the roadway, a yearling deer draped over his shoulders. Gregoria was outside, chopping wood.

He dropped the carcass at her feet. "Dinner," he said. He jerked his head toward the road. "Guests comin'." He leered at her and jerked his head toward the door. "Time for pergates."

"But the meal—" she protested.

He scowled at her. "I tol' you, stay inside!" he said. Then he grinned malevolently. "Want it here?"

"Lo siento," she said. She glanced toward the road, laid the axe against the chopping block, and moved toward the door.

He chuckled and followed her into the cabin. Gregoria maneuvered around him to shut the door, but he grabbed her and began groping her breasts. "Un momento," she gasped. She grappled with the latch as he pulled at her skirts. The wooden peg fell into place, then Charles was edging her toward the table. The hard

151

edge of its top cut into her thighs, but she spread her legs obediently.

As he moved against her, Gregoria thought about the meal for the approaching travelers. Perhaps they won't stop, she thought hopefully. Perhaps, like the stranger on the horse outside the cabin this afternoon, they will call out a lengthy greeting and go on. I will speak of the greeting to Charles after the travelers are gone, she promised herself. The man had sounded anxious and irritated. She hadn't fully understood what he'd said, but she didn't think it was a good message that she must deliver. She bit her lip and braced herself, waiting for Charles to finish.

~ ~ ~

Gregoria knelt in the shed beside the old blanket and began to pile the bones from the young deer into its center. It had been a small beast. The bones would not be difficult to carry up the hill into the forest. She paused, looking at its remains, and silently thanked it for providing them and their guests with sustenance. There were still a few scraps clinging to the bones. The small forest animals who found them would consider it a feast.

A sudden shadow blocked the light. Charles loomed in the outer doorway. "Whatcha doin'?" he demanded.

"Gathering the bones to take them onto the mountainside," she answered.

He shook his head. "Garden."

Confused, she frowned at him.

He jerked his head toward the hollow. "Garden!" he repeated.

"But they will attract small creatures," she protested.

"Garden," he growled. Then he grinned. "Fertilizer."

She opened her mouth, then saw his face. It had turned cold and hard. "Sí, mi esposo," she said meekly.

At least they are not human bones, she told herself as she dragged the blanket through the outer door. I will not bury them at the northern edge with the pieces of the man Evans. I am sure that is what mi esposo intends, but I will not.

Charles had paid no attention to the precise location of Evans' remains, so she was safe from his anger about this small act of defiance. She would dig between the rows of beans, as deeply as the rocky soil would allow, as far from the man's bones as she could. Where the bones and blood of the small deer would provide nourishment to her plants, instead of poison. She dropped her bundle at the end of a row, then turned back to the shed for the shovel.

~ ~ ~

Gregoria moved her basket to one side, straightened from the row of beans, and rubbed her back. It was becoming more difficult to bend over now, with the little one within her growing as it was. She patted her belly and smiled. Outside the cabin door, Charles was cutting logs into fire-size pieces, his shirt sleeves rolled up to reveal his massive arms.

It was good, this working together. Usually Charles had a guest break down the firewood for her, in exchange for a meal. But they'd had no guests recently and the pile needed to be increased before the cold weather came. Gregoria eased down into a crouching position and began carefully examining the bean plants to ensure that she'd harvested all of their fruit.

Her back was to the roadway, so she was startled when a man's voice bellowed "Hey you!" from the roadway. She looked up, then saw that he was addressing Charles, who still had the saw in his hand.

Three men on horseback rode into the hollow. They all had the look of men who stayed primarily indoors—pale skin and thick coats, though the air was warm in the sun. They were all about the same age and stayed on their horses as they spoke with Charles. Gregoria was too far away to hear what they said, but there was a tension in their bodies that made her glad they hadn't dismounted. Suddenly, they all turned at once, horse hooves spurting up dust in the dooryard, and trotted back to the road, heading toward Taos.

Charles stood watching them, his face impassive.

Gregoria hoisted herself awkwardly to her feet, lifted her basket, and carried it toward the house. As she passed him, Charles said, "Askin' fer that quack doctor."

Gregoria paused in the doorway. "The physician? They search for him?"

Charles shrugged and reached for another log. "Headin' t' Santa Fe. Didn' get there." He braced the wood against the chopping block and positioned the saw blade halfway down its length. "Wanted t' know, did we see him."

Gregoria frowned anxiously and went into the cabin. She sat beside the table and began cleaning the beans. He had been kind to her, the Doctor Applegate that Alma Kinkaid had sent to her. The tonic he'd provided was used up now and the child within her still moved. Charles had seemed to regret the medicine's purchase. He'd snorted whenever she took it, until she'd begun measuring out her dosage only when he was absent. Still, she thought it had helped.

Her thoughts moved toward the garden and the shallow grave in the shed, but she pushed them firmly away. The good Doctor Applegate was not there. Perhaps he had decided not to return to Etown or his letter to his friends there had been mislaid. She hoped he was well, that he had not fallen into the hands of— But again, she moved her thoughts firmly away from the dead and those who dispatched them to their graves.

~ ~ ~

"I seen it all," the little man said, stretching his legs in front of the fire. "Got me a few experiences, I can tell ya that!"

Charles grunted. He carried a Booz bottle to the fire and lifted it invitingly toward his guest.

"Naw, I'll take it straight from the jug, if'n you don' mind," the man said. "When I was huntin' Navajos with Kit, that's the way we drank it. When we could get it, o' course. Whisky was in short supply on that campaign. I hafta say, I kinda developed a taste fer it." Gregoria came forward with the jug and Charles took it from her and handed it to the man, who took it eagerly. He took one swig, then another. "This is almighty good liquor you got here."

Charles grunted sardonically.

The other man looked around the room. "Nice set-up," he said. "Whisky, travelers needin' food, a pretty wife to cook it fer you an' keep you warm at night, too." He turned and winked at Gregoria, who ignored him. "When I was huntin' Injuns with Kit, we got real hungry for civilized life." He swung back to Charles. "You in the Army?"

"Long enough." He sat down on the other stool and looked into the flames.

"Yeah, you got t' have the stomach fer Army life. Got t' have gumption. Ridin' trail ain't fer just anyone, I kin tell you that!"

Gregoria came forward and touched Charles on the shoulder. "The meal, it is prepared, mi esposo," she said softly.

"An' a pretty wife, in the bargain!" the man said. He grinned at Gregoria lasciviously.

155

She glanced at him and turned quickly away, but Charles had seen. As he rose from the stool, he gave her a sharp shove, and Gregoria almost lost her balance. She put a hand out, bracing herself against the fireplace. The man appeared not to notice.

"The meal, it is prepared," Gregoria repeated, as if nothing had happened. She glanced up at Charles questioningly. "If you are ready?"

He grunted and turned away, gesturing the smaller man toward the table. "Eat!" he said. "Eat up!"

"Raised biscuits!" the little man said as the men seated themselves. "Now that's a treat I ain't seen fer a while! Sure wish I could get my woman t' make biscuits!" He reached for the plate and helped himself to three, dropping them onto his plate. "And hot! Wowee! You got yourself some woman here!" He nodded approvingly at Charles. "A looker and a cooker and a breeder, too! What more coulda man want!"

Charles scowled. "You stayin' the night?" he asked. "We got bedding."

The other man shook his head and reached for another biscuit. "I can make it down the trail with this t' keep me goin'," he said. "Wanna get back to Etown before dark."

"Dark comes early."

"When I was with Carson, we rode in the dark all the time, gettin' the drop on them Injuns," the man said. "I developed real cats' eyes. There's nothin' I fear."

Charles fell silent. When the meal was finished, he spoke only to specify how much was owed for the whisky and food. The man paid in gold dust, tapping his small bag confidently. "More where that come from." He winked at Gregoria. "Even a laborer, so called, can rake in the gold if'n he knows what he's about. All it takes is energy and brains."

156

She gave him a fleeting smile, relieved he was going. Charles' sullenness worried her.

When he thudded the door shut behind their visitor, she knew she had reason to be worried, but she tried to act as if nothing was wrong. Sometimes that distracted him from his anger. She went to the table and began gathering the empty dishes.

But it didn't work. Suddenly, he was beside her, pulling her arm away from the dishes, twisting it sharply downward. "Child in your belly, still makin' eyes."

"No! I—"

"Yes!" He slapped her then, hard, the force of his hand sending her to the floor.

"Lo siento—"

But he wasn't listening. His boot bit into her side and instinctively she rolled away, wrapping her arms around her belly. "Por favor," she whimpered. "El infante."

"Hell! Ain't mine!" he growled. He kicked her again, then reached down, yanked her left arm away, and slugged her stomach. "Ain't mine!" he said again. "Doctor's, all I know!"

"Por favor, mi esposo," she gasped. "Lo siento mucho."

He punched her again, then straightened. "Bitch," he growled. "Keep yer eyes to yerself." He turned, picked up his rifle, and stalked out.

Gregoria sat on the floor, clutching her stomach and gasping from the pain. Never before had he beaten her like this. He must love me very much, she told herself. To be this jealous, this angry about a single look. I must learn to be more careful, she told herself once again.

~ ~ ~

She woke to darkness and sharp pains in her belly. Charles had not returned.

The pains were intense, grabbing her again and again, forcing her fully awake. She pushed back her disheveled black hair and sat up, but the pain cut through her again, pushing her against the bedding. "Ay!" she gasped.

These were clearly childbirth pains and there was no time to send for Alma Kinkaid, even if there'd been someone to send. Gregoria arched backward as another contraction ripped through her. She would have to do it herself. She closed her eyes, fighting her tears.

It is too soon, she thought bleakly. The baby shouldn't come for another cinco semanas, five weeks. Another spasm hit and she bit her lip to keep from crying out. She would need hot water, but both buckets were empty.

She eased off the bed, trying to move carefully so as not to trigger the pains. It took a long time to pull on her clothes. They weren't fastened properly, but it was dark outside and there was no one to see. Not even Charles. She bit her lip, then shook her head at herself. Thinking of that would not be helpful. She paused for a long moment, taking quick shallow breaths to keep the pain from coming again, then edged toward the bucket in the kitchen area.

Halfway across the room, she stopped, bending into the pain as it spasmed through her again, gritting her teeth to keep from crying out. Somehow she managed to reach the bucket, bend to grasp it, then straighten before the next spasm hit. She waited it out, then crept toward the door.

The cool air helped a little. She worked her way slowly across the hollow in the dark, pausing between contractions, fighting the urge to cry out. Just as she reached the stream, a jab of pain jerked her upward and the bucket dropped into the pool. Water splashed up, soaking her skirt.

She bit back the tears and knelt beside the stream, waiting for the bucket to fill, catching her breath. When the water had reached the half-way point, she slowly stood, lifted the bucket awkwardly, and began the journey back to the cabin. Halfway across the hollow, she was grabbed by a pain that felt as if it would split her in two. The bucket fell and Gregoria dropped beside it. "Ay!" she gasped.

Then Charles was there, swearing violently as he lifted her, carrying her into the cabin. As he laid her on the bed, the pain hit again, arching her back. She screamed in spite of herself. "Ya viene! Ya viene!" It comes, it comes!

"What's to do?" he demanded. She shook her head. There was a roaring in her ears and the pain was unbearable.

"What's to do?" he bellowed.

She closed her eyes. He seemed so far away. She could barely breath. Oh, just let it be over. She could feel him slipping away.

Suddenly he slapped her, hard, on the face. "Wake up!" he yelled.

She opened her eyes. His face was inches from hers, his breath hot and foul on her face, his blue eyes mere slits of anger.

"Stay awake!" he barked. He gestured toward her legs. "What's to do?"

She took a deep breath, her face stinging. He was only trying to help. "Pillows," she gasped. "Behind me."

He nodded. In two steps, he was through the entry to the shed and in a moment he'd returned with a bulging pack. He yanked her arm, pulling her up and shoving the pack behind her shoulders so she was half sitting, her knees bent upward. The pack was hard and lumpy, but it gave her the support she needed. Gregoria

159

clutched at the scratchy wool blanket beneath her and panted through the next spasm.

Charles watched her, his eyes narrow. "Christ," he said. "Why women want babies."

She shook her head, trying to tell him the child was too early, but the pain wrenched through her again. Wildly, she tried to sit up, even though she knew that she shouldn't. "Oh, Charles!" she screamed. "Ohhhhhhh!" There was another roar of pain and a fierce need to push, then she fainted.

~ ~ ~

Gregoria woke to a wave of sadness washing over her. A tiny bundle lay beside her, wrapped roughly in her faded red chal. She opened it with weak hands. "Está muerto," she said sadly.

Charles didn't answer. He was sitting on one of the fireplace stools with his face averted. The fire was out.

Gregoria shivered. "Mi esposo," she whispered. "Lo siento."

Charles rose and came toward her, his face hidden in the darkness.

"La culpa es mía," Gregoria whispered tearfully as he loomed above the bed. The blame is mine. She reached to touch the tiny body again. "El nene." She sighed. A baby boy. If only she had spoken to Charles differently, had not angered him.

"A boy," Charles agreed dully. He turned away.

She covered the child again and turned her face to the wall so he couldn't see her tears.

"No priest t' bury it," he said roughly.

"There is no need," she said. "It never lived." She closed her eyes. "It has gone directly to heaven."

Charles grunted without looking at her. "You an' yer flirting," he growled. "Yer fault. Said so yerself." He went to the cabin door. The sun was just coming up in an overcast sky. Charles went out, leaving the door open behind him.

The chill in the room intensified, but Gregoria didn't notice. She lifted the tiny body out of the chal, held it tenderly for a long moment, then carefully rewrapped it. She stared into the empty room, letting her tears flow unchecked, although silent.

She shook her head. Charles was right. Everything she did turned out badly. And yet he loved her. He had brought her with him, hadn't he? He kept her with him, guarding her like a treasure, fiercely jealous of other men's glances, reluctant to leave the hollow for fear of her being endangered. And he was all that she had, all that protected her from life on the streets, becoming one of the traídas y llevadas. She closed her eyes, letting herself feel her unworthiness.

After a long while, she struggled into a sitting position and looked around. The door was still open, the fire still out, the room in chaos, and there was no food prepared for Charles' return or if guests should arrive for a mid-day meal. She could at least try to make things clean and cheerful for him when he came back, like a dutiful esposa. Then perhaps he would be a little less angry with her. She sighed and turned to the tiny body on the bed. But first she must cleanse herself and there must be a burial. Not in the hollow. Perhaps beside the stream.

Gregoria took a long shuddering breath, moved the chal and its contents to one side, and lifted herself from the bed.

~ ~ ~

"I heard tell they arrested you," the miner with the battered hat said. He put his coin on the table and took the wooden noggin of whisky from Charles' hand.

161

Charles grunted. "Still here."

"What they want you for?"

Charles lifted the Booz bottle slightly and put it back on the table.

"Sellin' whiskey?"

"No license."

"Ah, the Governor wants his piece of your pie, is that it?"

Charles grunted again and put the cap back on the bottle.

The miner went to the fire and sat down. He took off his hat and set it on the floor beside him. "They always seem to be coming up with something to take our money. What's it my Daddy used to say? Only thing sure is death and taxes."

"Ain't payin'." Charles sat down on the stool at the other end of the fire.

"Still don't have a license?" The miner raised an eyebrow. "Ain't you looking for trouble, now that they have you in their sights?"

"I'll give 'em trouble." Charles leaned forward, reached into the fire, and pulled out a burning six-inch thick log. He whacked it against the edge of the fireplace, breaking the burning end into the fire, and swung the broken piece toward the miner, who gulped his whisky nervously and nodded.

"They want trouble, they'll get it," Charles said.

"Speaking of trouble—" the miner said. His voice trailed off, then he seemed to regain his courage. "I was in Letcher's store in Vegas last week. He asked me to give you a message." He paused and eyed Charles uncertainly.

Charles grunted. "Wants money."

The miner looked relieved. "That's right. He said he would send someone to fetch what you owe, if you'll just let him know when."

162

Charles grunted again. He lifted the piece of wood in his hand and examined its broken end carefully.

"He just asked me to tell you," the miner said apologetically. "Since I was coming this way." He set his empty noggin on the floor and stood up. "I'll be heading out now, I guess. Thanks for the drink."

Charles didn't answer. He only fingered the broken log absently as the man slipped out into the night.

PALO FLECHADO PASS, WINTER 1868

Two months had passed since her dead baby had been born. Gregoria was overcome with a deep sadness that only movement out of doors seemed to alleviate, even in the winter cold. The afternoon the mules strayed across the icy road and into the southern part of the valley in search of grass, she was glad of the chance to go after them. The cold air bit into her lungs and cleared the smell of fire and food from her skin and clothes. She was almost sorry when she found the animals and they turned obediently homeward.

As she came within sight of the cabin, she saw that two horses had been turned into the corral beside the house. With the return of winter, there'd been no visitors in two weeks, so there wasn't much food prepared. Gregoria hastened her steps.

As she entered the house, a sandy-haired young man turned from the fire, a noggin of whisky in his hand. "Ah, the preparer of provisions!" he said gaily, lifting the noggin to salute her.

Charles had been stretched out on the bed. He rose and came toward her. Gregoria looked up at him. "A meal?" she asked.

He nodded sullenly and went out. When he returned, he carried an armload of firewood. "An' a good host!" the young man said cheerfully.

Charles grunted irritably and returned to the bed. Gregoria began adding cornmeal to the stew, to thicken it.

"I hear tell you're famous for raised biscuits!" the young man said to her. In the corner, Charles growled disdainfully. Gregoria didn't answer either of them, but began carefully stirring the pot. There would be no time for biscuits. Perhaps the herbs she had dried in the summer would flavor the meat and meal sufficiently. She glanced toward the shadowed corner containing the bed. Charles appeared to be sleeping. She moved to the table without speaking or looking at the cheerful young man. He seemed to have finally grasped the situation, because he fell silent, gazing into the fire, moving occasionally to toss in a piece of wood or adjust the fuel with the thick stick propped beside the hearth for that purpose.

When the meal was ready, Gregoria went to the bed and touched Charles gingerly on the shoulder. "Not sleepin'!" he said sharply as he jerked awake.

They ate without incident, the visitor speaking from time to time, Charles grunting in response. Still, Gregoria's anxiety increased as darkness fell and it became evident that the stranger would be staying the night. She crept into bed and waited hopefully, but Charles' nap had refreshed him and he was a long time nursing his drink before the fire. Finally, he rose from the heavy wooden stool and the young man rolled into a blanket in front of the low-burning flames.

Charles lay down beside Gregoria and groped for her breast. She moved under him obediently. When he was done, they slept. In fact, Gregoria slept so soundly that she woke to full daylight and an empty cabin. She sat up, hope rising in her. Perhaps the young man had left early. Perhaps Charles had not been as angry as she thought. She went to the door and looked out. Two sets of footprints led toward the corral, then stopped in a smudged area. Then a single set of prints led around the house toward the shed. She bit her lip and followed.

Small rocks rattled on the rocky hillside above and she looked up cautiously. She would need to go back inside quickly if it was the young man and not Charles. But it was her husband, his face grim, carrying a large leather wallet.

"Catamount got yer friend," he said. "Couldn' save him."

He went into the cabin, came back out with a loaded pistol, and moved toward the corral. Gregoria stood for a long while staring up at the hillside, trying to block the pistol shots coming from the corral. Then, when she was sure Charles had stopped firing, she moved obediently toward the enclosure.

By that afternoon they had butchered the two horses and Gregoria had listlessly buried their bones in the garden, between the snow-covered rows of pole bean supports. The weariness had descended on her again. She should be thankful for the meat, she supposed. But Charles had killed the sandy-hair young man for the sake of his jealousy. She only felt tired with hopelessness.

There were few visitors after that and more snow arrived to cover the bare spot where the horse bones were buried. They are only animal bones, Gregoria told herself. It is part of the natural cycle of things. They will dissolve into the soil and create new life come spring. As my own body will create life, if Charles' interest in it continues. I have no choice. She waited passively for what was to come—whatever it was—to weary to truly care.

The winter was very windy and cold, and the snow drifted high in the pass. In places, the road was swept clear by the wind, but the cold and the uncertain terrain kept travelers to a minimum. When they did reach the base of the pass, most often they hurried on, bypassing the cabin tucked into the hollow. To Gregoria's relief, even when Charles stood at the door and gestured a welcome to them, they wrapped their clothing more tightly around themselves and kept going.

~ ~ ~

There was a slight break in the intensity of the weather in early December and guests returned to the Kennedy hearth. They came in groups now, never alone, crowding around the fire, sipping Taos Lightning and—if they were feeling rich—buying diluted whisky from the amber bottles shaped like small houses.

Gregoria slipped in and out of the house like a shadow, keeping the fire going, tending to the stew bubbling in the pot, carefully lifting the coals at the other end of the fireplace into position around yet another dutch oven full of raised biscuits.

She fed the guests without looking at them or the stew, her stomach churning in response to the smell of unwashed bodies and the meat breaking apart in the pot. She felt as if she couldn't breathe, as if she had a permanent feeling of nausea.

It is the fear, she told herself. The worry that one of these unwashed men will speak kindly to me and produce in Charles another frenzy of jealousy and death.

But there had been no deaths for weeks now and as long as the guests came in groups, there was little to fear. Yet the nausea would not stop. She fought against it bitterly, telling herself it was only the memories, that it was unlikely that she was with child so soon after the birth of the child lying beside the stream.

~ ~ ~

Gregoria added more wood to the fire, then looked at the small stack of fuel on the floor nearby. She would need more soon, wood that was not wet from the snow. She crossed the room, lifted the black chal she'd found in one of the packs in the shed from the row of nails by the door, and wrapped it over her head. She frowned as she tried to lift the door latch. It was very tight. The wind must be quite strong, to push the door against it like that. But

167

she put her hip against the boards and moved the door outward slightly, enough to lift the peg from its hole. When she did, the door moved inward sharply and a weight fell into the room, against her feet. "Ay!" she exclaimed, jumping away.

Charles half-rose from the bed. "What?" he growled.

"A man," Gregoria gasped. She dropped her chal and dragged the body far enough into the room to allow her to close the door. The man lay in a fetal position, his head and shoulders wrapped in a cheap cotton blanket. Gregoria touched his face gingerly, then turned a troubled face to Charles. "He is very cold."

Charles roused at this and crossed the room. He put a finger to the man's neck. "Dead Mexican," he said. "No loss." He grabbed a shoulder and rolled the man onto his back, then pulled the worn blanket from his shoulders and began searching his clothing for pockets.

Gregoria bit her lip, rose, and went to straighten the bed. When she turned, Charles was pulling the man's pants down. She averted her eyes and moved past him to bring in the firewood she'd been after when she'd first opened the door.

She stood a long time in the falling snow, brushing away her tears before they froze, fighting the nausea that rose unbidden. The man was obviously a poor peón. He would have nothing on him. Let him die with some dignity, be buried with respect. But she, a mere woman, what could she do? Charles would not listen to her. And if she spoke, he would be angry. She shuddered, piled another piece of wood into her arms, and went inside.

The man lay naked on the dirt floor, his cheap cotton clothing and tattered blanket tossed aside. Charles had brought an axe from the shed and was severing the man's legs from his torso.

"Hurry up," Charles growled at her.

She stared at him.

"Now!" he bellowed. He picked up a leg and threw it across the room, into the fire. "More wood!" he yelled.

There is a certain logic to what he is doing, Gregoria told herself dully. Even in the shed, the ground was too frozen to bury the poor mexicano. And if they left him outside, the catamount would be sure to go after his corpse. She pushed aside her irrational sense of guilt. After all, the man had died of the cold. Yet still her stomach wrenched within her as she deposited her armload of wood and turned back toward the door.

"It is not your doing," she muttered to herself fiercely as she stood in the doorway. There was a cracking sound behind her, as Charles wielded the axe again, and she plunged through the door and vomited violently. "It is not your doing," she whispered again, into the snow and the wind.

~ ~ ~

It was as she had suspected. She was with child again. Gregoria bit her lip and looked down at the mending in her lap. Charles' sleeve had caught on a splinter projecting from the logs near the bed. He had sworn sharply when it tore, and punched the wall angrily. She wondered if she could use the firewood hatchet to nip the splinter off so it wouldn't catch on anything again.

She nudged the edge of the patch with her finger and went back to work, leaning toward the fire to see the stitches more clearly. Fortunately, this thread matched exactly. She wondered what she would do when her small supply was used up. If William Kinkaid stopped by again on the way to Taos, would she be able to ask him to bring her some? If only Alma were with him!

Gregoria's work dropped into her lap and she gazed into the fire. She would need baby things. She closed her eyes. In a pack in the shed were the clothes she'd made for the child now buried by the stream. Those things would have to do. She sighed. Perhaps the making of them had not been in vain after all. Perhaps this time she would bring forth a living child.

She bit her lip. How would she bear it if she lost another baby? She took a deep breath and began sewing again. Perhaps it would be a boy. They could name it after Charles. Would he like that? She would be so glad, if Charles would be.

The door opened and she looked up shyly. Charles shook the snow from his coat and crossed to the fire, his boots tracking snow on the tamped dirt of the floor. He held his hands out to the flames. "Not hot," he grumbled.

"Lo siento," Gregoria said. "The wood, it is cold too, I think, and has trouble catching."

He grunted and moved closer to the flames.

There was a long silence, she working on his shirt, then she said shyly, "Charles? I hope you will be happy. I am preñada." She glanced up at him timidly. "Lo siento."

"Sorry? What fer?"

She focused her eyes on her needle and thread. "I thought you might not like it."

"A boy."

"I hope so."

Charles sank onto the other fire stool and stared into the flames. "My boy," he said. "Get what I need here, he'll be rico. No one'll look down on him."

Gregoria glanced up in surprise, then swiftly down again, to her work.

ELIZABETH TOWN, EARLY 1869

"Well, I hear we got ourselves a new County," Joseph Kinsinger said to the younger Middaugh brother as he huddled over the Middaugh Grocery's woodstove.

"So I hear," William Middaugh said over his shoulder. He was on a ladder, carefully dusting the tins stacked on the upper shelves behind the counter.

"An' Etown's the County Seat," Kinsinger said.

Thomas Pollock came through the door with a blast of winter weather. "By God, it's cold out there!" he exclaimed. But he didn't head to the stove. He turned to Middaugh. "Little Josie's got croup again. Sarah said to ask you for that powder we used last time."

The clerk nodded and began working his way down the ladder while Pollock went to the stove. He nodded to Kinsinger.

"I hear we got ourselves a new County," Kinsinger said conversationally.

"Do we?" Pollock asked.

"Happened 'bout a week ago." Kinsinger leaned forward to spit a slurry of tobacco toward the can left for that purpose on the floor nearby. "Etown's the capital."

"Capital of the Territory?" Pollock raised an eyebrow quizzically and cupped his hands over the stove.

"County seat," Middaugh said from the counter. "Elizabethtown was designated the seat for the new County."

"Colfax," Kinsinger said. "They named her Colfax County on account o' the new vice-president."

"Vice President elect," Middaugh said.

"Well, any little bit helps," Pollock said.

"Lemme tell you, this is important!" Kinsinger leaned forward. "With his connections, all sorts o' good things could happen for this County! We're movin' into the big time, I can feel it in my bones—"

"Here you go, Thomas," Middaugh said from the other side of the room. He put a carefully folded packet of paper on the counter and pulled out the store ledger book. "Is that a charge?"

"Yes," Pollock said. He nodded to Kinsinger and went to the counter. "Thanks, William. I hope it works. Listening to a one-year old cough like that is terrifying."

Middaugh nodded. "And you don't want the older ones catching it, either." He put both hands on the counter. "Give Sarah my regards. She'll remember how to mix it up, but I wrote the proportions on the inside, just in case."

"I'll do that." Pollock tucked the packet of powder into his pocket, nodded to Kinsinger again, and went out. He headed up the street toward home, shoulders hunched against an icy wind. Kinsinger was always running his mouth, he thought irritably. As if new counties were more important than a sick baby in a houseful of children.

~ ~ ~

Benjamin Franklin Houx was a big, sandy-haired man with an anxious face that hid a gentle heart. Why he wanted to be a lawyer was anyone's guess. To all appearances, he was a successful carpenter, though a slow one. No one but his wife Agnes knew how Ben's thoughts overtook his hands, how he could sit, apparently idle, for long stretches, the wood plane loose in his hands, the lumber lying on the bench, while he stared into the distance, lost in the intricacies of the legal case he'd been reading that morning before breakfast, before most of Elizabethtown or the rest of the Territory was even awake.

There were no children to interrupt his studies. At 39, Agnes knew it was unlikely there would be any and so she did not press him to be more about his business. They had enough on which to live, and if he found pleasure in his legal studies and his thinking, if he was not hungry for children to follow after him, she was content to leave him in peace. She herself would make her way to McCullough's stationery shop as often as they could afford it, to peruse his small stock of books for the occasional work she had not yet read. It was a quiet life she and Ben led.

Until the day Sheriff Calhoun showed up to ask Ben to be a deputy. Since the Sheriff lived in Maxwell's settlement at the eastern end of Cimarron Canyon, he needed someone on the spot in Etown. And Ben was his best hope.

"You working on knowing the law and all." The Sheriff leaned forward on Agnes' good parlor chair, causing it to creak anxiously. "You know more about that kind of thing than just about anyone in the County."

"Well, I wouldn't go that far." Ben shifted uncomfortably. "There's that new lawyer that's just arrived. Old Daniel Mill's son."

"Melvin? He'll be wanting to defend the people you arrest, not arrest them." Calhoun grinned companionably. "He wants the money. Besides, being Deputy's not a full time thing. It's just when someone is needed."

Ben nodded slowly and Agnes looked at her hands. He was going to do it, she knew. She pursed her lips disapprovingly, but the men were too focused on each other to notice. She sighed, shook her head, and offered the Sheriff more tea.

173

But after he left, she felt free to offer her opinion. "It's going to take away from your studies," she said as she placed the tea things back onto the tray.

"Oh, I don't think it'll be too time-consuming," Ben said easily. "The town's settled a bit since the mining first started. Things aren't as rambunctious as they were a year or two ago."

Agnes gave him a long look, shook her head, and carried the tray into the kitchen.

Moreno Valley, Spring 1869

And then winter was over and it began to be spring again.

In spite of the increase in paying guests and the resulting additional work, Gregoria felt a lift in her spirits as the weather warmed. New life sprouted around her and grew within her. Whenever she had the chance, she went eagerly to dig in her garden. She kept her face turned firmly away from the edge nearest the trees and instead dug forward into the hollow, tearing the grass out in great clumps, moving her garden plot steadily away from the trees and the bones, sorrow, and guilt buried there.

Charles watched her sardonically from the doorway but said nothing. Gregoria sowed beans on the northern edge, where the squash had grown the previous summer, and placed the poles for them carefully, effectively screening the burial area. Because she hadn't further disturbed the ground there, the grass was already starting to move in to cover the stretch between garden and forest. By next year the burial site would be obliterated. But Gregoria turned her mind firmly away from what lay under the soil, willing the new growth to cover her memories as well, digging steadily toward the hollow, moving the stones from the soil to one side as she worked.

~ ~ ~

In Elizabethtown, Judge Watts looked at the forms in front of him again and shook his head. "I take it Mr. Charles Kennedy didn't get himself arrested?" he asked drily.

175

Sheriff Calhoun chuckled. "I guess he wasn't at home." He gestured at the paperwork on the table between them. "Deputy Benitez travelled clear from Mora, then couldn't find him. The folks in Mora County must be glad to be rid of Colfax and its riff-raff."

The Judge laughed and shook his head. "Etown as the County Seat. You have to wonder how long that will last."

The Sheriff grinned. "Well, maybe it'll settle them down a little. But I've got Ben Houx as deputy up here and they've elected Patrick McBride as Justice of the Peace."

"McBride's a good man," the Judge said. "As long as he lays off the sauce. And I've heard of Houx. He's the carpenter who's reading law on the side, isn't he?" He looked back down at the Kennedy arrest warrant. "So we're transferring responsibility for Kennedy's arrest from Mora to Colfax County." He chuckled. "The first day of court in the new County and this is on the docket. Selling without a license. A full gill of liquor, too! That and a bunch of people caught gambling. As if that's anything new." He shook his head. "We worry about the damnedest things in this Territory."

Sheriff Calhoun shrugged good-naturedly. His hotel in Cimarron had its own set of gamblers, but he saw no reason to point that out to the Judge. "I don't make the rules, I just try to enforce them," he said, grinning.

"I wish you luck with this one." Judge Watts handed Calhoun the Kennedy paperwork. "From what I hear, he's not the most gentlemanly of characters. And there's a civil complaint against him, too, by Adolph Letcher. A debt and an unpaid bill of sale. When Kennedy hears about that, his dander's really going to be up."

The Sheriff grinned and shrugged. "That's what deputies are for. Though, even if we're better at finding him than Benitez was, we don't have much of a jail to put him in."

The Judge chuckled and stood, stretching his fingers. "Well, I guess it's time to go into court and see if we've got ourselves a full jury panel," he said. "Be ready to send out Deputy Houx to collect people. I doubt that they'll show up just because they were ordered to." He grinned. "Good luck with your new job, Sheriff."

"Collecting your jury members may be the hardest part," Calhoun said. "For the rest, I figure if I and my deputies stay friendly-like with everybody and keep our ears to the ground, we should be able to head off most trouble before it develops into anything much."

The Judge looked at him thoughtfully. "Well, that's one strategy," he said. "I'm guessing I won't be around to help you much after this session. President Grant has chosen to replace me with someone else. The Postmaster at Hudson, New York, or so I hear. I got the word just a few days ago."

"I'm sorry to hear that, sir."

"I'm not." Judge Watts grinned at him. "I'll be glad to get back to Santa Fe and private practice, and leave the enforcement of one-gill liquor offenses and gambling laws to somebody else."

~ ~ ~

A few days after the week-long court session had ended, Sheriff Calhoun and Deputy Houx consulted over lunch at Henry Lambert's hotel and restaurant establishment and decided that a light touch was needed in Charles Kennedy's case. For one thing, Etown didn't have what you could rightly call a jail. It was an abandoned miner's cabin that had been appropriated by the new

177

County and any man worth his salt could break out of it. In fact, two falling-down drunk miners already had. The other problem was that it was now mid-April and the circuit court wouldn't be sitting again until late August. It was unreasonable to jail a man for close to four months for selling four ounces of liquor.

The Sheriff left the issue of how to approach Kennedy up to his Deputy, but he made it clear that he didn't want the responsibility of a prisoner hanging around his neck until court was in session. "Besides, we'd have to feed him," Calhoun said as he pushed back his plate. "The county doesn't have the funds to feed a prisoner that length of time. Hell, they can barely afford to pay me and you."

Houx grinned and reached for another bread roll. "He's a big man, too, from what I remember. Bigger than me."

"Pretty wife, from what I hear tell." Calhoun winked. "Good cook, too."

"Guess I'll go up for a meal and see how the land lays," Houx said. "That might be the easiest way."

The Sheriff lifted his hat from the table and stood. "It's all yours, Ben," he said. "Just let me know if the steer starts buckin' so I can run for cover, all right?"

Ben Houx laughed, nodded, and reached for another roll. As he watched the other man leave the room, anxiety pricked at him, but he pushed it away. They said Charles Kennedy was a somewhat unreasonable man: given to temper and jealousy of his pretty young wife. He grinned. That would be a problem for Sheriff Calhoun. He had something of a roving eye. Benjamin F. Houx wasn't built that way. Agnes was all he needed.

Ben rose reluctantly from the table. Agnes wasn't all that happy about this deputy job. She'd be even less thrilled to know he was going to arrest someone with Kennedy's reputation. Arrest.

Now there was an interesting word. It didn't actually mean "take into custody." Just "stop in their tracks." Hmmm. Well, he'd try anyway.

~ ~ ~

It took three days for Deputy Houx to make it to a meal at the Kennedy way station. He'd had chairs to mend for Henry Lambert, a counter to install at the Middaugh Grocery, and a repair to the liquor shelving in Stinson's saloon after a miner had blasted the bottles and shelves with a shotgun. Finally, with nothing left to delay him, Ben headed down the Valley, ambling the horse past the sawmills south of Etown, watching the hydraulic miners hosing down the gravel-filled hillsides near Willow Creek.

Then he was farther south, riding through long-grassed ranch land and reflecting on the advantages and disadvantages of tying oneself to a piece of soil. For himself, once he'd established himself as a lawyer, he'd probably head east, down the mountains. Maybe into the area around Maxwell's. Someplace slightly warmer in the winter months. Agnes would like that.

Though it was warm enough here, this mid-May day, if somewhat muddy. The Moreno Valley got real rain in the spring, in contrast to most of the rest of the Territory. He splashed across several washes a foot deep in clayey muck and was thankful for the horse. Finally, he reached the point where the road divided. Southward, it headed toward Mora. West, it led up over Palo Flechado Pass, then dropped into the Rio Fernando valley and on into Taos. Now there was a warm spot for a man to winter, albeit drier than Maxwell's. He grinned. Agnes didn't think much of Taos. Too much adobe. According to her, houses should be built of wood by carpenters like himself. As the mare swung west in response to his signal, she stumbled on a stone in the road and he turned his attention to the track ahead.

Now here was a house made of wood that Agnes wouldn't think much of, he thought drily as he reined in at the edge of the Kennedy hollow. Wood logs chinked with moss, mud, and an occasional small stone. It was pretty rough. A man darkened the door, filling the space, and Deputy Houx nudged his mount forward.

~ ~ ~

"Well, that was a mighty fine meal," Benjamin Houx said. "I appreciate it."

Charles Kennedy grunted and lifted the Booz liquor bottle invitingly as his wife removed the wooden food platters from the table.

"Don't mind if I do," Houx said, grinning companionably. "The County will be paying the tab, since I'm deputizing for them."

Kennedy frowned, amber bottle in mid-air.

"Oh, it's all right," Houx said. "The Sheriff won't mind. In fact, I was dropping by to talk to you about your liquor sales issue."

Kennedy placed the bottle on the table and leaned back, his blue eyes narrowed. His big hands lay flat on the table, pushing against the boards.

Houx grinned at him, eyes twinkling. "You know those folks in Mora County wanted you in court for selling a gill of liquor? What is that? Four ounces?"

Kennedy grunted, watching him.

Houx leaned back casually and linked his hands together in front of his chest, stretching his fingers.

"Now Colfax County's got better things to do than harass a man about a thing like that, but Mora gave us their indictment papers, so we're bound by law to follow through in some way."

Kennedy was silent, watching.

Houx picked up his noggin, drank, then set it down again. "Pretty good stuff," he said. He smiled at Kennedy. "So the way the Sheriff figures it, you've got a nice operation here and you're not going anywhere in a hurry. If you'll just come into Etown when court sits in late August, we can talk this through, get the judge to drop the charges or whatever it is he needs to do. Then we can file the paperwork to make it all tidy."

"Tidy?" Kennedy looked at him contemptuously. "Got Letcher t' deal with."

Houx nodded. "I heard about that, but that's a civil case between you and him. This liquor sale charge is a criminal indictment, so the Sheriff gets involved." He shrugged. "So he sent me." He spread his hands apologetically, palms up. "Got t' keep the legal system happy, you know."

Kennedy's face darkened. "Waste o' time."

"That's as may be," Houx said mildly. He got up, put the coins for his meal and drink on the table, and went to the door. He lifted his hat from the row of nails set into the logs beside the door. "I thank you for your hospitality and look forward to seeing you in August. Court starts the 27th and runs for a week, so if you can get in anytime during that period, we should be able to take care of this." He nodded to Gregoria. "Ma'am."

Kennedy started to get up. "Now, just—"

Houx held up his hand. "That's all right. I can see myself out." He lifted the latch. "Good day to you."

He stepped outside, put his hat on his head, went to the mare and adjusted her cinch, then swung into the saddle.

181

Kennedy stood in the cabin doorway glowering at him, his black beard fairly vibrating with anger.

Ben raised a hand to his hat brim in a half salute. "I hope to see you in August," he said pleasantly and turned the horse toward the road.

Behind him, Kennedy roared, "You go t' hell!"

Houx's mare broke into a trot, but he tightened the reins, slowing her to a walk. They moved sedately up the bank to the road as Charles Kennedy's dissatisfaction darkened the cabin door behind them.

MORENO VALLEY, SUMMER 1869

As Gregoria's garden grew, so did her belly and her baby's activity within it. She felt the child's kicks with a sense of relief. Never before had she felt such activity in her womb. Surely it was a good sign, an omen that finally she would bear a living infant.

But the morning she felt the first stirrings of actual childbirth pain, she wasn't so sure. When she dropped onto a fireside stool and gasped, "Ya viene!" It comes! to Charles, he got up and headed toward the door.

He picked up his rifle and snapped it open, checking the load. "Goin' for meat," he said without looking at her. He gestured southward. "Coyote Creek." He turned his head, glaring at her. "Door stays shut," he growled. "No visitors."

She bit back her tears, gasping into the pain as she nodded, pushing her disappointment away. Men find the birthing process uncomfortable, she told herself. It is only reasonable that he wants to escape it. She wished she'd asked him to go for Alma Kinkaid, but she doubted he would have done so. He wasn't a man to ask favors of anyone. Perhaps he will return, as he did before, she thought hopefully.

But there was no point in wishing for something she didn't know would happen and she had more immediate things to concern herself with. She turned her attention to the contractions. They were still far apart, though painful. Another wrench twisted within her and she groaned against it, trying to relax. When it passed, she took a ragged breath and looked around the cabin, considering.

She would need water and clean rags. She closed her eyes, waited out the next pain, then pushed herself up from the stool to retrieve the small bag she'd already prepared.

She spread an old blanket on the floor beside the bed and carefully laid out the items she'd gathered: a narrow clean rag to tie off the cord, soft cloths for washing herself and the child, a small blanket for the baby. It was one she'd sewn for the child who now lay beside the stream. Gregoria smoothed it wistfully. Then another contraction seized her and she braced herself against the floor and gasped her way through the pain.

When it was over she pulled herself up and squared her shoulders. This was no time for sorrow. Surely it was bad luck to think about a dead child when another was about to be born. And there was still much to be done. She waited out another contraction, then made her way slowly across the room. The bucket had water in it. Thank God she had gone earlier than usual to the stream. She filled the kettle and put it on the fire to heat, hobbled to the rough wooden shelves in the kitchen to retrieve the paring knife, then sat down to wait.

~ ~ ~

Afterwards, Gregoria couldn't remember what happened, or in what order. She only knew that the water began boiling and she lifted it off the fire and began hobbling across the room. A contraction twisted through her, bending her double while the kettle was still in her hand.

She sank to the floor, hot water sloshing onto her skirt. "Charles?" she whimpered.

But the door didn't open. Instead, the pain ripped through her again, waking her from her stupor. She struggled to her feet and somehow made her way to the bed.

For the rest of her life, Gregoria would be unable to explain how she got through the next three hours. It was all a haze of pain and fierce determination. When it was over, she lay weakly on the bed, trying feebly to coax the tiny naked boy in her arms to begin suckling.

Then Charles appeared and lifted the child away from her. He stared at the baby in his big hands. "Boy child," he grunted. He looked down at her, eyes narrowed into mere slits. "My son."

The baby began to mew and Gregoria raised herself enough to reach for the small blanket on the floor and hand it to Charles. He tossed the cloth over the newborn and carried him to the door, which he swung open, letting in the June sunlight.

"It is drafty," Gregoria warned.

Charles ignored her. "My son," he said.

Gregoria smiled. The baby began crying and she stretched out an arm. "He has worked mucho," she said. "He is hungry."

Charles brought him to the bed and she rose gingerly to carry him to the fire. "Careful," Charles said, following her. He moved to add another log to the fire.

Gregoria glanced up in surprise as she settled onto a stool. "Sí," she said. She looked down at the child and a stirring of hope passed through her. Perhaps things would be different now. "What shall he be called?" she asked.

"Sam'l." Charles sat down on the other fireside stool, staring at the child. "Had a brother once. Samuel. He died." He shrugged and looked into the fire. "No food." His black head swung toward her. "This Sam'l be different. Hacienda and peons. Samuel the rico. No one'll bully him, say he's stupid!"

The baby latched on to her nipple and Gregoria drew in a quick breath.

"Hurt?"

185

"No. Yes, a little." She nodded at the sucking child. "The first feeding is difícil."

"Give 'im plenty." Charles got up, pushing his stool out of the way. "My son. Healthy an' strong." He gave her shoulder an awkward pat and headed to the door. "An' warm. Need wood."

She nodded and smiled at the baby. What a change a child created. Perhaps things would truly be different now. "Samuelito, mi nene," she said to the sucking child. My baby boy.

MORENO VALLEY, AUTUMN, 1869

The man in the buggy pulled his team to a standstill and looked west, along the road to Taos. He'd had a long drive from Mora and he was tired. He could just see a ramshackle cabin and corral off to the left. Kennedy's rancho. Thomas B. Catron studied it for a long moment, then snapped the reins, signaling the horses forward. Kennedy was said to have a temper and was probably only a squatter, but he was still a vote in the upcoming election. And there was a charge against him that Catron, as the Territory's Attorney General, could have dismissed without explanation.

It didn't take long. Catron was a stocky, no-nonsense man, not given to fine language, especially with men like Kennedy. A swirl of watered-down whisky from the amber Booz bottle, a few words, and it was done. "You still need to show up for court next week," the Attorney General warned as he got back into the buggy. "You've got that suit to settle with Letcher."

Kennedy grunted from the doorway, blue eyes squinted against the light. "Make it worthwhile," he said.

"I already did, didn't I? You won't have to pay a fine and you won't have a criminal record." Catron grinned. "Not that a record probably matters to you."

Kennedy scowled at him.

"If you're looking to keep this land for that baby boy in there, you'd better start deciding who your friends are," Catron said bluntly. "Remember, we're putting up Doctor Longwill of Cimarron for Probate Judge this fall."

Kennedy grunted again.

"I'll understand that as a vote for Longwill," Catron said.

Kennedy jerked his chin up, then down, and Catron grinned again. He flicked the reins at his team. "See you next week," he said as the horses swung toward the road. Though I'll be surprised if you show up, he thought grimly as the buggy lurched up the side of the hollow.

But Catron was a lawyer, after all, and his face showed neither surprise nor recognition the following Monday when he spotted Charles Kennedy at the back of the make-shift Elizabethtown courtroom. Instead, Catron continued to appear to listen to the arguments between a dry goods clerk named Samuel Cawker and saloon keeper Joseph Stinson and a bunch of local miners. Something about fraudulent claims and a missing witness. It was typical Etown activity: everyone seemed to have an interest in at least one claim if not half a dozen. And the ownership records could get complicated.

It wasn't a good way to start the day. Judge Palen's patience appeared to have already worn thin. The Cawker vs. Stinson case had come up on the first day of the session and still wasn't resolved. This clearly annoyed him. His annoyance continued during the following six civil cases, none of them as complicated as the one Stinson was involved with, but all of them requiring close attention on Palen's part. It was late afternoon before they were finished, and he was getting more and more irritated.

Then Catron rose. "Your honor, there are two criminal cases before the court that the Attorney General moves be dismissed," he said abruptly. "The first is number three on the docket, the Territory versus Charles Kennedy for selling without a license. The second is number 37, against Frederick Berger for permitting gaming."

Palen barely let him finish speaking before his gavel slapped the rough wooden table that was standing in for a bench and his head swiveled toward the court clerk. "Let it be recorded that the two named suits are hereby dismissed and that the said defendants as to this prosecution may go hence without delay."

There was a rustle at the back of the courtroom and Joseph Stinson re-appeared. "Your honor—," he said.

Catron saw Kennedy's eyes narrow as his head swiveled toward Stinson.

Palen's gavel came down, sharper now. "Any further discussion of your case will have to wait," he said sharply. He nodded toward a prosperous-looking young man sitting on a bench near the front, a gaudily dressed young Mexican woman perched beside him. "I believe we have a Bavarian immigrant who wishes to become a naturalized citizen." He glared around the courtroom. "A man who appears to have more appreciation for this great country than many of those who were actually born here."

Catron saw Kennedy's scowl deepen. As the Bavarian stood, the big man with the black beard stood and headed for the door, glowering at Stinson as he passed.

~ ~ ~

The Middaugh brothers catered both to the families of the town, with their grocery, and to the miners with a saloon. They did this from a building that was conveniently situated on a hilly corner lot, so that the grocery could be entered from one street and the saloon from the entrance around the corner and down the hill. Kennedy repaired to the saloon portion of the Middaugh establishment after he left the courtroom. He was sitting morosely at a table with a glass and a bottle of whisky, scowling at the walls, when Adolph Letcher came in. The older man spotted Kennedy, hesitated, then came forward.

"May I join you?" he asked formally as he removed his neat black narrow-brimmed hat from his head.

Kennedy grunted and continued to examine the walls.

Letcher smiled faintly and sat. "I understand there is now a child in your home," he said.

Kennedy's head swung around angrily.

"I went by your place on the way from Mora here," Letcher explained. "No one answered my knock, but I heard a child wailing."

Kennedy turned his attention back to the wall.

"It is a good thing to have a child," the merchant said. "A boy, I trust?"

Kennedy's face softened slightly and he nodded.

"I congratulate you. Have you chosen a name for the little one?"

Kennedy glanced at the other man. "Sam'l."

"A good Bible name," Letcher said approvingly. "Samuel the strong man. He will be a mighty one, with a name such as that."

Kennedy grunted and picked up the bottle. "Drink?" he asked.

"No, but I thank you," the merchant said. He gestured toward the door. "I must be speaking to the clerk of the court when today's session is complete and I wish to have my head clear."

Kennedy refilled his own glass.

"I must speak to him about the money you owe me," Letcher said, watching Kennedy's face.

Kennedy scowled.

"I understand that the cattle, they were sold to Joseph Stinson," the merchant continued.

"That bastard!"

Letcher smiled slightly. "I cannot disagree with you in that regard," he said mildly. "I am told that Stinson received a fine price from the butcher."

"Cheated me," Kennedy growled.

"Mr. Stinson also owes me a certain sum," Letcher went on. "Saloons can be expensive operations to maintain." He shook his head. "Personally, I don't understand why anyone would wish to own such an enterprise." He smiled mischievously. "Mr. Stinson has made a rather large payment to the bank on my behalf, slightly more than is truly required."

Kennedy scowled. "So?"

"It is only fitting that his payment account partially for what is owed on your cattle."

Kennedy frowned.

"If you can accommodate me with one hundred dollars, I will consider the account settled," the other man said.

Kennedy squinted at Letcher, moved a hand toward his pocket, then drew back. "That's it?"

"I can give you a receipt for the entire amount and will inform the court clerk that I have dropped the charges."

"Receipt first," Kennedy said.

Adolph Letcher smiled slightly, drew a book and pencil from a vest pocket, and began to write. Kennedy watched him sardonically. The man was a fool, but it was a small price for the loan and the cattle. The dent in his savings wouldn't be substantial.

191

DON FERNANDO DE TAOS, FALL 1869

The young woman looked tired but determined, the baby in her arms slightly older than the newborns usually brought to him for baptism. Father Ussel smiled at her perfunctorily and glanced at the father. He seemed familiar, somehow, but then that great bulk and the black beard and hair weren't likely to be easily forgotten.

If he looked in the records, he'd probably find them, this girl and her husband. The man said they'd been married in this church and he had no reason not to believe him. Ussel wrote their information in his record book and moved forward with the baptism. It was a Wednesday, so the church was quiet. As they proceeded, a thin worn-looking nuevomexicano man slipped in the door and knelt at the back of the sanctuary. This was to be expected in a church so near the Plaza. No one in the baptismal party turned to look at him.

When the ceremony was over, Father Ussel blessed each of the party and the husband grudgingly handed him the usual fee. As Ussel took it, he heard the young woman gasp. "Papá?" she asked.

The kneeling figure had risen and was standing, hat in hand, in the shadows near the door. The woman cast a swift glance at her husband, then hurried toward him.

"They told me you were here," the man said. "That you came from the Palo Flechado."

"Lo siento, there was no time to send—" the girl began, but the man shook his head.

"El nene?" he asked, laying a gentle hand on the form in her arms. The child?

She smiled and turned slightly so he could see, then pulled the blanket away from the infant's face.

Then the husband was beside them. "My son," he said harshly.

The woman's father looked up at him pleadingly. "Sí, " he said humbly. "Y mi nieto." And my grandson.

The husband scowled and turned to the woman. "Vamos." Let's go.

She nodded without looking at him, smoothed the blanket around the child's face, leaned to give her father a hasty peck on the cheek, and hurried out the door, husband at her back.

The girl's father stood for a long moment looking after them, then turned toward the altar, genuflected, crossed himself, and went out silently, his head bowed.

Still standing by the altar, Father Ussel suddenly remembered a wedding early in the year 1867: a rainy February day, a girl who shuddered from the cold as she said her vows. He shook his head. That had been over two years ago. Had she not seen her father in all that time? She was still only a child, seventeen at the most, and small for her age. They had come from the other side of Palo Flechado Pass. What it must have taken to convince her husband to bring the child in for baptism? And the trouble of such a journey with an unwilling spouse. She was a strong one, in spite of her frail appearance. He wondered if she knew how strong she was.

He turned to the altar and made his own obeisance, drawing his thoughts back to his duties.

Loretta Miles Tollefson

PALO FLECHADO PASS, FALL 1869

Gregoria sank onto the stool in front of the fire and closed her eyes. She was so tired. But there was no time to rest. Even in October, the guests trickled down from the pass and, because the Fall weather was colder than usual, they were more likely than usual to stop for shelter and food. Samuel was growing and would need winter things. She also needed to patch two of Charles' shirts and a pair of his trousers. But it seemed as if there was no time for mending. Or perhaps it was just that she was so weary. The very needle and thread seemed too heavy to hold.

And there was also the problem of food supplies. The money their visitors paid went into the old leather wallet and the pouch that Charles kept hidden away behind the bed and in the shed amongst the packs. She was reluctant to ask him for money for food supplies, much less cloth. He so clearly wanted to increase those funds, not to spend them.

Gregoria opened her eyes and grimaced at the fire. She would need to comb through the packs in the shed once again, the ones from the young merchant as well as the others that had been left behind. She thought of the young man, the first one, Charles Lamb, and found herself smiling gently. He had seemed a good man. Surely he would not object to the use of his goods for her child's winter clothes. She had abandoned his boots long ago. Fortunately, Charles hadn't noticed that she had not returned to them when the weather grew cold.

She was glad because, after the first few months of peace following Samuel's birth, Charles was again angry a good deal of the time. It didn't take much to set him off: a too-kind "thank you

194

ma'am" from a guest or too much expressed enthusiasm for her raised biscuits. Gregoria found herself dreading the arrival of guests for fear of another explosion, the danger of yet another man's eyes with the light gone from them. I must be more careful, she told herself.

On the other hand, the intensity of Charles' sexual demands when there were visitors seemed to have lessened. Although his lust seemed constant when they were alone. It is the cold, she told herself. While there had been little snow, the wind cut ice-cold across the valley. There was little incentive to go out and being cooped up in the cabin gave him nothing to do but lie on the bed and watch her work or tend to the child.

It had happened again that morning. She'd laid Samuel on the floor to clean his bottom, bending over him to remove his dirty clothes. Suddenly Charles' hands were on her skirts, flinging them over her head. She leaned forward, onto her hands and knees, bracing herself over the baby while Charles went at her, Gregoria biting her lip, the infant squalling with fear.

"Shut 'im up," Charles growled as he pulled out and began tightening his clothes. He slapped her bare rump. "Pull down yer skirt. Look like a whore."

She shook her skirt down without looking at him and spoke soothingly to the child. "It's all right, nene," she told him. "Nada to fear, baby boy."

"Hell there ain't." Charles was in front of the fire now, lifting the lid of the venison stew Gregoria had already prepared. "Fear Papa, if he's smart."

She finished with the child and gathered him into her arms. "Papá loves his Samuelito," she cooed to him. "Yes, he does."

"Love," Charles growled sarcastically at the fire. He stirred the embers impatiently. "Needs wood. Damn cold."

~ ~ ~

Edward Baker was an earnest young man with a shock of sandy hair and a habit of looking sideways at the person he was speaking to, as if trying to assess their sincerity, a sincerity that was written on every inch of his own freckled, brown-eyed face. Perhaps it is the paleness of his lashes that makes him seem so young, Gregoria thought as she moved past the two men on the stools before the fire to stir the bubbling pot of stew.

Baker leaned confidentially toward Charles, body tense with excitement. "I found me some gold!" he hissed. He patted his waistband. "An' I went to Taos and got it converted to paper! Over a hun'red dollars!" He shook his head, then grinned confidently. "I ain't gonna get my gold stolen, no sirree. Treasury notes'r safer by far!"

Charles grunted and looked at the fire.

Gregoria glanced into his face and went back to her stew. He didn't seem tense. The young man hadn't so much as glanced in her direction. It was a good sign. She moved back to the table to begin shaping biscuits.

"Smart," she heard Charles grunt.

"Yes sirree! I may just be a laborer, but I know me a thing or two!" Baker grinned gleefully. "Got me a new saddle an' trappings for my mule. Silver. Spanish silver." He leaned back and stretched his legs toward the fire. "Yes sirree." He gestured toward the two packs he'd left leaning against the log wall near the door. "An' I got me some calico an' other geegaws for tradin'."

Charles was silent. The young man continued to ramble, speaking of his childhood home, his friends in Etown, the Welch miner he worked for and bunked with there. Listening, Gregoria wondered if he was more clever than she had thought. Clearly, the men he lived and worked with in Etown would come looking for him if he should disappear. Or at least he thought that they would.

Still, Charles was silent, even for him. He wasn't drinking much, either. And when Gregoria told the men that the meal was ready, he gestured Baker to the table ahead of himself, instead of simply rising and expecting Baker to follow. Gregoria bit her lip.

After the meal, the men returned to the fire, Baker still talking excitedly about his good fortune and cleverness.

"Where you keepin' those notes?" Charles asked abruptly, cutting him off.

Baker grinned and patted his waist. "Got me a special belt," he said. He jerked his head toward the corral outside. "Same place I bought the saddle an' harness. That mexicano leather worker in Taos has some real talent."

"Humph," Charles grunted. He gazed into the fire. "Gonna sleep with it?"

"When I'm travellin' I will." Baker grinned at him. "I ain't stupid." He turned toward the fire. "And I ain't got nothin' to fear when I'm home."

"When yer laborin'?"

"I aim to put it with a banker. We got three of 'em that I know of in Etown."

"Banks'r dangerous," Charles observed to the fire.

"Well now, they get robbed, that's true. But that's always a risk." Baker grinned at the fire. "I could get robbed myself, fer that matter, but bankers got more protection, with their safes an' all."

Charles shook his head. "I wouldn't."

And that was all that was said. Until the next morning, when Baker made to pay for his bed and board. He'd pulled off his money belt, fished out the coins he needed, and was rearranging the leather around his waist when Charles put his hand on his arm. "I'll take that," Charles said. At the table clearing the dishes, Gregoria froze.

Baker shook his head, grasping the belt more firmly. "No thankee," he said. Then one hand lifted away and he opened his palm to display the money for his bed and food.

Charles waved it away. "Keep it safe," he said, grabbing for the belt and twisting it effortlessly out of Baker's grasp. Baker's mouth opened, but he only stared in helpless surprise as Charles wound the leather into a tight circle, then gestured toward the back of the room. "No one'll come lookin' here." He nodded toward Gregoria. "Rosa's witness."

Baker turned to look at Gregoria, who nodded without meeting his eyes, her fingers tightening on the platter in her hands. Go, she thought at him. Go quickly.

Baker nodded and turned back to Charles. "You might just be right about that," he said. "This'll be safer than Etown. I'll be back for it, come spring. Got me some investments I'm thinkin' on. Land, maybe. Houses."

Charles grunted. "Need more."

Baker nodded eagerly. "I'm figurin' I'll collect more, sell what's in the packs, than put it all t'gether and buy me some land."

Charles grunted.

"So I'll be back," Baker said. He nodded to Gregoria. "She's witness. It's one hundred three dollars."

Gregoria nodded again, not looking at him. Just go, she thought at him.

He nodded to Charles. "Thanks for the grub an' all." Then he turned and hurried out the door to his mule.

Charles left the cabin door open, in spite of the November cold, as he watched Baker cross the hollow.

When he turned back into the house, he looked down at the packs by the door and chuckled sardonically. "In a hurry." He poked at them with a booted toe and looked at Gregoria. "Shed," he ordered.

She nodded, left her work, and went to the packs. They were heavy with goods. As she dragged them across the room to the shed, she decided they would go behind all the others, where Charles wouldn't be reminded of them. Where they might have some chance of surviving unravaged until Spring, when Edward Baker returned for them.

Loretta Miles Tollefson

Palo Flechado Pass, Early Winter 1869

As soon as the man entered the cabin, Gregoria felt there would be trouble. The single room was already crowded with travelers sheltering from the raw late-November weather. The young man Baker had shown up early that day. To help Charles in any way he could think of, he'd said apologetically as his eyes roved around the room, searching for the packs he'd left behind. A few hours later, an Etown carpenter named Babcock and several of his friends, including two women, had arrived on their way to Taos.

Gregoria didn't like the look of the women, who seemed to think nothing of perching themselves on a man's knee, regardless of their relationship to that particular hombre. She had placed the sleeping baby on the bed and was in the kitchen corner, busying herself with the food, when the stranger came in and Baker went out to take care of his mules and buckboard.

As the newcomer took off his hat, revealing a close-cropped head of dark hair, his black eyes swept the room scornfully, his contempt palpable. Charles had gone out the back, to relieve his bladder, so no one went forward to meet him, which seemed to deepen his frown.

"Well, if it ain't Mister Coleman of Hattenbach n' Coleman's Dry Goods," the carpenter Babcock said jovially from his seat by the fire. "You got 'ere jus' in time." He waved his carved wooden pipe toward the table.

Coleman nodded. He jerked his head toward the roof overhead and the hail pounding against it. "The hail is quite large and the wind very strong." He spoke with a strong German accent.

"Sounds pretty hellish!" Babcock said with a laugh.

200

Baker came back inside and Coleman turned toward him. "The mules, they are covered?"

"Hope so," Baker said. "I turned 'em into the corral. They might get under the lean-to with the others, if'n there's room."

Coleman frowned, but then Charles came through the shed door. "Two bits fer food, one fer drink," he said abruptly.

Coleman's frown deepened, but he nodded and turned away.

"Ya pay now."

Coleman dug into a pocket. "I wish for just the food," he said. "No drink." He kept his eyes on the fire as he handed Charles the coins.

Charles grunted irritably and turned toward the table. "Rosa! 'Nother plate." He turned back to Coleman. "Booz'll warm you."

Coleman glanced at him and turned back to the fire. "Nein," he said.

Charles' eyes narrowed, but Gregoria intervened. "The dinner, it is prepared, mi esposo."

There wasn't room for them all at the table. Coleman and Babcock filled their plates and sat down on the stools by the fire. Gregoria took them noggins of water, then returned to serve those at the table. Charles gestured at the Booz bottles on the shelf and she took one to the fireside. She lifted it toward the men with an inquiring look, holding the bottle so that the amber glass glowed in the firelight.

"Just one," Babcock said, but Coleman shook his head again. "Nein," he said. He turned his head, raising his voice slightly so Charles could hear him. "I do not want your firewater."

Kennedy swiveled to glare at him, then looked away, apparently caught by something Baker was saying.

"Where you headin'?" Babcock asked.

"I have merchandise to collect in Mora." Coleman shook his head. "My partner has our team, so I was required to borrow the mules and buckboard of the brothers Kinsinger."

Babcock chuckled and cut into his venison steak. "Those two don't do nothing' for free. What'd they charge ya?"

Coleman smiled slightly, his merchant's pride slipping through. "Some cotton dress goods for Joseph Kinsinger's woman." He shrugged. "It is not a bad price for a team at this time of year."

Babcock popped a raised biscuit in his mouth. "Not bad at all," he agreed.

When they'd eaten their fill, the way station guests regrouped around the room. A conversation about firearms began, with Baker saying jauntily that he was thinking of buying himself a new pistol for Christmas.

While he talked, Charles went to the back of the room and rummaged through a pack leaning against the wall. When he moved back into the firelight, he was carrying a pearl-handled Colt revolver. "What you need," he said, holding it up. He turned the gun so the light glinted on the engraved barrel and grip. He touched the recoil shield. "German Silver. Paterson model."

Coleman's back straightened and he shook his head disdainfully. "That is an old gun," he said to Baker. "You come in to my shop, I sell you a new Colt at a good price. Pearl handle, engraved barrel, rim fire." He gestured toward the pistol. "Better than that."

Charles scowled in Coleman's direction. "Keep out," he growled. He turned back to Baker, produced a small silver powder flask, and poured black powder into the gun. "Flask, too," he said.

Coleman shook his head. "Those Paterson Colts," he said. "That powder makes a big mess, gums up the workings. The new rim fire Colts are made better."

"Powder's all right." Charles growled. He pulled a handful of lead balls from a trouser pocket. "No mess." At the table, Gregoria's hands stopped clearing dishes from the table. The others were watching, too.

The room held its breath as Charles slipped four balls expertly into the barrel, then spun the barrel and cocked the trigger. He gestured menacingly toward Coleman. "Wanna see?"

Coleman rose from his seat. There was a general scraping of stools and benches as the others shifted, too. Babcock stood and moved toward the door. Gregoria's hands tightened on the platter in her hands.

Charles moved toward the German merchant. "Wanna see?" he growled again.

The other man shook his head, raising his hands slightly. He nodded toward Baker. "The boy can do as he wishes," he said stiffly.

Baker moved forward, as if to put a hand on Charles' arm, but the big man shook him off. "Powder an' ball," he said. "No mess." He raised the pistol, aiming at Coleman's chest. "Wanna see?"

Suddenly, Babcock flung open the cabin door. As the heavy boards swung into the room, Charles' head swiveled and Coleman moved past him. The merchant grabbed at his coat and hat and rushed out into the night.

Charles barked a laugh as the man stumbled into the yard. Coleman paused, looking wildly toward the corral and the mule-less buckboard, then began running east-ward down the hollow, cutting toward the road.

In the house, Gregoria stood frozen at the table as the others spilled into the yard. She heard Babcock cry, "Kennedy!" as if to restrain him, then a pistol shot, loud in the darkness. A woman screamed.

There was a long and ominous silence, then Charles called, "Forgot your team!" and laughed harshly.

On the bed in the corner, Samuel began to fuss and Gregoria put down the platter she'd been holding and moved toward him. The man has escaped, then, she thought as she lifted the child. As she put him to her breast she realized how hard her heart had been beating, how anxious she had been. But surely there had been no real danger. After all, Charles killed from jealousy and the merchant had shown no interest in herself. It was for that reason that he had escaped. She was sure of it.

~ ~ ~

Early the next morning, after all the Kennedy guests had breakfasted and moved on, a group of men led by Deputy Houx rode into the hollow, hands on their guns.

Gregoria had been collecting deadwood for the cabin fire. As she came through the trees at the northern end of the hollow with her arms full of broken branches, a man vaulted from his horse, entered the corral, and led Coleman's mules out. She stopped and watched them, puzzled. This wasn't the same man who had fled the night before. She looked at the men on the horses. The merchant didn't appear to be among them.

Ben Houx moved his horse out of the pack and toward her as the other man began harnessing the mules to the buckboard Coleman had been driving. "Ma'am," the Deputy said, tipping his hat.

She nodded without speaking.

"Is your husband home?"

She hesitated, then nodded.

"Where might I find him?"

Charles had gone back to bed after the guests had left. He would be angry that she had spoken to these men. Angrier when he discovered that the buckboard was gone and she didn't know who had taken it. She bit her lip, unsure how to proceed.

As if he thought she hadn't understood him, Houx raised his voice. "Where might I find him?"

The cabin door opened. The men on the horses moved uneasily. Deputy Houx turned his head. Charles stood in the doorway, his massive frame filling the space. Behind him, the baby began to wail.

Gregoria moved then, hurrying toward the cabin with her armload of wood. The man fastening the mule harness stopped what he was doing and came toward her. "Lemme help you with that," he said.

"Leave 'er be!" Charles' voice stopped the man in his tracks. "Rosa!" He moved into the yard and jerked his head toward the house. "Get inside." As she moved past him, Charles' head swung toward the wagon. "What ya doin'?" he growled.

The men at the buckboard hesitated. Gregoria dropped the wood by the door and went inside, leaving the door slightly ajar. She picked up the baby and went back to the door. One of the men was nudging his horse forward. "We come fer our team," he said. "Coleman, he borrowed 'em from Pete and me yesterday to fetch goods from Mora. I guess he left 'em with you overnight."

Kennedy grunted and swung his head, looking at the men behind the speaker. "Got plenty o' help," he said sardonically.

The men on the horses looked at each other. Deputy Houx cleared his throat. "I understand there was an altercation between you and Joseph Coleman yesterday evening," he said. "And possibly Henry Babcock."

"Babcock's gone."

"Coleman filed a formal complaint this morning. You'll need to appear before the grand jury next spring to discuss last night's events and let them decide if they want the court to follow up."

"Nothin' t' discuss."

Houx's mare sidestepped impatiently and he reined her in. "It's against the law to assault someone with no cause," he said mildly.

"Cause?"

"Even with cause, it's generally preferable to settle these differences in court."

Charles snorted. "Didn't do nothin'," he said. His eyes swept over the men on the horses, then he turned, went into the cabin, and shut the door.

The only sound was the movement of horses shifting impatiently, then the creak of the buckboard as it turned away from the corral. Someone muttered an encouraging word to their mount and the horsemen moved out, following the wagon and mules onto the road and back toward Etown.

Inside the cabin, Gregoria sat down on the bed, her head bent over her child, and allowed herself to breathe again. Charles crossed to the fire, kicked at a log on the edge of the flames, then slammed his hand against the nearby wall. "Bastards," he growled and Gregoria's breath constricted again.

Palo Flechado Pass, December 1869

Gregoria tried to control her shivering as she carried the buckets of water from the stream. It was icy cold out here, but if the buckets shook, the water would spill and she'd have to make another trip for more. Tiny ice-hard flecks of snow had begun falling again and she was in no hurry to venture back across the hollow in the early December darkness.

As she neared the house, a thin dark figure emerged from the icy shadows at the end of the corral nearest the house.

She stopped, uncertain, the cold forgotten. "Papá?"

He came toward her, his battered hat and coat caked with snow. "Mi niña," he said as he took the buckets from her hands.

"What are you doing here?"

"I was waiting for you," he said. The water in the buckets began to tremble and she saw that his body also shook with cold.

Gregoria hurried to open the cabin door and her father followed her inside. On the bed in the corner, Charles slept heavily, face to the wall. The baby lay in a nest of blankets on the floor between the end of the bed and the entrance to the shed.

José put down the bucket, pulled off his coat and hat, then embraced Gregoria affectionately. "You are well?" he asked quietly.

"Sí, Papá. Desde cuándo estás aqui?" she said. How long have you been here?

He waved a hand in the air. "No por mucho tiempo." Not long.

She shook her head and went to the fire. "Here is soup. It will warm you."

He turned, looking around the room. "Y el niño?" And the baby?

She smiled, put the ladle back into the stew, and went to the pile of blankets on the floor. Samuel whimpered as she lifted him and Charles stirred.

Gregoria carried the baby to her father. As he reached for the child, Charles sat up. "Who's that?" he demanded.

Gregoria turned toward him. "It is mi papá," she said. She glanced at her father. "He has come to see Samuelito."

"Saw 'im in Taos."

"But that was only for a moment," Gregoria said pleadingly.

Charles grunted and remained on the bed with his eyes half-open, watching José with the baby.

José carried Samuel carefully to a fireside stool and sat down. He began rocking back and forth, murmuring a song as Gregoria began pouring cornmeal into the stew to thicken it.

"What's he sayin'?" Charles demanded.

Gregoria looked up. "It is a child's song. A song for Christ's birth."

Charles shifted impatiently. "What's he sayin'?"

Gregoria bit her lip, listening to her father's low voice. "Dijo el gallo: cocorocó, Cristo nació," he sang.

Slowly, Gegoria translated. "The cock said, 'Kokoroko! Christ is born'—"

"Garbage!" Charles rolled over, facing the wall. "Stupid greaser!"

Gregoria bit her lip and went back to her cooking as her father continued to sing.

~ ~ ~

As Gregoria's father, José had every right to be treated as an honored guest, but instead he made himself useful, carrying water, helping with the firewood and the mules. He kept his head down and nodded submissively at whatever Charles said. After a few days, Charles stopped scowling at the sight of him.

"Good peón," Charles told Gregoria, jerking his head toward the door. José had just gone outside to chop wood for the fire. "Might keep him. For the rancho." He shifted uneasily. "If it happens."

Gregoria glanced at him in surprise. They were sitting in front of the fire, she mending a pair of his trousers, he staring into the flames and sipping whisky from a wooden noggin. This was the first time in months that he'd spoken of his future plans.

"The money, it is enough?" she asked timidly.

"Course not." Charles gestured toward the door. "Be quiet."

"Lo siento." She went back to her work.

José came in with an armload of wood and Charles moved his legs to one side to let him pass. José crouched down to stack the fuel beside the fireplace.

"You good peón," Charles said abruptly.

José's hands slowed, but he did not turn his head. Gregoria's own hands stopped their work as her father looked at the small pile of wood and said, "Gracias, señor."

"You stay. Work fer me," Charles said.

He'd finished with the wood, but José remained where he was for a long moment. Then he turned his head toward Charles' legs. "Perhaps," he said.

"Work fer food," Charles said. "An' bed."

José glanced up at Charles' face, then at Gregoria and the wood. "For the time being," he agreed.

Charles grunted approvingly. "Tend mules," he ordered. He tilted his whisky to his lips.

When her father had gone out, Gregoria glanced at Charles, then looked back down at her work. "Gracias, mi esposo," she said.

"What fer?"

She gestured toward the door. "Mi papá."

He shrugged and stretched his legs toward the fire. "Long as he works."

She nodded and returned to her sewing.

~ ~ ~

The outdoor temperature had risen slightly and again there was little meat in the house. Charles took his rifle and headed into the valley, where the elk tended to congregate when snow was deep on the mountains.

Gregoria stood at the table kneading dough, preparing more biscuits. Her father sat on the bench opposite her, Samuel in his arms.

"You have learned to make el bísquete?" José asked.

Gregoria nodded. "There was a grandmother who lived nearby in Taos who taught me."

"The woman María?" he asked. "She is a good woman, though with strong opinions. It was she who told me you had gone."

Gregoria smiled. "She is certainly a woman of strong opinions," she agreed.

There was a long silence, while he watched her work, then her father said sadly, "You have learned many things."

She glanced up at him, then around the room. "Yes," she said.

"I also have learned." He waited, as if hoping for a response, but she kept her eyes on her work.

"Do you remember my friend Diego?"

Her hands stopped moving for a moment, then she continued more slowly, carefully kneading the dough. "Sí, " she said. "I remember."

"He recently came to talk with me."

She glanced up, then swiftly down. Her father's face was turned away, looking across the room at the fire.

There was a long pause, then José said, "He confessed to me what he did to you. That you did not provoke him."

Gregoria dusted off her hands and reached for the tin of lard. Her father watched as she greased the pan for raising the bread dough.

"I should have known that you would not do such a thing."

Silently, she moved the dough into the pan and covered it with a cloth.

"I should have guarded you against a man like Diego."

Gregoria carried the pan across the room and set it down in the corner, away from drafts from the windows or doors. She turned to face her father, who continued to stare into the fire.

"I did not understand." He turned, looking into her face. "I have asked God for forgiveness and made many penances, but still I bear the pain of it." He looked down into Samuel's face. "I am a bad person who does not deserve to hold a child so precious."

Gregoria felt a sudden rush of pity for this small man who held her nene so carefully. Yet he had done her a great wrong. "It cannot be undone," she agreed gently. "Yet it is in the past."

"Lo siento," her father whispered, more to the child than herself. But she moved forward anyway and gently put her hand on his shoulder.

"Gracias," she said.

Then Samuel squirmed in his grandfather's arms and began making sucking noises.

"He is hungry, I think." Gregoria bent to gather him into her arms.

José chuckled as he released him. "He grows quickly."

Gregoria retreated to the bed to nurse. José watched her for a long moment, then said, "More firewood is needed," and went out.

Gregoria smoothed Samuelito's dark hair as he suckled. She took a deep breath. She felt lighter somehow. As if a burden had been lifted from her shoulders, one she hadn't even known that she carried. "Mi nene," she whispered into her son's tiny ear. "Mi nene." My baby boy.

~ ~ ~

The cold and snow slammed in from the mountains behind them again and no guests ventured near the Kennedy way station for the next two weeks. It was a peaceful time for Gregoria, as she watched her father play with his grandchild, but she could see that Charles was growing restless. No guests meant no money coming in. How long would it be before he decided another mouth to feed was one too many?

But more money arrived on Christmas Eve, when a tall Americano man rode in from the valley on a big gray-mottled stallion. As she looked out the door from behind Charles' back, Gregoria could see that the horse's bridle and chest strap were richly decorated with silver. The man had the bearing of an aristocrat, even with the long red hair that curled over his collar below the smooth black hat.

Gregoria hurried to straighten the blankets on the bed. Turning, she tucked her hair behind her ears, then thought better of it and pulled it out again. No need to give Charles a reason for anger, though she felt instinctively that the man outside would not give offense with careless language or looks. Her father, sitting with Samuelito by the fireside, looked puzzled at these preparations but said nothing.

The americano entered the house slowly, removing his hat, looking around, smiling at José and the child, and nodding to Gregoria politely. "Señora," he said.

"Mi casa es su casa," she greeted him formally. My house is your house. She moved to take his cloak, which was dark brown and lined with fur.

Charles had followed the man inside. He took the cloak from her hands.

"I am Judge Michael Anthony of Missouri," the man told him. "I hope you can give me shelter? For a small fee, perhaps?"

Charles nodded and they negotiated terms. The man paid him for the night. "I hope to be with my friends in Taos tomorrow," he said. "I was detained in Cimarron this morning and Elizabethtown yet later, and so am not as far on my journey as I would have liked."

He and Charles moved to the fire. José vacated his stool and the Judge and Charles seated themselves and began speaking of Cimarron and Elizabethtown, politics and the weather. Gregoria began preparing a meal. When the Judge commented that he'd been detained due to discussions about the new tax collection process, she saw Charles stiffen.

"Taxes?" he asked sharply.

"Oh yes. You have not heard? The Territorial Legislature is considering a law that will require all citizens to pay a tax based on their real and personal property. A relatively small percentage, I must say. The legislation will almost certainly be approved and many arrangements must be made before the actual work of collection can commence."

"No right," Charles growled.

"There is a need for funds to cover the administration of government," the Judge said mildly. "The license fees have been insufficient to meet expenses." He spread his hands, palms up. "The housing and feeding of a governor and his staff, the maintenance of law and order, all these require a sum greater than license fees alone can provide."

"How much?"

"I do not have access to those numbers, of course."

"How much they take?"

The man shook his elegant red head. "The tax each man is assessed will be based on the value of his real and personal property."

Charles's eyes narrowed. "They know that?"

"There will be an evaluation and the establishment of a value by a government official."

"Who's paid." Charles scowled at the Judge as if he was the official in question.

The man smiled placatingly. "It is the way of government, my friend."

Samuel began wailing hungrily and Gregoria hurried to him. José handed him over and she settled down to nurse while her father finished preparing the meal. The americano watched her for a moment, then turned to Charles. "A son?"

Charles growled an assent as José appeared at his elbow. "The food, he is ready," José said apologetically.

It was a very quiet meal. José served them while Gregoria continued to nurse. Charles was seated facing her and she could see that he was still thinking about the new tax. He grunted for his

214

food when he wanted more, but said little else. He roused only when the Judge commented approvingly on Gregoria's cooking.

"A meal fit for a fine establishment," the visitor said, turning to nod to her. "The French cooking of Monsieur Lambert in his Etown Hotel cannot compare. It is a repast fitting for Christmas Eve."

Charles grunted irritably and the conversation moved away from the food and Gregoria. She moved Samuel into position to burp. She hoped the man's kind words would not make Charles angry. She pushed the thought away and made herself focus on other things. She had lost track of the days, had not realized Christmas was so near. Not that she had the materials or time to prepare gifts, anyway. She stifled a feeling of regret, put the child on the bed, and went to clear the table while the men retired to the fire.

José sat outside the circle of warmth, whittling on a stick and watching the other two men. Samuel began to fuss and he went to him and carried him back to the fire. Charles reached out a possessive hand and lifted the child awkwardly into his own arms. The Judge put a hand in one pocket, pulled out a small crystal, and held it toward Charles. "A Christmas gift for the child?" he asked. "With your permission?"

Charles scowled, then nodded begrudgingly. He jerked his head at José. "Take 'im," he growled. José rose and took the baby, then Charles took the crystal from the Judge. He held it up to the firelight for a long moment, then slipped it into a pocket without acknowledging the Judge's presence.

At the table clearing dishes, Gregoria watched anxiously. There was something about the set of Charles' shoulders that worried her, a tension she hadn't seen since the night the merchant Coleman had tried to intervene in the sale of the Navajo's pistol to Edward Baker.

When it was time to retire, José spread a blanket before the fire for the Judge, then curled up in his own blanket at the end of the fireplace, almost out of range of its warmth. The americano took off his jacket, unbuckled the gun belt at his hips, and laid them both on the table. He lifted his cloak from a nail by the door, wrapped himself in it, and lay down parallel to the flames.

Gregoria noticed that the Judge did not lie next to the fire, but away, as if it were too warm for him. Or as if he was being careful not to block the heat from her father, in his thinner covering.

She cushioned Samuel in his pile of blankets at the foot of the bed and laid down herself, between Charles and the wall, where he liked her to sleep when they had guests. As she did so, Charles stirred, and she willed her body to relax, to seem asleep. Surely he would not try to take her with the Judge in the room.

But what he did was far worse than attempting intercourse while others were present. In the middle of the night, Gregoria felt him stir, then sit up. He rose, and she rolled sleepily into the warm hollow his body had left behind. Then she realized he hadn't gone outside to relieve himself. She opened her eyes.

Charles was standing between the table and the fire, at the Judge's feet, the americano's pistol in his hand. He fired once, then twice, and the smoldering flames flared, lighting the blackness where the back of the Judge's head had been. In the same moment, her father jerked up from his blanket and stared at Charles in terror.

Samuel began to wail. Gregoria sat up and reached for him even as she wrapped a chal around her shoulders. She lifted him, instinctively pressing his tiny face against her chest to keep him from looking toward the fire. "Hush," she whispered. "Hush."

"Help me," Charles growled at José. "Shawl!" he barked, moving toward Gregoria.

She pulled off the one she was wearing and tossed it to him, still shielding Samuel's view. The two men wrapped the cloth around the mangled head and dragged the Judge's body across the floor and into the shed.

Against her breasts, Samuel began to whimper.

The only thing Gregoria could think to do was to sing him a lullaby. An old Christmas tune came back to her. "No lloréis, mis ojos," she sang, her voice trembling. "Niño Dios, callad, que si llora el cielo, quién podrá cantar?" Do not weep, my love; Child God, do not weep, for if heaven weeps, who will ever sing?

She gulped, forcing herself calm. On the other side of the wall, a shovel scraped against the shed floor. Gregoria raised her voice, trying to block the child's ears as well as her own. And now mi papá will be implicated in Charles' activities, she thought despairingly. But Samuelito must be spared this. She gulped, brushed aside her tears, and began the song again. "No lloréis, mis ojos." Do not weep, my love.

Her head was still bent, crooning to the child, when Charles came back inside. "Worthless peón," he growled, going to the fire. "I need help, he runs off."

Gregoria looked up anxiously. "Mi papá?" she asked. "But he will freeze in this weather."

"Catamounts catch him, he'll wish."

She shrank inside herself, biting her lip. She was glad her father had not allowed himself to assist Charles in his work. But still, she was afraid for him.

Against her, Samuel squirmed hungrily. She forced herself to smile down at him and uncovered her breast.

In the firelight, Charles was counting greenbacks. He looked up at her. "Empty house," he leered. "Good fer pergates."

She forced herself to smile back at him, though her mind was with her father in the sharp mountain cold. She worked fiercely to keep from thinking of the big Judge with his kind words and aristocratic red head, a head that was now only a black and empty hole.

~ ~ ~

Gregoria woke to Charles no longer in bed beside her, the sound of Samuelito crying, and the knowledge that there had been yet another death and that her father was gone. Despair smothered her like a heavy blanket, but the baby was wailing and she must respond. She rose, groping for him in the early morning half-light, and put him to her breast. He squirmed anxiously even as he sucked, reflecting her mood. She pushed the hair from her face and closed her eyes, willing herself calm, and the baby relaxed. She rested her back against the rough logs behind the bed and looked around the room.

It was Christmas day. A day to celebrate. She felt only sorrow at the death of the americano and anxiety for her father. She could hear Charles moving around in the shed, but she turned her mind firmly away from the sounds there. She didn't want to know what he was doing.

She sighed and shook her head at herself. There was no point in sorrow or anxiety. It wouldn't change anything. Samuel finished his feeding and she laid him on his stomach on the bed, dressed herself, and went to build up the fire and begin preparing the morning meal.

She was crouched beside the fire preparing tortías when Charles appeared from the shed. He carried a leather-bound box perhaps half a meter square. "For yer clothes," he said abruptly, placing it on the bench beside the table.

Gregoria rose and wiped her hands clean as she moved to the table. She stared down at the box. It was elaborately tooled in well-oiled leather. The red-headed americano had appreciated mexicano work, she mused, remembering the horse's trappings. Her mind flitted to the animal in the corral. She must be ready for the butchering, or Charles would be angry with her. It was not good for a child to see his father hitting his mother, even one as tiny as Samuelito.

She forced her mind away from the dead man and his animal and onto the box. Charles had moved to the fire and was leaning over it, pretending not to watch her as he warmed his hands. She lifted the box's lid. There had been initials gracefully carved into the leather on the underside, but these had been roughly scratched over with a knife, blurring their lines. She glanced at Charles. This is what he'd been doing, out there in the cold.

"Gracias, mi esposo," she said.

"Merry Christmas," he said roughly. He sat down, facing the fire.

Gregoria carried the box across the room and placed it next to the wall, near the bed. Samuel began to fuss and she lifted him and carried him back to the fire. "I have no gift for you," she said to Charles. "Lo siento."

He shrugged and looked into the flames. "Never had one before. Why now?"

"You have never had a Christmas gift?" she asked in astonishment. This was the first time he had ever given her one, but she knew what it was to receive them. When she was a child there had occasionally been small gifts from her father, when he had the funds. And they had always attended the navidad mass.

219

He shrugged and nodded at the fire. "Need wood."

She nodded, returned the baby to his bedding, and went to the door. What a destitute childhood her esposo had suffered. She pulled her chal over her head. No wonder he was so harsh sometimes, so anxious about money, so bitter in his pain. As she slipped through the door, she made up her mind to be more willing when he approached her with his physical needs, more patient when he spoke to her roughly.

The face of the americano judge flashed in front of her eyes. How she wished there would be no more guests, that Charles would find some other way to acquire the wealth he so desperately desired. And that, when they did come, the guests would not acknowledge her or Samuelito's presence in any way. She closed her eyes, fighting the pain and despair of it. And her papá. Where was he?

But then Charles bellowed "Rosa! Wood!" through the door and Samuelito began to wail. Gregoria roused herself. She had tasks to attend to. She piled a small stack of firewood into her arms and went back inside.

PALO FLECHADO PASS, EARLY 1870

The usual brief February thaw came early that year and more travelers came with it, going to and from Etown. Because it was the new County seat, there was much business to attend to there now. Or so Gregoria understood from the talk of those who stopped for a meal and drink before they pushed on for the night. There was also the new property tax that was to be levied. Whenever the talk turned to that part of the recent legislative activity, Charles' scowl grew deeper than usual and he growled, "Ain't payin'!"

The travelers rarely stayed the night and most of them were careful to avoid Gregoria's eyes even while they complimented Charles on the food she'd prepared. They'd pay for the meal and go on, camping along the roadside if they couldn't make it to Etown before nightfall.

Night fell quickly in the valley, the sun dipping behind the western peaks with little warning. Even while the tops on the eastern mountains still glowed golden in the reflected light, the shadows on the western slopes deepened, coyotes began howling, and bull elk bellowed in the cold. Catamount lurked in the night shadows as well, padding across the grassland in search of prey, and a wise man built a good-sized fire in a protected corner of one of the swales bisecting the valley, wakening often to replenish it. But even with these discomforts ahead of them, even with the February cold, travelers that year did not often linger at the Kennedy way station.

Gregoria was always relieved when they left, tipping their hats in her general direction, nodding to Charles politely. When they stayed, her sleep was restless and she woke more tired than ever. It wasn't just the worry about what Charles might do or the physical needs of the baby, who had begun to sleep through the night now that he was eating thin corn gruel. It was also anxiety about her father, pushed to the background by her daily tasks but creeping back as darkness descended. Where was he? Had he returned safely to Taos? Now that he had acknowledged his wrong toward her, her heart yearned for his presence, for the comfort of his worn face. The cabin was lonely without him.

~ ~ ~

Gregoria laid the baby on the bed and went out to bring wood in. The February thaw had given way to another storm and the snow was coming down steadily again, obscuring the view and closing the road from Taos to travel. Gregoria hurried to gather what she needed and went back inside. As she turned to shut the door behind her, she glanced outside again. Her eye caught a shadow moving at the edge of the hollow, next to the road as it headed into the valley. A hunched figure bundled in blankets, its face hooded against the cold. An old woman? Gregoria blinked and then it was gone, fading into the swirling wall of white as the storm moved inexorably across the landscape.

"What ya doin'?" Charles bellowed from the fire.

"Lo siento," Gregoria said. She fumbled with the door latch, her arms still full of wood, and peered eastward again. There was no one there. She'd better tell Charles. He would be angry if someone showed up and mentioned her seeing them. Especially if it was a man. She shivered and closed the door. "I thought I saw someone by the road."

222

"Pack animals?"

"No. I think perhaps an old woman." She began unloading the wood from her arms into the small stack beside the fireplace.

"Not likely." Charles stared into the fire, moving only slightly to let her add another log. His fingers squeezed her rump as she leaned forward. It was the cold, she told herself. With no visitors and nothing to do, he had only pergates to think of. She moved cautiously away from him and sat down at the table to sew. She had discovered that the leather the travelers' packs were made of could be crafted into clumsy moccasins. She'd made a pair for the baby and was now shaping a set for herself. These were better than boots, although not as warm. And she suspected that there were more packs in the shed than most families would own. It would be good to reduce their number. The leather didn't burn well, though Charles had tried.

She bit her lip. She wore proof of her complicity in Charles' actions in the cloth on her back and the leather on her feet. But then, she was complicit, whether she liked it or not. It was the men's attentions to her that caused their deaths, more than any-thing else. Her mind flicked to the americano judge. Perhaps he had looked at her lustfully when she had been unaware. Certainly, he had spoken kindly of her cooking skills. And Charles was al-ways glad to get money, no matter its source. But the blame? It was hers.

She shivered again. It is only the cold, she told herself. Winter lasts a long time in this valley.

~ ~ ~

He had failed her again. José Cortez huddled his thin shoulders as close as he dared to the tiny stove in the battered herder's hut

223

and felt the despair and oppression that only a winter wind can bring with it.

The hut was north of the Kennedy place a good two miles by road and hidden in the fold of one of the Valley's many swales. But still the wind found it and, because the building had been constructed for summer use, made its way inside.

He'd automatically headed for Taos that terrible night, that night that would forever stain his sentiments about the Christ child's navidad. José shook his head, trying not to think of it.

And Kennedy's face. The look of savage triumph as the smell of the gun's black powder wafted through the room. The glitter in his eyes as he went through the americano's pockets.

José had known in that moment that he'd given his daughter to a mad man. He covered his face with his hands, feeling the pain of it once more. And Samuelito. To grow up in such a home.

And he had run away. José shook his head, "Lo siento," he muttered, whether to God, his daughter, or his grandchild he couldn't have said.

But then he had returned. In the brief February thaw, he'd crept up the canyon from Taos and slipped through the forest past the Kennedy rancho and into the valley beyond. He had wanted to stay as close to the cabin as possible without being seen. He had a futile hope of being available if Gregoria should need him, although he knew that if he showed his face again, Kennedy would almost certainly kill him. After all, he knew too much. And then what of Gregoria and el nene? José shuddered and hunched closer to the inadequate fire.

He had been glad when he'd found this old hut. It appeared to have been unused for a number of years. Probably since the miners had arrived and the valley was overrun with them. The traditional herders from Taos seemed to have gone elsewhere with the advent of the gold mining. José had shoved the hut's fallen roof timbers back into position as best he could, covered them with juniper branches, and found the small stove still usable in spite of its rust. I am fortunate there is a stove, he thought now. And it does not smoke like the open fireplace Gregoria must use for her cooking.

José shook his head. "Lo siento," he muttered again, tears welling into his eyes. I am not much of a father, he thought bitterly. Yes, I am closer to her here than I would be if I were in Taos. But she is still there with Kennedy, that loco.

And José dared not show himself. He had taken a great risk last week, during the snowstorm. As he stood in the roadway watching her stack wood into her arms, then looking out the door, he'd thought for a moment she would come to him, the poor and stranded traveler, ask him to enter and warm himself.

But she wouldn't have dared, he reflected. Out of pity for the traveler, she would not ask a stranger to enter and endanger himself. And if she had—what would have happened then? I must not go so close to the cabin again, he told himself sternly. I must wait and find a way to watch from afar, to be ready when she needs me.

Palo Flechado Pass, Spring 1870

As the weather warmed and the spring rains came, travelers began once again to stop for food and occasional lodging at the Kennedy rancho. Gregoria baked raised sourdough biscuits and cooked venison and elk for them, but slipped outside as often as possible to begin preparing her garden for planting. It was early—there was still real danger of snow—but the ground had been softened by the rains and the grass was growing again, creeping into the area she'd planted the year before. She could feel her mind clearing as she set to work removing the grass, turning over the soil, enjoying the warmth of the spring sun on her back, the birds singing in the trees. It was good to be active again. It kept her mind from dwelling on other things.

Samuel distracted her, as well. He was growing rapidly now and she kept him with her as much as possible. He was on a blanket in the sunshine while she turned garden soil the day the Kinkaid wagon trundled down from the road. When Gregoria saw who it was, a wave of gladness swept over her. She dropped the shovel and moved to lift Samuel from his blanket.

The buckboard pulled up next to the corral and William Kinkaid climbed down. He nodded to Gregoria as she came from the garden, and circled the mules to help Alma and then Alfred down. The little boy smiled shyly at Gregoria as she and his mother embraced, Gregoria still holding Samuel.

"It's so good to see you!" Alma said, looking into Gregoria's face. "Is Mr. Kennedy here?"

"Oh yes," Gregoria said.

A flash of disappointment crossed Alma's face. Behind them,

the cabin door opened. "William wishes to speak with him," Alma said. "Something about the new County politics." She drew Gregoria toward the garden while William entered the house with Alfred by the hand. "I see you are gardening already. You are quite early, you know."

"It is a place of peace for me," Gregoria explained shyly. She glanced toward the northern edge of the garden. "Most of the time, anyway."

Alma pressed her hand. "And this is your little one? He is so fat and healthy!" Samuel smiled at her, then snuggled against Gregoria's shoulder. "He looks like you in the eyes," Alma said. "Babies are such a blessing." There was a trace of sadness in her voice.

Gregoria looked at her sympathetically. "He is growing very quickly," she said. "Soon he will be a baby no longer."

"And you will want more?"

Gregoria shook her head and glanced toward the cabin. "I do not think so." She shrugged. "But when he is no longer nursing, it will be as God wills."

Alma looked thoughtfully toward the house. "I have heard rumors," she said. She turned to Gregoria, brown eyes intense. "If you should find that you want to take things into your own hands—" She paused. Samuel was arching his back, leaning away from his mother. Alma reached toward him. "May I?"

Gregoria smiled and held him out. Alma scooped him into her arms and smiled down at him. "You are a handful, aren't you?" she asked. She looked at Gregoria, her face serious. "I think it isn't easy for you here. If you decide to leave—"

The cabin door opened. Charles' voice growled angrily. The two women exchanged anxious glances and turned. William came out of the house, still holding Alfred's hand. "It was so nice visit-

227

ing with you," Alma said, her voice louder than necessary. She handed the baby back to Gregoria and patted his face. "You'll be a good boy for your mamá, won't you, little one?" She leaned forward to give Gregoria a hug. "Come to us if you need to," she whispered.

Gregoria glanced toward the door, where Charles stood scowling. "It was so good to see you," she said. "I am glad that you came."

And then they were gone. Gregoria replaced Samuelito on his blanket and turned back to her garden, trying not to think about what Alma had said. Come to us. As if she could ever leave this place. As if Charles would let her. Involuntarily, she wondered again where her father was, if he was safe. If he was well. She shook her head at herself and dug sharply into the dirt.

~ ~ ~

Edward Baker entered the cabin without knocking, then hesitated just inside the doorway as if surprised by his own boldness. He twisted his cap between his hands and looked around anxiously. In the kitchen area, Gregoria looked up at him but did not speak.

Charles lay on the bed, hidden in the shadows. "Shut th' door," he growled.

Baker's head jerked in surprise, but he turned and latched the door behind him. When he turned back into the room, Charles had risen and was moving toward him.

"It's almighty damp out there!" Baker said. "Rainin' cats and dogs!" He moved toward the fire, then stopped halfway across the room and looked sideways into Charles' face. "I've come fer my money," he said anxiously.

Charles walked past him and lifted a jug of whisky from the shelf by the table. "What money?" he asked over his shoulder.

"The money I left you in November. The hundred an' three dollars. An' my goods, too." He grinned cheerfully. "I'll be needin' 'em once the weather clears. I'm thinkin' of goin' fer a peddler."

Charles poured himself a drink. He tossed back the whisky and set the noggin on the table. Without looking at Baker, he said, "Ain't got it."

Baker's head jerked around, looking into Charles' face. "You said you'd keep my money safe."

"Safe enough." Charles gestured toward the door. "Bought a mule."

"One o' those in the hollow?"

"'Nother one. Turned out lame. Hadta shoot it."

Baker's shoulders hunched. "I didn't ask you t' invest it," he protested. "'Specially in mules."

Charles shrugged, still facing the table. "What I did."

"So it's gone? All of it?"

Charles turned. "Yep." He grinned, blue eyes gleaming. "All."

Baker moved toward him, his sandy hair bright in the firelight, eyes burning with anger, hands clenched. "You should'na done that! You took my money! Everything I had! I was gonna invest that! You had no right!"

Charles raised his palm, as if to swat a fly, and Baker shrank away from him. "I mean, it was all I had," he said pleadingly, his face averted.

Charles shrugged. "Gone now," he said dismissively. He turned back to the whisky jug. "Drink?"

Baker shook his head. "No," he said. "No thanks." He stood staring sideways at Charles' back, but the big man didn't turn. Fi-

229

nally, Baker looked away, at the fire, then the door. "Well," he said. "I guess I'll be goin'." He looked again at Charles, but the other man made no response. Then he nodded to Gregoria, his face angry and confused at the same time, turned, and went out, shutting the cabin door behind him.

Charles grinned at the whisky jug, then at his wife. "That was easy," he said. He poured himself another drink and went back to the bed. "Pergates!" he called abruptly. Gregoria dusted off her hands and obediently crossed the room.

Elizabeth Town, Spring 1870

There had been an early April snowfall the night before and the courtroom floor was filthy with mud. Although three inches of snow had fallen after midnight, most of it was already melted, and half the street seemed to have been tracked into the room. Even Joseph Kinsinger, sitting with the other members of the grand jury, looked at it in disgust.

"Next case is number 89," the court clerk announced. "Mr. Coleman?"

The Prussian with the English-sounding name rose and came forward. He was duly sworn in and Stephen Elkins, the Territory's new Attorney General, walked him through the altercation at the Kennedy cabin, then called the other five witnesses.

Kinsinger leaned forward and frowned. There were stories enough about Kennedy, but the rumors said he did things when no one else was around, like the man supposedly killed by Indians that Joseph and his brother had seen. Threatening a man with a gun in a room full of people didn't sound like something Kennedy'd do. But that was quite a stack of witnesses. Joseph wasn't surprised when the grand jury vote resulted in a bill of indictment, although he felt himself hesitate before he nodded his own agreement. Who was going to get the pleasure of serving that warrant? he wondered. He was glad it wouldn't be him.

The jury trudged through the next case, then found Kennedy's name facing them again, this time on the lips of the young Edward Baker. The man was in his mid-twenties, but he seemed younger somehow. It was that way he had of looking anxiously sideways at you, like a dog who'd been whipped once too often.

"And he said he'd keep it safe but when I went back fer it, he said it was gone!" Baker said, twisting his cap in his hands.

"And what was the amount of the funds that you deposited with him?" the Attorney General asked.

"One hundred three dollars. And my tradin' goods, too."

"And there were no witnesses?" Elkins asked.

"No sir. Well, Kennedy's Injun wife."

"And you were planning on using those monies and the goods to work as a peddler?"

"Yessir."

Elkins turned to the foreman, who looked at the rest of the grand jury. They all nodded back at him, Kinsinger more firmly this time, indicting Kennedy once again. When this formality was recorded, the Attorney General turned back to the witness.

"I'm afraid that Judge Palen will require you to stand bond to return for the August session and Kennedy's trial on this matter," he said gently. "We don't have a case if you don't show up." He paused. "Bonds in this type of case are usually one hundred dollars."

Baker winced. His eyes closed and his lips moved, as if he were calculating his funds in his head. He opened his eyes. "I can do that," he said. "If'n I get my money back, it'll be worth it."

"There are no guarantees that your funds will be returned," Elkins warned.

Baker's chin lifted. "I'll do it," he said. "That bastard."

~ ~ ~

Samuel was at a remarkably young age to begin toddling, but he was suddenly mobile, though somewhat unsteady on his feet.

232

He was also beginning to work at communicating, although only his mother understood what he might be trying to say. With these new powers, the child had become full of interest in everything around him. He was holding precariously onto the wood pile one morning, babbling at the small birds that flitted around the stack looking for bugs, when a short round man dressed in black rode a brown and white pinto into the yard from the direction of Etown.

"Well, little man," the man on the horse said. "Where's your papa? Do you know?"

Samuel stared at the rider, one fist in his mouth.

Gregoria came to the door. "Samuelito," she said gently. "It is polite to speak when spoken to."

Samuel took his hand out of his mouth and smiled at the man.

"What do you say?" Gregoria prompted him, going to him. She picked him up so that he still faced the visitor.

"Hola," the baby said.

The man grinned, dismounted, and tossed the pinto's reins across the top rail of the corral. "Mrs. Kennedy, I presume?" he asked.

"Sí."

"Is your husband here?"

Charles appeared in the doorway. "Who wants t' know?"

The man put his hand out. "I'm Theodore Wheaton."

Charles studied him. "Yeah?"

The man dropped his hand. "I'm a lawyer. I live in Taos. I've come over for the court session this week and I understand you may be needing some representation. May I come in?"

Charles moved aside and the man entered. Gregoria followed with Samuel, who she carried to the far side of the room and put on the bed. He set up a howl of protest at the perceived confinement and she sighed. "But you must be quiet," she warned, lifting him down. "Papá is busy."

"Rosa! Biscuits!" Charles barked from the other end of the room.

"And Mamá is busy, also," she said to the child.

"'Sqetos?" the baby asked. Gregoria heard the lawyer chuckle.

"He's a hungry one, is he?" he asked Charles.

"Eatin' or talkin'," Charles said irritably. Gregoria moved quickly across the room to prepare the food.

After the men ate, they stayed seated at the table. "I thought you'd want to know what was happening before the Sheriff's deputy arrived," Wheaton said. "They've got you set for recognizance tomorrow afternoon."

"Recog what?"

"That's a fancy way of saying you promise to pay money if you don't appear at the Fall session to answer the charges. And the Judge wants co-signers. I took the liberty of lining up a couple men who say they'll stand for you." He made a face, as if he'd tasted something bad. "For a price. I got them down to twenty apiece." He shrugged. "Since they're promising to pay three hundred if you don't show, I guess that's not too unreasonable."

Charles pushed himself away from the table, as if to rise. "If I don'?"

"The Sheriff will come after you, the Judge will fine you for contempt of court, and you're more likely to get an adverse decision. Judge Palen doesn't go easy on what he sees as shirking. He's hauling Maxwell himself up on contempt charges. Apparently he didn't appear when Palen wanted him to come in and explain why he hasn't held Probate Court lately."

There was a long moment of silence.

"I hope I didn't overstep my boundaries by coming down here," Wheaton said. "There are serious charges against you. I thought you'd probably want some representation." He patted his belly. "Whatever you decide, I'm glad I did. That was a most delicious repast."

Charles grunted and reached for the whisky jug. "No money for lawyers." He hoisted the jug. "Want some?"

"Just a drop," Wheaton said. "Well now, that's the thing," he continued as Charles poured the drinks. "If you're worried about my fee, I'm sure we can arrange something." He grinned. "I've been working in Taos for twenty years. I know what it is to be short on cash." He leaned to one side to allow Gregoria to remove the food platters from the table. "Tell you what, I've got some business that's starting to develop south of here in Ocaté, so I'm going to be travelling by here fairly often on my way through. How about I take my fee in meals for the next half-year or so?"

Charles studied him for a long minute, then grunted. "Could do," he agreed.

"There'll be other costs, though," the lawyer warned. "The payments to your co-signers and then fines and court fees."

"How much?"

"Ten or fifteen dollars for the assault charge."

Charles scowled.

"That's nothing compared to what the embezzlement case might cost you, what with restitution and fees."

"Baker won't show." In the corner wiping down dishes, Gregoria's hands froze, then she went slowly on with her work, the too-familiar dread returning.

Wheaton tilted his head. "Do you know that for a fact?"

Charles shrugged and looked toward the fire.

Wheaton shifted on his stool. "Well, I'm not going to ask any questions, but if that happens, Judge Palen will toss the case for lack of witnesses and there'll just be the assault charge. The fact that Coleman has four or five witnesses is going to make that impossible to deny, though I can probably get it down from intent to kill to simple assault. That's likely to get held over to the Fall session as well."

"Damn law."

The lawyer chuckled and stood up. "Well, I might agree with you, but it's kept me and mine fed for a number of years, so I can't say much against it." He bent forward slightly, looking into Charles' face. "So we have a deal? I represent you and you provide me with meals when I come through? If you'll come into Etown tomorrow, we'll get the recognizance arranged and then I can take care of the rest. If Baker doesn't show up in August, you probably won't even have to be there. I can pay the assault fine and court costs and we can take my fee out in meals."

Charles grunted his assent. "Still gonna cost," he grumbled.

"You will need to bring money tomorrow for the recognizance fees," Wheaton acknowledged.

"Damn law."

Wheaton looked into his face for a long moment, then said, "Good day, then. I'll see you tomorrow," and let himself out the door.

Charles poured himself another drink. "Damn law," he muttered. "Law and taxes." He kicked at the bench on the other side of the table, knocking it to its side. "Sons of bitches!" he growled.

PALO FLECHADO PASS, EARLY SUMMER 1870

Charles' mood didn't lighten after he returned from the court session in Etown. He didn't speak of what had happened there, but there was a brooding sullenness about him that filled the cabin with tension. Gregoria tried to keep Samuel quiet, to have food prepared whenever Charles felt the urge to eat, and to keep out of his way as much as possible.

She knew there was still some danger of frost, but she began planting her garden seeds anyway. She thought the peas would be able to handle any sudden snowfall and that the wild onion seed she'd gathered the previous fall would be all right. After all, they normally lay under the snow all winter, waiting for spring. Besides, her arms yearned for the feel of the spade and shovel under her hands, digging into the earth.

She continued to expand the area she would plant, moving the garden's boundaries ever farther from the bones near the forest edge. She kept Samuel with her, though she had to watch him closely. He was still unsteady on his feet, but he could travel a remarkable distance in a short time. Fortunately, his curiosity saved him from going too far. He would stop, flop onto his bottom, and reach for whatever had caught his eye, intently examining the rock, insect, or flower that had caught his attention. Then he'd maneuver himself up and trot off again until stopped by the next interesting object. Gregoria found herself pausing to watch him explore his world, then returning to her work with a smile, the sun on her back, the breeze rustling the grasses in the hollow and the trees overhead, bird song from their branches.

237

She was digging in the garden, one eye on Samuel, the afternoon that a man on a bay gelding trotted up to the corral without appearing to notice her, then slipped off the horse and into the cabin without looking in her direction. Perhaps he only wanted a drink, she thought hopefully. She put her foot on the back of the shovel, feeling the blade slice smoothly into the damp soil. It had such a wonderful smell to it. At the end of the garden, Samuel chortled as he batted at a piece of grass sticking up from the turned earth.

"Rosa!" Charles bellowed from the cabin door. "Food!"

Gregoria turned, waved an assent, and scooped Samuel into her arms. "What a dirty nene," she teased him. "Too dirty for bísquetes." He giggled at her and wriggled in her arms, trying to get down. "Time to go inside," she told him. "Time to wash the nene." He pouted but didn't cry, and she was grateful. She had noticed before that he preferred the sunshine to the cabin. I must begin now to think of ways to entertain him when winter comes, she thought. To keep him from annoying his father with his frustration at being kept inside.

But her thoughts of the child were distracted by the men's talk when she entered. They were standing at the table, where Charles had just set down a cabin-shaped amber Booz bottle. "I'm tellin' ya, that's what they said," the visitor said as Gregoria closed the door.

"Boundary's east," Charles growled. "Top o' the Cimarrons."

The other man nodded. "That's what I thought, but I hear the bill o' sale Lucien Maxwell signed says it's at the top o' the Sangres." He gestured westward. "Which puts us all smack on his land grant." He shrugged. "Well, not his anymore."

Gregoria slipped around the men to the kitchen area, found a cloth, dampened it with water from the bucket, and carried Samuel to the fire, where she began wiping his face, shushing his protests as she did so. Behind her, Charles was growing ever more silent, which was never a good sign. She frowned anxiously.

"Maxwell sold out to some English group," the stranger said. "That Stephen Elkins had a hand in it, of course." He rubbed his right thumb against his fingertips. "Always after the money, that one." He shook his head. "I hear the new owners'll be lookin' for payment from those of us who don't already have title."

"Title fer what?"

"The land we're on. The claims we're workin'." He shrugged. "Anything they can find a way of claimin', I s'pose. They need to make back what they paid. I hear Maxwell ain't exactly walkin' away from this a poor man."

Charles grunted and poured himself a drink. He raised the bottle toward the other man, but the guest shook his head. "Nah, I'd better not. I need t' stay on my horse and that bay's got a mind of his own."

Gregoria finished cleaning Samuel and sat him on his bottom near the fireplace. She rose and came toward the table. "Food, mi esposo?" she asked cautiously.

The man swiveled toward her as if he'd just become aware of her presence, then turned back to Charles. "If you've got some of those raised sourdough biscuits, I'll take some along," he said.

Charles jerked his beard at Gregoria, who went to the kitchen shelf, found a bit of paper, and carefully folded it around half a dozen biscuits. As she worked, the man looked at Charles. "I hope you've got your papers in order," he said. "I wouldn't want you t' lose this place."

"Don't need papers," Charles growled. Gregoria heard the bottle scrape against the table as he lifted it again, then the soft sound of liquid pouring into a wooden noggin.

"Well, I hope you're right about that," the man said. He brightened as Gregoria came forward with the package of food. "Those'll be a real treat for me this evenin'," he said. Then his face tightened and he turned to Charles. "How much d' I owe you?" he asked pointedly.

"Two bits."

The man raised an eyebrow, but didn't argue. He produced the money, said goodbye without looking at Gregoria, and left the cabin.

Charles went to the door, watched him out of sight, then turned silently back inside. He sat down on the fireside stool nearest Samuel and shoved at the child with the toe of his boot. "Get him out o' my way!" he growled without turning his head. Gregoria scurried to obey.

~ ~ ~

With the news of the Maxwell Land Grant sale, Charles became even more taciturn and inactive than before. The travelers who stopped by spoke of little else than the sale as they tried not to looked puzzled at the lack of meat in the stews Gregoria served them. As long as there were raised biscuits, they didn't complain, although she wondered how long she'd be able to continue to bake them. There was not much wheat flour left, but the bread was essential now that there was so little meat for her to work with.

Charles hadn't stirred from the hollow for weeks and the elk and deer seemed to be avoiding the cabin's proximity. It is because the grass is greening higher on the mountains and the garden hasn't grown enough to attract them, Gregoria told herself. But she couldn't help but wonder if they somehow sensed the bones under the earth, both the human ones at the edge of the trees and the animal ones in the garden itself.

240

Gregoria couldn't bring herself to speak to Charles about the way the flour, sugar, and salt supplies were all dwindling. She wasn't sure how he would respond. He was so bitterly reluctant to spend his money. The scowl on his face when he'd pulled out the money for the legal fees had been terrible. There would be another death if she wasn't careful.

Though that is nonsense, she scolded herself. He didn't kill those men for their funds or goods; he killed them because he was jealous of their attention to me.

She turned her mind firmly back to the problem of her dwindling food supplies. The money Charles collected from the visitors who stopped to eat was important to expanding his resources. If she was to continue baking for their guests, he must purchase more flour and other things. Yet, she still didn't suggest it.

~ ~ ~

The bean plants in the garden were knee high when Gregoria woke one morning to see Charles sitting before the dead fire fingering a small leather bag. She sat up and he turned his head.

"Are you hungry, mi esposo?" she asked. She glanced at Samuel, still asleep. "I can prepare something for you before he wakes."

"Nothin' hot," Charles said. He stood up. "Etown fer supplies. You too."

Gregoria's eyes widened in surprise and she scrambled from the blankets and began gathering what she would need for Samuel, as well as cold biscuits and a little meat for the morning and mid-day meals. She had heard so many stories of Elizabethtown and now she would see it for herself. She tried to suppress her excitement. Charles would be angry if he thought she wasn't content where she was.

He was certainly morose as they made their way up the valley. The road was thick with rocks and the wagon jolted relentlessly. They reached the top of the swale that blocked the cabin's view northward. The northern part of the valley spread out before them. Small streams wound through the summer-green grasses. Here and there patches of purple iris glowed. Cattle dotted the landscape. Three white-headed eagles circled leisurely overhead. The sun was bright in the blue sky and small white clouds crowned the mountain peaks on both sides of the valley. Bright green patches of aspen brightened the mountainsides, contrasting sharply with the larger swaths of almost-black evergreens.

Gregoria noted a small herder's hut off to their left. A wisp of smoke rose from the chimney. The figure of a man moved beside it and she squinted at it, puzzled. She hadn't realized anyone lived that close to them. She glanced at Charles' set jaw and narrowed eyes, and turned her face from the hut. Charles might not like it that someone lived so nearby. She cuddled Samuel to her and felt his body relax into sleep in spite of the jolting wagon.

It was another hour before either of them spoke again. Gregoria noticed a low point in the mountains to their right. The various streams they had crossed all seemed to be headed in that direction. "Is the canyon of the Cimarron there?" she asked Charles, pointing.

He nodded without looking. "Git!" he growled to the mules.

She studied the landscape. She had heard their guests speak of the road through the Cimarron Canyon. Once only a mule track, Lucien Maxwell had improved it so that gold could be easily transported by stagecoach from Etown to the smelting plants in Colorado.

Alma Kinkaid had said she and William lived near the road that led to Maxwell's ranch. Yes, there was smoke rising in that direction. Gregoria squinted. And possibly the flash of sunlight on a glass window.

A small flock of blackbirds rose from a marshy patch beside the road and swirled around the wagon, flashing their red and yellow shoulder patches. At the sound of their whirring wings, Samuel stirred and opened his eyes. He laughed aloud and lifted his arms toward the birds.

"It is so beautiful," Gregoria murmured. "The flowers, the streams, the birds, the sky."

"Jus' valley," Charles grunted.

Gregoria tightened her hold on Samuel and fell silent again as the mules moved steadily northward. The hills appeared to be closing in ahead of them, the valley ending. The sun was well overhead, and warm. She wanted to ask where Elizabethtown was, when they would arrive, but Charles' mood seemed to be growing darker the farther they travelled.

Then she saw that the valley was only narrowing between the hills ahead, not ending. The wagon track pulled closer to, and then began to parallel, the stream that slipped between the tree-scattered hillsides. They passed two sawmills, their big blades screeching, then a scattering of wooden buildings came into view in haphazard rows along the sides of the small hills ahead and to their left. Etown, at last.

As the wagon moved up the road into the town, Gregoria sat up straight and hugged Samuel to her chest. There was an air of energy about the place, a kind of suppressed excitement and strain she'd never experienced before. The houses were made mostly of unbarked logs, like her own. There were men everywhere and only a few women.

Many of the men were americanos, although there were plenty of nuevomexicanos too. Some of them turned to look at Gregoria appraisingly and she glanced apprehensively at Charles, but he seemed to be focused only on the mules. They picked their way down the rutted street until he reined them to a halt before a wood plank-sided building with a porch roof that jutted out to shade two glass windows and the heavy wooden door between them.

"Middaugh Grocery," Charles said, without looking at her. "Stay 'ere." He got down and tied the mules to the hitching post.

Gregoria suppressed her disappointment at not going inside the grocery and looked down at Samuel. She tucked his blankets around him more securely while she tried to see her surroundings without appearing to do so. The grocery was located where two streets intersected. The street the building faced was flat, but the one beside it sloped sharply downward, toward the mountains to the west.

On the corner opposite, four men stood talking in front of a small building made of unbarked logs. Gregoria could feel them watching her. She hugged Samuel closer, but he began to fuss and poke at her dress. She sighed, carefully rearranged her black chal, and slipped him under it to nurse. He is getting too old for this, she thought wearily. But when he stops nursing, it is likely that there will be another child. She bent her head, trying not to feel the men's stares, and bit her lip.

"Wife," she heard Charles say from the door. A skinny man in a long white apron stood beside him.

"Ma'am," the man said, nodding.

Gregoria nodded back without looking into his face. Samuel began to make loud sucking noises. It was clear to anyone nearby what he was doing. She suddenly felt very poor and ugly. Charles and the man went back inside. Samuel finished nursing and pulled away to sit up in her lap. He leaned against her, eyes bright, absorbing Etown's sights and sounds.

As Gregoria rearranged her clothes as best she could under her chal, a group of men crossed the street toward the wagon and went into the store. A woman in a blue silk dress followed them. No one seemed to be watching Gregoria now and she relaxed a little, allowing herself to see the street as the child was seeing it: the activity, the mud, the glass windows in the rough-hewn cabins. There was so much to absorb that she was a little disappointed when Charles came out of the store with a bag of flour over his shoulder. The grocer followed him with the smaller items.

As they were loading the things into the back of the buckboard, a muscular dark-haired man in a blacksmith's leather apron came down the middle of the street, his hands in his pockets. He stopped at the corner of the wagon and looked up at Gregoria. "So you'd be his woman, I take it?" he said, an Irish lilt to his words. He turned abruptly to Charles. "It's you that I have somethin' here for." He pulled a folded piece of paper from his right pocket, transferred it to his other hand, then pulled out another of the same size and shape. "Two of 'em, to tell the whole truth."

Charles' eyes narrowed but he didn't respond. The grocer placed the last item into the wagon and edged away, back to his covered porch and glass windows.

"They'd be summonses for you to appear in the court," the man in the leather apron said. He took a step toward Charles, holding out the papers. Charles stood motionless, hands at his sides.

"You can't just go around stealing things and threatenin' people, now can you?" the man said. His voice rose. "We've got the law established here now!"

Charles moved forward then and for a brief moment Gregoria thought he was going to hit the Irishman, but instead he brushed past him, released the mules from the hitching post, and swung himself up onto the buckboard.

"You've gotta show up!" the other man said. He moved toward the wagon and thrust the papers into Charles' lap. "It's the damn law!"

Charles ignored him and swung the mules sharply away from the building, so that the buckboard turned and brushed against the man in the apron, forcing him to jump backward. "You've gotta show up!" he yelled again as the wagon moved away. The papers fell to the floor at Charles' feet and Gregoria set Samuel on the seat beside her and reached for them. She held them gingerly, not sure what to do with them. Would Charles be angry that she had retrieved them? Finally, she tucked them into the pocket of her skirt and gathered Samuel back into her arms.

Charles didn't speak until they were through the narrow pass and had trundled past the lumber mills with their screeching saws. Then he reached behind the seat to lift out a jug of whisky. "Got food?" he asked. Grateful for the reprieve, Gregoria reached under the seat for her bundle of biscuits and meat.

~ ~ ~

The cabin door was open when Benjamin Houx's horse trotted into the Kennedy yard. Charles was sitting on the chopping block just outside the door, a noggin of whisky in his hand. Gregoria was in the garden, Samuelito sitting in the grass nearby and look-ing intently at a small stick in his hand. Ben reined in at the corral and dismounted.

"Whiskey?" Kennedy asked him.

"No thanks," Ben said. "I'm here in an official capacity." He glanced toward the garden, where Gregoria had stopped working and was watching them. He raised his voice slightly. "I understand Deputy Fitzmaurice served you a couple of summonses yesterday."

"Deputy?"

"Fitzmaurice is the other Elizabethtown deputy. He's deputized at a few District court sessions and thinks he knows the law." Ben grimaced and pushed back his hat. "I guess he thought he'd save himself a trip out this way."

"Damn fool," Charles growled.

The deputy grinned. "I won't argue that point," he said. "I came out to say that they are official papers, even if you got them in an unofficial way."

Charles grunted and took a drink of his whisky.

"One of them's for that dust-up with Coleman last November. The other one's been filed by young Baker. He says you have some money of his."

"Embezzlement," Charles growled sarcastically.

Ben nodded. "That's what the grand jury called it. I think you know that both bills will be called at the August court session in Etown. The session starts the twenty-sixth. I wanted to make sure you knew the date. If you're wantin' a lawyer, Mills is in town. Or you can wait and sign on with one of the court circuit riders."

"Got a lawyer," Kennedy grunted and frowned into his whisky.

Gregoria had left her work and carried Samuel toward the house. She stopped at the edge of the corral and the child squirmed in her arms, wanting to be set down. Charles glanced up and gestured her impatiently toward the cabin door. She went inside without looking at either man as Charles continued to scowl into his drink.

After a long moment, Ben stirred, "Well, that was all I came to say. Guess I'll be heading out." He paused, but when Charles didn't look up, he resettled his hat and moved toward his horse. "I'll be seein' you in August, I guess."

As Houx mounted his mare, Charles grunted and looked up. "You tell Fitzmaurice t' stay out o' my way," he growled.

Ben chuckled. "I'll be happy to," he said as he turned his horse's head toward the road.

PALO FLECHADO PASS, MIDSUMMER 1870

Early in July, there was a thud on the door shortly after sunup, long before anyone was likely to be stopping for a mid-day meal. Gregoria was kneeling beside the fire, preparing tortiás. Samuel stirred uneasily in his nest of blankets and Charles stumbled from the bed and opened the door.

"Good morning, sir," a man said in a thin high-pitched voice. "How are you this fine day?"

Gregoria turned her head. She could just see a short thin man with pale hair clutching a thick book and holding a pencil.

"What d'ya want?" Charles demanded, blocking the doorway.

"Uh. Well sir, my name is McCullough." He coughed anxiously. "That is, I am J.B. McCullough, and I have been authorized to collect United States Census data for the Elizabeth City postal district. I'm here today—"

"Census?"

"Yes, sir. The United States Congress has established this year, 1870, as a census year and authorized funds for the collection of data from each of its residents." He coughed again. "As New Mexico is a Territory of the United States, it is necessarily included—"

"Fer taxes?" There was real menace in Charles' voice. Samuel whimpered, and Gregoria moved her griddle off the fire and stood, ready to go to him.

"Oh no, sir, I am not here to collect money of any kind." The man smiled placatingly. "I am just here to collect information."

249

He lifted his book. "I will write it in here and then turn it in to the authorities in Santa Fe."

"Ain't comin' in."

The man nodded anxiously. "Certainly sir. Whatever you say, sir. All I absolutely need is your name and—" He craned his neck, peering into the room. "That of your wife. And did I hear a child as well?"

"None o' your business."

The man coughed again. "Well, actually sir, I'm afraid it is my business," he said apologetically. "I am charged with recording the name, origin, occupation, and age of all the persons living in each household in Colfax County, as well as the amount of any real or personal property."

"Charles Kennedy."

"Sir?"

"Name."

"Oh! Yes, sir." The thin little man balanced the back of his book against the door jamb, licked his pencil, and wrote. "Occupation?"

There was a long pause, then Charles said, "Carpenter."

"And origin?"

"What?"

"Where were you born, sir?"

Charles studied the smaller man for a long moment, then grunted, "Tennessee."

"And your age, sir?"

Charles moved impatiently. "None o' your business."

"Oh, well, I can estimate, sir."

Charles grunted.

"And your wife's name, sir?"

"Rosa!" Charles bellowed over his shoulder.

Gregoria moved slightly, toward the door. "My name is Gregoria," she said from across the room, careful not to look directly at the anxious little man with his book.

"I'm sorry, ma'am, what was that you said?"

"Gregoria."

She saw him scribble something hastily, then lean forward to peer past Charles into the darkened room, trying to make her out. "And the child? There is just the one child?"

"Sam'l." Charles' hand was on the door now, pushing it shut. "That's all."

"And their ages, sir?"

"None o' your business."

The woman came closer. "I have diecisiete anos," she said. "El nene has uno—"

McCullough's eyes swung toward her, then looked at Charles. "I don't know Spanish," he said apologetically.

"She's seventeen," Charles growled. "Baby's one." He moved the door, narrowing the man's view of the interior.

"But sir, I am required—"

Charles shut the door in the man's face and latched it sharply. He scowled at Gregoria. "None o' his business." Then he grinned at her malevolently. "Think I was gonna hurt him?" He moved restlessly toward the fire. "Shoulda. Nosy bastard."

"Mamá?" Samuel asked. Gregoria moved to the bed, relieved that the man was gone, that Charles felt he had bested him.

Outside, J. B. McCullough mounted his horse and urged it away from the cabin. He was well into the valley before he stopped to finish his notations. The man Charles looked to be in his early thirty's, he thought. The cabin and real estate were worth perhaps six hundred dollars. The garden was large and obviously tended by the woman. Perhaps worth a hundred fifty. She seemed

251

a sweet enough thing. Clearly New Mexican. Certainly more informative than her husband. How she could stand living with that great hulk of a black-bearded bear was more than he, J.B. McCullough, could imagine. This had been the first of the many homes he was tasked with visiting on his census-taking duties. He hoped the others would be a little more gracious. He frowned, considering the last set of columns on the census form. There'd been no opportunity to ask if either of the adults could read or write. Surely they could. He shrugged, marked the boxes accordingly, then spurred his horse down the slope toward the next dwelling.

In the cabin, Gregoria completed her preparations for the morning meal with a sense of relief. Charles hadn't assaulted the man with the book and pencil, and he hadn't punished her for her interference. But there was still tension in his shoulders and face, a brooding anger that lingered long after the census taker had gone. The man's questions had reminded Charles of the looming threat of taxation and, with the sale of the Maxwell land grant, the uncertainty of his hold on the cabin and hollow. And then there was the lawsuit of young Baker. Gregoria hoped desperately that Baker would stay away until after the court met in August, though she refused to articulate to herself just what she thought Charles might do to prevent Baker from appearing there.

~ ~ ~

Gregoria straightened, hoe in one hand while she rubbed the small of her back with the other, and squinted at the dusty road leading toward Elizabethtown. A man walked rapidly toward her, dark against the golden grasses on the ridge behind him. As he came nearer, she saw that he was veering off the road, heading across the grass toward the hollow. She looked toward the cabin door. It was open, Charles looming just inside.

"Rosa!" he bellowed. Gregoria sighed. He would wake Samuel, who she'd left napping on the bed. She dropped her hoe and headed toward the cabin.

The visitor reached the door before she reached the corral. As she paused there, he took off his hat and her heart sank. It was Edward Baker. He tilted his head, looking up at Charles with a sideways glance, then down at the ground. Charles stood in the cabin door, blocking the way.

"I come to talk 'bout that money I left with you," Baker said apologetically.

"What money?" Charles growled.

"My hun'red and three dollars. An' my goods." Baker glanced up at Charles, then down at his own feet. He rubbed a spot on the ground with his left toe. "I swore out a complaint."

"Embezzlement," Charles grunted.

Baker nodded without looking up. "That's what the court called it." He glanced sideways at Charles. "All I know is, you still got my money."

"Tol' you I don'."

Baker raised his head with an effort and looked into Charles' face, then away. "You give me my money, an' I'll tell the judge it was just a misunderstanding. I won't even ask fer my trade goods."

Charles moved as if to come out the door, then pulled back. An instant later his rifle barrel was level with Baker's chest. Gregoria shrank toward the corral, reaching for the nearest rail.

Baker's hands went up. "I— I was just tryin'—"

"Tryin'," Charles sneered. He gestured with the rifle. "Try leavin'."

Baker nodded nervously and backed away, toward the road.

"Other way." Charles stepped through the doorway, gun barrel level with Baker's chest.

Baker looked into his face, naked terror in his eyes. Charles chuckled and gestured with the gun toward the mountainside behind the corral. Baker twisted toward the trees, almost falling in his haste. Charles snorted, pointed the barrel upward, and fired. The sound blasted across the landscape and the baby inside the cabin began to wail as Baker rushed past Gregoria and toward the trees at the northern edge of the hollow.

Gregoria bit her lip and slipped into the house. She gathered Samuel into her arms and carried him into the yard. The two men had circled the corral and were in the forest beyond the garden, Baker stumbling over the rocky ground as it sloped upward, Charles behind him, rifle pointing at Baker's back. As they disappeared into the trees, Gregoria heard another blast from the gun, then another.

There was a long silence, then another blast, farther up the mountainside. "Pobre hombre," she murmured. Poor man.

But she hadn't seen Baker fall. Perhaps Charles had only meant to frighten him, to make him go away. She released the breath she had been unconsciously holding. That was it, she was sure of it.

Samuel squirmed in her arms and she set him on the ground. He turned his head, looking around the yard. "Papá?" he asked.

She smiled at him in spite of her anxiety. How he was beginning to talk! And so early! What a smart child he was!

"Papá come soon," she told him. "Papá come soon."

PALO FLECHADO PASS, FALL, 1870

Two weeks later, Theodore Wheaton was back, riding in on the same brown and white pinto, still dressed all in black. His head was down, hat brim shielding his face from the sun and blocking his view of everything except the pinto's head and what lay just beyond it. He was so preoccupied that he didn't appear to see Gregoria cleaning the drinking water bucket beside the door. The pinto headed for the corral and Wheaton swung down, tossed the bridle reins over the top rail, and moved toward the cabin.

Gregoria paused in her work, prepared to offer a greeting, but Wheaton didn't acknowledge her. He knocked on the door, then entered without waiting for an invitation. On his first visit, he had not appeared to be this kind of person and Gregoria frowned slightly as she gathered up her kindling and followed him inside. She glanced automatically toward the bed, where Samuel lay sleeping, then her attention swung to the two men.

Charles had risen from his stool by the fire and he and Wheaton faced each other, firelight flickering across their faces. The lawyer had removed his hat and put on his blandest expression.

"Edward Baker didn't show, just as you predicted," he said. Gregoria moved toward the kitchen area and he glanced around in surprise, then turned back to Charles. "Judge Palen was rather irritated by that. Baker had guaranteed he'd be there the first day of court. When he didn't appear by the end of the third day, Palen declared his bond forfeited and dismissed the case." He shrugged and looked at the fire, his face troubled. "So that's settled."

Charles grunted. He moved toward the table. "Drink?"

"No, thank you." Wheaton continued to look into the flames. "The assault charge went quickly enough." A note of self-importance crept into his voice. "Just as I predicted." He turned his head. "I pled you guilty for simple assault and the fine was ten dollars."

The whisky jug thudded onto the table. "You said five."

"As I recall, I said it could be anywhere from ten to fifteen."

"Ten!" Charles growled in disgust. He lifted the jug, took a healthy swallow, then wiped his mouth with the back of his hand. "Bastard Coleman."

"I doubt he'll be stopping by to bother you any further," Wheaton said drily.

Charles lifted the jug again.

"I paid the fine for you, along with the court costs." Wheaton stirred, as if to leave the fire, watching Charles' face. "Since we agreed that my own fees would be paid in meals over the next half-year, if you'll reimburse me for the fine, I'll be on my way."

There was a long pause as Charles fingered the whisky jug and the lawyer watched Charles. Gregoria stood as if spell-bound, nerves tingling.

Then Samuel woke from his nap and whimpered "Mamá?" and all of the adults moved at once.

Gregoria crossed the room to the bed, Charles put down the jug, and Wheaton moved toward the table.

"It's only the fine that I'm asking you for," Wheaton said. "I covered the court fees myself."

Charles grunted and nodded unwillingly. He turned and crossed the room to the shed door.

Wheaton looked at Gregoria questioningly.

"I think he is finding the money," she said softly, without looking at him. She lifted Samuel from the bed and stood him on the floor. The baby wobbled a moment, then began walking carefully toward the fire. Gregoria and the lawyer watched him as if his steps were the most important thing in their world.

As Charles came back into the room, Samuel half-turned toward him, then sat down with a thump onto the floor. He laughed, rolled over onto his hands and knees, and began crawling toward the fire. Wheaton and Gregoria both chuckled, but Charles ignored him. He handed Wheaton a small bag of coins.

Wheaton looked at him in surprise, started to open the bag, then thought better of it. "That'll be all then," he said, starting for the door.

"Receipt," Charles said from behind him.

Wheaton stopped, turned, looked into Charles' face, then went to the table. He pulled a pencil and small book out of his pocket, scribbled some words in the book, tore out the page, and handed it over.

Charles glanced at the paper and folded it into his pocket.

Wheaton headed again for the door. "I expect I'll be seeing you in a few weeks' time," he said. "As I said, I have business developing in Ocaté, so I'll be travelling through and happy to take my fees in your wife's raised biscuits."

Charles grunted and followed him to the door.

Gregoria busied herself straightening the bed. When she turned, Charles was sitting in front of the fire with a scowl on his face. "Ten dollars," he growled. "More'n twenty meals!" He leaned forward and spat into the fire. "Damn law!"

On the floor beside him, Samuel reached up for his father's knee, to raise himself to a standing position. Charles shoved his hand away and the child slipped back onto his bottom. He turned and looked at his mother questioningly, his mouth open to fuss, and she put her finger to her lips, shushing him.

~ ~ ~

There was a rush of guests during the next few days, as people connected with the court filtered back to Taos and Etown merchants began bringing in the merchandise they'd need during the winter months, when the pass would be too dangerous for wagons. All the talk was of the events of the court session and of the changes coming to the area now that Lucien Maxwell had sold out. Apparently, there were agents for the new Maxwell Land Grant Company already making the rounds, collecting rents and asking to see title papers.

Charles became more silent the longer the talk continued and Gregoria became more anxious. His taciturnity was filled with a dense fury and she kept her eyes on the floor and Samuel out of the guests' way as much as she could. It would take little to set Charles off. She didn't want Samuel to be the cause of it.

After a week or so, the flood of visitors eased off and Charles' suppressed anger also seemed to cool. Still, there was a brooding quality to him. Gregoria eased carefully in and out of the house, trying to appease him without appearing to do so. This seemed to help and she had begun to think his dark mood had lifted when she came in from the garden one afternoon with a bushel basket of alverjones, peas, to be shelled and found him at the table with half a dozen stacks of gold and silver coins arranged before him. He sat scowling at them and fingering a thick wad of greenbacks. The discontent on his face warned her into silence as she went to her work sink.

Gregoria began splitting pods, dropping the peas into a separate bowl. She put a handful of the tiniest peas to one side, to feed to

Samuel, who lay sleeping on the bed. He would enjoy the sweet intensity of their flavor, the greenness of them.

"'Nother year," Charles said from the table. "If taxes don' get it."

She turned her head. "Yes?"

"Then I go." He gestured at the coins. "Homestead an' cattle."

She nodded. "In a place that is warmer in winter?"

"Without taxes." He grinned at her maliciously. "Too hot fer you. Just me'n the boy."

Her stomach tightened and her hands froze as she looked into Charles' face. Then he chuckled and began gathering up his coins.

Gregoria bit her lip and went back to her work. There was a great number of alverjones to be shelled. The summer had produced a bountiful crop. Charles is just toying with me, she told herself. He will need me for cooking and cleaning, if not to satisfy his physical urges. And for caring for Samuel. Not even Charles is cruel enough to separate a child from its mother.

A man who will kill for money. The thought rose unbidden and she pushed it and her panic firmly away as she dropped a handful of peas into her bowl and began removing yet another green covering. Charles was just trying to upset her. He didn't truly mean what he said. Besides, he didn't kill for money, he killed out of jealousy. Hadn't he told her often enough that the killings were her fault, that she should keep her eyes to herself? And yet— But she wouldn't let herself think about that or his threat to take the child away from her. She would think of something pleasant, like the good smell of the peas as she ran her thumb nail along the inside of the pods, revealing the tiny green pearls within.

~ ~ ~

Charles said nothing further about his plans and Gregoria drifted once again into living each day for its small beauties. As the weather cooled and the aspens on the valley's mountainsides began to lighten, then grow golden, she focused on preserving her garden produce against the coming winter, cooking and drying and making places for everything in the shed.

Charles spent most of his waking hours counting and recounting his coins, but Gregoria resolutely turned her eyes away from this activity and stayed outdoors as much as possible, taking Samuel with her.

They were in the garden gathering more peas when an Indian man rode down the trail from Taos. Two mules and a horse were linked on the lead rope behind his mount. Gregoria gathered child and basket and headed toward the cabin, entering it as the man turned off the road into the hollow.

"A guest," she said, a little breathlessly.

Charles looked up, scowled, and swept his stack of coins into its leather pouch. For such a big man, he could move swiftly when he needed to. He was across the room, money out of sight behind the bed, and at the door before the Indian and his animals had reached the corral.

Gregoria put her basket of produce aside. The man would want something hot and there was no time for shelling the sweet green alverjones. She still had biscuits from yesterday's baking. The broth on the hearth had sufficient meat in it, if she served it over the biscuits. She bent to stir it again. Perhaps she should add some corn to it. Or a few of the peas, if there was time.

The men came into the room, then Charles went out again, to tend to the animals. Gregoria nodded politely to the Indian man, eyes carefully averted. He had a kind but strong face, she saw, glancing sideways at him. Eyes that seemed to take in the room with one look. He sat down before the fire. Strands of white danced among the black in his shoulder-length hair, silver in the firelight. She could feel his eyes following her as she went about her tasks, but she was careful not to look up. He said something to her in his native tongue as Charles came in the door.

"She no Injun," Charles said sharply. He crossed the room and looked down at the man menacingly. "My woman." He shoved at the Indian's shoulder. "You wan' talk, you talk me."

"I apologize," the man said quietly in americano. "I thought she was Ute like me, or at least partly so."

"Ain't," Charles growled. He turned and nodded curtly at Gregoria. "Food ready?"

"Un momento," Gregoria said, her head bent. She knew the man hadn't meant to insult her. But he had four animals with him. Her stomach tightened and nausea burned in her throat. Pray Dios the Ute didn't look at her again.

But she knew the signs were not good. Charles was silent and sullen as they ate and, although their guest didn't speak to her again, he grunted approvingly at the flavoring Gregoria had given the meat and spoke softly in americano to Samuel, asking him if he had learned yet how to hunt.

Charles glowered at him. "Damn Injun," Gregoria heard him mutter as she stood behind him with a wooden bowl full of stew.

She bit her lip and touched him tentatively on the shoulder. "More food, mi esposo?" she asked. But his muscles were tight beneath his shirt and he didn't acknowledge her presence.

She turned away. How could she tell the man that he was in danger without Charles knowing, without making it more likely that Charles would harm him? There was little chance Charles would leave the cabin now. There was no reason. I am as trapped as the Indian is, she thought bleakly. There was nothing she could do, except somehow guard Samuel from seeing what was bound to happen.

A wave of hopelessness flooded over her. And how could she do that? She began gathering the dishes up and called the child to help clean them. He was old enough, she thought. The dishes were wooden and wouldn't break if he dropped them on the dirt floor.

"Out o' there!" Charles barked from the fire, where the men had retreated. Gregoria turned. He was gesturing to Samuel. "Women's work," he growled. He glanced at the Ute, who stared into the flames. "Go play," he told the boy sharply.

"Sí papá." Samuel used both hands to give his mother the wooden bowl he'd been trying to wipe out with a cloth and toddled to the floor near the bed. He sat down and began drawing designs in the dirt with his finger. Gregoria saw the Indian man watching him and turned away.

She heard the man get up and cross the room to the child. "You have marbles?" he asked. "How do you say it? Canicas?"

The boy looked up at him with a slight frown, then he reached under the branches that supported the bedding, biting his lip in concentration. He pulled out several small rocks, almost perfectly round and held them up with a smile. "Can'ca," he said.

The man nodded. "They are good." He reached into a pocket, pulled out a single golden cats-eye marble, and held it up to the light that flickered into the corner from the fireplace. "But they are not like this."

Samuel gasped in appreciation, his small fingers reaching up involuntarily.

The man chuckled and slipped the marble back into his pocket. "It is mine," he said reprovingly.

Samuel's face fell and he turned his head away, reaching for his pretty rocks.

Then Charles was standing behind the man, his hand in his hair, pulling his head backward, his knife flashing against the Ute's throat.

"Charles!" Gregoria cried, the dish in her hand thudding to the floor. "Not before Samuel!"

Charles ignored her. Instead, he looked down at his son. The child stared back at him, his face holding more fascination than fear.

The Ute's hands reached back, groping for a hold, and then Charles' hand moved downward and the knife went into the man's heart. He slumped onto the floor, eyes glazing, blood spurting onto the dirt.

Samuel stared down at the dying man, then looked up at his father, dark eyes puzzled. "Man die?" he asked.

Charles snorted. He turned to Gregoria, who was standing empty-handed beside the table, staring across the room. "Not before Samuel," he mimicked sardonically.

She looked at him, glanced at Samuel, who was leaning forward to look at the dead Ute, and turned blindly back to her wash basin. She clutched the side of the bench on which it sat and leaned forward, nausea assailing her. It is too much, she thought wildly. Already he is becoming like his father. I must get him away from here.

Behind her, Charles was going through the Ute's pockets while Samuel watched. Charles handed the child the golden cats-eye marble, then pulled out two more. "Holding out on ya," he said. "'Member that."

The boy looked down at the round spheres in his hands, the firelight catching the colors and making them glow. "Can'ca," he said.

"Marbles!" Charles said sharply. "Say it right."

263

"Mar— bel," the child repeated obediently, still looking at his new treasures.

"Yers now." Charles bent to lift the limp body. "Rosa," he barked. "Shovel."

Something inside her snapped. "There is no room in the garden," she said, without turning. "It is too dark to dig now and too cold. The burying must wait until morning."

Charles paused, the man still in his arms, and stared across the room at her for a long moment. Finally, he growled, "Morning," and carried the body into the shed, blood dripping onto his boots and the floor.

Samuel toddled to the fire, marbles in both hands. He held them up, gazing at the fire's reflection in their smooth surfaces. "Can'ca," he said contentedly.

Gregoria didn't respond. She stood in the kitchen area and stared at the wall, her hands still gripping the bench. Her son was becoming a monster. I must go, she thought. Yet, if I try to take Samuelito away, Charles will come after us. He wants a son so desperately. He will not let us go peacefully. But if I stay, how can I teach the boy that what his father does is wrong while I continue to watch him do it without protesting? Charles' jealousy and anger and greed are all so connected. How can I raise a child to distinguish between them, so he will understand, love, and pity, but not imitate, his father?

She was still reeling with the pain and uncertainty of it as she began preparing for bed. Even Charles noticed her silence and grief. His response was to take her roughly by the shoulders and pin her to the wall, reaching between her legs.

At the foot of the bed, Samuel stirred in his blankets. "Mamá?" he asked. But Charles growled "Quiet!" and the child subsided. Gregoria closed her eyes and submitted to Charles' demands.

He still desires me, she thought with a cold despair. He will come after me for my own sake, as well as that of el nene. And I have nowhere to go, no one to turn to, not even mi padre. I don't even know if he is still alive. He has abandoned me yet again. The tears rose unbidden but she bit them back, not daring to weep as Charles assuaged his needs.

~ ~ ~

Gregoria woke to a clear morning and rolled over to stare at the blood-spotted floor. Charles was not in the cabin. He is dealing with the Ute's body, she thought wearily.

The cougars would most likely get the kind-faced man, since Charles hadn't roused her to dig in the garden. A wave of revulsion shuddered through her.

But there was work to be done. She must dig out the bloody spots in the floor and bring in dirt to smooth over the resulting indentations. Samuel stirred in his blankets and she sat up.

She fed him quickly, then bundled him against the September chill and sent him outside to play. As she opened the door, she saw that the Indian's animals were still in the corral. She went back inside to begin cleaning the floor.

Left to himself, Samuel toddled straight to the corral. He was reaching up to stroke the nose of the smallest of the Ute's horses when a slender mexicano man rode a stocky black stallion into the hollow. He was leading two well-loaded pack mules and his horse's trappings gleamed with silver.

"Buenos días," the man said. He tipped his hat to the child and smiled, flashing brilliant white teeth above a carefully trimmed black beard.

"Hola," Samuel answered shyly.

The man rode up to the corral and dismounted. "Agua?" he asked.

Samuel frowned, confused. The man turned toward the door, saw the water bucket and dipper, and moved toward it, the child following.

The man took a long drink and replaced the dipper. "Gracias." He smiled at Samuel and looked toward the animals in the corral. "Your papá is a rich man. He has a great many horses and mules." He moved toward the corral.

By the cabin, Samuel laughed delightedly. "Rico!" he agreed happily. He pulled a marble out of his pocket. "Can'cas," he said. "Papa kill injun." He looked at the corral, then the marble. "Horsies y can'cas."

The man's well-groomed face lost its smile. He turned toward the child. Surely, he had misunderstood. The boy was still a baby, really. Then movement at the far edge of the rough-built cabin caught his eye. A great burly man with an unkempt black beard had come around the building and was glaring at him, a rifle in his hands. The big man strode forward and was beside the child in two steps. He shoved him aside with his foot, toward the house. As the child fell, the gun barrel roared.

The rico's hand reached for his holstered pistol, but it was already too late. He crumpled where he stood. Beside the corral, his stallion whinnied and crowded the pack mules as they bunched together, eyes rolling.

Gregoria was at the door, peering out. Charles glanced at her, then at Samuel, who still lay sprawled against the cabin's stone foundation. "Stupid!" he growled. He turned to the dead rico, slung him over his shoulder, and carried him around the cabin to the shed. He stripped the body of valuables, grunting with pleasure when he found the man's wallet. It was comfortably full of greenbacks. Maybe the land would come sooner than he'd thought. The man's packs had also looked heavy with goods.

Feeling more cheerful, Charles carried the body up the hillside behind the cabin and dumped it into a small ravine for the wild-cats. Then he went back to the house and corral. Gregoria was squatting next to the child, her hand on his shoulder. "Gettup!" Charles growled as he went by, but neither responded.

Charles stripped the saddle from the stallion and a pack from one of the mules and turned back to Gregoria. "Take 'im inside," he barked, but she only rocked backwards to sit in the dirt and look up at him, her face stricken. Her mouth opened, then shut again. Tears began streaming down her face. She shook her head wordlessly.

"Stupid bitch," Charles muttered, and turned away to carry the saddle and pack around the cabin to the shed. He made another trip for the rest of the packs, then paused in the shed to examine their contents.

When he returned to the yard, Gregoria was still sitting in the dirt. She'd turned her back to the cabin's foundation, lifted the child into her lap, and was staring at the mountains on the far side of the valley. Silent tears streamed down her face as she ran her hand over Samuel's black head.

Charles scowled at her. "Ain't got all day."

Gregoria looked up at him as if she'd never seen him before. Wordlessly, she pointed at Samuel's head. Charles leaned down to shake the child awake, then pulled back. He stared down at the boy's vacant eyes, then grabbed him from Gregoria's arms and half-ran into the cabin.

Finally, Gregoria spoke. "Samuelito!" she cried as she fol-lowed her husband inside.

Charles carried the boy across the room and laid him on the bed.

"What happened?" Gregoria looked up at Charles, her eyes dark with pain. "His head, it is broken."

"You don' teach him," Charles growled. He turned away, moving to the shelf that held the whisky jug. "Got in th' way. Fell." He sat down facing the fire and lifted the jug to his lips.

Gregoria moved swiftly to the door.

"Get back here!" Charles yelled. She ignored him and he slumped back onto the stool.

When Gregoria returned, she was silent. The water dipper freshly used, the packs she'd glimpsed in the shed, the animals in the corral, the blood near the corral and on the cabin's foundation stones. All this and Charles' actions when she'd first come out the door. The tale was clear enough.

Gregoria went to the bed. She sat down, lifted Samuel's body onto her lap, and looked across the room. Charles' face was morose in the firelight, the whisky jug in his hand. Her mind felt dull, and heavy with pain. She stared at the curve of her child's cheeks and felt nothing. It was too large an event. Her mind wouldn't allow it to be, couldn't feel what it meant.

There was a long silence, then Charles growled, "Fire's dyin'." Automatically, without looking at him, Gregoria moved to replenish it, then returned to the bed.

"Ya spoiled 'im," Charles said to the fire.

Gregoria didn't answer. Tears blinded her eyes as she stroked the battered head on her lap.

"Gone," Charles' voice was slurring already, as if his desire to get drunk was making the alcohol affect him more quickly than usual. "Yer fault!" he bellowed. He turned to glare at her, but his eyes fell on Samuel's body, and he jerked back to face the fire.

Gregoria lifted Samuel into her arms, cradling him. Her mind knew he was dead, yet her heart found it impossible to believe. She put her face in his hair. It still smelled sweet, of little boy sweat, even with the blood and the rocky debris from the wall. She stifled a sob and looked up at Charles. He glared at her and she lowered her face again.

Then a wave of anger swept over her. What did it matter if Charles didn't like her tears? Samuelito was dead. She raised her head defiantly and let the tears come. Quietly, though, not wanting Charles to cross the room and disturb her grief.

"Yer fault!" he bellowed again. He began to mumble at the fire, a low angry rumble that she blocked out with her own grief. But after a long while, her tears finally slowed enough that she could allow Charles' words into her consciousness.

"Been gone, wasn't fer you," he mumbled. "Me and him. Old enough. Shoulda gone. South. Warm." He turned slightly, steadying himself on the stool, and his boot caught the edge of the other stool. He kicked it out of the way and the stool fell on its side and rolled toward the fire. "Stupid bitch," he growled. "Lettin' 'im run." He lifted the jug to his lips, then jiggled it in front of his face. "Rosa!" he bellowed, eyes still on the fire. "Rosa! More whisky!"

Out of long habit, her body responded. Gregoria shifted Samuel's limp form from her arms and crawled off the bed. She slipped into the shed and rummaged for another jug. As she turned back to the cabin entrance, her eyes fell on the rico's gear and packs, truly looking at them for the first time. The packs had clearly been opened and their contents examined.

She stared at them, her mind processing what it meant. While she was crouched over Samuel's inert body, Charles had been going through the dead man's goods. Her husband was a cuadrúpedo, a four-footed beast. He hadn't even noticed that Samuel was injured, that he'd killed him with one blow. He'd been too busy searching the dead man's goods.

"Rosa!" Charles bellowed from the fireside. Automatically, Gregoria moved toward the cabin. Then she stopped. Why was she doing this?

But keeping him drunk will allow me to grieve in peace, she told herself. If only he will become drunk enough to be silent. The burden of her grief suddenly overwhelmed her. Her knees buckled and she leaned against the unbarked log walls and gasped at the pain of it.

"Rosa!" Charles bellowed again.

Gregoria straightened, wiped the tears from her face with the back of her hand, and carried the jug into the cabin.

He yanked it from her hand. "Whore," he said, without looking at her. "Bitch."

"Why are you angry with me, Charles?" she asked quietly. "I did not kill the child."

"Killed himself," Charles said. He pointed a finger at her. "Ya don' teach 'im. Always talkin' and babblin'."

"He was just a baby. And you loved him." She studied his face. He avoided her glance, staring sullenly into the fire. He lifted the jug to his mouth. "As you did me, once," she said wearily. She crept back to the bed to sit beside Samuel's body.

After a long while, she noticed that Charles had moved from the fire to the table, his back to her. The whisky jug sat on the floor beside him. There was a stack of coins on the table and a wad of greenbacks in his hand. He was counting the rico's money.

Suddenly, he lifted his shaggy black head toward the ceiling. "No reason!" he roared. He threw the greenbacks onto the table and swept a hand across the coins, flinging them onto the floor, where they rolled in every direction. Then he raised the whisky jug unsteadily to his lips. The liquid dribbled onto his beard. He wiped at his face with his free hand and turned to scowl at Gregoria.

"Love," he growled. "What love? Cheaper'n whores. Needed money." He gestured toward the child's body. "Shoulda been you." He glared at her with bleary eyes. "Shoulda been you!" he bellowed. He started to rise, then sank back to the table. "You." His head tilted forward, toward the table.

He is drunk, she thought. The drink makes him speak foolishly.

Yet part of her knew he spoke the truth and that she had known for a long time that it was so. He had never loved her. The coins nearest the fire glinted in the light and she stared at them in a grief-induced trance.

"Needed money!" Charles bellowed suddenly. His head came up and his fist slammed onto the table. More coins rolled over its edge. "Rico. No one lookin' down on me! Sons o' bitches." His head swayed toward the table again. "Shoulda gone." His words slurred into each other. "Take son. Leave whore. Sumplace warm. Goddamn. Sons o' bitches."

At last he was quiet, his head on the table, eyes closed and mouth open, greenbacks clutched in one hand while a finger of the other was hooked into the handle of the whisky jug on the floor beside him.

The fire was dying down and Gregoria was cold, but she had no wish to rouse Charles again. She maneuvered a blanket from beneath Samuel's body and wrapped it around her shoulders. She stared across the room at Charles' back. Her mind worked slowly, but more clearly than it had in a long while, perhaps ever.

She knew in her heart that what he said was true. He'd had a physical need to assuage, so he'd taken her to wife.

But we used each other, she acknowledged bleakly. I felt more gratitude than love, thankful to get away from the saloon, for food and clothes. Providing those was his part of the bargain. Mine was to satisfy his physical needs and give him a son.

She hunched forward, the grief hitting her again. Samuelito. Oh nene. How would she bear it?

After a little while, she sat up and blinked back the tears. Now that Samuel was gone, Charles had no reason to accumulate coins and greenbacks. She shook her head and a long shudder ran through her as she thought of where most of his money had come from. The deaths of those men had never been the result of Charles' jealousy. She saw that now, the thing she had denied for so long. Charles had used any attention to her, and then to the child, as an excuse to kill. The money was his true objective. How could she have been so blind?

She closed her eyes. He said it was all useless, that there was no need now for what he had accumulated, but she didn't believe him. Once his grief had calmed, the desire for wealth would return, perhaps even more strongly. The killings wouldn't stop. They had begun before the child was born and they would continue. He would still long to be rico, to revenge himself on anyone who appeared to have what he wished for. And he seemed to crave the increasing weight of the hidden bags of coins, the thickening of greenbacks in the old leather wallet. He would be unable to stop what he had been doing.

Gregoria smoothed Samuel's hair. She had considered leaving, but the child had held her back. She had known that Charles would not let him go and she could not go without him. She also knew that if she had taken the baby and gone, she would have had no way to care for him. She had no skills. She had only her body to sell and what kind of life was that for a child? And her father—

Even if she knew that he was still alive, even if she knew where he was, he had so little. It was pointless to ask for help that could not be given.

I was afraid, she thought dully. Afraid of what Charles would do if I left with the child. Afraid of his anger, my own inadequacies, that my father would fail me again, if he still lives.

A great sob choked her throat. She swallowed it down. So she had stayed and Charles had killed Samuelito. And he will probably kill me at some point, she thought wearily. In a fit of anger or just out of malice, if he feels so inclined. If he decides he no longer needs me physically.

Gregoria turned her head, the tears coming again. Not that it would matter if Charles should kill her. Death was preferable to life without her nene. He had been the one bright spot, her only joy. She would be content to go with him to the grave.

She wiped the tears from her cheeks with the back of her hand. All those men. Charles Lamb, the very first, with his smile and his innocence. The merchant Evans. The red-haired Judge with his courtesy and his Christmas greetings. The Ute, the strands of silver gleaming in his hair. None of them deserved to die for Charles' dream of wealth. And Edward Baker, running into the forest. Had she really thought he had escaped Charles' anger, his lust for blood? She had wanted so much to believe it was so.

She stroked her dead child's head, smoothing the hair away from his eyes. But she was also guilty. Not of provoking Charles' jealousy, but of not finding a way to stop him. For not leaving. She had been afraid, first for herself and then for Samuel. But he had killed Samuel anyway, in spite of all her precautions, and now she wasn't sure she really cared what happened to her. There is nothing left to fear, she thought dully.

A sudden stillness came over her. A log popped on the hearth and she looked toward it thoughtfully. At the table, Charles grunted in his sleep and another coin fell to the floor. There really was nothing left to fear. If Charles killed her, she would join Samuelito and the other little one in a far better place. But her hands were bloody, also. Perhaps Dios wouldn't allow her to be with her babies. But if she could evade Charles, then perhaps she could find someone who would put a stop to his madness. And she would be at least somewhat absolved of her part in what had occurred.

Her back straightened and she frowned. The only question was where to find help. Etown was closer than Taos and the road to it lay in the valley, not through the mountains. Even after all this time, the mountains at her back seemed forebodingly dangerous.

Gregoria closed her eyes, bringing up an image of the valley stretching northward, hearing again the swirl of blackbird wings just overhead. This made her think of Samuel and she opened her eyes, closing her mind to the pain, forcing her thoughts onward.

The fall nights were getting colder, although the days were still warm. And the moon was waning. The night would be very dark. She shivered. Mountain lions and other beasts roamed the darkness. But what did it matter? Charles or them— At least she would have tried.

She peered through the cabin's gloom, toward the table. Charles was still slumped across the thick boards, face toward the fire, greenbacks in one hand, the other still linked to the whisky jug.

Gregoria eased Samuel's head from her lap and placed it gently on the bed. She stroked his hair once more and leaned to kiss his forehead. She pulled the blanket off her shoulders and laid it over his body and face. Then she sat up, tightened the moccasins on her feet, and rose from the bed.

Halfway across the room, she turned to take one last look at her son's form, the stillness of him. Her stomach clenched and she felt a wail of grief rising to her lips, but she pushed the pain away with a deep, shuddering sigh. Perhaps it was just as well that it should end this way. How could he have grown up untwisted in this household, with this father? Already she had been unable to shield his eyes and his heart. Already he had looked not at the horror of a man's dead face, but at the contents of that man's pockets. A shudder ran through her again and she turned toward the door.

She hesitated at the row of nails beside the door, then pulled on her black chal and lifted Charles' heavy wool military coat down as well. He had worn it as long she'd known him. As far as she knew, there was no death attached to this garment, at least. As far as I know, she thought wearily as she buttoned the coat under her chin.

She folded the sleeves away from her hands and carefully lifted the latch, trying to be as quiet as possible. The wood scraped and she looked at Charles apprehensively, but he snored on, his face lit by the flames of the fire. Gregoria eased out the door.

The sun had already slipped behind the Pass and the hollow lay in deep shadow. Gregoria paused and looked at the animals in the corral. If she only knew how to ride, or hitch them to the wagon. But she didn't have time for that, anyway. Charles could wake at any moment. She crossed quickly to the road and began walking toward Etown.

There were clouds forming overhead, low and dark, heavy with moisture and cold. Gregoria shivered. She hoped it wouldn't snow. An icy rain began to fall. She paused to tug the chal up over her head and moved on. As she trudged through the gloom and the rain, she tried not to think about what lay behind her: the body of

275

the child, the man drinking his remorse into oblivion, telling himself she was to blame.

But there was no remorse in his soul for the others he had killed. And he would come after her and kill her too, if he woke and realized she was gone. She hesitated, looking behind her into the gloom, straining to hear any evidence of mule or wagon movement, but there was only the thin yip of a coyote in the distance.

Darkness had fallen completely now. She wished it was daylight, so she could watch for eagles overhead. Just the thought of the majestic birds made her feel stronger. She continued northward, trying to ignore the cold rain as it wet the shawl on her head and bit into her face.

Gradually, her anxious thoughts were numbed into silence by the effort to keep going. The ruts in the roadbed filled with icy rainwater and Gregoria tried to stay on the slight rise between them, but it was too dark to see well. Her moccasins were soon soaked through, her feet numb from the cold. She bent her mind toward the rise before her. Once she was past that, her figure would not be visible from the cabin. She turned to look at it again. Nothing stirred in the gloom. It looked so small from here, so huddled into the forest at its back.

She trudged wearily on, topping the ridge. After a long while, the valley will narrow and then I will be on the outskirts of Etown, she told herself encouragingly. But she was so tired already and her feet ached from the cold. A boulder as high as her waist loomed beside the road and she crept to it thankfully, grateful for something to lean against for a moment. The rain was coming from the southwest now, pushing against her left side, and she turned away, facing northeast. She blinked. There were lights shining from a house to the north, on the eastern side of the valley.

She thought back to the wagon trip to Etown. Were they here when she saw what she'd thought was the Kinkaid farm?

But she wasn't certain it was their farm. And if Charles found her there— She shook her head. The Kinkaids were kind people. They didn't deserve what was likely to happen then. No, she would go to Etown. Her fingers clung to the boulder as she moved around it to return to the roadbed.

But she was so tired. Just a few more minutes of rest. She closed her eyes and sank back against the big rock. She was so cold. So tired. Just a few minutes more.

But as she relaxed, she slipped and the rock did not support her. She landed on the edge of the road, its stony surface biting into her hands. The faces of the dead men rose before her eyes. "Lo siento," she moaned to them. "I cannot."

"What's the matter?" a voice asked from the darkness.

Gregoria shook her head. Surely she was dreaming. "Papá?" she muttered as she squinted into the darkness and rain.

Then a hand touched her shoulder. "Is it you?" the voice asked. "María Gregoria? Is it you?"

She rubbed a hand over her face. "Papá?"

His arms were around her then, lifting her up. "Come," he said. "My hut, it is near."

She shook her head. "He has killed Samuelito," she said. Her voice broke and she gulped back the tears. "And the others."

The arms around her stiffened, then relaxed. There was a long silence, filled only with the sound of the icy rain slapping against the wet earth and the rock.

"Mis pecados fueron la causa," her father said at last, his voice muffled. It is on account of my sins. "I was afraid and ran away."

Gregoria shook her head. "I should have taken el nene and gone," she said. "But I was afraid. Also, I didn't want to believe

277

what I knew to be true." A deep shudder ran through her and he moved to pull her closer, but she shook her head and straightened her shoulders. "And now I have nothing to lose," she said. She turned her head, searching for her father's face in the darkness. Her chin lifted. "It is time."

"Sí." His voice trembled a little. "It is time." Together they moved forward into the icy wet night, his arm around her waist, heads bent against the wind.

They trudged northward for what seemed like hours, supporting each other wordlessly, working their way carefully along the icy yet muddy road, feet numb with cold. Finally, the valley narrowed. They passed a track that angled up toward the Baldy Mountain mines, then the lights of the first Etown buildings twinkled out from the hillsides ahead.

Gregoria and her father halted at the same moment, wiped the rain from their faces, then clutched each other more tightly as they moved forward again.

ELIZABETH TOWN, FALL 1870

By the time they reached the buildings on the outskirts of Etown, Gregoria had begun to shiver uncontrollably, despite her father's arm around her waist. The rain had penetrated even the heavy wool of Charles' coat and small shards of ice clung to the chal covering her head. Her vision had narrowed to the few feet of frozen ground directly before her, a tunnel of blackness and cold. She focused only on moving forward, although she couldn't have said where she was going. She was barely conscious of her father's presence. He also seemed unsure of their destination, moving blindly up the frozen mud of the street that led into the town.

As the buildings began to grow closer together, Gregoria forced herself into awareness. I will need to make a decision, she thought dully. His arm is all mi papá has to give me.

As they neared the first building with lights at the window, a door swung open. Gregoria glimpsed a group of men sitting at a table, bottles at their elbows and cards in their hands. There was a burst of raucous laughter. She and her father moved onward.

Her mind worked slowly, trying to remember. Charles had driven the buckboard straight into town and up this street to a grocery in the center of town. Señor Middaugh's. Perhaps that would be a good place. She thought she remembered a porch with a roof. A protection from the icy rain.

Just ahead, another saloon door swung open. A woman with hard bright eyes looked out. "Don't see 'em!" she called over her shoulder to someone inside. "Looks all clear t' me!" Then a man stumbled past her and down the steps. He leaned into the street and began retching into the icy mud.

Gregoria and her father moved on. The icy rain had turned to tiny drops of hail that slanted sideways in the wind. It stung her face, but she was so numb she could hardly feel it. Only the thought of Middaugh's covered wooden porch kept her going. When they finally arrived there, she saw that only the boards directly under the glass windows were dry. The wind-driven rain had soaked everything else. She huddled against the wall below the window to the right of the door and sank down, her father kneeling beside her.

The burning in her feet had stopped. She couldn't feel anything, really. Just cold. So cold that she didn't even really feel cold any longer. She closed her eyes, her mind as numb as her body. She didn't notice when her father rose, moved to the end of the porch, stood for a long moment looking downhill, then returned to her side.

Only the pressure of his hand on her shoulder brought her back from the fog that enveloped her. "Gregoria!" he said. "María Gregoria!" She shook her head, curling toward the tiny bit of warmth remaining at her core, but he wouldn't stop. "María Gregoria!" There was real panic in his voice now. "Daughter, please wake yourself!"

Gregoria blinked, trying to focus. In the darkness, through the haze blurring her vision, she could just make out her father's face. He was removing his coat.

But he would be cold. She shook her head, her numb hands trying to gesture to him to cover himself, but he pulled her to her feet and wrapped the coat around her shoulders. "Come," he said. "There is a place there." He gestured toward the intersecting street.

She shook her head, confused. How could there be warmth in the street? It was warmer here on the porch. Her eyes closed again and she felt herself tilting toward the window. So cold.

"Come!" her father insisted, his arm around her shoulders. "Please, María Gregoria! Come!" Her legs were stiff and her feet felt like blocks of wood, but Gregoria made a great effort. She felt herself moving over the wooden boards.

Somehow he managed to get her down the set of steps at the end of the porch and into the icy hail once again. She shuddered against it and they turned and stumbled downhill. Gregoria's closed eyelids sensed light and she squinted them open. Golden rays streamed from a window to their left. She frowned, puzzled. Where had the window come from? She tried not to lean so heavily against her father, but her feet were heavy and wouldn't move properly.

Then they were on another porch, this one much smaller than the other. There was no room to lie down. Men's voices sounded from the other side of the door and she tried to focus on what her father was doing. He couldn't seem to get the door open and support her at the same time. Then someone opened it from the inside and they stumbled through, into a sudden silence.

A chair scraped on bare wooden floor and more hands were on her, guiding her to a seat by a pot-bellied stove that crackled with heat. A tall man with gray eyes and a carefully trimmed dark beard was helping her to sit and saying "Brandy!" sharply over his shoulder. Long white fingers lifted a glass to her lips. So unlike Charles' rough hands or the rough wooden noggins he served whisky in. She shuddered at the taste of the alcohol and the sudden thought of Charles, and the man bending over her said, "I apologize, ma'am. Is it too strong?"

She shook her head and he again lifted the glass to her lips. She tried to drink a little more, but her frozen mouth refused the curve of the glass and some of the liquid dribbled down her chin. She turned her head away, so the man wouldn't see, and lifted her hand to her face. A fine cambric handkerchief was slipped into her palm. She put her hands toward each other, pinching the cloth between them, and touched it to her face.

"We need hot broth," the man said, turning away from her. There was a soft southern drawl to his voice. "Gordie, do you have soup on hand?"

There was a babble of voices as the men consulted. Dazedly, Gregoria looked around the room. The bar was a long sort of table at one end, with liquor bottles and a long mirror behind it. Her father stood near one end, his hat in his hand, watching her. The merchant Coleman stood near him. Someone had taken both coats from her shoulders and replaced her wet chal with a small blanket. Two other chairs stood beside the stove where she sat. A table holding a litter of glasses and playing cards stood in one corner. Several men stood near the door, watching her. One of them seemed familiar, but her eyes blurred and then he was gone. Her feet were beginning to thaw and she winced from the pain. "Kennedy's wife?" she heard someone ask.

"Alone," Coleman answered. "Mein Gott."

She looked toward her father and saw that he'd retrieved his coat. He stood by the door, hugging it in his arms as if for warmth, his eyes on her face.

"That's ten miles at least!" a man exclaimed.

The man with the trimmed beard came back, moving carefully toward her with a bowl of hot liquid in his slim white hands. He was tall and slender. More elegant than any man she had ever seen. His blue eyes were watchful but gentle.

He carried the bowl to the table in the corner and turned to the men by the door. "May I gather your cards, gentlemen?" he asked. They nodded and he moved the playing cards and glasses to the far end of the table. Gregoria closed her eyes. The heat and the weariness. The pain and the sorrow. She wanted desperately to lie down.

"Ma'am, if you could gather the strength to take some refreshment, I believe it would benefit you greatly." The blue-eyed man was standing over her again. Gregoria closed her eyes, tightened her muscles, and rose unsteadily. He bent his elbow toward her and she grasped it gratefully. Limping slightly, he led her carefully to the table and pulled out a chair. As she collapsed into it, another man brought a napkin, spoon, and small loaf of bread.

Gregoria looked toward the door, wanting to ask that they bring food for her father, but he gave her a barely-perceptible shake of the head and moved toward the bar.

"Whisky?" the bald-headed man called Gordy asked him.

"Put it on my account," the man named Coleman said.

Gregoria gazed into the bowl of soup and tears sprang into her eyes. Such kindness. She looked up into the sympathetic eyes of the stranger, who had seated himself at the corner of the table.

"And now, ma'am," he said. "Mrs. Kennedy, isn't it? My name is Clay Allison. How can I be of service to you?"

She felt the tears beginning again and covered her face with her hands. "He has killed Samuelito," she said. "My baby boy."

There was a muffled exclamation from the men in the room.

"So many he has killed." She shuddered and looked up. "But now our son."

The eyes of the man across the table had gone hard. "How many?"

"Ten." She shrugged. "Perhaps more. For their gold."

"She speaks truly, Señor Allison," her father said. "The americano last Christmas. The Judge they say vanished to Texas." He moved restlessly, toward the door. "Kennedy killed him when I was there. He ordered me to help him with the body, but I ran away to Taos."

"You didn't tell anyone?" the familiar-looking man demanded. "Damn greaser."

"Shut up, Kinsinger," someone said. "Knowing Kennedy, would you have told?"

José looked at Clay Allison. "I was afraid," he said. "He kills without thinking. Mostly for gold, as she said. But also for anger."

Gregoria nodded, her hands pulling the blanket closer to her shoulders. She was suddenly cold again, in spite of the heat from the stove and the warmth rising from the bowl of soup. The man across the table had gone icily still.

"It is true," Gregoria said. "I thought he killed for jealousy, but truly it is for possessions." She shuddered. "And now el nene. In his anger."

Allison looked toward the bar. "Gordy, can you find this lady a bed fit to sleep in tonight?"

"Sure thing, Clay. Soon as she finishes her soup."

"If you'll excuse me, ma'am," Allison said. He rose from the table, eyes sweeping the room. "Would any of you gentlemen be interested in assisting with the apprehension of a foul murderer?" There was a coldness in the soft southern drawl that sent a shudder down Gregoria's spine. He looked down at her. "I am sorry for what you have endured, ma'am," he said gently. "We will see that justice is done." Then he rose and strode toward the door.

Gregoria shuddered again as she watched him go. Such icy-cold anger. Her eyes strayed to her father, but he was crowding with the others toward the door and didn't turn to look at her.

The room emptied of everyone except the barkeeper Gordy. He came toward her, head gleaming in the light. "Can I get you anything else?" he asked. He stopped beside the table and looked at the untouched bowl of soup. "It would be well if you could just eat a little of that, ma'am," he said gently. "It's a wonder what a little broth can do for a body. And Mr. Allison and me, we'd both appreciate it."

She lifted her spoon obediently.

"And while you're at it, I'll see about a warm bed for you," he said.

Gregoria bent her head over the bowl and Gordy moved away. He added more wood to the fire, then thumped up a set of steps behind the bar as she tore a small piece of warm bread from the loaf.

~ ~ ~

José stood on the porch of Middaugh's Grocery and watched as Clay Allison began organizing his posse. Everyone in Etown knew the location of Kennedy's place. There was no need for a guide. And José had no horse. He would be long left behind by the time the posse's mounts had reached the wider section of valley southward.

All these things he told himself, but he knew deep within that he was still afraid. Kennedy would guess that Gregoria had help getting to Etown and if José was with the posse, he would know instinctively that it had been he who'd assisted her. She could not have gone so far on her own in this cold. Kennedy must have let her go thinking she wouldn't make it, hoping she'd freeze to death, José thought bitterly.

285

Revulsion and a fierce anger against his son-in-law swept through the small man's frame. The man Allison was known as a gun fighter. Perhaps he would just kill Kennedy there and then.

But then José shuddered and crossed himself. No matter the sin of the man, it was still a sin to wish him dead. Even after what he'd done to Samuelito. And all the others, José reminded himself. There is no doubt that mi hija spoke truly, that there have been more deaths than the one that I witnessed, he thought grimly.

The sleet had turned to a light snow and he squatted down against the wall, shielding himself as best he could. There is another thing I fear, he admitted to himself. I am too small, too insignificant, to religioso to be of use to mi hija in this matter of revenge. The americano men are taken by her beauty and her goodness, and they will help her. If they knew I am her papá, that I have failed in my duty toward her, they might not be so willing to come to her aid.

José had felt this instinctively the moment he'd half-carried Gregoria into the Middaugh saloon. Fortunately, she had not spoken to him while they were there. No one need know of their relationship. Until this is over, he told himself.

He stirred uneasily. Whatever "this" was. What would happen now? Would the posse capture Kennedy? Would he escape them? If he did, where would he go?

Perhaps he should go back to the herder's hut. Or at least pretend he was going that way, in the hope of meeting the posse on their return trip and learning what had occurred when they reached the rancho. But José had walked far that night and supported Gregoria much of the way. He was weary beyond measure and could go no further. He wrapped his still-damp coat around himself and eased off the porch in search of shelter from the cold.

~ ~ ~

Benjamin Houx was settled for the evening with his law books at the round wooden table near the parlor fire, Agnes across from him with her novel, when a knock sounded on the outer door. They looked up simultaneously and exchanged uneasy glances.

The knock came again. Ben went to the door. Rain blew in as Joseph Kinsinger entered. He pulled off his hat and nodded to Agnes apologetically. "Howdy ma'am." He turned to Ben. "We finally got the goods on Charles Kennedy an' Clay Allison's roundin' up a posse. He sent me t' ask if you'd come. Keep it legal an' all. Coleman's goin', too. He's still pretty wrought up 'bout that intent to kill charge bein' reduced t' assault."

Ben and Agnes exchanged glances, then she shook her head ruefully and rose. "Your boots are in the kitchen," she said. "I'll get them."

The posse was to gather outside Lambert's Hotel. Allison and some of the others had been drinking inside as they waited for Houx and anyone else who might straggle in. When Houx rode up, Allison came out to the porch.

"I understand you have a witness to a killing at the Kennedy rancho," Ben said.

"Two witnesses, in fact," Allison told him. "And more than one killing. Though one of the witnesses is his wife. I'm not sure how her testimony would stand in a court of law."

Ben's horse moved impatiently. "The first thing we need to do is find out if Kennedy is still there," Ben said.

Allison nodded and disappeared inside for a moment, then the posse members came trooping out. Henry Lambert followed them. "They're somewhat liquored up," the little Frenchman told Ben from the doorway. "Good luck to you."

The Deputy grinned, nodded, and guided his horse into the middle of the street. In the absence of the Sheriff, he was the de

287

facto leader of any legal posse, but the men and horses surged past him, grouping around Allison, whose mount moved toward the edge of town as if glad of the exercise. Ben shook his head grimly. If they were as liquored up as Lambert had implied, his primary role tonight was going to be keeping Charles Kennedy alive. He spurred his horse down the dark street.

~ ~ ~

Once again mi papá has deserted me, Gregoria thought drearily the next morning. I have no one. She huddled next to the potbellied stove in the Middaugh saloon and tried to ignore the two miners conversing at the bar and the man Gordy as he wiped glasses and rearranged bottles. She felt as if all of them were watching her and she shrank closer to the stove and clutched her now-dry chal to her shoulders, acutely aware of the dried mud on her skirt and the battered moccasins on her feet.

When Clay Allison came through the door, she looked up eagerly, then at the stove, suddenly embarrassed. Allison took off his hat, spoke to Gordy, then came toward her.

"Good morning, ma'am. I trust you have recovered from yesterday's journey?"

She nodded. "Sí. Gracias." She flushed. The man would think her ignorant, speaking only español. "Yes, thank you," she said. "Thank you for your concern."

"De nada," he said, smiling. He had the darkest blue eyes. She gazed into them for a split second, then dropped her own guiltily. "I thought you would wish to be apprised of the outcome of last night's events," he said.

Something gripped at her heart. She nodded, eyes on the battered wooden floorboards.

"We buried the child at the edge of the garden," he said gently. "We thought you would like that. We found a good-size stone and used it as a marker. One of the men carved a cross into it." He smiled a little. "It's rather rough. There was no moonlight to speak of."

She nodded again, wanting to thank him, but not trusting her voice. She blinked back the tears.

"Your husband—"

A shudder ran through her.

"Kennedy was drunk when we got there, tryin' to burn the papers of the mexicano he had shot."

She nodded. "Safety in fire," she murmured.

"I beg your pardon?"

"In fire is safety," she repeated. "He says it is so."

"He came willingly enough. Ben Houx saw to that. No thanks to Joseph Coleman." He chuckled and shook his head, then turned his attention back to Gregoria. "Kennedy's in custody. Justice McBride has ordered a search of the property. We couldn't do much last night, given how dark it was. Deputy Houx and some of us are going out today to do that—to look for evidence. Is there anything I can retrieve for you while I'm there? Anything you need?"

She shivered. Just thinking of the cabin made her feel cold. Yet she did need clean clothing. She swallowed. "There is a small leather box containing my clothes." She paused, remembering the source of that box. "I do not need the box itself. Its contents would be enough."

Allison nodded, studying her with gentle eyes. "Forgive me, ma'am, for asking this question, but is there any assistance you can give us in our search?"

She looked again at the stove, then said slowly. "The shed behind the house. And the garden. Also, there are two horses and some mules in the corral. They belonged to the man who died yesterday." She shivered and moved closer to the blazing stove. "Lo siento. I am so cold."

Allison looked around the room. "And this is no place for a decent woman."

Gregoria smiled faintly and huddled closer to the stove. It was kind of him to call her "decent."

"Unfortunately, the hotels aren't much better," he continued. "Generally, the only guests there are men. Although Henry Lambert would do his best to accommodate you."

"I have no money," she said, thinking of Charles' horde, the coins on the dirt floor, shining in the firelight. She shivered and bent her head, biting back the sobs that suddenly choked her, the fear. It had been dangerous enough to slip across the room and remove Charles' coat and her chal from the nail by the door. To have collected money also would have been impossible.

Señor Allison rose from his chair. Gregoria raised her head. He had crossed the room to the bar and was speaking with the man Gordy. When he returned, he said, "I think it would be best if you were to remove to Mr. Lambert's hotel. You will be more protected there from prying eyes. The attached restaurant is as much a saloon as anything else, but there will be no need for you to enter it."

"I have no money," she repeated.

"That is of no consequence," he said. "Henry will extend me credit and we can arrange something later."

She shrank back. He had called her a decent woman. Surely he would not expect payment of a physical kind.

"You can trust me," he said gently. "I will strive to be as true to you as I am to myself." He paused, smiling slightly, as if surprised at his own words, then asked, "Do you have any friends that I can call on in your behalf?"

She started to shake her head, then thought of Alma's kind face. "Mrs. Kinkaid," she said.

"Alma Kinkaid? Do you know her?" There was real relief in his voice. "I will escort you to Lambert's hotel and then go directly to the Kinkaid place to tell her of your need."

Gregoria felt a glimmer of hope. "Gracias," she whispered.

LAMBERT'S HOTEL, FALL 1870

Gregoria had never been in a room so luxurious as the one Henry Lambert assigned her in his Etown Hotel, with its fireplace, three chairs, rag rug, iron bedstead, and curtained glass window. She had just gotten settled and was sitting in the rocking chair beside the fire when Justice McBride knocked on the door. A chubby youngish man with an Irish lilt to his voice and the smooth hands of a politician, he was brimming over with nervous energy in his store-bought suit and vest, and anxiously jovial beneath the short brown beard on his round face.

"As Etown's Justice of the Peace, I've come to ask you a few questions, ma'am, in preparation for the grand jury, you see," he said as he followed her to the fire. "I'm the judge here until the circuit court comes back in the Spring and I'll be wantin' to decide as soon as I can whether to hold your man for trial or to let him go."

She drew back. "Let him go?"

"Yes, ma'am." Patrick McBride bounced slightly upward, onto the balls of his feet. "If there's not enough evidence to hold him, that's most likely what I'll find I'm required to do."

She nodded, feeling dazed.

"This conversation may take some time to get through," he said, bouncing upward again. "I hope you won't take it unkindly if I sit down."

She nodded shyly and motioned him to the upholstered chair by the window, then realized he would not sit until she did. She placed herself in the rocking chair and he sat bolt upright in the other chair. He pulled a small black book and a pencil out of his

292

vest pocket. "Now, if you will be so kind as to tell me all that has happened, I'd be most highly appreciative," he said.

She repeated what she'd told the men in the saloon the night before, then he asked questions: where she and Charles had lived before building the cabin, how long they had been together, whether they were legally married, where she was born and to whom. She struggled to understand his long and rapid questions and answered as best she could, often staring into the fire, glad she was not facing an entire roomful of men.

Somehow, telling this man of her impoverished upbringing made her feel smaller, more anxious. Would anyone believe what she said: she, the daughter of a mexicano laborer, against Charles, an americano with money at his disposal? And she wasn't even sure where her father was. It all seemed like a dream, his appearing beside her in the rain and cold, his arm around her waist, leading her into the saloon, disappearing into the night. She forced her thoughts away from her father and onto the questions the Justice was asking her.

Finally, it was over. "I expect that'll just about do it," he said cheerily. He saw the look of relief on her face and lifted a hand, as if in warning. "It's certainly enough to give me the license to convene a grand jury," he said. "But the jury itself will make the decision about whether to file charges an' all."

She frowned in confusion.

"Kennedy will still be locked up good an' tight," McBride said reassuringly. "It'll take a couple of days to get enough jury members together, though I expect we'll be set to go by early next week."

She nodded uncertainly, still confused.

"The grand jury is a group of men who consider the evidence in hand and determine whether to call for a trial," he explained.

He bounced to his feet. "I understand there was a man with you, a Mexican, when you came into the saloon yesterday evening." He consulted something at the front of his book. "I believe they call him José Cortez. Is that correct?"

Gregoria nodded.

"And how may it be that you know the gentleman?"

Something in her raised a warning. "He lives north of the pass. He found me by the roadside."

"They tell me he said he'd been at the rancho on Christmas last. Is that also correct?"

She nodded.

McBride rocked onto the balls of his feet. "Well, now, I'm going to need to speak to the man, or at least call him before the jury. You wouldn't happen t' know his whereabouts, would you?"

Gregoria shook her head.

"Well, it's most likely that someone will have had a sight of him." He tucked the little book and pencil back into his vest pocket. "In the meantime, all I ask is that you just sit tight." He peered into her face, his expression softening. "If we can find him, we won't need you to testify before the jury, and that'll be more comfortable for you, I'm quite sure."

Her eyes widened in alarm. "Testify?"

He nodded. "But I'm thinkin' you won't be called upon to speak, if we can find this Cortez fellow. You say you don't know where he might be?"

She shook her head and he shrugged and turned away.

"It appears that your husband has already found himself an attorney," he said as he headed for the door. "That Quaker fellow Mills." He shook his head. "There's a pair for you. They do say the law makes strange companions."

Gregoria and the Justice stood looking at each other. Finally, McBride said, "If there's anything at all that you need, ma'am—"

She shook her head. "Mr. Lambert has been very kind. He has said a servant woman will bring food to me here and he has not asked for payment."

McBride grinned. "They do say that Clay made it quite clear that you were to be left in peace, as it were."

"Mr. Allison has been very kind."

McBride laughed and shook his head. "He's a true Southern gentlemen, is our Clay. I'm wishin' he was as kind to the men as he is to the ladies."

Gregoria smiled uncertainly, not sure what he meant. The Justice bounced forward onto the balls of his feet again, giving her a half-bow. "Well, I'll just let myself out," he said. "Someone will come for you if you're needed to testify, if we can't find that Cortez fellow." He frowned. "Clay Allison said somethin' about looking up the Kinkaids. I take it that you might be going to them?"

She hesitated. "When they hear what has happened, what I have helped with, they may not wish it."

He shrugged. "Alma Kinkaid's known far and wide as a fair and good woman. She'll do the right thing." He looked at her sharply. "But don't you go gettin' too far away now, in case we can't find that Mexican."

She nodded numbly and watched the door close behind him, then sank back into the rocking chair by the fire. She'd thought all she had to do was tell someone what Charles had done, that they would take him away and she would never have to face him again. She huddled closer to the fire and buried her face in her hands. Her father— Had he fled back to Taos? Would the Justice and his men find him? Would he also shrink from testifying? And when

295

they discovered that he was her father, would they believe what she said? If they didn't believe her, would they let Charles go?

She shuddered and pulled her chal tighter around her shoulders. If Charles was freed, he would come for her. Of that, she was certain. And he would be more angry than ever before. She gulped back the acid of fear that rose in her throat.

And Alma. What would be the right thing for her to do? Charles had not killed for Gregoria's sake, out of jealousy and anger, but out of his own greed. Yet she, Gregoria, had aided him: not only providing an excuse, but also burying the bodies, using up the tell-tale food and goods as quickly as possible. Her very skirt was made of cloth from a dead peddler's pack. She shivered. What would Alma think when she knew? She was well-known here and respected. Would she be willing to be Gregoria's friend?

When Clay Allison came to her door later that day, he said little to calm her fears. His face was somber as he gave her the bundle of clothing, inquired after her health and comfort, and told her that the Kinkaids had gone south to Watrous on business.

"I have sent word, but it may be some days before they respond," he said, moving to the window. "It's gettin' colder out there and looks like we're in for a healthy storm here and out on the plains," he added. "I doubt she and William will make it before the jury sits. They've got to get from Watrous to Cimarron and then up the canyon. The ice along the river is already so bad that the stage hasn't been through in two days." He moved toward the fireplace, where Gregoria had reseated herself. "In the meantime, I hope you have everything you need." He fumbled in his pocket and pulled out a wallet.

She shook her head. "I cannot take your money," she said. She rose from the chair. "I will speak with Mr. Lambert. Perhaps he has cooking or sewing that I can do."

"This isn't my money." He smiled, a hint of mischief in his eyes. "I liberated it from the cabin this afternoon. It seemed to me that you would need something to tide you over. The rest of it is in Justice McBride's safekeeping."

She sank back into the rocking chair. "It is blood money," she whispered. "It is why Samuelito is dead." A shudder ran through her and she raised her eyes to Allison's sympathetic face. "Charles stole it from those men." She clutched at her chal. "Surely there is something respectable I can do in exchange for my lodging and food."

Allison slid the bills back into the wallet. "It is but a small portion, but I honor your feelings, ma'am. More than I can say. Shall I speak to Mr. Lambert?"

"Yes, please."

But Henry Lambert did not come to her. Gregoria was left in her room with nothing to do but stare out at the frozen mud in the street, grieve for her dead child, wonder if Alma would come, and wait for word of the gran jurado.

The next few days passed slowly. Gregoria tried not to let her mind wander to Watrous and Alma Kinkaid, to the Etown jail where Charles waited, to the grave by the garden, to wherever her father had gone. She found herself straying often to the window, but she couldn't have said why. She could take no pleasure in the pine-covered hills beyond the frozen mud of the street and the unpainted wooden buildings that lined it, the men going in and out of the shops and saloons, and the occasional woman or child making their well-bundled way through the cold.

She caught a glimpse of someone who she thought might be the lawyer Melvin Mills. He was different from the other men. Young and dressed in a smooth broadcloth suit and vest that fit precisely over his round shoulders and slightly protruding stomach. He looked out of place among the roughly-clad miners.

As she watched, he approached an old man in a tattered blue hat who had been lounging on the other side of the street. The younger man's arm went around the old miner's shoulders and their heads bent toward each other, deep in conversation. The old man gestured toward the hotel and Mills looked up, toward her window. He had dark eyes and hair and a flexible mouth in a smooth-shaven face. Gregoria shivered and drew back, toward the fire and away from the view and the gray skies overhead.

MIDDAUGH SALOON, FALL 1870

There was a knock on Gregoria's hotel room door on Monday, just as she finished eating her morning meal. Her spirits lifted hopefully. Alma? But no, it was the man who had come to the rancho to explain about the papers the man Fitzmaurice had thrust at Charles that day in Etown. The man in the doorway was as tall and his face as kindly as she remembered.

"Mrs. Kennedy?" Benjamin Houx asked. "I've come to ask you to attend the grand jury session this morning."

Gregoria's stomach contracted. It must have shown in her face, because the Deputy said gently, "It is possible that you won't have to testify, but Justice McBride has asked that you be there in case Señor Cortez doesn't appear."

She nodded distractedly and turned into the room for her chal.

"There's a real chill in the air," he said. When she turned, he was holding out a woman's wool coat, shabby with age but spotlessly clean. "I took the liberty of bringing this with me, in case you needed it," he said apologetically. "Someone said you were wearing an old Union coat when you came in. I thought you wouldn't want to wear that this morning." He lifted the garment slightly. "It's an old one of my wife's. She was happy to lend it to you."

"You are very kind." She covered her head with her chal and he helped her into the coat, then guided her out of the hotel and into the street.

As they picked their way along the frozen mud, he explained that the town still didn't have a courthouse, though it had been named the county seat over a year and a half before. District Court was held in hired rooms when it was in session. Since this wasn't a regular session of the court, there was no money to hire space. The Middaugh brothers had offered the saloon behind their grocery. No liquor would be for sale before hand, but they hoped to make up for that loss immediately after the grand jury met.

"To the jury members themselves and all the people who wish they could serve," he said with a grin. "There's been no shortage of volunteers. With this winter weather settling in, no placer miner in his right mind would want to be washing ice water through cold gravel when he could be one of twenty-one men in an overheated room participating in the most sensational thing that's ever happened around here."

Gregoria shrank a little as he said this. Twenty-one of them? Twenty-one pairs of eyes watching her, judging her? And Charles, too, with his angry scowl.

But she saw no sign of Charles when she entered the room. There were men everywhere, perched on the bar room chairs, leaning against the wall, and clustering around the pot-bellied stove. Deputy Houx guided Gregoria through the crowd to a chair in a back corner and she slipped into it gratefully. The men ignored her. They were too busy talking among themselves and watching the small table at which Justice McBride was seated, just in front of the saloon's bar. An empty chair sat next to it, angled to face the rest of the room.

Charles wouldn't be coming, Gregoria realized as she listened to the men around her. Apparently, it wasn't the custom for the accused to be present at a grand jury hearing.

She craned her neck, watching the door. Where was her father? Surely he would come. Surely he would speak for her. He would be afraid, she knew. And she doubted that he understood any more than she did how this americano justice worked, or that Charles wouldn't be here to swear and rage, reaching out in anger to wreak vengeance.

She continued to watch the door throughout the jury selection process, which felt interminable to her, although Justice McBride seemed pleased that it had gone quickly. Other than those acting as witnesses, only a few were not eligible to sit on the jury panel: Joseph Coleman, who had gone to law against Charles, and William Henderson and Samuel Cameron, who had stood bond with him. This left almost all the men in town as potential jury members. It seemed to Gregoria that all of them were present in the crowded room.

Justice McBride asked some questions, the jurors were chosen, then the room was cleared of everyone except Deputy Houx, the jurymen, the witnesses, Melvin Mills, and Gregoria. The jurors dragged their chairs into two rough rows against the wall opposite the door to the street and chose a man named Thomas Pollock as their leader. Then the court got down to business. Her father had still not arrived.

Gregoria forced her eyes away from the door and watched Clay Allison limp forward to sit in the chair by the Justice's table. He described what had happened when Gregoria, who he called "Mrs. Kennedy," had arrived at the Saloon.

Melvin Mills walked toward him. "You had seen Rosa Kennedy on previous occasions?" he asked.

"I believe she came into town this summer with Kennedy and their baby son," Allison said.

"And you saw her then?"

"As you may have observed, ladies are not that common in Etown, Mr. Mills." Allison smiled at him, his eyes cold. "Any lady coming into town is bound to be noticed."

301

"Especially a woman as attractive as Rosa Kennedy," Mills said. "It is well known that you have an eye for the ladies, Mr. Allison."

"I do appreciate a good face and figure." Allison glanced around the room, his eyes pausing on Gregoria for a split second, then moving on to the jury. "I also have a great deal of respect for beauty and virtue. That Mrs. Kennedy possessed both these qualities was apparent to me on the single occasion that I glimpsed her in town with Mr. Kennedy and again when I actually met her on that unfortunate night."

"And why do you call it an unfortunate night?"

"Why, she was cold and wet and in great tribulation. That was clear at the first sight of her."

"Because she had run away from her husband like a cheap Mexican half breed." Mr. Mills turned away and nodded to the Judge that he was finished with the witness. Gregoria shrank back into her chair and looked toward the door. Please, let it open, let mi papá appear, she prayed. She knew now why Justice McBride had wanted to shield her from testifying. Please, let mi papá appear.

But the doctors were speaking now, the ones who had been asked to examine the bones found in her garden. It took a long time, while they used technical terms and appeared to disagree and then to agree and then disagree again. Attorney Mills looked disgusted when he finally said, "So in your informed medical opinion, you cannot ascertain whether the bones found in the garden are of animal or human origin."

"That is correct," the man in the chair said in a Scandinavian accent. He opened his mouth to explain further, but Mills turned on his heel and walked away. "I have no further questions, your honor," he said over his shoulder.

An irritated look crossed Justice McBride's round face, but he only said, "Thank you, Doctor Westerling," and looked across the room at Deputy Houx. "And now, since it appears that we have no further witnesses—"

The door opened and Gregoria's father entered the room. He pulled off his hat and looked around, blinking. His eyes glanced over Gregoria. The men on the jury stirred impatiently.

"Mr. Cortez?" Justice McBride asked.

"Sí, señor." José walked toward the Justice's table, his shoulders hunched. Deputy Houx moved forward and was at his elbow when he reached McBride.

"It's thanking you I am for arriving so promptly," the Justice said drily.

"Lo siento señor," José said humbly. "I did not know until this morning."

The jurymen looked at each other and muttered among themselves, but McBride ignored them. "And is it ready now you are to testify?" he asked.

José nodded, was sworn in, and told to sit down. He sat on the edge of the chair, fingering his hat, eyes straying occasionally toward Gregoria as McBride asked him about the events of the previous Christmas. He said nothing to indicate his relationship to Gregoria and did not mention Samuel. He explained that he had eventually returned to the Valley to work as a casual laborer. There was no cost to live in the abandoned herder's hut, so he had remained there, walking to Etown and the mines to search for work. He'd been returning to the hut when he'd found Gregoria beside the road.

When he'd finished, Melvin Mills moved forward. "Your honor, I have only one question."

Justice McBride nodded.

303

Mills took two quick steps to stand directly in front of the witness chair and scowled down at José, who blinked up at him nervously.

"You say you witnessed a murder and ran away to Taos," Mills said severely. "If you witness a crime, you are bound to report it. Don't you know that?"

José nodded nervously.

"Then why didn't you report it?"

"Lo siento. I was afraid."

"You were in Taos, in another county. Charles Kennedy was here in the Valley, over twenty-five miles away. Of what were you afraid?"

"That he would find me and kill me."

"I say you were afraid of being caught in a lie!" Mills leaned forward threateningly.

José's face blanched and he jerked backward, the chair's wooden legs scraping the floor. "It is not true," he protested. "I saw him. He told me to help. I ran away."

"And what did you take with you?" Mills demanded. He straightened and moved disdainfully away.

José pulled the chair straight and sat down again. "Qué?"

"What did you take with you?"

"Nada."

"You didn't return to the cabin for your goods?"

"I ran away. I took nothing."

"What did you have hidden in the woods?"

José looked at the Justice beseechingly. "Lo siento, I don't understand."

McBride looked at Mills. "A wee bit of clarity might be of use," he said mildly.

Mills didn't move. He glared at José. "You ran away through the mountains in the middle of winter and headed to Taos, twenty-five miles away, with only the clothes on your back," he said slowly, as if speaking to a child. "Elizabethtown was closer, but you didn't come here. You went to Taos instead. You could not have made it to Taos at that time of year without clothing, food, and an animal to carry you."

José stared at him speechlessly.

Mills jabbed a finger at him. "I say that you stole what you needed from Mr. Kennedy," he said. "You had goods cached nearby, probably stolen. You stole an animal from Charles Kennedy and you lit out for Taos. When you got there, you didn't go to the authorities because you are a liar and a thief. You didn't want them asking any questions!"

José shook his head and turned to Justice McBride. "It is not true."

"Are you telling the court that an officer of this court has stated an untruth?" Mills was standing directly in front of him again, looking down belligerently.

José looked up at him in confusion, but Mills turned away. "I have no more questions," he said over his shoulder.

José looked at Justice McBride. "You are free to go," the Justice said.

José nodded uncertainly, stood, bowed his head, and went out without glancing toward Gregoria's corner. She watched him anxiously, pity in her heart for the way the lawyer had treated him, gratitude that he had been willing to endure it for her sake, wondering what he would do now, if she would see him again.

She turned her attention back to the chair by the Justice's table. Mills was speaking now with the man Chester Landry, who said heartily that he and his son and son-in-law had stopped at the

305

Kennedy rancho for a night in '67. Everything seemed smooth as silk to him. His son? Oh, he'd given up on gold and headed eastward to work on the railroad that was comin' this way. His son-in-law Henry had cashed in his claim and gone back to Landry's daughter, who thought a man ought to stay home and play sheep dog. This got a chuckle from the jury and Landry looked pleased with himself.

Gregoria looked down at her hands. Then Landry moved from the chair and she heard her name. She looked up. All the eyes in the court room were on her. She bit her lip and straightened her shoulders, preparing herself. Then the Justice shook his head, and Melvin Mills shrugged and turned away and began speaking to the jury, telling them Charles Kennedy was guilty of nothing but impatience with a stupid Mexican laborer and a wife who was undoubtedly playing him false.

Gregoria shrank against the back of her chair, willing herself not to listen, praying that the men in the two crooked rows of chairs would see that her father spoke truly, that Charles would not be allowed to go free.

But she was not to know just yet what those listening to the attorney thought of it all. When Mills finished speaking, Justice McBride spoke a few words and then she and the others were ushered out so the jury members could speak among themselves.

"This may take a while," Deputy Houx said as he assisted her down the saloon steps. "If you would like, I'll return you to your hotel."

Gregoria nodded. Suddenly, all she wanted to do was lie down. She doubted she'd be able to rest, though. Not until she knew what the men in the room behind her had decided.

LAMBERT'S HOTEL, FALL 1870

She had been right about not being able to rest. As Gregoria lay fully clothed on the iron bedstead, her thoughts remained firmly fixed on the Middaugh saloon, where the grand jury was still meeting. Outside, the sky was growing dark. The clouds that had hovered over the western mountains as she and Deputy Houx made their way to the courtroom now covered the valley sky. They had drifted so low that the mountain peaks on either side were completely obscured, but no rain or snow had yet fallen. It was almost as if the clouds themselves were holding their breath.

Gregoria rose and went to the window. There seemed to be men everywhere. They grouped in small huddles up and down the street, occasionally ducking into a saloon for a drink. When they came out, they stamped their feet and gazed gloomily skyward, then leaned toward each other again with tense faces, looking occasionally toward the Middaugh building. They seemed as anxious as Gregoria felt.

And then it was over. The clusters of men joined together in the middle of the street, then surged in a mass toward the saloon. After a long while, they began to trickle back down the street in twos and threes, some into the saloons, others back to their mountainside mining huts or Etown cabins.

It had finally begun to snow: tiny icy pellets that slanted in the wind. As Gregoria watched, Clay Allison appeared at the end of the street, moving swiftly in spite of his limp. Deputy Houx was beside him, hat tilted against the weather.

When they appeared in her doorway, Gregoria saw immediately that there was a problem. Clay Allison's eyes were tight with anger and even Ben Houx's usually placid face looked anxious. Kennedy would be held for trial at the Spring court session, but the jury had almost released him. Even those who'd agreed to the indictment believed he would ultimately go free. There'd been a great deal of discussion about the cost of holding a man for a trial which was bound to end in an innocent verdict.

"They all seem to appreciate Mr. Mills' extraordinary legal skills," Clay Allison said drily.

Benjamin Houx smiled slightly. "I don't believe he's actually attempting to bribe anyone," he said. "It's more likely that he's just trying to sow doubts in the minds of the men who might end up on that jury, come Spring."

Allison turned to Gregoria. "Mr. Mills has been very busy these last few days."

She nodded. "I have seen him from my window. Every hour he has spoken with another person."

"The other concern was that the jail might not be able to withstand a serious escape attempt," Allison said. "I am especially concerned for your welfare, ma'am, if Kennedy should get loose."

She frowned. "Get loose?"

"The jail is not very strong," Ben Houx explained. "Although I've been doing my best to correct that deficiency."

"He is very angry with me," Gregoria said.

"He's a low-down cowardly Yankee bastard," Clay Allison growled. "Begging your pardon, ma'am."

She found herself smiling in spite of her anxiety.

"What it amounts to, ma'am, is that Etown isn't a truly safe place for you right now," the Deputy said.

Gregoria lifted her hands, palms up. "I have no place to go."

"I understand the Kinkaids left Watrous yesterday," Clay Allison said. "If the Cimarron road remains clear, they should be here in a day or two."

"They have no obligation to help me," Gregoria said. She looked at him with troubled eyes. "If Charles escapes and I am with them, they will also be in danger." She looked down at her hands. "Perhaps I can find work in Las Vegas or Santa Fe. Some place away from here."

"I believe you would need to be somewhere far from New Mexico Territory to be truly out of harm's way," Allison said.

"Some place back east," said Deputy Houx. "Or maybe California or Oregon."

"I have no money."

Allison shifted his feet and Ben Houx looked at him. "There may be ways to address that concern," Allison said, looking away.

"Well, one way to ensure your safety is to make sure the jail can withstand even a man as big as Charles Kennedy," Houx said. "Which means I have work to do."

"And I have responsibilities also," Allison said. He looked at Gregoria with regret in his face. "I would sleep in the hallway outside your door myself, ma'am, if I thought it would help you." He grinned. "If Henry would let me."

Gregoria smiled in response, but when the door closed behind the two men a few minutes later, she bit her lip in distress. Then her chin lifted defiantly. She would not go with Charles. If he killed her here, in this room, then perhaps a jury would know what he was. Even the attorney Mills would know. But whatever happened, she would not go with him. She would not be party to his actions ever again. Because she was certain the killing would go on if he was freed.

~ ~ ~

Gregoria shivered and hunched closer to the fire. It was easy enough to say she would not go with Charles if he was set free or escaped. But would she really have the courage? Her stomach churned with anxiety. It was one thing to say "let him kill me," but another thing entirely to imagine herself responding to his anger with anything other than submission.

Suddenly, there was a sharp rap on the hotel room door. Gregoria's head jerked up and she stared at it as if it were alive, her heart pounding. Had it already begun? Was it Charles? What should she do? Then a woman's low-timbered voice called, "Mrs. Kennedy? Gregoria? May I come in?"

Gregoria felt a leap of hope. She had wished it with all her heart and it had come true. She stumbled across the room. "Oh, Mrs. Kinkaid!" she half-sobbed as she opened the door.

Alma's sturdy body filled the doorway and her eyes smiled into Gregoria's. Her serviceable brown woolen coat was damp with melting snow. "May I come in?" she asked.

"Oh yes! Please do!" Gregoria drew her in, helped her with her coat, and sat her down by the fire.

Alma drew her chair up close to the rocker, leaned forward, and took Gregoria's hands. "Mr. Allison told us about Samuel," she said, looking into Gregoria's face. "I am so sorry."

Gregoria's eyes filled.

"Can you tell me what happened?" Alma asked gently. "Can you bear to speak of it?"

Gregoria nodded wordlessly.

"Take your time." Alma squeezed Gregoria's hands gently. "As much as you need."

Brokenly, she began with Samuel's death, and then went backward, explaining about the other babies, Charles' jealous rag-

310

es, his insatiable physical appetite, his desire for wealth, the travelers and their deaths. Alma listened calmly, her mouth tightening occasionally, her pupils expanding and contracting at the deaths of the infants and guests. She asked an occasional question but mostly just listened.

Finally, Gregoria had spoken it all. It was much more than she'd told Justice McBride and this telling was more cleansing, somehow. When she was done, the two women stared silently into the fire for a long while, Alma still holding Gregoria's hands.

Eventually, Alma stirred and drew away. "Do you think it would pain you to live again in a household with a child?" she asked gently.

"There is no pain greater than the pain I bear now," Gregoria said. Her chin lifted. "Except returning to Charles."

Alma chuckled. "Yes." She looked into Gregoria's face. "Would you consider coming to us? As you know, I'm not much of a cook and I could use some help."

Gregoria shook her head. "If they let him go or if he escapes, he will come for me. I cannot place you and your family in such danger."

Alma's jaw tightened. "I'm not afraid and William won't be either."

"You have asked him? He has agreed?"

Alma smiled. "No, I haven't asked him. But he will agree." She looked into Gregoria's face. "Do you agree?"

Gregoria smiled and nodded, tears springing into her eyes. "Con gusto," she whispered, reaching for Alma's hand. With pleasure.

Alma pressed Gregoria's hands between hers and stood up. "Then, if you'll gather your things, I'll go down, tell Henry that you're leaving, and settle the bill."

"I have no money," Gregoria said anxiously. "Mr. Allison—"

Alma nodded. "Yes, Clay told me what he'd done about the money. And your response." She shook her head. "I told him you were absolutely correct and he was foolish to think you would feel otherwise." She chuckled. "Poor Mr. Allison. Every time I see him he stands corrected about something or other."

"And so I have nothing," Gregoria said.

Alma shrugged. "No es nada," she said. "That's not a problem. We'll take it out of your salary for helping me with the cooking."

Gregoria nodded and smiled. She followed Alma to the door and closed it behind her. She stood for a long moment, savoring the feelings washing over her. Friendship and safety. Acceptance, in spite of what she had done. And Alma had said "salary."

Gregoria shook her head in dazed disbelief. To cook was not demeaning, did not make her an outcast. A sob of relief swept over her. She didn't deserve such consideration. The sobs shook her shoulders for several minutes, then she took a deep breath. Alma and Mr. Kinkaid would be waiting for her. She must gather her clothes.

ELIZABETH TOWN JAIL, FALL 1870

Charles Kennedy moved his shoulders restlessly against the cot's iron headboard and took another swig of the whiskey he'd bribed the guards to buy for him. The lawyer Mills didn't think he should be drinking. Charles grunted dismissively and gulped the whisky again. He grinned, remembering the look on Mills' face when he'd arrived at the jail late Monday afternoon and discovered Charles half-drunk.

"Are you sober enough to understand what I have to say to you?" Mills had asked. Greenhorn Quaker. Didn't know how a man could hold his liquor. "The more time I spend with you, the more it will cost you," he'd warned.

But Charles didn't need to have things repeated to him twice. He knew where he stood. The grand jury was sendin' him to trial and he was gonna be stuck in this hell hole 'til Spring, 'less he could find a way out. And when he did, he'd deal with Rosa. The bitch. Not that he wanted her back. He was through with women. He stirred on the cot. He could still get it going when he wanted to, but the urgency wasn't there anymore.

His need for Rosa was different now. Now it was punishment: fear in her eyes, her saying "Lo siento" the way she did. It'd be more often now. Now that she'd gone and lied to these dirty hypocrites. They'd of done the same as he had if they'd had half the chance. Half the guts.

"Cowards," he muttered. "Cowards!" he said again, louder. "Cowards!" he howled. When he stood up, he could see through the cell bars to the single jail window and the street beyond. At

313

the sound of his voice, a passerby stopped and turned to gaze at the jail.

Charles fell silent. The man was tall and slender, in store-bought clothes. Not a miner, but not as polished and sleek as Melvin Mills, either. Full, neatly trimmed black beard. Must be that Allison that had headed up the mob at the cabin. It had been dark and Charles had been drunk, but certain things he remembered: the air of command, the beard, the Southern drawl. Unreconstructed Reb making himself out a gentleman.

Charles gulped more whisky. Damn rico. Kept talkin' 'bout Rosa like they was friends. Called her "Mrs. Kennedy" and "your lady wife." Lady? Half-breed bitch. Lyin' whore. He'd teach her t' talk to other men.

It had been two days since the grand jury session, with nothing to do but lie here and drink and eat an occasional meal. Weren't giving him enough to eat. Man his size needed food. If he ate like this 'til the Spring session, there'd be nothing left of him t' try.

Charles turned his back to the cell bars and fumbled at his money belt. It was still fat with greenbacks and coins. He pulled out a silver coin and rubbed it between his fingers. Should be good for a decent meal or two, even with the guards' cut.

"Guard!" he bellowed as he refastened his clothes. "Guard! Food!"

They were quick enough to respond. They'd already figured out that he had money and a large appetite.

Melvin Mills arrived at the same time as the food. He sat on the single chair and watched Charles, on the edge of the cot, wolf down his meal.

"Bail?" Charles demanded, his mouth full.

Mills shook his head. "Justice McBride is unwilling to allow bail," he said. "He believes you to be a flight risk."

"'Fraid fer himself," Charles grunted.

"He's learned that you don't own the land on which your cabin and corral are situated," Mills said evenly. "So you can only give a cash bond, which would be easily forfeited." He nodded toward the whisky bottle. "He's also aware of your whisky consumption. Alcohol can cause a man to act recklessly, making you a possible danger to the community if you're on bail."

Kennedy lifted his head from his food and glared at Mills. "Danger? Ya lettin' that drunk say that? Some lawyer." He bit off a chunk of bread. "Yer case," he said, pieces of bread crumbling from his mouth. "Paid ya good money."

There was a long pause, then the younger man said grimly, "Yes, my case." He stood up. "But as I told you when I agreed to represent you, I can't guarantee anything." He moved toward the cell door and rattled the door, signaling to the guard that he was ready to go. "A little less of that Taos Lightning could very well improve your chances of walking out of here a free man, Mr. Kennedy. And perhaps sooner than you might think."

Charles snorted. "Break out, instead." He lifted the whisky jug to his mouth as the guard unlocked the door and Melvin Mills stepped out.

"I wouldn't advise that," Mills said from the other side of the bars.

Charles grunted and hoisted the jug at him.

Mills looked at him for a long moment, then turned away.

Charles chuckled sardonically and took another swig.

~ ~ ~

Ben Houx and Patrick McBride were in McBride's office, discussing how to fund Charles Kennedy's incarceration, when John

315

Fitzmaurice flung the door open. He pushed a Taos Pueblan man ahead of him into the room.

"I found this fine gentleman at the Kennedy cabin, burying somethin' in the shed," Fitzmaurice said, gesturing toward the Indian. "He was destroyin' evidence, from the looks of it." He glared at the Indian. "You in cahoots with that Kennedy?"

The man gave him a puzzled look.

McBride leaned back in his chair, hands linked on his chest, and studied Fitzmaurice. "And what were you doin' out there, your own self, if I may ask? Looking for Kennedy's treasure, were you now?"

Fitzmaurice bristled. "I'm a deputy too, ain't I? I was just checkin' to make sure we hadn't missed anything!"

McBride and Houx exchanged glances, then the Justice looked at the Pueblan. "And you? What was it you were doin' out there?"

The man gave him a long look, then said, "My father disappeared two years ago. When I heard about the man Kennedy I thought his body might be there." He shrugged. "So I went to look."

"Did you find anything?" Ben Houx asked.

"Not my father."

"Somethin' else?" McBride's chair creaked as he leaned forward. "Speak up, man!"

The Indian nodded reluctantly. "In the room behind the house is a body with red hair." He glanced at Fitzmaurice. "I was covering it again when you came."

"Why'd you cover it up, man? That's evidence!"

The man shook his head. "He is not my dead. My duty is to my father."

McBride and Houx looked at each other, then Fitzmaurice. "Red hair," McBride said. "You don't say." He bounced out of his

316

chair. "Come on, let's get us a doctor and go see what that body can tell us!"

The three americanos headed out the door, then Ben Houx turned back into the room. "Thank you," he said to the Taos man. "I believe you may have helped us enormously."

A grim smile flashed across the other man's face. "I am free to go?"

"Of course." Ben grinned. "I apologize for Fitzmaurice. He's Irish and quick to judgment sometimes."

The other man grunted and followed him out the door.

"You'll come with us on your way back?" Ben asked.

The man shook his head and gestured toward the mountain slopes to the west. "There are other paths."

And he doesn't want to have anything more to do with John Fitzmaurice, Ben thought, as he watched the Pueblan head up Broadway, toward the western mountains. Smart man. There was supposed to be a lake up there somewhere that was sacred to the Taos people. Ben wondered if the man would stop there to cleanse himself of his recent association with a body that wasn't "his dead." But, as Agnes would say, that wasn't any of his concern. Ben shrugged and turned to follow the others.

Middaugh Saloon, Fall 1870

"He was a great brawny guy with a lotta red hair," John Fitz-maurice said. He gestured to Gordy for a refill.

"That does sound like a description of the man," said Joseph Coleman from the other end of the bar. He nodded toward Clay Allison, who was sitting at a table nearby with several compan-ions. "Judge Anthony was a big man in more ways than one. He had a great many friends here."

Allison stroked his beard and opened his mouth, but Fitzmau-rice wasn't finished. "Six inches under the dirt, hole the size o' my fist in the side o' his head." He grimaced. "That gun musta been close."

"So what happens now?" Gordy asked as he refilled Fitzmau-rice's glass.

"Nothin' that I rightly know of," the Deputy said. "McBride figures the grand jury did all we can do. Now we just hold on 'til the Spring."

"When's the Spring session?" Allison asked. "April?"

"End o' March." Fitzmaurice put down his glass and wiped his face with the back of his hand. "I got t' get back t' work, supervisin' the jailers."

"And the jail?" Coleman asked. "It is strong enough to hold that big bastard?"

"Aye, that's a concern, all right." Fitzmaurice shook his head. "Ben Houx is doin' his best, but that Kennedy's got some power-ful brawn."

"Those jailers've been feedin' him whisky, too," Gordy said.

Six more men came in and crowded up the bar, Joseph Kinsinger, Chester Landry, and his son among them.

"How is Kennedy when he's drunk?" Allison asked.

"Dangerous," Kinsinger said. "I've seen him an' he's crazy. I'm thinkin' that jail won't hold him long, no matter what Houx does to it."

"An' he eats like a pig," Landry said. "I was in Lambert's yestiday when the young jailer came in sayin' Kennedy wanted more food. That's taxpayer money he's gobblin' up."

"We'll be payin' for him from now until the Spring," Fitzmaurice said.

"It occurs to me that the grand jury process was extra-legal," Allison said. "Why couldn't we hold a trial the same way?"

The men looked at each other. Fitzmaurice nodded slowly. "It may take some talkin' to convince the Justice to go along with that idea," he warned.

"'Nuff of us tell him what we think, he's bound to agree," Chester Landry said.

"If he wants to get himself re-elected Justice," Kinsinger said. "Or higher."

A general chuckle ran through the room. They all knew Patrick McBride's political ambitions didn't stop with being Etown's Justice of the Peace.

"Let's go ask him," someone said. There was a surge of men toward the door, with Fitzmaurice willingly propelled at its head, Kinsinger, Landry, and the rest following behind. Allison stayed seated for a long minute, then tossed back his drink and sauntered after them.

Ben Houx had been giving the Justice an update on his efforts to fortify the jail when the group from the saloon knocked on McBride's office door and entered at the same time. "There's not

319

much more I can do," Ben was saying apologetically as they pushed inside.

Clay Allison had caught up with them by now. He stopped in the doorway and took off his hat as McBride leaned back in his chair and hooked his thumbs into his vest pockets. "And what can I do for you gentlemen?" the Justice asked.

"Well, we're thinkin' we have a solution to the problem of what to do with Kennedy until the Spring session," Fitzmaurice announced. "We figure, since we've got a grand jury decision, we'll just go ahead an' hold a trial now an' get the entire thing over with."

McBride frowned.

"It would certainly save County funds," Clay Allison pointed out mildly. He stepped into the room. "And then there's the very real possibility that Kennedy will escape, no matter how securely that jail is reinforced. He seems to have the funds to pay for assistance." He glanced around the room. "There's no tellin' who might die if that happens." He focused on McBride. "When's the election? November? Kennedy runnin' loose about then wouldn't be very safe, now would it?"

There was a long silence, then McBride sighed and stood up. He leaned forward, hands flat on the desk. "All right. From what Ben here tells me, it does appear that holding Kennedy until the Spring is going to be almighty difficult. I suppose holding a trial immediately makes a certain kind of sense."

"Immediately?" Ben Houx asked. "You don't want to hold off a few days?"

McBride looked around the room and shrugged. "I'm thinkin' its most likely better held sooner rather than later."

There was a general outburst of excitement from the men with Fitzmaurice, then McBride held up his hand. "We want to make sure we do this legal, though," he said. "It's a full slate of jurors I'll be needing for the lawyers to choose from." He paused, considering. "And we'll be needing a prosecutor as well." He looked at Ben Houx, who shook his head.

"I haven't been called to the bar yet," Houx said. "Besides, I was the arresting officer. It would be inappropriate for me to act as prosecutor, too."

"Hell, I'll just do it then," Fitzmaurice said. "I've sat through enough court sessions. I know how it works."

They all looked at him. Fitzmaurice spread his hands. "Now how hard can it be? The man's guilty as sin!"

McBride frowned, then nodded reluctantly. He turned to Ben Houx. "You'll need to notify Mills."

"Notify me about what?" asked a voice from the doorway.

The crowd parted to allow Melvin Mills to enter the room and station himself in front of McBride's desk. He looked at McBride, pointedly ignoring the crowd. "Was there something of which you needed to inform me, Justice McBride?"

The Irishman sank back into his chair. "Well now, I'm thinkin' that a trial just might be in order." He leaned back and hooked his thumbs into his vest again. "It does seem to me that Charles Kennedy's trial might advisedly occur sooner rather than later. We can get this whole thing dealt with instead of lettin' it stew from now until the end of next March."

Mills studied McBride's face, then nodded slowly. "Yes," he said. "It may be better to take care of this now."

A rush of excitement ran through the men behind him. He turned to face them, his youthful face grim. "But I will be playing my part in these proceedings with all the respect that is due to the law, gentlemen," he said sharply. He looked at McBride. "I expect a full complement of potential jurymen and an examination of them strictly according to court rules."

"That's already been arranged for," McBride said smugly.

"Fine." Mills raised an eyebrow. "I'm assuming the Middaugh saloon is as available for the petit jury as it was for the grand."

McBride glanced at Ben Houx. "I'll see about it," Houx said. He stood, pushed his way through the room, and went out.

"All right," McBride said to the rest of them. "Let's get this over with."

It took a mere two hours to make the arrangements. The Middaugh brothers were willing to turn their space back into a courtroom. The room was set up identically to the arrangements during the grand jury: two rows of mismatched chairs for the jury members opposite the saloon's street door, Justice McBride at a rough wooden table in front of the bar, the chair for witnesses beside it.

Charles was marched in and placed in the front row of spectator seats, facing the bench. He sat with his arms across his chest and his legs straight out before him, his bulk dominating the room. His breath reeked of whisky, but his head was straight and his blue eyes narrow and alert, watching the proceedings as he combed his fingers through his black beard.

There was no lack of men willing to participate as jurors. Mills and Fitzmaurice made short work of that part of the process. A reluctant Thomas Pollock was named foreman and the jury was sworn in. Then, to save time, Justice McBride summarized what Gregoria had told him and had the grand jury testimony from the doctors and José Cortez read into the record.

When Melvin Mills rose, he ignored Gregoria's statement completely but sharply questioned the reliability of both Cortez' and Doctor Westerling's testimony. "Neither speaks English well," he pointed out. "Doctor Westerling is a native of Sweden and Cortez an illiterate Mexican. Where there is a difference of language there is always the possibility that a question has been misunderstood and so not answered properly or completely." He paused for effect. "Then there is also a question as to the fully-developed mind of a witness who is an illiterate Mexican."

There was a buzz in the back of the room, where a group of nuevomexicanos were clustered, and John Fitzmaurice raised his voice to object to Mills' comment. Justice McBride ordered the jury to ignore Mills' remarks, but Charles smiled grimly. It was a good trick. In the back of the room, Clay Allison's face darkened. While he didn't have much use for foreigners himself, Mills wasn't playing fair.

The discussion turned to the body that had been unearthed in the shed. Doctor Bradford took the stand. Since he hadn't had a chance to consult with Dr. Westerling, he was hesitant to speak definitively, but in his opinion, the corpse had been buried within the last twelve months.

Mills pounced on this answer, demanding how the good doctor could tell when the corpse had been buried. Wasn't decomposition significantly affected by soil moisture and temperature? It was well known that temperatures were lower at that end of the valley as compared to, say, Etown. There was certainly more snow. Could Bradford guarantee that the body hadn't been buried there before Kennedy built his cabin and shed? Doctor Bradford shook his head uncertainly, flushed with annoyance but unwilling to state categorically what his science told him was an inexact estimate, at best.

Charles smirked and leaned back in his chair. They'd only found the one body. Careless bastards. He was thirsty, though. He wished the thing was over. He needed whisky.

The sun had been down an hour before Mills was through interrogating the doctor. McBride announced a dinner break and ordered the jury sequestered in the Middaugh storage room, their dinner brought in from Lambert's.

"Leastways they'll get a free meal out o' it," someone behind Charles said as he was herded out the door by his jailers.

"I'm hearin' they'll get more'n that from the prisoner hisself," a voice answered. Charles jerked his head around sharply, but the faces around him were blank, eyes carefully averted.

After the break, there were a few preliminaries, then Mills called Charles to the stand. The witness chair creaked dangerously as he sat down. Charles shifted his weight and it groaned again. He scowled at Mills. "Lousy chair," he said.

Attorney Mills looked toward Justice McBride.

"Can we locate a sturdier chair?" McBride asked Ben Houx.

Jury foreman Pollock rose. "Your honor, he can use my chair, if you'd like. It seems plenty strong enough."

McBride shrugged and nodded. The exchange was made and Charles sat down again. He grunted approvingly when the wood made no sound, but he didn't look toward the jury and nod his thanks. Thomas Pollock frowned.

Melvin Mills walked Charles through his version of what had happened the day Samuel died. Accident, Charles explained with his usual terseness. Pushed the boy out o' the way, he fell. Didn't want him trampled. Horse and two mules were loose. Sorry? Course he was! His son.

When Fitzmaurice came back to this point, Charles became surly. Yes, there'd been other children. Couldn't say how many were his, though. He'd been gone. Had t' put food on the table. Couldn't know what she was up to, he wasn't there.

Suddenly, Fitzmaurice switched topics. "And after you settled in the pass, how many people did you kill?" he demanded.

Charles' face darkened. "No one," he growled.

"You already admitted that you killed the child."

"Accident!"

"Be that as it may, you did kill him. How many others did you kill, Mr. Kennedy?" Fitzmaurice looked around the room with a self-satisfied air.

"Just him." The voice was low but menacing.

"And mayhap Allan Lamb?"

"Who?"

"Maxwell O'Connor?"

"Huh?"

"And what about the Ute Indian they call Walks Quietly?"

"Injun?"

"And Juan Antonio Archuleta?"

"Nope."

Fitzmaurice raised his voice and looked toward the jury. "All o' those men disappeared on the road between here an' Taos. Truth to tell, they disappeared in the pass near the Kennedy rancho, so called." He turned back toward Kennedy and pointed his finger at him. "Judge Michael Anthony's dead body was found lyin' buried in the shed behind your cabin. Now just how did he get there if you didn't kill 'im? I say you killed those men I named to you just now and then stole all their goods. What do you say to that?"

Charles' arms were still crossed. "Never heard of 'em."

"Animals that aren't yours were found in your corral, now weren't they?"

"Mountains." Charles shrugged. "People die. Mules smarter'n people."

"You, sir, are a murderer! And a wicked thief!"

Charles came out of the chair in one movement. Instinctively, Fitzmaurice backed away. Charles moved toward him, fists clenched.

"Mr. Kennedy!" Melvin Mills said sharply as McBride rapped his gavel.

Charles dropped his hands. "Lyin' bastard!" Charles snarled into Fitzmaurice's face. He turned and stalked back to the chair, which creaked in protest as he thudded into it.

Fitzmaurice stayed where he was. "So what do you have to say about all of those bones that were found lyin' buried in the garden?" he asked. "Are you for sayin' those were all from elk and deer you killed for meat?"

"Some horse."

Fitzmaurice frowned. "You killed horses for meat?"

The audience stirred uneasily. Horses weren't worth what mules were, but eating them was something a man did only in desperation.

"Found 'em injured." Charles shrugged. "Dangerous pass."

Fitzmaurice opened his mouth as if to pursue the topic, then appeared to change his mind. "An' it's your own wife who swore to Justice McBride that you killed those men. Men who stayed in your cabin, broke bread at your table, drank your watered-down whisky." He raised his voice. "You took their goods an' then cut up an' buried their bodies." He turned toward the jury, then back to Charles. "She said you even tried to burn some of 'em!"

Charles leaned back in his chair again, his arms crossed. "Lying half-breed whore. You got nothin'."

"If she's so worthless, why did you continue to live with her then?"

Charles smirked. "Man's got needs."

326

Fitzmaurice grimaced and looked at the jury again. "So mayhap it is that the doctors' can't tell the difference between what's animal bones and what's human," he said. "But that's not to say those weren't human parts in that garden, not just butchered horses." He raised his voice, clearly enjoying himself, and stabbed his finger in the air. "That body in the Kennedy shed was Judge Anthony sure enough, a man a great many of us knew personally and well."

He took a step closer to Charles. "An' where is it that all those animals in the corral came from? You can't show us bills of sale or give us the names o' the men you bought 'em from." He shook his head. "I'm thinking these pieces of information are all apt to put a negative light on what you say."

He turned to the jury and pointed dramatically toward Charles. "His own wife says he did it! Any jury with a lick of sense is bound t' find him guilty of at least one count of murder." Fitzmaurice paused, seemingly impressed with his own logic. "If not many more," he added. Then he turned to sit down.

But Melvin Mills was equally persuasive and a good deal more eloquent. He called into question the doctors' evidence and wondered why Justice McBride had not seen fit to require Rosa Kennedy to testify before either the grand jury or this court. Was it because she was an unreliable Mexican half-breed who chose to stay with Charles Kennedy even while he was supposedly killing and robbing guests in the home that they shared? If she was truly horrified by his alleged activities, she could have left at any point. But she hadn't done so. There was only one inference to draw from her supposed lack of action: She was lying. "What self-respecting woman would stay with a man who did what she claims Kennedy has done?" he demanded.

In the back of the room, Clay Allison's face grew paler and his eyes glittered as Mills proceeded. He watched the jurors, who merely looked thoughtful. They didn't appear to have already made up their minds. But then, they haven't had a chance to talk among themselves, he reflected. Or consider the value of whatever Mills promised in all those little chats he's been having with the various men of the town.

Mills and Fitzmaurice finally finished speaking and the jury was sent into the Middaugh storage space to discuss their verdict. They were secluded for three and a half hours. In the meantime, the Etown saloons—including Middaugh's—were open and busy, the crowd restless with suppressed energy. Allison drifted through the crowd, taking a drink himself now and then, growing more and more quiet as the time wore on.

When the jury returned and the saloon settled back into something resembling a courtroom, Foreman Thomas Pollock was visibly angry. They'd been unable to come to an agreement, he reported, his face tight. He glanced at Mills, Charles beside him, then looked back at Justice McBride. The jury was officially hung. There was no chance that they would reach an agreement. Two of the jury refused to budge in their doubt of Charles' guilt. The trial had been of no use.

"Hell and damnation!" came from the back of the room.

"I'm guessin' Mills didn't spend quite enough," someone said.

"That bastard's usin' stolen gold to buy 'im a verdict!" a man behind Allison growled.

Justice McBride leaned forward. "You're sure you can't reach an agreement?"

Pollock nodded unhappily.

McBride looked at Kennedy. "Well, I'm guessin' that we'll be feedin' you for a while yet." He jerked his head at the jailers standing near the door. "Take him on back to the jail and make sure he gets there." He looked around the room, then slammed his fist down on the table. "Court is dismissed." He gestured behind him. "I'm thinkin' the bar'll be openin' again soon enough." He turned and stomped after Kennedy and his keepers.

"Well, that just beats all!" someone near Allison said.

"Wonder how much Kennedy spent?" a voice asked from the front of the room.

"I need a drink," a voice answered.

The crowd surged toward the bar, but Allison stood silent, his blue eyes focused on the door to the street.

Elizabeth Town Jail, Fall 1870

Ben Houx met Kennedy and his entourage outside the jail. "We've commandeered Jasper Sears' new grocery storehouse to house you instead," he told Charles. "You'll be safer there." He glanced at Mills. "You're welcome to come along, of course."

As they went up the street, the whole town seemed to stop to watch them pass.

"There's more'n one way to get justice," a man's voice growled as they passed the doorway of Stinson's saloon.

"That's why McBride's puttin' him in Sears' storehouse," another man answered. No one in Charles' small group turned their head.

As they neared the log storehouse, Charles glanced at Mills. "Best you could do?" he asked contemptuously.

Mills looked at the building, then realized Kennedy was referring to the trial. "I did the best I could, given the circumstances and your instructions," he said defensively.

"Ain't gettin' more money." Charles brushed past the guards and into the windowless storage building. It was solidly built of heavy Ponderosa pine. Near each inner corner, thick L-shaped iron bars linked the logs to one another. They'd been attached with hand-hewn nails the thickness of a man's thumb. The building had clearly been designed to protect its contents from break-ins and thieves.

"I'll leave you now," Melvin Mills said from the doorway. "I thought I'd consult with Justice McBride again about the potential for bail."

Charles grunted and Mills moved away from the door, leaving it slightly ajar. Charles looked at the logs. Maybe the mob couldn't get in to him, but he sure as hell wasn't gettin' out of this cage, either. He turned toward the door and bellowed "Whisky!"

The two guards looked in. "We ain't neither of us supposed t' leave our post," the older one said.

Charles dug into his pocket and pulled out a coin. It gleamed in the light from the door. The guards looked at each other.

"It'll just take a minute," the younger one said. "It's just two steps 'cross the street."

The older one shrugged. "It's yer head." He gestured at Kennedy with the muzzle of his gun. "Just you keep there an' toss that coin to Junior here," he ordered.

Charles flipped the coin toward the younger man, who caught it deftly. He pocketed the coin and said "I'll be back" as the older man swung the heavy door shut.

Charles blinked in the sudden darkness, then saw that the cabin's logs hadn't been chinked. Slivers of sunlight gleamed through the narrow slits between the timbers. As his eyes adjusted, he saw an iron-framed cot in one corner, a slop bucket in another, and little else but a scuffed-dirt floor and a chair much like the first one he'd sat on in the courtroom. He kicked at it and dropped onto the bed. Mills. Waste of greenbacks. Well, he wasn't gettin' any more 'til Charles was out o' this hell hole.

The latch rattled and the door cracked opened. A hand appeared, clutching a whisky bottle. Charles crossed the room and took the bottle with a grunt of acknowledgement. The door shut with a thud. Charles saw that it, too, was well bound with iron. Wouldn't break down easily.

He returned to the bed and sat, tilting the whisky to his mouth. He patted his money belt with his free hand. Enough to cover

331

whisky and food. Bail when he needed it. Nothin' to do now but drink and eat 'til Mills did his job. Damn lawyer.

Charles lay back on the bed and started making plans. Mills'd get his bail set and he'd pay 'im off, then head back to the cabin, unearth the rest of his money. It wasn't all hidden behind the bed or in the shed. Rosa didn't know about the cache in the rocks up the mountain. Couldn't tell Allison what she didn't know. Lyin' whore.

Then he'd take off south long enough for Etown to forget him. Be back, though. Had scores to settle. That bastard Fitzmaurice. Stinson, too, damn him. And that bitch Rosa.

He tipped the bottle again, thinking about Rosa and what he'd do to her, wondering when she'd begin to wish she was dead, whether he'd kill her then or make her suffer a little longer. He could feel his manhood harden at the thought of it. He chuckled and swallowed more whisky.

He'd gone through two more bottles before noon the next day. When the younger guard came back with the fourth one, he opened the door farther than usual. "There's some folks pretty riled at you over at th' saloon," he said, blocking the sunlight.

"How's that?" Charles heaved himself from the bed and staggered toward him.

"They're sayin' you bought the jury and that Mills'll keep spendin' 'til you're free."

Charles grunted and put his hand on the bottle, but the guard didn't release it.

"How much money you got stashed in that cabin, anyhow?"

Charles jerked the bottle out of the guard's hand. "Go t' hell," he growled.

"You gonna kill me too? With your bare hands?" The young man's face smirked into his. There was whisky on his breath.

Charles raised the bottle at him threateningly, then lowered it. "Waste o' whisky," he said, turning away.

"I think you're just a coward, really. One o' those bully types, pickin' on women and shootin' sleepin' men."

Outside the door, the older guard muttered a warning, but the young one kept his eyes on Charles. "Ain't you?" he asked.

Charles' fist balled into a mass. He raised it. "Want this?" he growled.

The heavy wooden door swung shut and Charles slammed it with his fist. "Want this?" he yelled. Suddenly he was filled with a fierce restlessness, almost sexual in its intensity. He slammed the door again, its boards groaning under the impact.

"Want this?" he howled. He paced along the storehouse walls, slamming his fist into the logs. "Want this?" he yelled. He slammed again. "Want this?" Over and over, he walked the room, fists ramming against the wood, howling at the men outside. "Want this? Want this?" The anger felt good, the need to smash something intensifying with each blow.

~ ~ ~

Gradually, Charles' fit subsided and the whisky began to work. He sank onto the thin mattress and slept.

He woke the next morning to a sudden slash of light across his face as the door opened. Melvin Mills entered, carrying a lantern. When the door swung behind him, he fumbled with the wick and the light flared into Charles' eyes.

Charles put up a hand. "Damn you," he said. "Turn it down."

"I apologize," Mills said, adjusting the wick. "Given the lack of windows in here, I thought some light would be useful while

333

we talked." He put the lantern on the floor and gestured toward the chair. "May I?"

Charles grunted and Mills sat down, his hands folded in his lap. He looked into Charles' face. "I understand that you had a little whisky yesterday evening."

Charles grunted.

"It seems that you became somewhat excited."

Charles shrugged.

"I must ask you to calm yourself," the lawyer said.

Charles' head swiveled toward him. "Calm!" he snarled. "Get me out o' here! Then I'm calm!"

"I am taking action toward that end," Mills said evenly. "I have spoken to Justice McBride about establishing your bail. Due to the cost to the County, he has no desire to hold you until Spring. However, he does wish to first consult with Sheriff Calhoun in Cimarron, since the Sheriff is the official actually responsible for making the formal bail arrangements."

"Takin' long enough," Charles growled.

"The wheels of justice move slowly," Mills said. "Patience is all that's required." He looked around the room. "And how are you doing? Is there anything I can get for you?"

"Whisky."

Mills opened his mouth to object, then shrugged. "I'll see what I can do," he said. "But do try to keep your outbursts to a minimum. Drawing attention to yourself is not helpful. You must be patient." He leaned down to pick up the lantern, then stood. "Justice McBride seemed to believe that he would hear from Sheriff Calhoun sometime tomorrow or possibly Monday," he said. He turned toward the door. "I'm travelling to Cimarron today to inquire as to how I can speed up the process."

Charles grunted and stayed where he was as Mills went out, the door thudding shut behind him. Slivers of sunlight found their way through the uncaulked logs. Fifteen minutes later the older guard swung the door open and handed in a whisky bottle along with the basket containing Charles' morning meal. As he took them, Charles glimpsed a knot of men on the other side of the street, watching the building. He moved to a slit between the logs and peered out. Thomas Pollock, the man who'd acted as jury foreman, was talking to the men, moving his hands as if to encourage the group to move on, but they only nodded impatiently, their eyes fixed on the storehouse. Finally, Pollock moved away, shaking his head.

Charles carried his food to the bed and opened the whisky bottle. Patience, Mills had said. Charles grunted and dug a spoon into the container of stew, then gulped down a slug of whisky. He'd be patient, all right. Once he was out o' here, he'd patiently track Mills down and break his liver-hearted neck.

He devoured the food, then sent for more and another bottle. After he'd finished them both, he settled back on the bed, mind hazy with alcohol, body finally relaxing. "Don' know how t' feed a real man," he muttered. Had t' provide for himself, if he wanted enough. He'd learned that early on an' it was still true.

~ ~ ~

The jailer who brought his evening meal was strangely subdued, but Charles hardly noticed. He ordered another bottle of whisky and drank from it while he ate, then lay down on the bed and watched the trickles of light between the logs fade into nothingness.

He slept heavily, then woke to stumble to the opposite corner and the chamber pot. He'd been using it since he'd first arrived and it hadn't been emptied. Its contents sloshed over the pot's edges as he used it and he turned impatiently away and directed his stream toward the wall. As the urine splashed the logs, he snorted with laughter. This'd fix whoever thought they were gonna store groceries in here. He'd smell it up for 'em. "Real nice," he growled and grinned drunkenly.

Then he blinked and squinted uncertainly at the logs. Flickers of light came through the chinks, casting fitful shadows into the room. Was it daylight again already? He shook his head, trying to clear it, and moved his face closer to an unchinked slit, the pine catching at his beard. Torches. And men. A mass of them, bundled against the cold.

Charles fumbled at his crotch, refastening his clothes as he backed uneasily across the room to the bed.

Outside, there was a murmur of voices as the men with the torches moved closer.

"What d' you want?" a guard asked sharply. Then there was a grunt and a thud.

Charles' head swiveled toward the door. He felt for his half-empty whisky bottle, took a long drink, then shook it irritably. Waste o' liquor. There were voices just outside the door and someone demanded a key. Charles took another gulp, then poured the rest of the alcohol onto the dirt floor and flipped the bottle over, gripping its neck. He cracked the other end sharply against the iron bedstead and the bottom of the bottle split off, falling to the floor just as the door crashed open and a mass of dark shapes poured into the storehouse.

Charles faced the mob head on, the jagged bottle end protruding like a knife from his right hand. "Want this?" he snarled. "Want it?"

~ ~ ~

His size was an advantage, but not for long. The uncertain torch light made it difficult to see where they all were. Indeterminate shapes rushed him from every direction and he swung out in a wide arc. The bottle's jagged end met flesh and he heard a yelp of pain.

Charles chuckled and slammed his left fist into the middle of the dark mass coming at him from the right. Then a club hit him from behind as someone else thrust a torch into his eyes.

He staggered, shook his head, and let out a roar of pain and defiance, striking out aimlessly. But then ropes were snaking around his biceps and another club smashed into his right hand, dashing the broken bottle to the floor.

"Careful o' the glass," a soft Southern voice drawled.

Charles blinked in the torchlight, turning his massive head. "What d' ya want?" he demanded. They were all wearing hoods, except Clay Allison, who materialized two feet in front of him, face pale and eyes glittering in the flickering light.

"We desire justice." Allison's voice was icily quiet. He stared into Kennedy's face. Allison was much thinner than Charles, but they stood eye to eye, the one massive, hair and beard wild, eyes dulled with whisky, the other tight as a wound spring, hair sleek and face sharply alive. If Allison had been drinking, it was only apparent in his voice, which tended to become quieter the drunker and angrier he became.

"You got justice," Kennedy growled. "Jury justice."

"Bought jury!" someone near the door yelped.

"Hung jury!" someone else said.

"You purchased your so-called justice with the gold that you stole," said the man at the end of the ropes that bound him. It was the voice of the Prussian man Coleman.

"We'll show you real justice," another voice said.

"What we'll do to you ain't half 's bad as what you done," growled a voice behind him.

Clay Allison smiled slightly, his eyes on Kennedy's. "The people have spoken," he said sardonically.

Charles looked toward the door. "Guard!" he bellowed. "Guard!"

"Your guards are somewhat indisposed at the moment," Allison said. "But do not concern yourself with their welfare. They'll be hale and hearty again when morning arrives."

"But you ain't!" a voice said from the back of the crowd.

Allison stepped to one side and motioned toward the door. "After you," he said.

Hands tightened on the ropes binding Charles' arms and he was propelled across the room, the mob parting before him. Then he was in the dark and frozen street and the faceless shapes closed around him again, hands grabbing at his shirt and the ropes, someone even pulling on his beard. He shook himself with a roar and the grip on his beard loosened.

"You can' do this!" he bellowed. "I got a lawyer!"

"I hear Melvin Mills has left town," a man's voice said. "And he has your gold with him, too."

"Deputy Houx is out o' town, too," another voice said smugly. "No one t' protect you now, you bastard."

"I'll kill you all!"

"Now, I do believe that to be a most unlikely prospect." Allison's silky voice was just behind him. "Gentlemen, shall we proceed? The slaughterhouse seems appropriate, somehow."

Charles reared back, twisting away from the hands holding the rope. "No, you ain't!" For a single moment he stood alone in the street, bound but with no hands grasping him, then the hooded figures crowded in again.

"Oh, yes we are!" a voice said in his ear. "And we'll do it right here in th' street if you ain't careful. We wouldn't want blood on the street now, would we? Not like that Evans you said th' Injuns killed?"

Someone else chuckled. Charles jerked away, but then multiple hands were shoving him downward and he was on the ground, his ankles being fastened together with rope. The dark shape of a mule appeared. More hands grabbed Charles' legs and ropes were wrenched into place around his thighs. Then he was on his back, feet in the air, head and shoulders scraping against rocks and frozen mud as the mule surged forward, urged on by the mob.

The animal kicked out in panic, striking Charles' legs, but he made no sound. It was a long half-mile to the slaughterhouse at the edge of town, but he bore the rough ride stoically. His torso bumped over the frozen ruts and he focused on keeping his face upright, away from the rocky ground tearing at his shirt and back.

The big wooden slaughterhouse stood off from its neighbors, surrounded by empty corrals now that summer had ended. It was the ideal location for an indoor lynching. Charles glared at the hooded men untying his legs from the mule, but said nothing. He made no move to stand. It took eight men to lift him into the empty building and onto the rough-hewn bench in the center of the barren room, which stank of dried blood. Thick ropes swung from pulleys attached to the massive beams overhead, ready to suspend newly slaughtered cattle for gutting.

They hoisted Charles onto the bench, shoved him into a standing position, and looped a rope around his neck. Then they brought the unwilling mule inside and positioned him behind Charles, facing the other end of the building. The free end of the rope was run through a pulley overhead and tied to the mule's harness. Two men stood at its wild-eyed head, holding it steady.

Charles faced the hooded crowd and glared belligerently.

Clay Allison stood at the front of the group, head and face bare. "Do you have anything to say before you go to your Maker?" he asked. "Would you care to make your confession in the hope of obtaining peace with the Almighty?"

"Ain't no peace," Charles snarled at him. "Cut you in pieces, if I could." He snorted. "Like those other sorry souls." He glared around the dark room. "Wish I'd taken more." He jerked his head toward the town. "Stinson and that bastard Fitz."

Allison's face darkened in disgust and he stepped back. He gestured to the men holding the mule and they coaxed the animal forward, toward the other end of the building. The rope strained through the pulley overhead and lifted Charles' heels only slightly from the bench. He snorted derisively.

Two hooded men leapt forward and shoved at the bench, pushing it out from under Kennedy's feet. As it toppled out of the way, he snorted again, then there was a snapping sound and his body was dangling in the glare of the torches, the rope straining overhead.

The mob stared for a long silent moment, then someone near the door yelled "Yippee!"

"It was justice he got this time," Joseph Coleman's voice said. "The bastard."

"So he did kill all those men," Joe Kinsinger's voice said. "I'll be damned."

"And cut them to pieces," Clay Allison said grimly. "Ya'll heard him." He nodded to the men with the mule. "You can release the body now." He turned away. "And get that long-sufferin' mule out of here."

Charles' big body fell to the dirt floor with a thud and the mob crowded around it. Someone prodded his shoulder with a booted toe. "He don't seem all that big now," he said.

~ ~ ~

There was a long silence as the men stared down at Kennedy's body. Clay Allison had disappeared. Then someone said, "Guess we should put him back in Sears' storehouse."

"Or give 'im a taste of his own medicine. Cut 'im up and bury 'im in separate pieces."

"Naw, then Satan couldn't find him on judgment day."

There was a general chuckle.

"That mule still here? We could give him a taste o' more dirt."

"Naw, that mule's seen enough fer one night."

"It ain't night much longer."

"I've half a mind to shoot him up, just for good measure."

"Waste o' bullets."

"Hangin' was too good for him."

Clay Allison emerged from the shadows, a slaughtering knife the size of a machete in his hand. The men around Charles' body moved back silently, suddenly cautious. Allison was unpredictable when he'd been drinking, especially when blood had been shed. He stood over the massive body for a long, silent moment. Then he nudged Kennedy's head with the toe of his boot, straightening the neck, and bent forward. The knife flashed out, then down, in the torchlight.

Kennedy's head rolled away from the base of his neck. There was a sound from the mob, somewhere between a gasp and a chuckle.

"That'll do it, Clay!" someone laughed.

"Cut 'im up just like he did them!" another voice said.

"Gimme the knife!"

"No, that's enough." As Allison straightened, he lifted the dripping head by Kennedy's black hair. "We'll need a container for this, then you all can drag his carcass back to the storehouse or bury it. But cutting any more would make us as savage as he was." A smile flickered across his pale face. "And 'was' is the operative word here, gentleman. The beast is dead and retribution has been paid." He turned toward the door. Someone handed him a gunny sack and he dropped the severed head into it.

"What ya gonna do with it?" someone asked.

"We ought to put it up somewheres, as 'n example," a voice suggested. "Or take it to Mrs. Kennedy."

"Take it to Lambert," someone said. "He's the great chef. He can cook it like Kennedy did those horses."

Allison grinned. "Now that's an interesting idea. Let's take it to Henry. We'll put it outside his place as a warning to Attorney Mills when he comes riding back into town. We do justice here, regardless of the amount of one's money or the so-called law of the Union." He lifted the gunnysack shoulder-high and raised his voice. "We do justice!"

There was a ragged cheer, then the crowd followed him outside and down the street. The darkness in the eastern sky was starting to lift as daylight approached, though a quarter moon still hung low in the west. As they moved up the street, men in dark hoods began peeling off into the shadows, so that there was only a small group to face Henry Lambert when he met them at his hotel door.

"And what is it that you have there?" he asked. His French accent leant an extra level of politeness to his tone, but his body blocked the doorway firmly. It was clear that he'd already been informed of the sack's contents and the group's purpose.

Clay Allison held out the gunnysack as if presenting Lambert with a gift. "A warning to those who kill miners and abuse women."

"Ah," the Frenchman said, peering into Allison's face, his hands on his hips. "And what is it you plan to do with this warning?"

"Vamos, Frenchy!" someone behind Allison muttered. "Come on!"

"Hoist it!" someone else hissed.

"It's cold out here," a voice complained. The men jostled closer to Allison and the sack, but neither he nor Lambert moved.

"It would appear that justice has been served," Lambert observed, crossing his arms across his chest.

"Executed," Allison said with a slight smile.

Lambert smiled back at him. "And now? What is it that you intend?"

"To enhance the likelihood that no further depredations are made on the gentlemen or ladies of these parts, it seems appropriate to inform and remind the populace of the repercussions of such acts," Allison said formally. "It occurs to me that a prominent position in the environs of the most distinguished establishment in Colfax County would serve as an appropriate device for such a reminder."

Lambert smiled. "And Lambert's Etown hotel and restaurant is so fortunate as to be this establishment?"

Allison flourished his free hand toward the men behind him. "It has been so designated by the consensus of those who assisted in implementing the justice of which we speak."

Lambert chuckled, but there was no mirth in his eyes as he looked at the hooded men behind Allison, then into Allison's face. "You are certainly in fine form this morning, Clay." He shook his head. "But a severed head, that would not be appetizing to my guests." He glanced at the windows above him. "Or aid in the peaceful rest of my wife or any other lady who might honor my establishment with her presence."

Allison and the others looked at him silently. No one moved.

"Perhaps it could be placed on a pole in the garden." Lambert gestured toward the back of the building.

Allison shrugged and turned from the doorway. The men behind him muttered, but moved aside. A few of them followed him to the back of the building, where he gingerly peeled the gunnysack away from Kennedy's bloody head and lifted it carefully onto a metal stick that had supported a bean vine a month before. He held out his hands, filthy from his work, and one of the hooded miners proffered a canteen.

As the liquid splashed over Allison's palms, he looked down sharply, then lifted his hands to his face. He sniffed. "That's good whisky, man!" he said with a laugh. He slapped the man on his shoulder. "Now that's a quite unnecessary sacrifice for the sake of justice!"

They all laughed and moved back around the building, toward the street and their various dwelling places.

As they went, the sky began to turn a pale, translucent blue. The rays of the morning sun touched the snow atop Baldy Peak to the east, highlighting its pristine whiteness. A light breeze sprang up, rustling the needles of the pines that darkened the valley's sides. And the open eyes in Charles Kennedy's severed head gazed blindly at it all.

Moreno Valley, Fall 1870

When Gregoria woke that Saturday morning, it was full daylight. Since she had arrived at the Kinkaid place earlier in the week, she'd risen before the others each day, just as the mountain tops on both sides of the valley were beginning to glow, to prepare the morning meal. They had been good days, filled with calm and enough work to keep her mind occupied, to save her from thinking about her loss. She liked rising so early in the peaceful household.

But today when she woke, the sunlight was streaming through the small window in the lean-to where she slept just off the kitchen and she could smell eggs and bacon frying. Burning, in fact. She grimaced as she sat up, then shook her head and smiled. Alma must be cooking.

But there were voices in the next room that she did not recognize. Male voices trying to speak softly, but not those of William Kincaid and the child Alfred. They seemed constrained and a little anxious. Gregoria's stomach tightened and she frowned and reached for her clothes. Something had happened. Something was wrong.

Word had come yesterday that the jury had failed to reach a verdict, that Charles was back in jail. Had he escaped? Fear clenched her stomach. She dressed hurriedly, smoothed her hair behind her ears, and opened the door to the kitchen.

Alma turned from the big black cooking range and smiled at her, a long metal fork in her hand. "We were trying not to wake you," she said apologetically. Three strange men sat at the table, egg-stained plates and full coffee cups before them.

"Buenos días," Gregoria said. She moved to the table to begin clearing dishes. "I overslept. Lo siento."

"No need to be sorry," Alma said firmly. "I wanted you to sleep." She looked at the men at the table. "There was news from Elizabethtown and I thought a little rest would help to prepare you for it."

Gregoria's hand froze as she reached for a plate. She felt her breath stop. "Qué?"

Alma and the men shared a glance. The oldest one took his hat off his knee and stood up. "I'm thinkin' we'll be goin' now." He nodded to Alma. "Thankee kindly for the fixins." He bobbed his head at Gregoria. "Ma'am. Good day to ya." He put his hat on his head and backed out of the room.

The other two men murmured "Thank you" and "Good morning" and hurried after him.

Gregoria stared after them, her anxiety building. Alma chuckled and shook her head ruefully as their footsteps receded down the hall to the front door.

Gregoria swallowed against the thickness in her throat. "There is news?"

Alma sobered and put the metal fork on the counter beside the stove. "Please sit down, Gregoria," she said gently. "Would you like coffee?"

Gregoria nodded numbly and sat. She stared blindly at the dirty dishes still on the table. Charles has escaped, she thought despairingly. I have brought danger to my friends.

Alma filled two cups and brought them to the table, then sat down across from Gregoria.

Gregoria clutched the coffee cup between her hands but did not lift it to her lips. She looked at Alma. A shudder went through her

347

and the hot liquid sloshed dangerously. She set the cup on the table. "What is it?" she asked. "He has escaped?"

Alma shook her head. "He is dead," she said gently. "A mob broke into the jail last night. They hanged him."

Gregoria stared at her.

"There is more." Alma's lips tightened. "You might as well know all of it. You're bound to hear, sooner or later." She looked at the table, then into Gregoria's face. "After Kennedy died, Clay Allison cut off his head with a slaughter knife and stuck it on a pike outside Henry Lambert's hotel."

Gregoria stared at her in horror. She reached for the coffee cup, but her hands were shaking and she couldn't lift it without the hot liquid spilling. She covered her face with her hands.

"It is too horrible," she said. She took a deep breath and put her hands palm-down on the table, staring at them. "He killed those men and my nene." She looked up. "If he had escaped, he would have come here and put your life in danger. Yours and William's and little Alfred's." She shook her head. "But he suffered too. He wanted so much to be looked upon with respect. He thought money would give him that. And stealing was all that he knew. He didn't know how else to be. His anger and his lust and his fists." She closed her eyes. "It was all that he knew," she repeated. She looked at Alma beseechingly, tears streaming down her face.

Alma smiled through her own tears. "You have a good heart."

"No. I was afraid and I didn't try to stop him." Gregoria shook her head. "When I finally acted, it was because I was angry about what he had done to my poor Samuelito." She closed her eyes. "I thought I would be happy if he were punished. Glad that he could no longer hurt me or anyone else." She grimaced. "But to lynch him and cut off his head—" She opened her eyes and looked into Alma's face, shaking her head. "Mr. Allison seemed like such a

nice man. Such a gentleman." She shuddered. "It is too horrible."
She shook her head again. "I don't know what to think. How to
feel."

Alma nodded sympathetically and stared into her own coffee
cup for a long moment. "Clay Allison is a complicated man," she
said slowly. "And he finds men who abuse women very difficult
to understand. Also, it seems that there was some fear in the town
that Charles would escape or be set free." She shook her head.
"And I don't think Clay knows how to look at things from someone else's perspective," she said ruefully. She got up and moved
around the table to sit in the chair next to Gregoria's. She put an
arm around the younger woman's shoulders. "But whatever you
feel, that is what you should feel," she said. "Both the pain and the
sorrow."

They sat for a long time, Gregoria sobbing quietly, Alma's arm
comforting her.

~ ~ ~

"And now I have no one," Gregoria murmured. She bit her lip
and gazed out the small glass window of her lean-to bedroom. She
could see Alma in the bottom of the garden which sloped away
from the house. She was placing straw over the cabbages and car-
rots she hoped to carry through the winter. Alfred ran between the
rows, grabbing at his mother's apron strings each time he trotted
past her. She would turn, scolding laughingly, then return to her
work. Gregoria smiled, then the tears came again. Samuelito
would have done that, when he was a little older.

Her child's smiling eyes rose in her memory and she groped
her way to the bed. Her nene was gone. Charles had taken him
from her. She felt only pity for Charles, now that she was safe

from him, but his greed and impatience had taken Samuelito from her and now she had no one. The pain of it overwhelmed her.

There is still mi papá, she reminded herself. Wherever he is.

How grateful she had been to him the night he found her beside the road! She might have died, as cold and weary as she was. Certainly she wouldn't have had the strength to walk to Etown by herself. But she had not seen him since he'd testified before the grand jury. He had simply disappeared.

As he has disappeared from my life so many times, she thought wearily. Disappeared emotionally after the death of mi mamá, sided with the man who molested me, ran away when he saw what Charles was doing. She felt the self-pity rise and she accepted it, weeping into her hands. "I have no one now," she murmured again.

She looked around the tiny room. It was clean and warm and she was safe here, but she would be a servant for the rest of her days. Alma was kind, but there had been a subtle change in their relationship since Gregoria had arrived. Alma was in charge.

As it should be between employer and employee, Gregoria told herself. Yet the feeling between them had shifted away from friendship and Gregoria didn't like it. I should be thankful for what I have, she told herself sternly. And she did feel thankful. But she also felt trapped.

Gregoria sighed and rose from the bed. It would be time for the midday meal soon and she should begin preparations. But as she moved toward the door, it swung open and her father stood before her.

His shoulders were as hunched as always and his battered brown hat was twisted in his hands, but his eyes were bright as he looked at her. "You are safe," he said.

Gregoria nodded mutely, too surprised to speak.

"I did not know where you had gone."

She returned to the bed and sat down, motioning him to the single chair.

"Lo siento," he said. He twisted his hat again, looking at it intently. "I was afraid to ask where you were."

"For fear of the questions," she said, watching him.

He nodded at his hat. "No one seemed to guess that I was your papá."

She smiled slightly. "Yes. It was a good thing."

He looked up. "But now it is done. He is dead."

She shuddered in response and looked away.

"We are blameless?" It was more a question than a statement. Gregoria peered into her father's face, which was twisted in pain, his eyes avoiding hers. "It is a horrible way to die," he said.

"We are blameless," she said firmly. "He had done great wrong. The americanos chose to punish him as they did. We did not choose it."

He nodded absently and looked around the room. "You will stay here?"

She started to nod, then shook her head. "I do not know," she said. "The Kinkaids are kind to me, but—"

"I had thought to go home."

She gave him a puzzled frown.

"To Ranchos," he explained. "Or Taos. Perhaps north." He shrugged. "Wherever there is work."

She nodded and looked at her hands.

There was a long silence, then he said, "You will come with me?"

She looked up in surprise. He looked into her eyes, then away. "I have very little," he said apologetically. "A few coins."

351

"I can manage with very little," she said. "It has always been so."

He smiled at her tremulously, then he crossed himself, his lips moving in a prayer of thanksgiving.

~ ~ ~

"Lo siento," Gregoria said. "I cannot stay." Her eyes followed Alfred as he headed across the field toward his father, who was examining the hooves of a horse in the south pasture.

Alma shook her head. "Do not be sorry." She gestured toward the dark green of the mountains surrounding them. "This valley holds too much pain for you now."

Gregoria's eyes followed her gaze. "Its beauty reminds me of what I have lost," she admitted.

"As does my son."

Gregoria shook her head, but Alma smiled sadly. "It is natural enough." She reached for Gregoria's hands, holding them gently within her own, and looked into her eyes. "Perhaps someday you will return. When the pain has softened."

"That doesn't seem possible."

Alma smiled again, a shadow crossing her face. "Pain does fade, a little. Over time. As does the sorrow. I have experienced it." She sighed. "Although I'm afraid it will always be there somewhere, marking you."

Gregoria straightened her shoulders. "But I must somehow continue."

Alma nodded. She released Gregoria's hands and reached into her skirt pocket. She pulled out a battered brown leather wallet. "Clay Allison sent this to you. It contains the balance of what he retrieved from the cabin, after he'd paid the hotel bill."

Gregoria drew back.

"You earned this," Alma said. "With your cooking and cleaning and raised biscuits. You fed weary travelers and guarded them as well as you could from Kennedy's intentions. It is rightfully yours." She held it out. "There isn't much in it. Perhaps twenty dollars. And I've added a little for what you have done while you've been here."

Gregoria took it gingerly. "Gracias," she murmured. "You have been most kind to me."

"No hay de que," Alma said. There is nothing to thank me for.

The two women smiled into each other's eyes, then Alma reached out, hugged Gregoria tightly, and released her. "Go now, before I start crying," she said with a damp smile.

Gregoria turned away, toward her father and the waiting road.

~ ~ ~

Dread knotted Gregoria's stomach as she and her father crested the swale south of the cabin at the foot of Palo Flechado Pass. She stopped and stared down the slope, toward what remained of her garden. Her father reached for her hand, but she pulled it away, focusing on the hollow and its contents.

The cabin and corral looked so small from here, though they'd loomed so large in her experience. There was no sign of the mules or the buckboard. Taken by the men of the town, she supposed. Most of what was left of the bean crop had collapsed in the early October cold. The elk and deer would feast well this winter. A smile flickered across her face. She didn't begrudge them the work she'd put into the garden. It had been a pleasure. A relief. And some of their fellow creatures had given their lives so that she and her child might eat.

353

Gregoria closed her eyes, hearing Samuel's laughter as he played with the small stones she'd turned up. A long shudder went through her and she opened her eyes. Her father was watching her anxiously and she smiled at him.

"They told me that Samuel is buried near the garden," she said. "I would like to stop for a moment."

"Is there anything you wish to collect from the cabin?" he asked. "Food or cooking utensils?"

She shook her head. "I think it has probably all been removed," she said. "By the men who came for Charles and those who undoubtedly came after, to look for his gold."

"And there are too many memories," he said.

She nodded and her father patted her arm awkwardly, then they started down the slope toward the hollow.

~ ~ ~

Gregoria knelt beside her child's grave and ran her fingers lightly over the roughly-carved cross someone had chipped into the piece of granite that had been placed at its head. Her father stood waiting beside the road, but still she lingered, thinking over all that had happened in the last three years, and the men in her life: the man who had blamed her for the atrocities he committed and the man who now stood, hat in hand, thin shoulders hunched against the October breeze, lips moving in prayer.

Her father had failed her. He would fail her again. She knew it for a certainty. "As we all fail each other, sooner or later," she murmured, tracing the cross once again. She looked toward the stream and the tiny grave that lay beside it. As she had failed that child and Samuel and even Charles. Certainly, as Charles had failed her. And Samuel. She shuddered and her mind turned away from the pain of it.

She closed her eyes. What had Clay Allison said to her? "I will strive to be as true to you as I am to myself." And yet he had led the lynching and beheading. How true to himself had he been? She shook her head, eyes still closed. He was a complicated man, Señor Allison.

"As are we all," Gregoria murmured. A complicated mixture of failure and strength. She turned her face to the sunlight that filtered through the ponderosas at the edge of the hollow. And none of us really know which will be uppermost at a given moment, failure or strength, she mused. When we will fail ourselves or those about us. We cause each other such pain and such sorrow. Yet all we can do is try to forgive, learn from our failures, and move on.

She bowed her head for a long moment in wordless contemplation, breathed in the sharp-sweet smell of the pines, opened her eyes, and stood up. An eagle cried overhead. Gregoria looked across the valley, at the landscape she had grown to love in spite of everything. But it too was complicated, with its serene summer beauty and its bitter winter winds. Just now, the afternoon sunlight glinted off the mountains to the east, bathing its peaks in a serene brightness. Gregoria smiled at the reflected beauty and gently patted her son's headstone.

"Adiós, mi nene," she murmured. "Rest in peace. It is a good place to rest." And then she rose and moved forward to join her father at the edge of the road.

THE END

Postscript: On December 20, 1871, about fourteen months after Charles Kennedy's death, María Gregoria Cortez Kennedy married Antonio Chavez of Placita de los Dolores at the Nuestra Senora de Guadalupe church in Don Fernando de Taos, New Mexico Territory. This was the same church where Gregoria had married Charles and where Samuel had been baptized. It is likely that Padre Gabriel Ussel officiated at this wedding, as well.

Note to Reader

There is a northern New Mexico legend goes something like this: On a dark and stormy night in late September 1870, a young woman burst into a saloon in the mountain mining town of Elizabeth City (aka Elizabethtown or Etown) with a gruesome tale. Her husband, Charles Kennedy, had been robbing and killing guests in their home. The victims that weren't buried under the floor had been chopped into pieces and burned. That day, he'd killed their young son. A group of miners went to the cabin that night, arrested Kennedy, and hauled him to Etown. A few days later, they held an impromptu trial. When two members of the hurriedly-assembled jury refused to make his guilt unanimous, Kennedy was returned to jail. A mob led by gunslingers Clay Allison and Davey Crockett, Jr. liberated Kennedy from jail, lynched and be-headed him, then stuck his head on a pike in front of a Cimarron saloon thirty miles away.

It's a story that seems too gruesome to be true, but newspaper accounts from the period support its basic outline. As I read the modern retellings of these reports, I couldn't help but wonder what would prompt a woman to marry a man like Kennedy in the first place. And why would she stay with him as he killed and then killed again?

Why she left seemed clear enough: he'd killed her child. But some of the popular retellings indicated that there were other children. These same retellings also contradicted each other on important points such as Kennedy's wife's name and origins, whether she was actually married to Kennedy, and the age of the child he killed.

All of this made me curious. With the invaluable assistance of staff at the New Mexico State Archives, Colfax County Clerk's Office, Raton and Silver City Public Libraries, Taos Latter Day Saints Family History Center, University of New Mexico-Taos Southwest Research Center, Moreno Valley locals Jacqui Binford-Bell and Jack Schweitzer, and others, I began digging. What I discovered clarified critical information about the people involved and also helped me to imagine a possible rationale for the actions of both Kennedy and his wife—the rationale that became the basis for this novel. Here is what I learned:

Charles Kennedy may not have been his real name. The marriage record for Kennedy and his wife, the baptismal record for their son, most of the District Court records for Charles, and the 1870 Colfax County probate record following his death, all refer to him as Charles Canady. However, the 1870 Census data, some of the court records, and the October 1870 *Daily New Mexican* account of his death refer to him as Charles Kennedy.

Given the similarity between the pronunciations of Kennedy and Canady, it's easy to see how this confusion might have occurred. Because the Kennedy spelling is used in the modern retellings as well as in the Moreno Valley where the events occurred, I chose to use it in the novel. But for research purposes, discovering the Canady spelling opened up quite a trove of artifacts. I am grateful to Nita at the University of New Mexico-Taos Southwest Research Center for pointing out this important piece of information early on in my research process.

Kennedy/Canady was married to a girl of Spanish heritage. Some of the modern retellings of the Kennedy legend claim that the woman who reported his misdoings was Kennedy/Canady's common-law wife and a Ute Indian. Neither of these assertions are supported by the historical record. According to Our Lady of Guadalupe Church records in Taos, Charles Canady married María Gregoria Cortez (alternatively spelled "Cortes") on February 28, 1867. She was from Ranchos de Taos, a village just south of Taos, and the daughter of José de Jesus Cortez and María Antonia Lucero. Her mother was dead at the time of the marriage. Other records indicate that her mother may have died some years earlier, following the birth of a son who also died, and that María Gregoria was not quite fifteen years old at the time of her marriage. The 1870 census data lists her as "Gregoria," a common nuevomexicano custom at a time when many girls bore the first name "María."

Nothing in the marriage or census records indicates that Gregoria, her parents, or her grandparents were Native American—a fact which was usually stated in these types of documents during that era. Given the status of Native Americans in the mid-nineteenth century, especially in the eyes of the Anglo population, Gregoria's silence about Kennedy's activities might be more easily understood if she had been Indian. This would have been a fruitful topic for fictional exploration. However, there is no evidence in the church or census records to support this claim and therefore I did not incorporate the idea into the novel.

A number of the modern retellings of the Kennedy/Canady story also report that his wife was named Rosa. Although there is also no historical evidence for this claim, I chose to use the name in the novel by having Charles rename her Rosa instead of using Gregoria's birth name. I saw this as a possible strategy in what I imagined to be Charles' attempts to undermine her sense of self as part of a larger campaign of abuse and domination. That she was sexually and emotionally abused is, of course, my assumption. It seems a plausible explanation for her silence about Kennedy's activities during the three and a half years she was married to him.

The Kennedy/Canadys lived at the base of Palo Flechado Pass, which is approximately twelve miles south of what remains of Elizabethtown. The modern retellings of the Kennedy/Canady story locate the rancho anywhere from the outskirts of Etown to twenty miles away. However, a homestead claim filed about six months after Charles' death on "a place known as Canady's Ranch ... commencing at the Palo Fletchorio (sic) and extending 1/2 miles square from said point at the mouth of Taos Cañon" corresponds to the Moreno Valley tradition that the Kennedy cabin lay at the base of Palo Flechado Pass.

A road through the pass still connects to San Fernando River canyon, then through it west to Taos. East of the pass, the road to Etown is joined by a road that travels south to Mora. The base of Palo Flechado Pass would have been a prime location for waylaying travelers looking for a place to rest on their way to and from Taos, Mora, Elizabethtown, and Cimarron (also known at the time as "Maxwell's Place") to the east.

The child Charles killed was very young and their only living child. Samuel Kennedy was born in June 1869 and baptized at Taos' Our Lady of Guadalupe church on September 29, 1869 at age three months and five days. Thus, he would have been about fifteen months old in late September 1870, when he is said to have been killed. Some of the modern retellings state that the Kennedy/Canady child was ten years old when he died, while others make him three. Neither age is supported by the historical record.

Samuel is the only child listed in the Kennedy household in the July 1870 Census record. Since Charles and Gregoria married in early 1867, it seems highly likely that she had been pregnant prior to bearing Samuel and had lost those children in some way. This idea is supported by some of the modern retellings, which state that there were previous pregnancies or children who did not survive prior to Samuel's birth. I chose to incorporate this idea into the novel as a way of further demonstrating the abuse that I imagine Gregoria suffered at Charles' hands.

Charles had been in trouble with the law prior to Gregoria's flight. Thanks to the research skills of the staff of the New Mexico State Archives, I know of four cases in which Charles Kennedy/Canady was named as a defendant in New Mexico's courts:

In Fall 1868, Charles Kennedy/Canady was charged in Mora County with selling a gill of liquor without a license. Mora County was split into Mora and Colfax counties in early 1869, with Etown as the Colfax County seat. That Spring, the Kennedy case was transferred to Colfax County. It was dismissed by Judge Joseph Palen during the Fall 1869 District Court session in Etown at the request of New Mexico Territory's then-Attorney General Thomas B. Catron.

In Spring 1869, Adolph Letcher, a merchant who'd recently moved his operations from Taos to Las Vegas via a burro train across the Sangre de Cristos, sued Charles Kennedy/Canady for nonpayment of funds owed on some cattle, as well as an additional $75 loan. Letcher informed the court at the Fall 1869 session that he wished to dismiss the case.

In Spring 1870, Charles Kennedy/Canady was charged with assault with a deadly weapon against Etown merchant Joseph Coleman. Details of the encounter and weapon, as well as a list of witnesses, are provided in the court docket. At the Fall 1870 court session, with Attorney Theodore D. Wheaton of Taos acting for Kennedy/Canady, the charge was reduced to simple assault and a fine of $10 and court costs was assessed.

Also in Spring 1870, Charles Kennedy/Canady was charged with embezzling $110 and "the goods and chattels" of Etown laborer Edward Baker. Baker and Kennedy/Canady both signed bonds guaranteeing their appearance at the Fall 1870 session, when the case was to be tried. Although Baker is listed in the Etown precinct's July 1870 census data, he did not appear for court in late August, thus forfeiting his $100 bond. Because there was no witness, Judge Palen dismissed the case. Although there is no direct evidence that Charles killed Baker to prevent his appearance, it seems likely, given Kennedy/Canady's other activities, which were reported in some detail to the Silver City *Southwest Sentinel* in 1885 by Joseph Kinsinger, who was living in Etown in 1870.

Charles Kennedy faced two juries. Although the modern retellings generally report only one trial, which resulted in a hung jury and Kennedy's remand to jail, the mid-October 1870 Santa Fe *Daily New Mexican* report of his trial and death provides details from two trials. The first seems to have occurred soon after Kennedy's arrest and to have been a formal legal proceeding, apparently a grand jury investigation. This is the trial at which José Cortez and Doctors Westerling and Bradford testified. A second trial followed a few days later, after the exhumation of a body at the Kennedy cabin which fit the description of the man José Cortez said he'd seen murdered the previous Christmas Eve.

This second trial is referred to by the newspaper as a "public meeting" and "impromptu trial" (implying that it wasn't a truly legal proceeding) and resulted in a hung jury. The newspaper reports that, following this second trial, "a party of men, armed and disguised, surprised the guard, took Kennedy from prison, carried him to an old slaughterhouse about half a mile from town," and lynched him.

Charles Kennedy probably didn't die on October 7, 1870. Although it is commonly accepted in northern New Mexico that Charles Kennedy's lynching and death occurred on Friday, October 7, 1870, there are discrepancies in the historical record that make this date highly unlikely.

At first glance, the October 7 date is correct: in mid-October 1870, the *Daily New Mexican* reported that Kennedy was tried "last month" and then lynched on Friday, the 7th. Since September 7, 1870 did not fall on a Friday, the newspaper account has been interpreted to mean that Kennedy was killed on Friday, October 7. The October 7 date is repeated in all of the modern retellings as well as on the replica tombstone in today's Elizabethtown cemetery.

However, the Colfax County Probate Court entry that names Kennedy/Canady's lawyer Melvin W. Mills as executor of the deceased Charles Canady's estate is dated Tuesday, October 4, 1870. This is three days prior to October 7. Clearly, Kennedy did not die on October 7, 1870, after his death had already been recorded in the County Probate records.

I can only surmise that the *Daily New Mexican* reporter was confused in his time sequence and, in an attempt to be precise, misreported the date of Kennedy's death. (As a former newspaper reporter, I know how easily this type of confusion can occur!) For the purposes of my story's timeline, I've assumed that the statement that Kennedy/Canady died on a Friday night is correct and that only a few days passed between his lynching and Mills' appointment as executor. This would place the lynching on Friday, September 30, 1870, a week prior to Friday, October 7. Given the local tradition that Gregoria's walk to Etown occurred across a cold and stormy landscape, it seems logical that her trek, about ten days prior to Charles' death, would have taken place in late September, during a period when the Moreno Valley typically experiences more erratic than usual weather patterns.

Davey Crockett, Junior didn't participate in the lynching. A number of the modern retellings of the Kennedy lynching place Davey Crockett, Jr. at the scene. The nephew of Congressman Davey Crockett, who died at the Alamo in 1836, Crockett, Jr. would himself be killed in 1876 during a Colfax County War shootout in Cimarron. According to Clay Allison's biographer Chuck Parsons, Crockett, Jr. was in Texas at the time of the Kennedy lynching. In fact, Parsons says it's not even certain that Allison was in Etown at the time, although he concedes that it's possible.

I've chosen to incorporate Allison into my storyline because, given his reputation for loving excitement, it seems likely that, if he was in Colfax County at the time, he would have been in Etown, where the action and the gold were. Allison was also known for his gallantry towards women, so it's plausible that he would be involved in any activity that redressed a wrong done a woman, especially a pretty one. He also had a propensity for sticking up for the underdog, a characteristic that would be demonstrated more fully during the soon-to-begin Colfax County War.

Kennedy's severed head didn't end up in at Lambert's Hotel in Cimarron. Legend has it that Clay Allison and Davey Crockett, Jr. carried Charles Kennedy's severed head to Cimarron in a bloody gunnysack and placed it on a pike in front of Henri Lambert's Hotel and Saloon (now the St. James Hotel), as a warning to passersby of the consequences of evildoing in Colfax County. However, Lambert's establishment was still located in Elizabethtown in 1870. He would not move to Cimarron until 1872.

So, while my storyline includes the portion of the legend involving Charles' head being severed and placed on a pike, it does not include the ride through Cimarron canyon, blood-soaked gunnysack in tow. As picturesque as that ride might have been, it is highly doubtful that it happened. Even if it had, Kennedy's head wouldn't have ended up outside Lambert's establishment, which was still in Etown in 1870. I believe my interpretation of the legend is probably closer to what actually occurred.

As fascinating as the research for this novel has been, many of my questions have remained unanswered. I would like very much to know if the José Cortez recorded in the 1870 Census as living near the Kennedy/Canady cabin really was Gregoria's father, what actually motivated Charles' killings, what Gregoria grew in her garden (listed in the Probate Court inventory as being 4,000 yards and containing produce worth $250, a decent sum for the time), what she and other historical figures looked like, how many people Charles actually killed (in 1885 Kinsinger reported that he claimed twenty-one deaths), and a thousand other details.

As I see it, the historical novelist's role is to gather the historic record, fill in the gaps in that record as plausibly as possible, and then (most importantly) imagine the emotions and motives of the people who lived those events, trying to understand what drove them and what we can learn from their lives today.

Writing about Gregoria and Charles Kennedy has taken me deep into the past and the human psyche. I hope this novel will take my readers there, also, and bring them forward into the present with a clearer understanding of themselves as well as what might have driven Charles, Gregoria, and the Etown mob to do what they did. After all, our fears and motivations today are not so very different from theirs then, though the resulting events may not be enacted in quite the same way.

.

HISTORICAL CHARACTERS

Allison, Robert Clay (1841-1887) Confederate Civil War veteran and gunslinger who claimed he never killed a man who didn't need killing, but who also had a soft spot for ladies and children. Allison was responsible for a number of deaths in Colfax County. Some of the related bullet holes are still visible in the tin ceiling of the historic St. James Hotel bar in Cimarron. He was active during the Colfax County War in the 1870s, but moved to Texas in the 1880s, where he died. Allison is reported to have been involved in the arrest and eventual lynching of Charles Kennedy. For more information, see Chuck Parsons' Clay Allison, *Portrait of a Shootist*, Pioneer Book Publishers, 1983.

Ashurst, Merrill (circa 1808-1869) Alabama attorney who arrived in New Mexico in 1851 and was noted for his ability to speak Spanish before juries. He was elected to the New Mexico Territorial Legislature that same year and was U.S. Attorney General for New Mexico from 1852 to 1854. Ashurst was reappointed to the position in 1867 and served in that capacity during the Spring 1868 Mora County District Court session before resigning in early 1869 due to illness. He was, however, apparently still well enough to practice law, because in the Spring of 1869 he acted as counsel to Lucien and Luz Maxwell in a Colfax County case involving the unauthorized harvesting of timber on their lands.

Babcock, Henry S. (circa 1830-?) Forty-year-old New York-born carpenter who lived in Elizabethtown (aka Etown) in 1870. Babcock was present at the 1869 Kennedy/Coleman incident and was one of five men who, during the Spring 1870 Colfax County

367

District Court session, swore to testify against Kennedy at the next term. He served as court bailiff during that same session.

Baker, Edward (1844-?) Twenty-six-year-old Elizabethtown laborer who in April 1870 complained to Colfax County officials that Charles Kennedy had embezzled $103 worth of goods and chattels from him the previous November. Baker had also been a witness to the 1869 Kennedy/Coleman incident. Although he swore at the Spring District Court to appear against Kennedy at the August 1870 session, he did not. As a result, the embezzlement charge was dropped. There's no direct evidence that Baker was killed by Charles Kennedy, though his disappearance was convenient.

Beaubien, Charles 'Carlos' (1800-1864) Quebec-born trapper of aristocratic French-Canadian descent who arrived in New Mexico in early 1824. Beaubien gave up trapping relatively early to become a merchant in Taos. He married María Paulita Lobato of Taos in 1827 and applied for Mexican citizenship two years later. In 1841 Beaubien was co-grantee, along with Provincial Secretary Guadalupe Miranda, of what would become the Maxwell Land Grant in Colfax County. Beaubien's oldest daughter Maria de la Luz married Lucien Bonaparte Maxwell. Together, they consolidated ownership of the land and in 1870 sold it to what would become the Maxwell Land Grant and Railway Corporation.

Benitez, Frederico (? - ?) Mora County Sheriff's deputy who was sent to Palo Flechado Pass to arrest Charles Kennedy for selling liquor without a license. He was apparently unable to complete this task.

Berger, Frederick (? - ?) Member of the Petit Jury during the Colfax County District Court Spring 1869 session, despite the fact that the grand jury charged him during that same session with one count of permitting gaming. The case against him was dismissed during the Fall 1869 term.

Bradford, Doctor Fred G.H. (circa 1837- ?) Thirty-two-year-old Elizabethtown doctor who, along with Doctor Westerling, provided evidence during the Charles Kennedy trial in the Fall of 1870. According to the 1870 census, Doctor Bradford was born in Maine.

Calhoun, Andrew J. (1823 - 1889) Illinois-born Sheriff of Colfax County, New Mexico in 1870. He lived in Cimarron, where he kept a hotel. Although he was Sheriff, he was not above the law and was fined $50 at both 1870 court sessions for allowing gambling. He was also a partner with Kit Carson in a copper mining company claim near Coyote, New Mexico, north of Mora. By the mid-1870s Calhoun was a forage agent for Fort Union, supplying them with hay from his Ocaté ranch, where he also operated a stage station. He died there in 1889.

Catron, Thomas Benton "Tom" (1840-1921) Successor to Merrill Ashurst as U.S. Attorney General for New Mexico. While serving as Attorney General during the 1869 and 1870 Colfax County District Court sessions, Catron also practiced as a private attorney. He represented Adolph Letcher in an 1869 suit against Charles Kennedy for nonpayment of debt and later acted for Letcher to inform the court that he "will not further prosecute his said suit but dismisses the same" (Colfax County District Court Transcript, Fall 1869 Session, Day 8, Saturday, September 4, Case #9). For more about Catron, see *Thomas Benton Catron and his era,* by Victor Westphall, University of Arizona Press, 1873.

Cawker, Samuel (1845 - ?) Illinois-born dry goods clerk in Elizabethtown who participated in a long-running property dispute with Joseph W. Stinson throughout 1869 and 1870. Cawker owned $4,000 in real estate in 1870 and lived with his mother

Mary, who owned real estate valued at $40,000. His mother was among the top seven property owners (by value of land) in the County at the time.

Coleman, Joseph (circa 1836 – ?) Civil War veteran and 33-year-old dry goods merchant in business with fellow Prussian Isaac Hattenbach in Elizabethtown in 1870. Coleman was assaulted by Charles Kennedy in late 1869. Although the initial charge against Kennedy was assault with intent to kill, this was reduced to simple assault and Kennedy was fined $10 and court costs.

Colfax, Schuyler (1823-1885) Vice-President of the United States from 1869 to 1873. Colfax County, created by the NM Territorial Legislature in 1869, was named in his honor. Schuyler Colfax had visited northern New Mexico Territory in late 1868, shortly before being sworn in as Ulysses S. Grant's Vice President. He was a journalist and politician from Indiana and was expected to be President one day. Unfortunately, the Grant administration scandals ruined those hopes, as well as the hopes of those who thought naming the County after him would be a smart move.

Cortez, José de Jesus (? - ?) Maria Gregoria Cortez Kennedy's father. A José Cortes, age 44 and listed as a laborer worth $200 in real estate, is listed in the 1870 census as the nearest neighbor but one to the Kennedy family. The Santa Fe newspaper story about Kennedy's death, reports the testimony of a José Cortez regarding the death of a redheaded American at the Kennedy cabin in December 1869. For the purposes of this novel, I have assumed these were all the same person.

Cortez, María Antonia Lucero (? - ?) Gregoria Cortez Kennedy's mother. Taos baptismal records reflect the birth of a child named Jose Ramón to María Antonia Lucero and J. de Jesus Cortez in 1854, but the marriage record for Gregoria and Charles indicates that María Antonia died prior to February 1867. I have found no further information about the baby. Based on this information, I have assumed that María Antonia and Jose Ramón died around the same time.

Edwards, ? (? - circa 1869) Merchant from Taos. The Southwest Sentinel interview with Joseph Kinsinger names Edwards as one of the men Charles Kennedy killed, along with an unnamed "friendly Indian," and a Mexican man Kennedy killed for "a small sum."

Elkins, Stephen (1841 - 1911) Missouri attorney who arrived in New Mexico in 1863 after resigning as a Union Army Captain in the middle of the Civil War. Elkins was elected to the New Mexico Territory House of Representatives the following year and became Territorial U.S. District Attorney in 1867. As was common practice, while District Attorney, Elkins also practiced law. His first Colfax County case in 1869 was as counsel to the first woman to obtain a divorce in the newly-formed county. Elkins served as New Mexico's Congressional Delegate during the 1870s. He used this position to delay New Mexico statehood, an event he and his law partner, Thomas Catron felt would be detrimental to their business activities, which included land grant speculation and other questionable practices. Elkins left New Mexico in 1877 and moved to West Virginia. He served as Secretary of War during the Benjamin Harrison administration, then was elected to the U.S. Senate, where he remained until his death.

Fitzmaurice, John (circa 1836 - ?) Iron molder from New York who served as a bailiff for the Colfax County District Court in the Spring and Fall of 1870 even though he had been charged at both 1869 sessions with keeping a gaming table. Fitzmaurice paid a $25 fine for the first charge but the second one was dismissed. In the Fall of 1870, he also served as interpreter for the Grand Jury. According to Joseph Kissinger, Charles Kennedy said he would have died happier if he'd killed Fitzmaurice and Joseph Stinson as well as the 21 people he'd murdered.

Foley, Tim (? - ?) One of the men who discovered the Aztec Mine on the east slopes of Baldy Mountain in 1867. The Aztec was said to be richest gold lode in the West up to that time. It produced around $1 million in gold within the first four years of production. Tim Foley didn't participate in the ownership of this mine and seems to have left the area before 1870. He isn't listed in the 1870 Colfax County Census.

Henderson, William, "Wall," W. (circa 1831 - ?) One of two men who stood bond for Charles Kennedy in response to the embezzlement and assault charges against him. The Pennsylvania-born Henderson may have felt some sympathy for Kennedy due to his own experiences in April 1868. A gold prospector, he killed a man in Humbug Gulch east of Elizabethtown early that month and, being a law-abiding man, turned himself into the authorities. When those authorities didn't act as quickly as local residents thought they should, a mob of about eighty men threatened to take matters into their own hands. Fortunately, a messenger was able to reach a troop of Fort Union cavalry thirty miles away in Cimarron in time for them to return with him to Elizabethtown and save Henderson from being lynched. Henderson was apparently absolved of blame in the death, because he served as a member of the Colfax County District Court's petit jury during its 1869 Spring session as well as standing security for Charles Kennedy.

Houx, Benjamin F. (circa 1829 - ?) Michigan-born Elizabethtown carpenter who served as bailiff during three of the 1869 and 1870 Colfax County District Court sessions, as well as providing legal counsel for at least one case. Court records indicate that Houx was Elizabethtown justice of the peace in the Fall of 1870, although newspaper accounts of the Kennedy "trial" and lynching say Patrick McBride held that position. By 1875, Houx (also sometimes spelled "House") had moved to Rayado, south of Cimarron. In the early 1880s, Santa Fe Land Office receiver Elias Brevoort identified him as one of nine men in the area who were involved in land fraud in the Territory.

Ilfeld, Charles (circa 1847 - 1929) German Jew who arrived in Santa Fe in 1865 at age 18 and became a leading territorial merchant, sheep rancher, and land owner. By 1867, Ilfeld was in business with Adolph Letcher in Taos. When they decided to transfer to Las Vegas, the two men packed their merchandise onto seventy-five (some say it was 100) burros and crossed the mountains to Las Vegas. The store they opened there eventually became the flagship location for the Charles Ilfeld Company, one of the largest mercantile firms in New Mexico. Ilfeld was active in Las Vegas affairs and served as director of what is now New Mexico Highlands University.

Kennedy, Charles (circa 1839 – 1870) Tennessee-born man who settled at the foot of Palo Flechado Pass in the late 1860s and proceeded to fleece and kill unwary travelers. The 1869 and 1870 Colfax County District Court record, as well as newspaper articles in the October 13, 1870 Daily New Mexican and the November 24, 1885 Southwest Sentinel, all reflect portions of his activities. The articles also provide information about Kennedy's trials and subsequent lynching and death. See the Note to Reader for details.

Kennedy, María Gregoria Cortez (1852 - ?) New Mexico-born wife of Charles Kennedy who was 14 years old when they married in Taos in February 1867. They settled in the Moreno Valley at the foot of Palo Flechado Pass, on the road from Elizabethtown to Taos. There they kept a way station for travelers, and Charles Kennedy became embroiled in a series of lawsuits: one for selling liquor without a license, another for assaulting an Etown merchant with a deadly weapon, and still another for embezzling a local laborer's money and goods. He was suspected of other nefarious activities, but nothing could be proven until the Fall of 1870, when Gregoria appeared in Etown and denounced him. The subsequent trial and lynching would make the Santa Fe, Silver City, and Indianapolis newspapers.

Kennedy, Samuel (1869-1870) Son of Charles and Gregoria Kennedy, born in June 1869 and baptized three months later in Taos. According to news reports about his father's lynching, Samuel was killed by Charles Kennedy in September 1870, an event that resulted in his mother's flight to Elizabethtown and his father's subsequent lynching.

Kinsinger, Joseph (circa 1835 - ?) Ohio-born laborer employed at the Etown Quartz Mill and Lode Company in 1870. While Kinsinger seems to have been quartered at the mine, his wife Desideria Baca and daughter Amanda resided in Elizabethtown. Kinsinger served in the Union Army in New Mexico during the Civil War as part of the First Cavalry, Company K. He may have fought at Valverde and Pigeon's Ranch and after the war participated in Col. Christopher Carson's Navajo Expedition. In 1885, an interview Kinsinger gave to the Southwest Sentinel served as the basis for an article about Joseph Coleman's late 1869 experience at the Kennedy cabin, the death of a young doctor from Elizabethtown, and Kennedy's arrest and death.

Kinsinger, Peter (circa 1831 – before 1908) Ohio-born cooper employed at the Etown Quartz Mill and Lode in 1870. Peter Kinsinger was Joseph Kinsinger's brother. They apparently bunked at the Quartz Mill and Lode Company site while their families lived in Elizabethtown. Peter had been one of the three men who discovered gold in the Baldy Mountain drainage in early

1867. While his brother Joseph seems to have left the Elizabethtown area some time in the 1870s, Peter stuck around as a part owner of the Spanish Bar mine near the mouth of Grouse Gulch below Etown. Peter and his wife Elmira had a one-year-old son named Franklin in 1870. By 1880, he and Elmira had several more children and were living in the Ute Creek precinct east of Etown. He was dead by 1908, when Elmira, now living in Ohio, filed for a widow's pension based on Peter's service during the Civil War.

Lambert, Henry/Henri (1838-1913) Frenchman who, after various seafaring and other adventures served as cook for the Fifth Army Corps in Washington D.C. and, as part of that service, for President Lincoln. Lambert seems to have been with the Union army at Petersburg, Virginia, but stayed behind to open a restaurant. He remained there two years, leaving in 1868 with a bride, Mary Stepp, and the resources to travel to Denver, then to the new mining camp of Elizabethtown, New Mexico, where he opened a hotel. It is this location that tradition says served as the final resting place (before burial) for Charles Kennedy's head. In the Fall of 1871, the Lamberts moved to Cimarron, where Henri opened the saloon that would form the first story of today's St. James Hotel.

Letcher, Adolph (1828 - 1903) German-born Taos merchant who loaned money and sold cattle to Charles Kennedy in 1867. In April 1869, Letcher instituted a civil suit against Kennedy for nonpayment. The suit was apparently settled out of court that summer, because Letcher withdrew the suit during the Fall court session. Letcher and his clerk Charles Ilfeld moved the Letcher operation from Taos to Las Vegas in the late 1860s. Eventually, Letcher sold out to Ilfeld, who built the operation into one of the largest mercantile firms in New Mexico Territory.

Longwill, Doctor Robert (circa 1837 - 1895) Cimarron-based medical doctor, who arrived in the area as a contract surgeon and served as Fort Union medical officer in the late 1860s. Longwill was elected Colfax County Probate Judge after Lucien Maxwell left the county in 1870. The doctor was connected with the Santa Fe Ring and was a member of the Maxwell Land Grant and Railway Company's board of directors. He was also an associate of Melvin Mills and was implicated with him in the 1875 death of Reverend Tolby. He eventually left New Mexico for Pennsylvania, where he died in 1895.

Lynch, Matthew (circa 1844 - 1880) One of the three men who, in 1867, discovered the lode that would become the Aztec Mine, a mine that produced over $100,000 in gold between October 1868 and July 1869 and would yield about $1 million in the first four years of production. The Irish-born Lynch was involved in various enterprises in the Elizabethtown area, including a system that redirected streams into the Moreno Valley and allowed miners, including himself, to implement hydraulic mining methods. He died after being hit by a falling tree and passed the water system on to his two brothers.

Martinez, Padre Antonio José (1793-1867) Catholic priest at Taos from 1826 to 1857 and member of a prominent Taos family there. Although Padre Martinez plays a very small role in *The Pain and The Sorrow*, he was a major influence in Taos, where he operated a printing press, co-educational school, and seminary. He also played a leading role in nuevomexico politics under both the Mexican and American administrations.

Maxwell Land Grant The land grant originally known as the Beaubien/Miranda Grant (see Charles Beaubien entry), but which took on Lucien B. Maxwell's name when he and his wife Luz acquired it following Beaubien's death (see María de la Luz Maxwell entry). After the Maxwell Land Grant & Railway Company purchased the grant in 1870, most people in New Mexico continued to refer to it as "Maxwell's Grant."

Maxwell, Lucien Bonaparte (1814 - 1875) Illinois-born trapper and merchant who married the oldest daughter of Charles Beaubien. Maxwell and his wife acquired the entire Beaubien/Miranda Land Grant after her father's death and sold it in 1870 to a consortium of English investors, when it became known as the Maxwell Land Grant & Railway Company. Maxwell was elected the first Colfax County Probate Judge. There seems to have been some irregularity in the way he carried out his duties, because the Territory of New Mexico brought a lawsuit against him for neglecting to hold probate court. By the time he paid the $50 fine for this offense in the Fall of 1870, he and his family were in the process of moving to the recently-abandoned Fort Sumner on the Pecos River. Maxwell died there five years later. For more about Maxwell, see Harriet Freibeger's *Lucien Maxwell, Villain or Visionary*, Eagle Trail Press, 2016.

Maxwell, María de la Luz "Luz" Beaubien (1829 - 1900) Daughter of Charles Beaubien and the wife (at age 12) of Lucien Bonaparte Maxwell. The year before Luz' marriage, the Mexican government had granted her father and nuevomexico's Provincial Secretary Guadalupe Miranda joint ownership of the vast swath of land that would become the Maxwell Land Grant after Beaubien's death in 1862. Luz seems to have been an active partner in Maxwell's land transactions: the land grant sale was held up until her signature could be added to the paperwork and wired to New York City. Luz died at Fort Sumner in 1900.

McBride, Patrick (circa 1845 – circa 1877) Irish-born gold miner worth $4,500 in July 1870. He was reportedly a hard drinking man with a hail-fellow-well-met persona and political ambitions. Around the time of the quasi-judicial trials that led to Charles Kennedy's lynching, McBride became involved in the effort to elect Robert H. Longwill as Colfax County Probate Judge, an effort which included trying to bribe Samuel Cameron. A few weeks later, his home was burned down by angry miners rioting in response to the Maxwell Land Grant & Railway Company's attempts to throw them off their claims. McBride seems to have left Etown shortly thereafter. By 1873, he was in Los Alamos County, where he served as Probate Judge and occasionally interim justice of the peace. He died a few years later of alcoholism.

McCullough, John B. (circa 1844 - ?) Pennsylvania-born merchant in Elizabethtown who also acted as census taker for the County in 1870. By 1873, McCullough had moved to Cimarron and was serving as the new County Seat's postmaster. He was the uncle of Dora and Kate McCullough, the two women who married Clay Allison and his brother.

Means, Thomas (? – 1867) American-born man who was lynched in Taos in early January 1867. During a drunken spree, he'd drawn his knife and fired his pistol at several people, then assaulted and nearly killed his wife. Following his arrest, a mob broke into the room where he was being held, took him to an adjoining room, and hanged him from one of its roof beams.

Middaugh, William (circa 1848 - ?) The younger brother and clerk for Asa Middaugh, owner of an Elizabethtown mercantile and dry goods store as well as a land office business. The brothers were from Pennsylvania and ran a store that stood at the corner of Third and Columbia in Elizabethtown. Because Columbia, the street that ran beside the store, sloped down the hill, the lower portion of the building was accessible from it. When John Pearson owned the building in the 1890s, this door opened to a saloon or what the 1905 Souvenir of the Great Elizabethtown Gold and Copper Mining District, called a "social club". Although there's no way of knowing whether the Middaugh brothers operated the same business there, it seems like a safe assumption.

The Middaugh's apparently did a thriving business. Asa was sufficiently wealthy to join Lucien Maxwell in a $5000 bond for Sheriff Andrew Calhoun in Spring 1869. The bond was subject to forfeit if Calhoun didn't "well and truly discharge all his duties as such Sheriff according to law" (Colfax County District Court Record: Spring 1869 Session. Day 1: Tuesday, April 6). The Middaugh's moved their operations to Cimarron in the early 1870s, part of the exodus to the new Colfax County seat.

Mills, Melvin Whitson (1845 - 1925) Canadian-born Quaker lawyer who represented Charles Kennedy in the Fall 1870 extra-judicial proceedings against him. Melvin graduated from the University of Michigan law school in 1869 and began practicing before the Colfax County District Court in the Spring of 1870. He is said to have been part of the Santa Fe Ring and was instrumental in moving the Colfax County seat to Cimarron in 1872 and then to Springer in 1874. He served two terms in the Territorial Legislature as delegate for Colfax County. Mills and his wife moved to Springer in the late 1870s, where they built a three-story mansion with over 20 rooms and a maple interior trim. They also owned a large ranch in eastern Colfax County, where they planted fruit trees in what is now Mills Canyon.

Moore, William (circa 1818 – after 1880) Post Sutler at Fort Union who commissioned Joseph Kinsinger and others to look for copper in the Moreno Valley and got gold instead. Although Moore was involved in various ventures in the Baldy Mountain area and operated a store in Elizabethtown in the early years, he and his family were still at Fort Union in September 1870. Elizabethtown is purported to have been named after his youngest daughter. By 1880, he had settled in the Mora, New Mexico area.

Palen, Judge Joseph G. (1812-1875) Palmyra, New York postmaster, who replaced John S. Watts as Chief Justice of New Mexico's Territorial Supreme Court and Judge of the First Judicial District Court (which included Colfax County) in 1869. Palen quickly found a place among the men who were making the most of their time in New Mexico, joining Catron and others in incorporating the 1870 Rio Grande Railroad and Telegraph Company and other ventures. He died in December 1875, while still on the bench.

Pollock, Thomas (1826 - ?) Ohio-born gold miner who lived in Elizabethtown in 1870 with his wife Sarah and four children. Thomas Pollock served on the Colfax County District Court's grand jury during the Spring 1869 session and was called to serve on the petit jury that fall, but ended up being transferred to the grand jury and made foreman. He would have had the experience to serve as foreman for the quasi-judicial proceedings against Charles Kennedy, although so far I have not found a record of the men who sat on that jury.

Romero, Dolores (? - ?) Sheriff of Mora County in the Fall of 1868.

Santa Fe Ring A loose-knit association of businessmen in New Mexico who, from around 1865 to the end of the century, sought to control events and land to their own benefit. Many of them (Thomas B. Catron, Stephen Elkins, Robert Longwill, and John S. Watts) also played a role in the Maxwell Land Grant & Railway Company, either helping to incorporate the company, serving on its board, or providing legal services. For more information about the Santa Fe Ring, see *Chasing the Santa Fe Ring*, David L. Caffey, University of New Mexico Press, 2014.

Schiffer, Herman (circa 1845 - ?) Bavaria-born man who became a citizen of the United States during the Fall 1869 court session in Elizabethtown. The census data for Schiffer indicates that he was a dry goods merchant with $1000 in real estate and $3000 in personal goods.

Sears, Jasper (circa 1808 - ?) A grocery man who owned real estate in Etown, including a lot on the corner of Fourth and Columbia, directly behind the Middaugh grocery. At 62, he was one of the oldest men in Elizabethtown in 1870.

Sibley, Major George Champlin (1782-1863) One of three United States Commissioners appointed by Congress to complete the 1825-1827 survey of the Santa Fe Trail. Sibley was the only Commissioner to cross the international boundary into Mexico. When he arrived at Point of Rocks on Wednesday, October 19, 1825, he announced that it was too late in the year to travel safely to the capitol and headed west across the Sangre de Cristo mountains to Taos, where his business associate Paul Baillio was located. Sibley completed his survey and map work in 1827 and returned to Missouri, where he and his wife established what is today Lindenwood University.

St. Vrain, Ceran (1802-1870) Taos-based trapper and trader and a descendant of French nobility who arrived in Santa Fe in March 1825 and remained in New Mexico the rest of his life. A big man, who made friends easily, St. Vrain is said to have fathered at least four children, each by a different woman, and is buried at Mora. His son Vincent plays a small role in this novel.

St. Vrain, Vincent (? - ?) Son of Ceran St. Vrain. Vincent was a merchant in the southern part of New Mexico when the Civil War broke out and Confederate forces occupied the area. He was instrumental in providing behind the lines information to Union side. He was in Mora in the Fall of 1868 and acted as the foreman of the Grand Jury which found evidence that Charles Kennedy had sold liquor without a license.

Stinson, Joseph Whitmore (circa 1838 - 1902) Private in the Union Army in the 1st California Infantry, who was discharged at Los Pinos, New Mexico in the Fall of 1863 and did not return to California. By 1868, Stinson was in Elizabethtown, where he operated as a saloon keeper and was involved in real estate transactions. During the Spring and Fall 1869 and the Fall 1870 court sessions, he admitted to various counts of permitting gaming and dealing cards and paid the related fines and court costs. Stinson subsequently moved to Santa Fe, where he continued as a saloon keeper. He eventually returned to California, where he was admitted to the Old Soldiers Home in Sawtelle in 1896. He was still in California when he died of gangrene of the foot in September 1902.

Ussel, Gabriel (1838 - 1907) French priest recruited by Bishop Jean Bautista Lamy to assist in reforming the Catholic Church in New Mexico Territory. Ussel arrived in New Mexico in 1856, and served initially in Arroyo Hondo and then Taos. He remained there until 1875, when he transferred to Walsenburg, Colorado where he served until his death in 1907.

Watts, John Sebrie (1816 - 1876) Indiana native who served as Chief Justice of New Mexico's Supreme Court and Judge for First Judicial District from 1848 to 1854. Watts stayed in New Mexico and operated a legal practice based in Santa Fe. He was reappointed to the court for a short period in 1868 and presided over the Mora court session during which Charles Kennedy was charged with selling liquor without a license. When Joseph Palen was appointed Chief Justice, Watts returned to private practice. He represented Lucien Maxwell during three of the four 1869 and 1870 Colfax County District Court sessions and was also part of the group who incorporated the Maxwell Land Grant & Railway Company, then handed it over to the consortium of English capitalists who were buying the Grant.

Westerling, Doctor Richard (circa 1834 - ?) Physician and native of Sweden who provided evidence during Charles Kennedy's quasi-judicial trial in late September 1870. Westerling became a U.S. citizen during the Spring 1870 court session in Etown. He served in the U.S. military and had been honorably discharged prior to obtaining citizenship.

Wheaton, Theodore (1819 – 1876) Lawyer and member of the 1st Missouri Volunteers who arrived in New Mexico with General Kearny in 1846. Originally from Rhode Island, Wheaton remained in New Mexico after the Mexican-American War and practiced in the Territorial courts. One of his first actions was to assist in prosecuting the men who killed Governor Charles Bent in early 1847. Wheaton settled in Taos, represented the County in the Territorial Legislature in 1852, and was speaker of the House during the next two sessions. He was United States Attorney for New Mexico Territory from 1861 to 1866. He represented cases at all four Colfax County District Court sessions in 1869 and 1870. He is the only attorney whose name is associated with Charles Kennedy in those records.

Williams, William Sherley "Old Bill" (1787-1849) North Carolina-born mountain man who spent his formative years in Missouri. At sixteen, Williams left home to live among the Osage Indians. After the death of his Osage wife twenty-one years later, he headed west. Based in Taos, the lean, red-headed Williams had a taste for gambling and Taos Lightning, a locally made whisky, and a propensity for trapping on his own or with only a camp keeper as companion. A self-confident man with strong opinions, he eventually ran afoul of John C. Fremont, who hired Williams to guide his 1848 expedition across the Rocky Mountains. The party became trapped by harsh winter conditions and Fremont refused to follow Williams' advice, then blamed him for the subsequent death of twenty-one of the group's thirty-two men. Williams himself died during an attempt to retrieve the equipment and records left behind in the expedition's scramble to safety.

Wootton, Richens Lacey "Uncle Dick" (1816 – 1893) Virginia-born mountain man and unreconstructed rebel who turned to road-building in his late 60s. He settled in Raton Pass on the mountain route of the Santa Fe Trail and built a toll road that eased travelling and also provided him and his family a reliable income, grossing an average of $700 a month. When the Atchison, Topeka and Santa Fe Railway Company track reached the Pass from Denver in 1878, Wootton negotiated the purchase of his toll rights in exchange for $50 a month compensation for the remainder of his life and that of his fourth wife, Maria Paulina, who was some 40 years his junior.

Made in United States
North Haven, CT
23 August 2022

23103797R00215